New York Times bestselling author
Jeff Long scales new heights of
terror and suspense in
THE WALL

"Heart-stopping vertical adventure. . . ."
—*Kirkus Reviews*

"Jeff Long delivers a palpable sense of the Zen-like concentration and hand-straining physicality needed to conquer a big hunk of rock. A bravura description of a forest fire and the truly shocking ending . . . elevate *The Wall* far above an increasingly high pile of pedestrian thrillers."
—*Entertainment Weekly*

"Keeps the reader enthralled. . . . *The Wall* is Long at his piercing, probing best."
—*The Denver Post*

"The surprise ending is a true shocker."
—*Publishers Weekly* (starred review)

"Thrilling. . . . Heart-stopping. . . . Powerful. . . . The steep granite setting is both exotic and harrowing."
—*Boulder Daily Camera* (CO)

This title is also available as an eBook

Jeff Long creates riveting suspense and chilling scenarios—in novels that are "superbly original . . . terrifying and exquisite" (Dan Brown).

THE RECKONING

"Gripping . . . menacing. . . . A neatly tied, portentous thriller."

—*Kirkus Reviews*

"Packed with satisfying shocks."

—Scripps Howard News Service

"Suspenseful, tightly written. . . . Long superbly depicts war-scarred [Cambodia], its people, and its beautiful, hazardous landscape."

—*Publishers Weekly*

"Excellent storytelling. . . . Jeff Long's books have always been must-reads for me. . . . He's the best thriller writer you've never read. Rectify that by picking up *The Reckoning*."

—*Rocky Mountain News* (Denver)

YEAR ZERO

"Jeff Long writes with poetry, style, and pace . . . crafting his twists and doling out his delectable details with exceptionally gratifying results."

—Dan Brown

"Wow! There's no other word for *Year Zero*."

—CNN.com

"A dashing, exciting thriller. . . . The sum of this complex tale is more than its parts of medical thriller, archeological fiction, action/adventure, and doomsday scenario, as Long thrills with an intricate puzzle. Long doesn't miss a step. . . ."

—*Publishers Weekly*

"[A] clever, apocalyptic thriller. . . . Long writes stylishly and tells a good yarn."

—*Kirkus Reviews*

THE DESCENT

"A remarkable novel, an imaginative tour de force that somehow succeeds both as sober-minded allegory and nail-biting thriller. . . . A rip-roaring good read."

—Jon Krakauer, author of *Under the Banner of Heaven: A Story of Violent Faith*

"Absolutely bone-chilling—every bit as good as Stephen King at his best."

—Charles R. Pellegrino, author of *Dust*

"This flat-out, gears-grinding, bumper-car ride into the pits of hell is one major takedown of a read. Jeff Long writes with force and unearthly vision. . . . It is one page-burner of a book."

—Lorenzo Carcaterra, author of *Sleepers* and *Gangster*

"A dizzying synthesis of supernatural horror, lost-race fantasy, and military SF. . . . Long's novel brims with energy, ideas, and excitement."

—*Publishers Weekly*

Also by Jeff Long

JEFF LONG

THE WALL

POCKET **STAR** BOOKS
New York London Toronto Sydney

A Pocket Star Book published by
POCKET BOOKS, a division of Simon & Schuster, Inc.
1230 Avenue of the Americas, New York, NY 10020

This book is a work of fiction. Names, characters, places
and incidents are products of the author's imagination or
are used fictitiously. Any resemblance to actual events or
locales or persons, living or dead, is entirely coincidental.

ISBN-13: 978-0-7434-9870-8
ISBN-10:   0-7434-9870-4

This Pocket Star Books paperback edition November 2006

10 9 8 7 6 5 4 3 2 1

POCKET STAR BOOKS and colophon are registered
trademarks of Simon & Schuster, Inc.

Cover design by Jae Song

Manufactured in the United States of America

For information regarding special discounts for bulk
purchases, please contact Simon & Schuster Special Sales
at 1-800-456-6798 or business@simonandschuster.com.

To Helena,
my Trojan woman

THE
WALL

ONE

When God throws angels down, it starts like this.

A breeze stirs. It carries the slightest distraction, a scent of trees perhaps, or a hint of evening chill, or a song on a radio in a car passing three thousand feet below. In some form, temptation always whispers.

High above the earth, toes smeared against the stone, fingers crimped on microholds, the woman turns her head. Not even that: she turns her mind, for an instant, for even less. That's all it takes.

The stone evicts her.

The wall tilts. The sky bends. Her holds . . . don't hold.

She falls.

By now, eight days high, her body is burning adrenaline like common blood sugar, one more fuel in her system. So in the beginning of her fall, she doesn't even register fear. She is calm, even curious.

Every climber knows this rupture. One moment you have contact, the next it's outer space. That's what rope is for. She waits.

Her mind catches up with her body. A first thought forms, a natural. *My hands.*

All our lives, from the cradle to the grave, our hands are our most constant companions. *Like the back of my hand.* They give. They take. They roam and shape the world around us. But hers have turned to stone. Or time has stopped.

Each finger is frozen just so, still hooking on holds that no longer exist. Her high arm is still stretched high, her low arm still bent low. One leg is cocked, the other is straight to the tiptoe of her climbing slipper. She could be a statue of a dancer tipped from its pedestal.

Her paralysis does not alarm her. Hollywood shows victims swimming through air, limbs splayed and paddling. In reality, when a climber is climbing—really climbing, not fretting the fall, but totally engaged—and the holds blow and you peel, what happens is like a motor locking. "Rigor" is the formal term, as in rigor mortis. Your muscles stiffen. Body memory freezes, at least for a moment. It doesn't matter what your mind knows. Your body stubbornly believes it is still attached to the world.

What surprises her is the length of the moment. Time stretches like a rubber band. The moment is more than a moment. More than two. *Patience,* she tells herself.

There will be a tug at her waist when the rope takes over. Then there will be an elastic aftershock. She knows how it will go. She's no virgin.

Her synapses are firing furiously now. She overrides her Zen focus on what civilians call pulling up, and what climbers call pulling down. The rock has let go of her. Now she forces her body to let go of the rock. Her fingers move. She starts to inhabit her fall.

For the last day, they have been struggling to break through a transition band between two species of granite, one light, one dark. In this borderland, the rock is manky and loose. Their protection has been increasingly tenuous and their holds delicate as sand castles.

And so she was—necessarily—way too high above her last piece of protection, climbing on crystals of quartz, almost within reach of a big crack. She had the summit in sight. Maybe that was her downfall. It was right there for the taking, and maybe she grabbed for the vision too soon.

From the ground up, the beast has begrudged them every inch. They have done everything in their power to pretend it was a contest, not a war, nothing personal. Now suddenly it bears in on her, the territorial imperative of a piece of rock. El Cap is fighting back.

Part of her brain tries to catalog the risks of this fall. Much depends on the nature of the rope, the weight of the falling object, all 108 pounds of her, and the length of the drop. Any point in the system could fail, the runner slings, the carabiners, her placements, their anchor, the rope. The weakest link in that chain of mechanisms is the human body.

On her back now, helpless, she glances past her fingers. The rope is making loose, pink snake shapes in the air above her. She's riding big air now.

A dark shape flashes past. It is last night's bivvy camp, gone in a blink of the eye. *Do they even know I'm falling?* At this speed, the camp is the last of her landmarks. The wall is a blur. Her braids with the rainbow beads whip her eyes.

Except for the grinding of her teeth, she falls in silence. No chatter of gear. No whistle of wind. Oh, there's a whiff of music, a spark in the brain. Bruce, the Boss. "Philadelphia." Faithless kiss.

She's fallen many times. At her level of the game, no climber has not given in to gravity. You build it into the budget. It comes to her that she's counting heartbeats, six, seven, eight. . . .

Her freefall starts to ease. Finally.

The serpent loops straighten. A line—hot pink—begins to form in the dead center of her sky. The seat harness squeezes around her pelvic bones.

Abruptly the line snaps taut with a bowstring *twang*.

The rope claims her. She gains weight, a carload of it, a solid ton of shock load.

The catch—or its commencement—is brute ugly. Her arms and legs jack down like puppet jumble. Her spine creaks. Head back, medusa coils flying, throat bared to the summit, she comes eye to eye with the abyss behind and below her.

It's totally still in the valley. Autumn is in high gear. The leaves are blazing red and orange. But there's hunger in the beauty. Pandemonium. You could get swallowed alive down there. She jerks her head from the hypnotic sight. She tunes it out. Turns it off.

The rope. She grabs for it.

The summit. She centers herself.

Eyes up, she takes a breath, her first since coming off, a deep, ragged drag of air. Like breaking to the surface again, she gasps.

Her fists lock on the rope. Sunshine is painting the rim. She curses, full of fighting spirit. They were so close, just hours shy. The fall will cost them.

She blames herself for rushing. They were banking on making land by night. They had gorged on all but the last gallon of their water, and eaten all but some scraps. They'd even high-fived their victory. Dumb. Jinxy. The wall moves with a tempo all its own. Full of wishes, too ready for flat land, she'd pushed too fast.

She yo-yos on the rope.

The recoil dangles her up and down in the depths. Eleven-millimeter kernmantle is built for shock. A fifty-meter section—the standard for climbing—has a break strength of five thousand pounds. Cavers shun "dynamic" climbing rope: it's too bouncy for them in dark, bottomless shafts. But for a climber, elasticity is the very hand of the lord and savior.

Her mind brims with next thoughts. She doesn't offer thanks. Fate is action, that's her mantra.

The rope's still quivering, and already she's doing damage control. The fall could have been bad. She could have hit the wall or blown her harness. The line could have tangled in a limb or wrapped in a noose and snapped her neck. If not for years of yoga practiced everywhere, in gyms, dorm rooms, friends' apartments, and campgrounds, her vertebrae would be scrambled eggs. But she's whole, unwounded, not even a rope burn. The soreness will come, but not, by God, before she gets back on the horse.

Twisting in midair, she gathers herself together. The woods are darkening below. The sun band is creeping higher up the headwall, ebbing away. No way they'll beat night today.

Knowing it will never work, she tries pulling herself up the taut, thin line and gains not an inch. It's too thin, too taut, like a wire. She quits to save her strength. She settles into her harness, waiting. She needs a pair of jumar clamps and stirrups so that she can ascend the rope. One of her partners will lower the necessary gear, they'll know.

She is impatient to return to the headwall above their hollow and finish what she started. It's more than stubbornness, more than getting back in the saddle. She's raving on endorphins, wild with energy. Her memory of the moves is crisp. She knows the holds. She's cracked the code.

Come on, girls. "Yoo-hoo," she calls. And waits.

As the moments go by, she rehearses the sequence of moves: left toe here, pinch the white quartz crystal, reach right, stack her fingers on a seam hidden in a splash of sunlight.

In her mind, she makes it all the way to the big crack running straight to the skyline. The crack was so close, just a move away, and then she would have owned the stone. Now she's forfeited the day. They'll have to wait until tomorrow night for their seafood and wine at the Mountain Room Restaurant.

At last a voice seeps down from their camp in the vertical hollow. It is a single syllable, her name. But also it is a warning. Pain, she hears, and desperation.

Something is wrong up there. Her fall has wreaked some kind of havoc in the camp, there can be no other explanation. Clutching the rope, still as a fawn, she peers up in time to see the pink sheath blow.

For all its strength, a rope is a fragile thing. A grain of sand inside the sheath, a spot of acidic urine, even the rays of sunlight can destroy the core's integrity. In this case, the rope fails at the threshold of their sanctuary. The hollow's rim is not a knife edge, but it's an edge just the same.

Fifty feet overhead, right where it bends from sight, the rope bursts into flower. It happens in a small, white explosion of nylon fibers. It looks like a magician's trick, like a bouquet springing from a wand.

Chrysanthemums, how pretty. But she knows the truth of it.

Quick as a bird, she steals a sip of air. *Faith.* She grips the rope with all her might and wills the world to freeze, the rope to weave itself together, her body to be light as a feather. Abruptly she is weightless.

It breaks her heart. She whispers, "No."

It was not supposed to end this way. You climb hard, get high, tango with the sun. When you fall, you fall with grace and the rope takes over. You heal, if necessary, and reach into your heart. Chalk up, tighten the knots, and get on with the climb. That's the way of it. Ascent abides. Always.

The physics of the breaking rope flips her sideways, and then facedown. Like that she goes, chest first into a hurricane of her own making.

She could close her eyes. She wants to. But of course she can't. This is the rest of her life.

The air cools instantly. The light changes. It goes from that golden honey to starved blue steeples. She has dropped into the shadow zone. *Already?*

This is a different kind of falling. This one is full of forbidden thoughts. She has never not known hope. That's the greatest shock. She is staring at the end of time. There is not one thing she can do to improve her situation. And yet she hopes. She can't help herself.

Her mind goes on grasping. Command, of a sort, comes second nature to her breed. Even as she plunges, she calculates madly. In the back of her mind, *Like a cat, land like a cat. On your hands and feet. Light as a cat.*

Climbers have a natural fascination with falling. Its discussion, usually held by a campfire or on long road trips, draws heavily on legend, anecdote, and personal experience, and includes falls one has survived and falls one has witnessed and even falls one has merely dreamed about but forgotten they were dreams. You learn from the fuckups. The accident reports almost always come with names, if not of the victims, then most certainly of their routes, and dates, and the type of gear and precise condition of the rock, ice, or snow involved. Often they list the temperature. Anything to make the unknown seem known.

For many climbers, "terminal velocity" refers to a death drop, sometimes known as "cratering." In fact, the term specifies that point when a falling object reaches zero acceleration. Air resistance from below becomes equal to the mass of the object times the force of gravity. You don't slow down, but for what it's worth, you quit falling any faster.

All of this occurs to her in an instant. A million synapses are firing now. Images, words, forgotten smells, and emotions all spring loose in a flood. She remembers sparks from a campfire, the exact scent of cedar smoke, that taste of his lips, his finger. *Butterflies, the seashore, Mom, a singsong alphabet.* More and more.

The terminal velocity of a human averages 120

miles per hour, or roughly 165 feet—the length of a fifty-meter rope—per second. But it takes time to reach that state of zero acceleration.

In her first second, she falls just sixteen feet. By the end of her third second, she has covered 148 feet; by the end of the sixth second, some 500 feet. That leaves roughly a half mile to go, and she is just reaching terminal velocity. What it comes down to is this. She has eighteen more seconds to live.

The wind robs her lungs. It just sucks her empty. It makes her deaf, that or the blood roaring in her head.

She commands herself to see. She keeps her eyes bared. This is for keeps.

The ground does not rush up at her. If anything, it opens wide, growing deeper and broader. She is a pebble tossed into still water, except the ripples precede her in great concentric expanses of earth.

Swallows make way for her.

The forest becomes trees.

Out beyond the road, the river runs black through the white autumn meadow.

Such beauty. It fills her. It's like seeing for the first time.

She knows the blood chemicals must be taking her away. How else to explain this sense of being chosen? Of being received. Of being freed. She's never felt such rapture. It's glorious. *I'm going right through the skin of the world.*

And yet she fights paradise. The glory is too glorious, the abyss too welcoming. It means to kill her. That quickly she despairs.

If only she could catch her breath. There is no in between. Fear, ecstasy, anguish: each extreme, all amok. *Death.* She keeps that word at bay. She tries.

And yet here is the sum total of every climb and every ambition and every desire she's ever felt. Stack them end to end and they reach to the moon, and for what? It strikes her. She has wrecked her life. Her barren life. *A fool's trade.* All for nothing.

It is then that she spies her savior.

The trees part and there he is, a tiny, lone figure moving along the valley floor. He is approaching El Cap. But also, impossibly, and yet absolutely, he is making a beeline for her.

Everything changes. Her fear dissipates. Her wolves lie still. A great calm pacifies the storm.

I'm not alone.

It's so simple. Whoever he is, he's coming for her. Nothing else explains it. Random chance does not exist for a woman with no chances left.

From high above, settling through the air, she watches him labor between the trees, bent beneath his loaded pack. He's a climber, plainly, and well off the main trail. In forging his own path, he is marrying hers. It's deliberate. It's destined. There is not the slightest doubt in her mind. Whoever he is, he's traveled the earth and followed his dreams and timed his days exactly to receive her.

If only he would lift his head. She wants his face. His eyes.

Above the trees, she opens her arms. She arranges herself like some beatific creature. The air sings through her fingers. The feathers of her wings.

And still he is unaware of her. She wants him to look up and see her. She wants him to open his arms and embrace her. With all the love in her, she loves this man. Every memory she contains, all her being, lies in his hands now.

Her heart swells, her giant heart. Oh, she loves this life. There was so much more to do. Even one more sunset. And children, God.

She pierces the forest, thinking, *Forgive me.*

TWO

The pear.

Hugh moved the way giants do, head down, driving against his pack straps, planting each footstep with an eye to his next. Sweat stung his eyes. *The pear.*

Other thoughts crowded in.

Water weighs eight pounds per gallon, and he was humping ten jugs, like some eager kid. Knee joints crackling like popcorn. Some kid. Fifty-six going on nineteen.

He didn't need to be bushwhacking straight upslope. The main trail would have been easier and probably faster, and clear of the poison ivy and oak woven among the underbrush. For that matter, he didn't need to be here at all, slaving this load through the forest on his final afternoon on the ground. His partner Lewis had said the extra water was overkill. He'd insisted they had plenty to last them on the wall. Hugh could have been back at the cabins resting right now.

But what if we aren't who we were? They had been young once, and now they were not. And El Cap was no longer necessary to him.

The pear. He returned to it. Keep it tight. Simple. Small thoughts for grand designs.

It was an eighty-nine-cent Bosch pear, the type Annie used to love. He imagined the blade of his Swiss Army knife cutting neat sections. He would eat it at their cache at the base of El Cap. He would have it in slices, resting on his back. That kept him in motion, casting himself at this thing that did not need him.

For the moment, he could pretend to be a pilgrim lost in a dark wood at the foot of the mountain, though the woods were not so much dark as the walls above were so bright. And climbers never called El Cap a mountain.

The forest thickened. It had been a drought summer. The leaves were dry as old newspaper. Twigs scratched against his pack. Acorn shells lay scattered, emptied far ahead of winter by hungry animals. Deprived of rain, the dusty rhododendrons looked unwashed. The locals were all quoting the *Farmers' Almanac* to each other, predicting an early winter and tons of snow.

Not much more now, a few hundred yards at most. There is a way to rest while walking that he'd learned by watching porters in Nepal. With each step, you trade the whole weight of your burden from one leg to the other . . . then lock and pause . . . then step again. Done right, a person can go all day with it.

He stopped abruptly, on instinct.

The water rocked on his back like ten tiny seas. One foot forward, the other knee locked, he stood in place. Something had changed. *But what?*

He waited with his head and body pitched against the pack weight. He let his senses roam. The forest had quit moving. There was no scurry of squirrels. The jays had fallen silent. The air was still.

Whatever the animals had sensed, he was sensing it last. It made him feel dull and vulnerable. A moment before, he'd been synched into the forest's flow. Now, suddenly, he was alone. And yet not alone.

It might be a predator. There were bears, though the decades of tourism had turned them into garbage mutts. Or a coyote gone rabid. Or a mountain lion. During his long absence from the States, they'd migrated throughout the Sierras. Joggers and mountain bikers were getting dragged down on the outskirts of L.A.

Something was watching him.

He waited patiently. Not a motion broke the jungly screen. No birds sailed through the trees. Hugh turned heavily, and there was nothing downslope either.

With a glance up at El Cap, he decided it was all

inside his head. He had doubts about the climb, and so now his doubts were prowling the forest.

He shrugged the pack higher and continued on. The little seas sloshed by his ears. Sweat hit the rocks in polka dots. *The pear.*

The air took on a smell. It reminded him of a hunter's camp. But this was Yosemite, and there were no hunters.

A kill, he guessed. That would explain the stillness and this scent of fresh meat. One animal had taken another.

He reached the edge of a small clearing. A woman was in there. The red bark glistened. It didn't register at first. He almost went around.

She was taking a nap, obviously. This was her privacy. But with a second glance, a guilty one, a widower's glance, he realized this was the crux of the forest's sudden hush.

She rested on her back on a flat talus slab, face up to the wall of golden light. He took it in. Small breasts. A jut of pelvis. Brown hair braided with beads the color of a rainbow. Her chin was tucked just slightly.

For a moment, his mind refused the awful truth. She was at such peace, one hand over her heart, the other dangling from the stone as if she were drifting on a boat in a stream. She had searched out this perfect view. She had laid herself down in a stone trough that cradled her skull and shoulders and womanly hips.

He took a step higher, and of course this was no

cradling trough. The slab was flat. The underside of her lay crushed against the stone.

Hugh flinched once, but did not back away. The lizard king had caught her, that starving, patient thing. People talked about Mother Nature. Mother, hell. One false move and you ended up in its belly like this.

He held back, piecing together the details. A seat harness girdled her thighs and waist. She was a climber, not a suicide or a murder victim. He knew roughly when she'd fallen and from where. Just a half hour ago, before setting off from the road, he had seen her and her two partners working it out twenty-five hundred vertical feet off the deck, closing in on the summit. Until now, he'd had no idea one might be a woman.

He set his feet and tipped back his pack to get a proper look. The vast, radiant panels of El Cap gleamed through the darkening trees. It took a minute for his eyes to adjust to the immense scale and orient himself to the cracks and shadows. A dark hole on the wall was his landmark. If there were any survivors, they would be cowering in there. If not, the rest of them were probably lying close by in the forest.

He lowered his eyes to the woman. She had crashed within the last few minutes. The first flies had yet to arrive.

He must have been within a hundred feet when she landed. How could he not have heard such an earth-shattering thing? There should have been the

sounds of tree limbs snapping and a body—a life—
exploding. Where was the thunder of her collision?
Where was the howl?

And still Hugh remained on the outskirts. He
did not have to be part of this thing. Many people
would have bolted from the scene, some to run for
help, others to be shed of the horror. Even among
climbers, with their vaunted brotherhood of the
rope, some would have fled, some would have
reached for their cameras, and some would have
just made a wide detour and continued with business.

The smell was mounting. Blood and shit.

His horror aside, the crash would steal hours
from his day, right when he had his own climb to
tend. He had no obligation to her, no duty as a wit-
ness. She was a stranger to him. And though he
had traveled among Bedouins who lived their lives
like books already written, Hugh did not traffic in
predestination. He did not believe he was meant to
be here to help her to the other side.

But her quietness pulled at him. And—again—
he had that sensation of being watched.

He resigned himself. "Ah, Glass, you're in it
now," he said, and ponderously backed against a
boulder to ease off his pack. Released from his
cargo, he had an odd moment of separation. The
death chained down his mood, even as his body felt
buoyant and thankful for the release.

He approached her warily. She frightened him.
From this side, she seemed too perfect. Where was

the ruin? Her lips were parted. She had white teeth, and five small earrings like silver fringe along one lobe. Her beads were real minerals, not plastic.

As a geologist, Hugh could pick out the turquoise, agate, jade, and ruby, and even their likely value and source. She wore no rings or bracelets, of course, not on a climb. But it was easy to imagine her adorned for the street, like some barbarian loose among the lowlanders.

A few colorful slings and a gear rack crossed her chest like bandoliers. Hugh eyed the equipment, reading in it her last minutes on the wall. The rack held little gear. She'd either exhausted her protection just prior to the fall, or had deliberately gone up with next to nothing. The latter, he decided. The few pieces of "pro" had small heads on thin wire, the sort that favor very delicate placements. That told him much. She'd been deep in Indian country up there, and had selected for a deft, light strike, for ballet, not biceps.

He touched her shoulder. It was basic and necessary. He had to make contact, and introduce himself, and get steady. This was real.

She was still warm. Before his eyes, even as he touched her, she lost her color. The rosy cheeks went gray. Her lips bleached to wax. He drew his hand away.

He circled the slab, and it was like going to the dark side of the moon. The real destruction crouched back here. Her envelope of skin had ruptured up and down her side. With all the blood, it was hard to tell the rope from the entrails. Her snapped ribs showed like something in a butcher shop. Her face—so pretty from the other side—sagged in buckled folds.

"Why you?" he whispered, partly to her, but mostly to himself. He regretted finding her. He regretted her death. Most of all, he regretted the waste.

She was young, maybe twenty, but that was not the real pity of it. Climbers are realists. Risk confers both gain and loss, and youth had nothing to do with it. Living in other lands, seeing the ravages of famine and disease, Hugh had come to view this kind of risk as an extravagance, a kind of personal theater. For him, the tragedy was that he would forever remember this young woman, who had sewn precious stones into her hair and silver into her earlobes, as nothing more than a carcass.

He'd seen worse. Ride the mountains long enough and you were bound to meet the dead. He'd found avalanche victims squeezed into packages no bigger than a TV set, their faces looking up from under his boots and crampons. He'd watched climbers take videos of quick-frozen limbs and torsos scattered on the glaciers beneath Everest. He'd helped retrieve a climber from the base of the Diamond on Longs Peak, just rags and sticks.

He went to his pack, glad to turn away from the stench and ugliness, and found an old green tarp. He snapped it open and covered what he could of her, head first. Only now did he notice one foot turned upside down. Her bones would be jelly.

He began pinning the tarp in place with chunks of granite. For the time being, there was no wind to disturb it, and a few rocks weren't going to deter animals from rooting underneath while he went to report her. But his handiwork gave shape to the mess. It closed off the bedlam in his mind. When the rangers arrived, they would find her neatly tucked atop the slab. The stones and tarp made final his part of her burial. It signed him out of the terrible event. They could have his tarp.

As if approving, the forest rustled.

Hugh glanced around. The trees gently creaked and dry leaves rattled like coins. A primal thought sprang up: *Her spirit's still lingering.*

He didn't dismiss the possibility. People assumed geologists were earthbound and geocentric, but even the ones who were carried lucky coins or a rabbit's foot. Searching for oil and gas involved the hard data of shot graphs and core samples, but also a good bit of the witching rod and a vigilance for secrets layered deep underfoot.

In the Arab countries, and Nigeria, and Louisiana, he'd shared field camps with experts trained to decipher the stratigraphy of hundreds of millions of years, who nonetheless spoke of biblical creation as a fact. Upon discovering Hugh was a mountaineer, one geologist had begged him to help explore Mount Ararat in Turkey, convinced the ark was frozen into its summit snow. Some oilmen lived like desert ascetics in four-wheel drive, in constant motion through faraway sands, chewing khat, smoking hash, taking peyote, having visions. These were the soothsayers who provided Tony the Tiger with his oil.

Hugh knew the species. He knew himself. Superstition came with the territory.

His progression to geology—from a rock hound in second grade, cracking open egg-shaped geodes, to a master of science with a license to roam the ends of the earth—had left him more pagan than American. Climbing in the Himalayas, he'd passed among villagers who believed in monsters and goddesses perched on the summits, and the river of consciousness.

He never talked about such things. But he saw life forces dodging everywhere, in everything from man to lizards and bugs, but also in trees and rocks and crystals of salt and ice. At the same time, he believed to his core that none of it mattered at the human level. It just was.

"Go on now," he murmured to her spirit. "We'll take care of this." This. The wreckage.

The trees settled.

Done. He finished with the tarp and stood back to memorize the exact location. He would go down and make his report to the rangers. He wanted rest and a hot shower. And distance. He needed a few hours away from El Cap and its consequences. Because, this aside, first thing in the morning he and Lewis were heading up.

But the more he tried to settle on a landmark, the more the forest seemed overrun with the trees and thatches of manzanita and rhododendron. It was not like him to be so illiterate with the land. Even deep in the Rub', Saudi Arabia's Rub' al-Khali, or Empty Quarter, there was always some way to pinpoint your position. He felt lost suddenly.

The death, the brutality of her collision, had him more unsettled than he thought. That was not good on the eve of his launch. *Bear down, Glass. Walk on.*

High on the towering wall, the sun line was draining higher. The earth was moving. He faced downhill, and there was not a trace of his way. He glanced at his watch, as if by knowing the time he could extract a longitude at least, anything to fix this rootless, spinning site in place.

The breeze stirred again. The shoulders and back of his shirt were soaked. The chill leaped on him like an animal. While he was getting his sweater from the pack, he had an idea. A sentiment.

That high on the wall, after so many days in the sun, she would have been thirsty. He left a Clorox jug of water near the head of the slab, an offering. Let the rangers think what they wanted.

THREE

Going down, he had to fight to not race. There was no urgency. She was dead. He would only trash his knees by rushing. And yet he wanted to get away. No desperation, mind you. Just a natural desire to leave the death far behind. It was not the first time. The desert surfaced in his mind, the red, alien desert, the dunes at sunset. Annie. *Thy will be done.*

He had brought two collapsible ski poles for the descent. Long ago he would have gone loping down the talus, agile as a goat. Now the poles clicked on rocks and snagged on branches.

Without the pack bearing down on him, the forest was a different place, a taller place. Instead of staring at roots and rocks, he could look up and around. The redwoods soared like cathedral spires. The sky was blue. A glorious day.

He eased himself down a clutter of stones. No

snakes to worry about at this time of year, only the venomous oak and ivy. And his left ACL, and that tickle of torn meniscus in his right knee, and the bum ankle, and his hips. *Save it for the Captain.* The climb was when the sum of him could be greater than his failing parts.

The undergrowth thinned. He saw a figure coming through the trees. "Ha-low," he called. "Here. Up here."

He slowed. He was back among the living. The presence at his back slid away, that sense of stilled waiting.

What emerged from the trees was a strange brew of leather, rags, and a parka bandaged with *X*s of duct tape. He looked like a time traveler, wearing a John Muir–style slouch hat with an eagle feather in the band, and blackened buckskin pants that had shrunk to midshin. He wore Air Nikes and carried a hiking stick with animal heads whittled along the shaft.

The man limped closer, winded from his slog. He was skinny, with a junk-food paunch. At first Hugh was so glad to have someone to share his news with that he ignored the peculiarities.

"There's been an accident," Hugh said.

"Do you think I'm blind?" The man glared at him, and coughed. "What have you done?"

Now Hugh saw the palsy laming the man's entire left side. "I covered her."

"Well, you shouldn't have come. Everything was fine. She wouldn't have come off. The rope wouldn't have broke. They were almost to the top. Then you show up."

Hugh looked closer, startled by the hostility, trying to rationalize it. Shock, he thought. "You saw her fall?" he asked.

"Right from where she went, the whole damn way, all of it." The man leaned on his stick and coughed again.

"How did it happen?" Knowing wouldn't change a thing. She was dead. But Hugh was curious. Here was an eyewitness.

"You tell me, mister." Tree sap had glued goose down and needles to his beard. He'd bent too close to a campfire and frizzled a patch to the jawline.

"I don't know," said Hugh. "It was over by the time I found her."

"You call that an accident? You find her in the middle of nowhere? You? By accident?"

"I was talking about the fall."

"Because there's no such thing as accidents. I'm here. You're here. She was up there. Now she's down here. Get it? You see the gist of it, all coming together? You?"

"Not really," said Hugh. Driftwood, he thought. You saw his type curled on grates in the cities and climbing out of Dumpsters. This was simply Yosemite's version. They came up from the cities and towns, stealing into the Valley, full of demons. Some were war vets with nightmares, or drug addicts, or college runaways full of *Black Elk Speaks*. Hugh saw the necklace inside his parka now, little animal bones and fetishes strung together. This was no college kid, though.

"You don't believe me. It's starting to happen now, just like I dreamed it."

"We need to tell the rangers," Hugh said. "Do you have a car? My friend dropped me off. I was going to thumb back."

The man went on raving. "You think I don't know about you? You and your buddy stashing gear and food at the base. I know you're going up."

Great, thought Hugh. Mr. Muir had been following them. There was no sense in asking if he'd stolen anything, he'd only lie. Now they'd have to waste time going through the haul bags to see what might be missing.

"Big men. Big walls," the man said. "Big mistake."

He was getting more aggressive. Hugh sized him up. He might have a limp, but he was bigger than Hugh, and that hiking stick was thick enough to break bones. But if it came to a footrace, Hugh figured he was quicker, even with his hobbling and ski poles. And suddenly he didn't like the idea of this man going up to the body.

"Come with me," he said. "We'll do this together."

"Do what?"

"The rangers need to know."

"Give her away to them? You?" The slouch hat filled with shadows. "She don't belong to you."

Not good, thought Hugh. But what could he do, drag the man down to the road? Tie him to a tree?

With what? Their rope was up at the base. And it was their climbing rope. "She can't stay here," Hugh said. "The animals will be coming. We need to get her in before night."

"Just because you go up on the walls, you don't own the place."

"None of us do. Not me, or you." Hugh gestured up at El Cap where the other climbers were, or had been. "Nor them."

Tears beaded down the greasy face. "I knew them. Kind ladies. They brought me food. Yes. They knew my camp. We had secrets. I watched over them. They said I was their homeboy."

Hugh didn't buy a word of it. "Well, I'm sorry."

"If you were sorry, none of this would be happening. Now we're in for it."

"Look at me," Hugh said. "Right in my eyes. Have you ever seen me? Because I've never seen you."

The man grimaced. "The devil's a dog. A black dog. You ever seen that?"

Like talking to the wind, thought Hugh. Time was wasting. He started to walk around him.

The hermit lifted his hiking stick, as if to block him. "Now all hell's loose because of you." His breath stunk of road kill.

Hugh knew madness. He'd lived with it. He'd seen it make Annie not Annie. It had stripped the soul right out of her. He'd watched her wither away, mind and body, until his heart quit breaking. There was only so much suffering you could stand by and just watch. And then you had to walk on. God willing.

"My friend," he said, "this has nothing to do with us."

"Liar." The man was weeping.

"Let me go. Please." Hugh let the stick rest against his chest. He could feel tremors through its wood. The man was harmless.

"You killed her."

"Enough," said Hugh.

"I should have stopped you."

Enough.

Taking him down was as simple as grabbing the staff and giving a pull. The man spilled to his weak side, and Hugh heard his skull, like a coconut shell, knock on a rock. The hermit gave a sharp cry, and Hugh felt a twinge of regret at his pain and surprise. But he was fighting away the animals, no more or less. Hugh didn't offer him a hand up.

"Get out of here," Hugh said.

"My stick," the man pleaded.

Hugh held it out of reach. The stick was a worthy thing, the product of many days and nights of loving attention. Knots had been carved into faces and forms, images of nature rising up from the wood's surface, a whole Eden in his hand.

"I'm going to break this. If I find you anywhere near here, I'll break your legs." *Christ, Glass, a poor gimp?* He could never do such a thing. But of course he could. Lift a rock, drop it, cripple the animal once and for all.

"Don't." The slouch hat fell off, and with it fell the hermit's menace. He gained a forehead, a pale spray of constant worries. A few wisps of hair lay matted across his soft, white scalp. It looked like a mushroom growing from quiet rot beneath a log.

Something about that bared head brought out Hugh's pity. Harm this poor thing? The sun was his harm. The moon was his harm. All he had was this stick to shepherd his nightmares.

"Get going," Hugh said. Again, he didn't offer his hand, not out of meanness, just caution. The man had carved the stick with something. He had a knife on him somewhere.

"My stick."

Hugh heaved it like a spear far into the woods.

The man scrambled to his knees to track its general course. It went out of sight and Hugh hoped the thing didn't hang up in the boughs.

The man got to his feet. He tugged the hat onto his head and went in a crooked line after his stick.

"That's poison ivy," Hugh called after him. It was a small act of mercy. The fool didn't need any more misery in his hard life.

The stranger glanced back at him. "I'll see you here again," he said. "Right where you left her."

Hugh bent as if to pick up a rock, like you'd throw at dogs. But the man was already off through the thicket, noisy for a minute, then gone.

FOUR

Near eight, Hugh walked into the bar at Yosemite Lodge. Thirty years ago, it would have been packed with climbers. But the nightly banquet of high-plains drifters was a thing of the past. The park service had contained the once rowdy climbing scene with rules and regs, and the beer had gotten too expensive. Also, this new breed of climbers took their training more seriously, and the semesters were back in session, and the season was wrong.

So the place was empty. In place of audacious young bravos and their braless girlfriends, the bar was occupied by five TV sets running an endless stream of extreme sports, all scored to deafening hip-hop. The bartender was fishing for customers, or just indulging himself.

Lewis Cole perched on a stool nursing a tonic water with lime, tossing peanuts at his mouth, waiting like it was no wait, just killing time. Tall, with the neck of a wrestler, he was too big to be a rock climber, though in the face of conventional wisdom he'd proved to be a very good one, a small legend, the Great Ape. He'd never been pretty to watch in action, but he had ungodly reach and speed and fists like iron chunks, perfect for slugging it out with Yosemite's famous cracks.

Hugh took a seat at the little table with Lewis. Suddenly his legs felt heavy. He let his back muscles sag, and gave a silent sigh. For the first time in many hours, he could afford to be weak.

Lewis didn't greet him outright. There was no need. They had a shared history that went back to second grade at Whittier Elementary School, and they were about to be tied together every minute for the next seven days or so. To Lewis, Hugh had been off on a chore, no more. He threw another nut at his mouth. He offered the paper cup of them to Hugh. He waited.

Hugh was famished, but waved it off. "I'm a little dry," he said. *The creature had eaten his pear.* Hugh couldn't get over that. When, at their insistence, he had led the rangers back to the site, his pack was lying open. The hermit had stolen his pear. Which was the least of it. But also the essence of it. The monster had felt so comfortable in stealing her body, he'd paused to help himself to Hugh's piece of fruit. It was all about territory.

Lewis called to the bartender. The man took his time coming over. He was shaved bald with some kind of Chinese calligraphy tattooed at the base of his skull. "More peanuts?" he said. Hugh got it. Lewis hadn't been much of a customer.

"Water," said Hugh. "And I'll have what he's having."

"Water with your water." A wise guy. "You want some gin or vodka to go with it?"

Once upon a time, you drank the demon and raged all night, and next morning cleared the toxins out of your system on the wall. Or took the party with you, jugs of wine, hits of acid, doobies, mushrooms, name it. Great routes had been climbed in a hallucinogenic fog. But that was a thousand years ago, and tomorrow morning was almost upon them. "Just straight tonic water, the same as him," Hugh said.

"While you're at it," Lewis said, "how about changing the channel? And tweak the volume. Oh, and yeah, more peanuts."

The bartender signed "cool" with his horn fingers, and moseyed off.

"We almost went looking for you," Lewis said. "Almost. Rachel wanted to. She drove up in a rental car this afternoon and thought you'd be here. I told her you were out communing with the bewilderness. I said to just let you ramble in the brambles."

Hugh smiled faintly. Lewis was clowning with his Beat speak, dishing up vestiges of auld lang syne, trying to set the tone. He saw El Cap as their time machine. It was going to take them back and make life simple and sweet again.

"It's good she didn't come," Hugh told him.

"That's what I told her," Lewis said. "Glass is having his usual struggle session. Like Sisyphus rolling his rock up the hill. So who won, you or the water?"

"You didn't hear?" Hugh was surprised. The past four hours loomed in him. The earth had split open and swallowed a woman. Surely word had spread.

Lewis heard his tone. His face clouded and he darted a glance at the TVs perched in the corners to search out his own information, looking for news of some disaster or terrorist attack.

Just then the screens flickered to a new channel and the volume dropped to a reverent hush. Hugh looked up and the bartender had found them a nearly comatose PGA Seniors tournament.

"Cute," said Lewis.

The bartender brought Hugh's tonic water. He set down a bowl brimming with too many peanuts, as if feeding beggars. Lewis didn't look at him.

Hugh told Lewis about the fall and his return with the rangers, and the unbelievable body theft, and their search, still ongoing. He kept it brief, on purpose. The last thing two aging mountain men needed was a bloody foreboding. Superstition could kill a climb before you ever left the earth.

"You are shitting me," Lewis said when he finished. "Here, in the Valley? That's straight out of Frankenstein or Poe."

"He bundled her up in the tarp and took her

off," said Hugh. "A special friend. By the time I got there with the rangers, he'd had a good hour's head start."

"You should have broken his legs while you had him down," said Lewis. "You threatened him. You should have just done it."

"How could I know he'd do a thing like that?"

Lewis frowned.

Now what? Hugh waited. He'd had time to think their choices through. But Lewis would need to catch up with it and reach his own conclusions.

Lewis got quiet. His big fingernail—carefully clipped to the quick for their climb—tapped on the photo in the center of the table. It was a photo of El Cap, though nothing pretty. The frame was filled with everyday rock and just a sliver of sky. Most people would have thought it was a reject. But for these two men, it was both past and future, a black-and-white portrait of Anasazi Wall, the route they had pioneered back in 1968. They were its fathers, and it marked the greatest year of their lives.

Shortly after making Anasazi's first ascent, life had taken them off in different directions. Hugh had become a doodlebugger in the bayous of Louisiana, dynamiting the mud in seismic search of oil. When a job came up with British Petroleum, he'd jumped at it and taken his bride off to Egypt, Saudi Arabia, and Dubai, to vast desert country. Lewis had strayed back to Colorado and earned a graduate degree in Ezra Pound and Wyndham Lewis, and done with it the only thing he could, opening a used bookstore that had evolved over the years into a poets' hangout and a latte bar. Now, like old warriors, the two of them were returning to their battleground, Anasazi.

Lewis quit tapping. His finger pinned the photo flat. "I don't mean to be insensitive," he started. "That could be me lying out there, or you. But . . ." But it wasn't.

Right away Hugh knew in its entirety how their decision would unfold. They would go back and forth a little, paying lip service to what was proper at such times, but end with the fact that, really, the death—even her stolen remains—changed nothing. El Cap was a matter of orbit, the pull of gravity, a fact of life, their life. And she'd had her chance.

For years, they had been tempting each other to take one more stab at the beast. Once upon a time, big walls and big mountains had been their glory. They came from a bygone era. Vietnam, Camelot, and Apollo had all been parts of their vocabulary. They had lived hand to mouth, working construction jobs, digging ditches, and one summer hiring onto the Alaska pipeline, to pay for gear and more climbing. They'd slept in caves and under picnic tables and on high ledges, subsisting on Jif peanut butter and Charlie's tuna. A can of peaches and a tin cup of glacier melt were virtually sacraments. And at the center, always, El Cap remained their holy grail.

In its day, the 3,600-foot-high monolith had been hailed as both the American Everest and the last Eiger. But like Hugh and Lewis, the proud Captain had grayed and slid from grace. El Cap had turned into a circus ground with a whole new breed of speed climbers, bolt gunners, and parachutists performing stunts and bagging records. Once mighty routes, including Anasazi, were now viewed as milk runs. The well-heeled adventurer could even buy a guided ascent of El Cap at the rate of $1 per vertical foot. Coming back, going up, leaving a bit of blood, it seemed the least Hugh and Lewis could do to restore some of the nobility they had known.

And their time for the grand, absurd suffering of a multiday big-wall ascent was now or never. Anasazi would be their swan song, and they knew it. Each had kept climbing over the years, but it couldn't last. In preparation for this climb, Hugh had made a daily diet of ibuprofen for pain and inflammation, along with vitamins and whey protein powder. Lewis had gone further, getting testosterone shots that left him bigger than ever. They were steeled and tempered and psyched for this thing. Once Anasazi was finished, Hugh reckoned each of them could slide back into the arthritis and skin cancer and mortality that awaited them.

Lewis spoke his condolences to the young woman's departed soul. He saluted her as "one of us," and raised his glass of tonic water.

"Bismullah," whispered Hugh. Lewis looked at him. Louder, he said, "In the name of God."

"God? We're dabbling in religions now?"

"Cultures," said Hugh. "The Arabs say it before entering a place. It keeps them safe."

"Do tell." Lewis wanted to see how infected he was.

"You know," Hugh waved at the air. "From them."

" 'Them'? You've been in the land of the heathen too long. This is America, bro. Not eleventh-century Islam."

"It goes back before Islam, long before that. Primal fears. They have their names for them, we have ours."

"To guilt, ignorance, and the id," said Lewis.

Hugh eyed the photo, and it showed sections of the doomed climb off to the side. In the upper corner, like a bullet hole, stood Cyclops Eye.

"The rangers will find her," Lewis said. "They'll get her home." He was studying Hugh, looking for chinks in the armor. It was Hugh who had dealt with the slaughter, Hugh who had blood on his sleeve, Hugh who might have weakened.

"She'd want us to carry on," Hugh reassured him. "It's what I'd want."

"Me, too," said Lewis. "So we're good for it?"

"Of course."

"Do me a favor." Lewis paused, eyes furtive.

"Sure."

"How about some teeth?"

"What?"

"A smiley face. Or at least keep the worst of it under the table, you know, about the body getting stolen. Rachel's not in the mood."

"She's not feeling well?"

"We had a little argument." Lewis tossed more peanuts at his mouth. "No worries. She'll be coming any minute. She can't wait to catch up with you."

"Me, too."

Lewis suddenly noticed the photo, as if it had sneaked up on them. "I hit Camp Four and did some more due diligence."

Camp Four was a sort of dumping ground for climbers from around the world, a motley base camp for all the big walls. People had once occupied it like homesteaders, planting themselves for years. The petrol station that hid it from civilian view was gone, but so was much of the camp's ghetto comportment. In theory at least, the park service limited climbers' stays to a couple of weeks. The worst of the shantytown shelters had disappeared and been replaced by ordinary dome tents, if only because a used dome tent could be had for the price of a good sheet of plastic. The nightly twinkle of campfires surrounded by hard-core storytellers was a bygone thing, especially this year when the drought had parched the forest to dry tinder. But for all the changes, Camp Four was still the place to get your information. The latest beta pooled there like water in an oasis.

Hugh and Lewis were not staying at Camp Four. Lewis was chagrined. He felt like a traitor for taking a room at the lodge, but Rachel had put her foot down. She said she'd paid her dues in Camp Four, crawling up off the ground and out from tents for too many mornings of her life. Either they rented a room or she stayed home. When Lewis had called him about the matter, Hugh told him he was on Rachel's side. *Let's save our suffering for the wall.*

Until the climb began, Hugh was very happy to have his own shower and toilet and a bed with sheets and a pillow. And his own rental car, his own entrance, his own exit. Friendship was one thing, but Hugh had outgrown the sort of camaraderie that once fueled their stolen rides on freight trains from Denver, and their hitchhiking in storms, and their making claustrophobic fear-and-loathing marathons through Utah and Nevada packed in Hugh's VW Beetle.

Hugh took out a small, thick, leather-bound book. Lewis called it the bible. Filled with hand-drawn maps and topographical sketches and notes, it contained a lifetime of adventures. He opened it near the beginning, to a page neatly titled "Anasazi." Lines met hatch marks and dots and numbers, the puzzle pieces of their climb.

Lewis reached for the Bible as if it were his own, and aligned it beside the photo. With the tip of the little plastic sword from his lime slice, he very precisely matched sections of Hugh's topo with the photo. He looked faintly silly, a fifty-six-year-old man stabbing with what looked like a child's toy at a treasure map.

"Remember that expanding flake on the ninth pitch, how it gave us fits? Well, the flake's gone. It fell off when no one was looking. There's a bolt ladder now. It misses the flake altogether. We can save hours. They say it cuts out the extra night."

"I'm for that," said Hugh.

The sword tip moved. "And the vegetated crack on the twentieth pitch, where we used knife blades? You can hand-place three-inch angles now."

Hugh let him go on. Beta or not, he was taking nothing for granted, not the bolt ladder, nor the eroded crack on the twentieth pitch, nor the summit. Anasazi had changed, and they had changed. As a young man, he'd used other men's maps and their prior knowledge to explore the mountains and rivers and deserts. But at some point, conventional wisdom didn't matter. You had to draw your own maps, make your own rules, and find your own way.

Lewis went on taking them up the route with his sword tip, pitch by pitch, thrashing out details they'd covered a dozen times, burning off nervous energy that neither wanted to admit to. Hugh let him go on. Just as Hugh had needed to carry water this afternoon, Lewis needed to recite the route yet again.

Hugh had his back to the door. When a new customer entered, he felt the night chill against his neck. The bartender straightened. Lewis glanced up from the book of maps.

Hugh turned, thinking Rachel was finally making her appearance. Instead he saw a man, probably half their age, with a long thatch of sun-bleached hair and the wide back and mason forearms of a

climber, a Tarzan in old Levi's. Wearing a white
T-shirt and Teva sandals with white socks, he was
neat and clean, and a local. Hugh could tell he
belonged here. He carried himself directly, with no
nonsense, no bluff or mannerisms.

The bartender said hey, to no response. "Anything?" he said.

Tarzan shook his head no.

"Let me get you a beer."

The man didn't answer. He looked straight at
Hugh and Lewis and came around the big unlit fire-
place with its odd, squat, Soviet-style skiers on the
metal plaques of the pillars. "Hugh Glass," he said
to them.

"That's me," said Hugh.

No logos on the T-shirt, no body art, no excess.
It stressed his intensity, that and his eyes, which
were Hollywood blue. He was deeply tanned, the
way laborers get. The only paleness Hugh saw was
at the edges of his wristwatch. The guy probably
combed his hair once in the morning when he
shaved, then was done with the burdens of image.

"I'm Augustine," he said. "With SAR. I got there
late. You'd left."

After this afternoon, Hugh knew the acronym:
search and rescue. "You're a ranger," he said.

"Nope, an eighties hire," he said. He stood
there, not exactly aggressive, but not friendly either.
Lewis sensed it, too.

"That's a new one," Lewis said.

"Back in the eighties, the park service would go

to local bars and draft men to fight fires. You got paid by the hour. The term stuck. That's what they call us now."

"You're a firefighter?" Lewis said.

Hugh put two and two together, SAR and the hourly pay. "A rescue climber," he said.

Augustine nodded, wound tight as a clock.

"We kind of missed the eighties. And nineties," Lewis said. "Back in our day, they used to let you guys live in Camp Four year-round." A gilded role, rescue work marked you as one of the best of the best.

Augustine's name tickled Hugh's cultural memory, something about a scandal or an epic. But he'd been out of the clannish, larger-than-life climbing scene too long.

Augustine cut to the chase. "You're the last one who saw her," he said to Hugh. There was no question about the "her." Obviously they were still searching for the body. His tone held accusation.

"I told them everything I knew," Hugh said. "But ask me again. Pull up a seat." He gestured at the bartender and pointed at Augustine for that beer.

"I'm not staying," Augustine said. "I just want to hear it straight from you."

"Sit, damnit."

Augustine eased onto the stool, but stayed distant, hands to himself, not propping his elbows on their table, not leaning into their society. He kept his gunslinger vigilance. But Hugh saw when his eyes recognized their photo. "Anasazi," Augustine said. They became less strange to him.

The beer arrived, and along with it two more tonic waters, though no one had asked for them. The bartender gripped the back of Augustine's neck, nothing sloppy, then released him and left. A minute later, the golf joke flickered dead. The TVs went blank. They had their privacy.

"How can I help?" Hugh said. He hoped Augustine was not here to recruit them. He was tired. It was an aberration that he had become part of her mystery. He had nothing to add.

"You said she had beads in her hair."

"Little stone beads." Hugh sized them with his fingers. "Some turquoise and jade and agate. Very pretty."

"But you said her hair was brown."

"That's right."

"Not blond? Maybe with the blood in it?" Augustine's back was rigid, but something in his tone loosened. *Hope,* thought Hugh. *The man wants hope.*

"Brown. Light brown," Hugh said. "I don't know, dirty blond maybe."

Augustine hardened himself. He put away his hope. "What color were her eyes?"

"I didn't look. I didn't want to."

"How tall was she?"

"She was flat on her back." Flat.

"What kind of shoes was she wearing?"

"You mean a brand name? I can't tell the difference anymore. They were these modern climbing shoes, you know, these slippers." One turned upside down. Hugh emptied the image from his mind.

Augustine's frustration showed. "She had earrings?"

"Silver rings, five or so. Up here along the edge of her ear. They stood out. I guess it's the fashion."

"Both ears?"

Hugh reached in his mind to the far side of her. "I don't know about that," he said.

Augustine pressed it. "You saw them in the one ear."

"I don't remember."

"But you said they stood out. You would have seen them."

"To tell the truth, I'm trying to remember if she had another ear. She came down through the trees, and the other side of her, it was unpleasant."

Augustine stared at him.

"Look," said Hugh, "it's obvious you know these girls." No surprises there. The Valley was cloistered and tight-knit, especially the climbing community, like tribal settlements in every mountain valley he'd been through, from the Solu Khumbu to the Appalachians.

Augustine's jaw tightened.

"Tell me how to help you name her," Hugh said. "Keep asking me questions. Maybe something will come clear."

"Just tell me, was it her?" Augustine opened his wallet. He showed a photo of a young woman drenched with sunshine. Her hair was white with light. Augustine was in the photo, too, practically transparent in the radiance. He had his arm around her.

Hugh might have guessed. The woman—or one of the women on the wall—was his lover. "No," Hugh said. "It wasn't her."

"Forget the hair," Augustine said. He was plaintive and skeptical. He was afraid Hugh might be wrong. "Look at her face. You saw her face."

The more Hugh examined the face in the photo, the less certain he became. There were resemblances, but maybe he was imagining them. He tried to remember the face he'd covered with the tarp, but its features melted in his memory. And this face in the photo was so ethereal, like a face in a dream. What if he was wrong? What if this woman was the same one he'd found in the forest?

"You don't know," Augustine decided.

"Who the hell would steal a body?" Lewis said.

Hugh started to describe the wild man, but Augustine interrupted. "Joshua," he said. "He's one of the cavemen."

The rangers had used the same term that afternoon, "cavemen," as if the hermit were part of a rare, dying species, an American yeti.

"Joshua?" Lewis said. Hugh looked at him. "Didn't he used to work in housekeeping? This was thirty years ago, a kid. A crag rat. He got hit by lightning. I thought he died."

"It was before my time. But he lived," Augustine said. "He kept coming back. They finally gave up and let him stay, a charity case. Ever since, he's been living in caves and animal dens, eating tourist leftovers and downed game, foraging for nuts and berries. He rants and raves. We thought he was harmless."

"Somebody must know where to find him," Lewis said.

"Do you know how many places there are to hide?"

"What about dogs?" asked Lewis. "Can't they bring in dogs?"

"It's not her," Hugh said. "I'm telling you."

Augustine didn't believe him, though.

"Have you spotted the others?" Hugh asked. He wanted Augustine to hold on to his dignity, or at least not come apart in front of them. "There were three of them. They couldn't all have disappeared."

They could all have fallen, of course. Their anchor could have pulled and sent the other two to their deaths. But the rangers knew that and Hugh had watched them looking everywhere, including the treetops.

"We've been calling. There's no sign of anybody up there."

"They'll find them," Lewis said.

"I know," Augustine said. It was spoken without emotion, a promise to himself, to fetch the dead and wounded. To keep on hoping.

FIVE

Hugh looked at their reflections in the dark window.

Over the next days, El Cap was sure to peel them open and see what grit each contained. Hugh and Lewis would run their stone gauntlet. Augustine would probably kiss a cold forehead, or a hand, something still recognizable, and learn grief, the hardest lesson of all. No matter what happened on the wall or in its forest, their shapes would shift. Each of them would come away changed. El Cap was like that.

Even as Hugh gazed at the dark glass, a woman's face surfaced in the mirror. Lewis and Augustine didn't notice as the ghost gradually joined them from the other side of the window. Her eyes stayed fixed on Hugh.

At first, rising from the darkness, she could

have been any woman, old or young, practically an idea. Closer to the glass, her features grew more distinct. The pallor took on color. Her lips were a lush red. She seemed to be boring in on Hugh, seductive and dangerous at the same time. Was he imagining the dead girl? At the last instant, she reached her chin forward and pursed her lips and pressed them against the glass, a kiss for Hugh.

"Rachel," he murmured.

She rapped at the window, and the other two men started. With a silent laugh, she vanished back into darkness. A minute later, she came through the door. The men rose to their feet, Lewis last of all. "My wife," he explained to Augustine.

Hugh had never seen her this way, in designer jeans and a black sweater that sparkled and played with her curves, and with exact makeup, and a stride that suggested daily tennis or aerobics. Her beauty confused him. It was so different from the beauty he remembered. Over three decades had passed.

Gone was the granola girl with her hair in a ponytail tied with a bandana. She and Annie had been the closest of pals, bonded by Yosemite and camp life, and by the dangers their boyfriends courted on the walls. The four of them, the two couples, had traveled up and down the West Coast, from Baja to Vancouver, thousands of miles.

"Finally," she said to Hugh, and kissed him on the mouth. She gave him thirty years' worth of a hug. Hugh was surprised by how good she felt. It was almost embarrassing. Over her shoulder, Lewis was grinning from ear to ear. She held Hugh at arm's length, looked him over, and gathered him in for a second long, hard embrace. "Just like you were," she said.

She had been their gypsy spirit, forever on her feet, eyes closed, arms up, twisting and curling like smoke, ready to float off into the cosmos it seemed. Everything was so fresh and present in those days, the music, the poster art and flowers in your hair, the Conan comics, even the ancient war. He remembered driftwood campfires on Pacific nights, the ocean going in and out under the stars.

Annie had perfected a drop-dead Janis Joplin impression, with every high, rusty, piercing note. Hugh had memorized on his harmonica a fair John Mayall riff that basically worked for any occasion. All of nineteen, Lewis would drunkenly preach the orthodoxy of the Beats, and the spontaneity of art, and the art of climbing. Between songs, he would chant his precious Ginsburg, who was, to the rest of them, already old, fat, and hairy. Hugh would argue with him as if it really mattered. Forget the elitism of the junkies, queers, anarchists, and urban hipsters. In the wilderness lay true freedom. In the stone.

She let go of him.

"This is Mr. Augustine," Lewis said, and Augustine gravely shook her hand.

"You're going with them?" she said.

Augustine frowned uncertainly. "El Cap, you mean?"

"You're not a guide?" she said. "I thought they'd come to their senses."

"A guide? Them?"

Hugh was grateful beyond words. *Them*. They were not forgotten. Until that moment, he had not realized how profoundly he was waiting for such a judgment. He still belonged. They might actually pull it off. Lewis heard it, too. His eyes were suddenly bright.

Rachel didn't miss a beat. "Did you know this is where I met them?" she said. "Before you were born, I'm sure, right here, this very room. It wasn't a bar back then, just a gathering place. It was raining. There was a fire. Some of the Camp Four refugees had come over to dry out. I was just this young thing, sixteen, all bedraggled. And here were these two boys in the corner, totally serious, totally business, the walls, you know, the walls. They saw me across the room, but I had to go up to them. Do you remember?"

"I remember," said Hugh.

"And a little bit later, Annie came over, soggy as a hound, a total stranger just like me. It happened like magic, great loves, everything, our whole future born out of one wet afternoon. I ended up with Lewis. And Annie got herself the lone wolf. I can't remember how we got all sorted out and paired up. We just followed the stars."

It was strange to hear Annie's name spoken so gaily, without the solemnity people seemed to think Hugh required. Five years had passed, but because this was his first trip to the States since her death, they acted like it had happened just yesterday. Lewis was the worst in that respect. He seemed afraid to even mention her, as if Hugh might have a breakdown.

Then Hugh noticed Augustine. He looked trapped by all the happy talk about great loves. The pain on his face was unmistakable. Rachel had no way of knowing.

"Let's walk outside," Hugh said to him.

"No need," said Augustine. "We've covered it all, I guess."

"At least have some of your beer."

"Another time, that would be good." Augustine's big arms hung like string.

Hugh didn't insist. The man had a long night of the soul ahead of him. On balance, Augustine had given more than he had received. Without knowing it, he had declared Hugh and Lewis's legitimacy. Now he was going off empty-handed. Hugh left it at that.

"Keep the faith," Lewis said. He looked sheepish. He knew it was lame.

Rachel looked at the men, mystified by their unease.

Augustine nodded to them. "When you're up there, if you see something . . ." He didn't finish. By then it would surely be too late.

"We'll report," Hugh told him.

"Great." Augustine turned and stepped through the obstacle course of bar stools. Hugh watched until the door closed behind him.

"What was that all about?" Rachel asked.

Lewis gave Hugh a warning look. "He's with the park service. He wanted some information."

She wasn't stupid. "He looked like the Grim Reaper."

"There was an accident this afternoon," Lewis said.

"On El Cap." Rachel nodded. "You thought I wasn't going to find out?"

Lewis's twinkle dimmed.

"It happened near the top," Hugh said. "Three women. One fell. The rescuers are getting it figured out."

"Three women?"

Rachel seemed more surprised by their gender than by the accident. In the old days, girlfriends tended the campsites and worked on their bikini lines down along the Merced River. They were trophies the men returned to from the heights. If a woman tied into a rope, it was only for something very short and very easy that involved a picnic at the top.

"And what did the ranger want?"

"He's not a ranger, babe," Lewis said.

She stared at him.

"I found one of the girls," Hugh said. Then he recalled Lewis and Rachel's two daughters, each grown up and moved away now, but an echo nonetheless.

"And you're still going up there?"

"It's different," Hugh said. "They were off on something new. We're doing a victory lap on

Anasazi. Only the weekend warriors bother with it anymore."

She wasn't buying it. "A girl died today. On El Cap."

"They were pushing a first ascent. A radical first. Off the scale."

"And when you two did Anasazi Wall thirty years ago, what do you think everyone was saying? The same thing. Radical. Crazy."

Hugh shut up.

"We're way under the speed limit here," Lewis said.

"Act your age," she snapped at him.

"We are. It's this or really loud golf slacks. Come on. El Cap, our old stomping grounds. A little Viagra for the soul."

"God, Lewis." She sounded sad.

The bartender came over. He was respectful this time, almost fraternal. Their powwow with Augustine had elevated them. Rachel ordered a glass of Australian wine.

It was too late to turn over the photo. El Cap occupied the table. Their silence lasted until the wine arrived.

"The girls," Hugh finally said. "Your girls. You must have pictures."

Rachel sighed. She had a small purse, more like a leather wallet on strings, very chic. It held a credit card, a lipstick, and snapshots.

"Look at them," Hugh said. The daughters were truly beautiful. "Tell me about them."

"As of this college semester, we're official empty nesters," Lewis said. "Trish made Bucknell, and Liz is in her third year at UT Austin."

"A Yankee and a rebel," Hugh said.

"Business, and engineering," Rachel pointed at one, then the other. "No philosophy. No poetry. I think Ezra Pound is finally dead."

She couldn't have been clearer. The daughters were moving on past Lewis. And Rachel was, too. Hugh suddenly realized that she was going to leave Lewis. She hadn't told him yet. But El Cap figured into her strategy somehow, or else she wouldn't have bothered to come.

Lewis stood up. Rachel didn't. "We're still good for four in the morning?" he said.

"I'll be ready," Hugh said.

Rachel saluted her husband: "0400."

Hugh started to get up, but she grabbed his wrist. "No you don't. I have a glass of wine to drink, and Lewis gets you for the next week. I think I'm worth a half hour, don't you?"

Hugh lifted his fingers in surrender and sat again.

"Make her understand," Lewis told Hugh. To Rachel he added, "And don't kill my messenger."

Once Lewis was gone, Rachel stretched her long swan neck. She breathed out. "This is our grand reunion. Lewis really wanted it to be that for us. The way it was."

"I know."

"It's no good, of course. We grew up, some of us anyway. And Annie's gone."

Hugh aimed for the high road. "Lewis always was one for the past. It's one of the things I love about him. He wants utopia so badly, and he wants us all right there with him."

"Have you ever tried driving forward while you're looking in the rearview mirror? That's life with Lewis." She sighed. "Lewis."

"And Rachel?" said Hugh.

He wasn't sure where to begin with her. She had grown up. Grown away. Her perfume was perfectly stated, not a whiff of her heady musk of yore. Her laugh lines were smooth, the almond eyes younger than ever. She had an excellent surgeon, and stylist. Her waist-length mane had been cut to a shag, feathered and highlighted. Her nails were bright as plastic.

The changes were all her doing, Hugh decided. Lewis had always been an earthy man. He liked hippie girls' armpits. Without him, or despite him, Rachel had gone beyond that. She had turned herself into a trophy wife. Hugh couldn't help but admire her conviction. She knew her beauty, and had chased it.

"And Annie," Rachel said. There was going to be no avoiding Annie.

"Hayati," Hugh said. "That's what I used to call her. It's an Arab endearment. My life."

"Mine, too." Rachel took his hand in her cool hands. "She was my best friend. Even after you took her off to those places."

Those places. The desert surged in his mind. The

wadis and wastelands and infinite sunsets. The dunes. He stanched it.

"Did you know we tried to come to the funeral? But the Saudis wouldn't issue us visas."

"They're tough about that," Hugh said. "Anyway, there was no funeral. The sand took care of that. I let her go."

"You know what I mean, we wanted to be there for you. I don't know how you survived the whole ordeal."

"You walk on," he said. The wind had altered the dunes. Even the Bedouin trackers had given up. God's will, they'd said.

"We never thought she'd last as long as she did over there," Rachel said.

Hugh grew very still. "Why do you say that?"

"She hated it so much, the heat, the submission, the compound life."

"Is that all she told you about?"

" 'Like a bird in a cage,' she wrote me. Arrogant expatriates. Arrogant Saudis. More than anything, she hated the hatreds. The wars. After Desert Storm, she said that was it. But she stayed. I could never figure that out."

"Did she tell you about the wedding we went to?"

"The one with the twelve-year-old girl?"

"Yeah, I know," said Hugh. "And Annie almost refused to go. But it turned out to be the beginning of something big for her, like a secret garden. It was an old-fashioned wedding. The women had their own tent, a black Bedouin *bait sha'r,* a house of hair. They sang and danced, and when Annie showed them a few modern moves, she was like a long-lost sister. They begged her to teach them."

"She said something about dance lessons."

"It was more than that. The dance was just a cover. She was their window on the world. They adored her, and vice versa. She taught them things. They taught her things. Henna patterns. How to pluck her eyebrows with a loop of thread, one hair at a time. How to belly dance. And make coffee from scratch. Green coffee."

"She was surviving, Hugh. It was just a way to keep her sanity."

"Her sanity?"

"Yes, while you were gone looking for oil and climbing mountains. Did you know I told her to leave you? To come home? I told her you would follow."

"Yes, we talked," said Hugh. "But there was nothing for me here. My job was there. And this will sound old-fashioned, but she was my wife."

"Don't put it that way," Rachel chided him. "Marriage wouldn't have stopped her from coming home. Love, yes. The wifey thing, not a chance. Not the Annie I knew."

"The Annie you knew was only the Annie she let you know," Hugh said.

"We had no secrets."

"Everyone has secrets, Rachel."

"Not us."

Hugh could have let it die there. But he was tired of hiding the truth. He was tired of the pity and the whispers. "Did she ever say anything to you about her Swiss cheese?"

" 'Swiss cheese'?"

"I didn't think so," he said. "It was our little code for the holes in her memory. The little lapses that started turning into big ones. Her spells."

The slightest storm appeared on Rachel's taut forehead.

"She did her best to hide it," Hugh continued. "For a while we thought it was just the summer heat or maybe a bacteria in the air-conditioning. Or menopause. That was the great hope, that it would get better. She quit drinking alcohol, then coffee and her Diet Cokes, thinking, you know, it might be the artificial sweeteners or the caffeine."

"What are you talking about?"

"I came home one day and she was sitting in front of the TV. But it was off. I touched the set and it wasn't even warm. She'd been there all day. Watching nothing."

"I don't understand."

"I didn't either, not for the longest time. She was too young. It crept up on both of us, and then it was too late."

"What, Hugh?"

"Alzheimer's."

"Annie?" said Rachel.

"We stopped going to parties because there would be these lapses. She would fumble little shared moments, or get a friend's name wrong. It got worse. She did everything to keep up appearances, even in front of me, but we both saw what was happening. The pounds just fell off of her. She'd forget to eat during the day. The expat wives all wore gold bangles from the medina, just like the Arab women. But Annie's wrists got so thin the bangles dropped like rain. I'd find them on the floor. One day I stepped on her wedding ring, by the front door."

"I had no idea." Rachel was in shock.

"While it still mattered to her, she didn't want anyone to know. By the last year, she didn't know herself."

"This is so . . . I thought she shared everything with me."

"She felt like a leper. She dropped from sight."

"How long did this go on?"

"In retrospect, years. Like I said, at first it seemed just a lapse here and there."

"How did you manage?"

"You mean the doctors? We tried them all. I took her to Switzerland. They all said the same thing. A losing battle. They didn't use those words, but that's what they meant. It was just a matter of waiting for the end."

She squeezed his hand. "I'm talking about you. How did *you* manage?"

"I didn't want it to be true either. I was in denial just as much as she was. But then one afternoon, there was a knock on my door. It was the *mutawaeen*, the religious police. Holier than holy. They roam the streets with camel switches, looking for vice, stuff like a woman's hair poking from her head scarf, or nail polish on their toes."

"She wrote about them. Vicious fanatics."

"Some are good men, some are very bad," Hugh said. "But Annie was right. She was a bird in a cage. There are so many rules to follow over there, especially for the women. There's the dress code and the head scarf. And every guest worker has to carry an ID card. Married women have to carry a copy of their husband's identification or they'll arrest you. This can get very serious. The *mutawaeen* take Sudanese or Ethiopian women, black women, into the desert and rape them, and leave them to die."

Rachel looked stunned. "And they came to your house?"

"That day I answered the door, and there were two *mutawaeen*. They had Annie with them. That was bad enough. She had wandered out of the compound in shorts, and with no head scarf, and no I.D. She didn't know her own name. They could have disappeared her. Instead they made inquiries and were returning her to me. It was the most terrifying moment in my life."

"Because she had wandered away?"

"Because they were so kind about it. Because they could see what I had been refusing to see. They have a word for the insane, *majnoona.*"

"She wasn't insane, Hugh. Alzheimer's is a disease."

"It's just a matter of which century you live in. *Majnoona*. It means possessed. Possessed by jinns."

"Genies?" Rachel scoffed. "Like in a lamp?"

"That's the American version, sanitized. Among the Arabs, they're beings from a parallel universe, created before Adam. Some are like devils, but some can be like archangels who watch over you. The Arabs believe they live in deserts and the ruins of cities and graveyards and empty wells, even in toilets. Scholars debate why Allah made them. The Koran talks about them in 'Surah Al-A'raf,' the Heights. They have powers. They can inhabit people, or animals, even trees."

"You're serious," she said.

"I'm just telling you what they believe. It's a different world over there. And however you want to explain, after the *mutawaeen* came, I couldn't deny we had a problem. Annie was not Annie anymore. They might have returned her to me, but she wasn't ever coming back again."

"Hugh, this is awful."

"I resigned myself. It was like the end of my life. But it was going to be a very long ending, possibly decades. I thought about putting her in an institution. But she would have hated that, so I kept her at home. I hired help. We took a few trips into the desert. She used to love that open sky. Then I screwed up. Our last trip, I lost her."

"I thought she wandered away."

"I don't know how it happened. I left her in camp, and when I returned, she was gone. Vanished. It was almost like the jinns really had kid-napped her."

"So she *did* wander away."

"I should never have taken her into the desert. But I did, and now I have to live with that."

He waited to see what Rachel said. She touched away a tear that threatened her mascara. "Poor Annie, my God."

They had gone deep enough. He backed off. "I didn't mean to surprise you with this. All I'm saying is that it wasn't all peaches and cream. But it was our life together, *hayati* and me."

"I'm so sorry," Rachel said. "It *was* your life together. And I'm one to talk. Look at the mess Lewis and I have made of ours."

"He's a good man," Hugh said.

She didn't contradict him. Her mind was made up. Lewis was history. Hugh understood. There comes a time.

She turned Hugh's hand in hers, palm up, then down. She touched the lines and callouses and knuckles and hairs and pale scars. Long, long ago she used to read their palms.

"What's it like now, Hugh? What kind of life do you go back to?"

"Without kids, less and less, to be honest," he said. "I've got a Hobie out in the bay. I swim and take my vacations in the mountains wherever, Nepal, Africa, Europe, South America. Other than that, security's so tight these days, we rarely leave the compound. The walls keep getting higher, literally. Big concrete walls. They won't keep the madness out. It's only a matter of time before someone breaches the fortress and kills more of us."

"You could leave," she said.

"I think about that. They'd love to retire me. But then where would I go?"

She turned his hand again.

"I remember this," she said. "How you go up whole and come back skinned and raw and starving. It made sense back then. Both of you needed to see the emptiness for yourselves. You've been there, though. You've seen what there is to see. Why go tilting at windmills when you know they're just windmills?"

Hugh started to say that Lewis was out to show his women—his wife and daughters—that he was still their knight in shining armor. But she had basically just said as much.

"It's not going to work," she said. "He wants to win me back. El Cap figured so large in our romance, and in yours. Bless him, he thinks we can still be saved, even Annie, somehow. But my mind is made up."

"I know," Hugh said.

She glanced at him. "It's that obvious?"

"No."

"He doesn't know."

"I know that, too. I can tell."

She took a sip of wine. "At first I blamed Lewis. Then I blamed myself. I thought it might be the big M, or boredom. All I can say is, we reached a fork in the road. I want to see the world, Hugh. I waited until the girls went off. Now it's my turn. Do you understand? El Cap is useless."

"Then why bother coming to Yosemite at all?" he asked.

"Because, Hugh. I'm tired of missed opportunities."

Hugh was stunned. She had come for him?

He looked at her face, and this time he saw the desperation. She was holding his hand for dear life. She wanted to be rescued from her decision.

He was tempted. She was beautiful. He was lonely. He could catch her hand and pull her to firm ground. They could be perfect together. It might even last.

But there was El Cap.

Quickly, before Rachel could speak to his desires or build more secrets between them, before she pulled him into her, he rejected her. He let go of her hands. He didn't draw away, nor did she. But she let go, too.

"Maybe I'm still shaking off the sand," he murmured.

Rachel didn't even blink. Probably she had expected nothing from him. "This should be easy then," she said.

"What's that?"

"While you're up there, slaying your dragons together, will you do me a favor?"

Hugh knew what she was going to ask.

"Make him understand," she said.

Lewis had made Hugh his messenger. Now she was making him hers, using Lewis's very words. Hugh started to protest. "Rachel . . ."

"You know what it's like to lose a wife," she said. "You'll have the right words for him."

Abruptly, she released him. There was one more sip in her wineglass. "I should warn you," she said, too cheerful, "it's been a long day, and four is early. I'm going to look like holy crap in the morning."

Hugh started to stand to guide her to her husband's room.

She pressed his shoulder, making him sit. "Oh, Hugh," she said, as if his chivalry was the silliest thing.

SIX

Hugh stood outside the front lobby in the darkness. It was colder than he'd expected, near freezing. He could tell by the fog off the Merced River. It could seem like whole parishes of souls when that mist smoked up and marched across the meadows. Sometimes people got lost just getting back to their tents.

He bent and hefted his rucksack, which contained next to nothing. The little pack was a vintage Mammut made of indestructible canvas and leather. He'd had it since high school, when he and Lewis had first started daring each other up the crags.

He looked for the sky, and there were no stars, no moon, no sign of any rim. The night felt deep. He faced the bully line of trees crowded up against the asphalt. Behind him, the lobby was well lit and warm, with a Mr. Coffee machine in one corner. But that would be the end of him, Hugh knew. If he took one step away from this cold post, he'd be gone.

Somewhere beyond the park's boundaries there was bound to be a breakfast shop with a booth by a window. He could watch the sun come up. It had been decades since his last visit to San Francisco. Drive down the coast and he could lose himself in a thousand coves. Head north and he wouldn't have to stop until the Arctic Sea. Why repeat himself on El Cap? He could take Rachel and go off into the world, armed with a Visa card and a map.

He kept his back to the lobby. He passed his hand through the mist, opening and closing his fingers. By turns it was a young hand, then an old one.

The parking lots were largely empty. It was another California October full of Armageddon. There'd been an earthquake along the coast, more fires, more floods. And terrorism weighed heavily on everyone he'd met since returning. They had been a traveling people, Americans, but now he found them bunkered in their homes and neighborhoods, with their cities under siege. Airlines were going bankrupt. The tourist industry was in near collapse.

Just beyond the reach of the light, night animals were scavenging the joint, rustling about, hunting down every human remnant. He could conjure up their feast: the crumbs from trail snacks, the cigarette butts, chewed gum and Band-Aids with X-Men and Disney creatures, the backing peeled off new bumper stickers declaring "Yosemite—The Best of the West" and "Go Climb a Rock," and dropped yen notes, and even the salt off discarded hiking sticks. That reminded him of Joshua.

Where are Lewis and Rachel?

He crossed his arms. The sleeves of his fancy new all-weather shell crackled and whisked. He uncrossed his arms, self-conscious, and saw the Nike trail hikers with their royal purple ankle sleeves. Should have stuck with the old gear, he thought. Things that showed pedigree and the violence of high places, like his rucksack. Instead he'd gone shopping.

An animal squealed suddenly, a tiny, piping shrill. Hugh held his breath and listened. The piping rose and fell, then ebbed to silence. He imagined fur being ripped open.

He felt impaled.

Dawn would break the spell, of course. The crystal forest always thawed. The mist burned off. The birds sang again.

A pair of headlights materialized. Hugh picked up his rucksack. He half-expected Lewis to be hanging from the passenger window like a bird dog, but the window was shut. When Hugh opened the back door, the signal went *ding-ding-ding.*

Rachel was driving. She didn't greet him. Lewis twisted to give him a smile, but by the green dash light he looked weary and awful, as if he had not slept for nights.

They left behind the few lights of civilization.

The fog opened in rags. Hugh peered through the window and found stars blinking like sniper fire.

They took a bend in the road. A vast darkness blocked the lower two-thirds of the night sky. That would be El Cap's shoulder. More trees swooped in, blotting it out. But Hugh could feel it, like a magnetic force, a great northern presence hanging above them.

There are objects so large and forbidding they become benchmarks, giving scale to the world. El Cap was like that. The closest thing to it that was man-made, that wasn't a force of nature, was war. But when all was said and done, war seemed to Hugh mostly a matter of failed imagination, and El Cap was just the opposite.

Abruptly, a big meadow opened to their left. The meadow lay stark and frigid, like a bad Polaroid shot. Autumn grass poked up, white and reedy. There was a cluster of people and vehicles up ahead. From a distance, they looked like another team preparing to embark.

"So much for solitude," Lewis muttered.

"It's a big rock," Hugh said. There were dozens of routes spread across the face of El Cap, and the odds were slim these others were heading for Anasazi. But it would be a mess if they were. Even the idea of competing for his own route soured Hugh. He hadn't come from around the planet to dodge dropped gear and share ledges with strangers.

Then Hugh recognized the green park trucks

and some of the faces. "It's the SAR crew," he said. Rachel slowed to a halt along the gravel shoulder.

"They're still looking?" she said.

They got out and walked ahead. There were a couple of National Guard troops among the rangers. Hugh could tell which ones were the eighties hires this morning. They weren't wearing guns and Sam Brown belts.

"Glass?" said a short, sturdy man, one of yesterday's rangers. He had a pair of binoculars, which Hugh thought curious. It was pitch-black out there.

"Morning," said Hugh. They shook hands. "Still nothing?" He smelled fuel. They were tinkering with an engine back there.

"Bastard hid her body good," the ranger said. "But some tourist called in a sighting."

Rachel edged closer. Lewis tried to block her.

"So you've found her," Hugh said.

The ranger shook his head no. "This would be another one of them, on a rope. A couple from Florida spotted it last night leaving the park. They thought it was normal, just another climber up there. Then they heard about the accident on the late news. We got their call about midnight. It took until now for the guard to bring up one of their big guns."

"Try now," someone said. A generator roared to life.

The soldiers tugged at a canvas shell, unveiling a trailer-mounted spotlight. They flipped a switch, and it was as if a false sun had suddenly landed among them. Hugh's night vision blew to pieces.

They swiveled the machinery around. White light hosed the meadow and trees like a Flash Gordon death ray. In the really old days, rangers would push flaming logs off Yosemite Falls to entertain the tourists. Lewis had toyed with the idea of using the walls for a giant drive-in movie screen. He wanted to show climbing movies, what else. That was in the pre–*Eiger Sanction* era, when the pickings were slim: Walt Disney's *Third Man on the Mountain,* and the Spencer Tracy movie *The Mountain,* and a sci-fi flick about the yeti. On slack nights, he said they could do slide shows about El Cap on El Cap.

The beam made a round circle on the stone above. It made the hulk of rock seem even more enormous. Hugh heard several eighties hires trying to direct the soldiers' aim. The soldiers told them to keep their hands off. The circle of light wandered aimlessly for a minute, crisscrossing features famous to climbers, but meaningless to the layman. At last they got oriented, and the beam crept higher, a few feet at a time.

The ranger lifted his binoculars. All eyes focused on the circle. It was like looking through a giant, ungainly microscope.

As best he could, Hugh followed the women's line of cracks and dihedrals. But without binoculars, and probably even with them, the route kept disintegrating into great blank patches devoid of cracks. Twice the rescuers lost their bearings in the blankness and had to scour the rock for cracks to restore the logic of the women's ascent.

There was no missing her, once she appeared.

She was dangling upside down at the tip of a rope. The SAR team called back and forth to one another, compiling their individual observations. She looked too still to be alive. They followed the thin thread of rope higher to where it sank into Cyclops Eye. They splashed light into the depression, but saw no sign of the third woman. Maybe she was lying in the woods somewhere.

The ranger lowered his binoculars.

"You mind?" asked Hugh.

Through the binoculars, he saw the woman entangled with rope. A slight breeze rocked her gently back and forth. Her body was less distinct than her shadow, stark black against the brilliant white stone.

"I don't understand," Hugh said. "How could I have missed her yesterday? Right underneath them and I didn't see a thing."

"None of us did," the ranger said. "Maybe they tried to evacuate themselves after dark. Maybe they had a second accident."

Someone flipped on a megaphone and began throwing names at the wall. "Cass. Andie. Cuba." Three names, not two.

Then it struck Hugh that they still didn't know whose body he had found yesterday. The megaphone repeated the litany over and over, each monosyllable distinct.

"The meadow's going to be jammed today," the ranger said. "One corpse missing, another on a string. A thing like this beats the hell out of reality TV."

Hugh looked and Rachel's face was metallic with anger.

"How soon can you get to her?" Hugh asked.

He knew the park service would be swift about it, as much for image as humanity. In one notorious incident on the Eiger, a German alpinist had dangled out of reach on the Eiger for almost a year. But it had been notorious only because it was so public. High peaks, particularly Everest, could be like open graveyards, with bodies and snapped-off parts scattered on both sides of the mountain. On one expedition, Hugh had watched climbers from a half dozen countries pass a dead Frenchman sitting in a perfect throne of ice beside the trail. He'd been there so long he'd become a landmark. At those altitudes, it cost too much time and effort to bury any but the ones that blew down to the flats, usually many years later.

"We've got a team on the way to the summit," the ranger said. "They've been going all night. Once day breaks, Augustine will lower down to her."

"The man we met last night?" Rachel said.

Hugh studied the situation. The shadows were useful, a way to gauge how far the body hung from the wall. Ten feet, he guessed. But above the hollow of the Eye, a brow of stone jutted out still farther. Even if Augustine could line up his descent just right and hit the dime, he'd still be facing a gap of twenty or thirty feet to the body. "It's going to be tricky," he said.

"Augustine's the best we've got," the ranger said. "Meanwhile we'll keep searching the floor. It's going to be slow going. There are niches and crannies all over, and we're shorthanded. After nine-eleven, half the rangers got pulled from Yosemite to help guard dams and bridges."

It was an invitation to join them. But Hugh saw the Kirk Douglas dimple in Lewis's chin tighten. His vote was no. Hugh handed back the binoculars. "We'll keep our eyes peeled from above," he told the ranger.

The ranger didn't beg. "Good enough."

"The season's getting late," Lewis explained. "Every day counts."

"There's always next season," the ranger said.

"No there's not," Lewis said.

"Oh, they'll quit," Rachel told the ranger. "But first they have to go through the motions for the sake of pride. They'll come down. They'll sneak out from the forest when no one's looking."

The ranger smiled at her little joke, then realized it was no joke. No one spoke for a moment. The generator roared, pouring light into the darkness.

"You'll be close to the rescue team's fall line," the ranger finally said. "Watch your heads."

They walked back to Rachel's rental car. She was in a quiet fury. "You're not going to help? You're obsessed." She was close to crying. "They could be your daughters."

"Rachel," said Hugh. "If there was a chance anyone might be alive, we'd join them in a heartbeat. But you saw for yourself. It's over for them."

She glared at him. He was the traitor, not Lewis. She'd given him a chance at her last night. He could have chosen romance. Instead he was going off toward death. She was trembling. "This is so ugly, I can't tell you."

Hugh had wanted things to be all right between them, to get her blessing, or a simple good-bye. That wasn't going to happen. He felt momentary panic, an old nightmare, the lizard king rearing up from the desert. *You'll lose her forever.* Did he dare?

He forced himself to breathe. You go forward. That's why he'd come, not like Lewis, who wanted to go back. Searching for the dead . . . he couldn't do that anymore.

Lewis started to change his mind. He saw an opening with her, or thought he did. "I could stay, if it means so much to you," he said.

Rachel pointed at El Cap. "Go," she said, "just go."

Hugh slugged his rucksack onto one shoulder and stepped back to let Lewis say his good-bye. Without another word, she climbed into the car and closed the door and left them standing by the road.

SEVEN

It is a strange fact that tourists never venture through the screen of trees between the road and El Cap. They park their cars and pull out their picnic baskets and lawn chairs and cameras and binoculars to watch from the meadow, always sticking in safe numbers to the far side of the road, never suspecting that the strip of forest separating one world from another is scarcely a quarter mile deep. The trees serve as a no-man's-land.

On a sunlit day, the crowd might wait hours to see climbers start in like they were warriors going off to battle. They usually kept a distance, as if only the lost and disaffected dared come in here, and they weren't completely wrong. Draped with ropes, sporting scabbed knuckles and the eyes of old-fashioned cross-and-sword *entradas*, the big-wall boys—and girls now—were either the chosen or the damned. They were poet-commandos, psychological riffraff, and rock and roll Galahads. In their boldness, they seemed to certify El Cap's monstrosity.

Briskly now, Hugh switched on his headlamp and descended from the road. The autumn field was dry and brittle. At first, their passage went unencumbered. Shins and knees, Hugh threshed through the grass, leaving broken, dead stems. Overhead, the spotlight seemed to connect heaven and earth. The roar of the generator dwindled.

Draped with coils of rope, Lewis followed like a prisoner, a happy one, perfectly resigned to his fate. He was whistling. Rachel's harangue had given him hope. She cared enough to be angry. He thought El Cap was working its magic once again.

Hugh wasn't about to spoil his delusion. Rachel was angry because she was afraid. There was an irony to it. All three of them—she, Hugh, and Lewis—were creating a void, she by divorce, and he and Lewis by climbing. Now they had to survive their choices.

They came to the edge of the trees, and Hugh hesitated for an instant, long enough to glance up at the treetops forming a ragged blackness against the stars, and then back at the road and the ethereal figures manning the light. There was safe harbor among them, it was not too late.

"Lost already?" Lewis said.

"Just letting you catch your breath, dad."

Hugh entered the forest. Shadows jumped

ahead of his light. He clambered up a junk heap of talus that marked the beginning of the shatter zone. In this region girdling the base, rock from the summit landed in great explosions that smashed trees and mowed down the manzanita scrub.

He did not mean to revisit the accident site, but suddenly they were upon it. Bright orange tape marked the slab where she had landed. Trees were flagged to help the SAR people locate the site. All that remained of her was dried blood.

The place was empty. Not just empty of the body and the searchers and the crime-scene rangers with their cameras and vials and Baggies. It was empty of that presence he'd felt yesterday. Empty.

Lewis crossed himself. Hugh remembered receiving the baptism and first-communion announcements for the Cole daughters, and the Christmas photos and birthday thank-you cards that had always delighted Annie, but also saddened her. They'd never managed to get pregnant, but talked about adoption, and then it was too late. In her dementia, she'd made a baby out of towels and would hold it for hours.

The trees were feverish looking, cold and sweaty with glassed-over bark. The Spanish moss hung in strands. Except for the cold, they might have been in some dank bayou.

"What are we doing here?" said Lewis.

"I was trying to avoid it."

"Yeah?"

"Believe me, I didn't need to see this again."

"You're right. It's not healthy, Hugh."

Did Lewis think he had a morbid fixation? That he was joining one missing woman with another? "It has nothing to do with Annie," Hugh told him. "I got turned around in the woods."

They peered up through the opening in the trees, and that tube of white light was glued to the wall overhead. It had tricked the day birds into flight. Hugh could see starlings flitting in and out of the beam. From this angle, the body on the rope was hidden from view, and he was thankful for that. Days from now, by the time they reached that height on Anasazi and looked across, Augustine would have cleared El Cap of its prey.

Lewis said, "Let's keep on truckin', *compañero*."

Hugh's pack sat where he'd propped it. He'd told the searchers to slake their thirst with his water, and empty plastic jugs stood in a neat line. His water offering to the girl was still full, though. They'd guessed its significance. It sat untouched by the head of the slab.

Hugh and Lewis divided the remaining five gallons and continued up the slope. Their cache wasn't far now. Things were almost familiar again.

Climbers' garbage began to surface in Hugh's light. A piece of black metal glinted in the pine needles. Lewis rooted it free with his toe, a rusted, pitted piton from the iron age, back before chrome-moly steel came into use. Empty, flattened cans glittered like tin and aluminum leaves. There was a hat, and a paper bag with human feces, and a mangled Pentax camera.

The pilgrims had been busy. Bits and pieces of sling hung in the limbs, red and green and peppermint striped. He spied an inexplicable lone ski pole, then suddenly, with a billowing huff, the torn remains of a parachute shroud. All in all, it spelled a crazy surge of events, whole generations of activity that he had missed out on since their last visit.

Very suddenly, Hugh's light splashed back into his eyes, blinding him.

El Cap sprang straight from the earth.

He slapped his palms on the hard, slippery flank with something like joy. Black mica crystals glittered in the white granite. Its touch stabilized him.

He stepped away and craned back with his headlamp. His light faded to darkness about fifty feet up. There at the fifty-foot mark, by government decree, Yosemite's walls officially became wilderness.

Lewis came up from the trees behind him. In the beam of his light, Hugh cast a huge shadow. They were in the land of giants now. But as Lewis approached, the shadow quickly shrank to mortal size.

"Oh, yeah," said Lewis. He set down the water jugs and slapped the source, just as Hugh had, grinning. "Now tell me, heathen, dare I eat a peach?"

More ritual. "Should I roll my trousers?" Hugh dutifully supplied. Sometimes they would keep reciting right to the ropes.

Everything began here. They hurried along the

stone root, following the trace of a path worn by countless climbers.

Their cache of gear was waiting where they'd left it, two waist-high haul bags carefully—scientifically, one might say—packed. The bags contained their life-support system for the vertical world. They hadn't bothered with any elaborate camouflage to conceal the bags. Thefts happened, but so did vigilante justice. Anyone with brains knew better than to pilfer a fellow climber's haul bags. But also, anyone with brains knew better than to leave anything of real value—like good ropes and expensive hardware—in a haul bag overnight.

Lewis checked the sailor's knots he'd used to tie the haul bags shut. It was not a complicated knot, resembling a regular square knot except for the lay of the working end. For centuries sailors had used it in lieu of a lock, not as a security but as a seal. If a thief had tampered with the knot, you could usually tell at a glance.

"I don't think he got us," he said, meaning Joshua. "Too busy stealing a bride, the sick bastard."

Dawn was still more than an hour away. Even when it came, direct light would take another two hours to reach the floor and heat the stone. But they acted as if the day were already slipping away. With little talk, they went to work.

They opened the haul bags and pulled out two old "beater" ropes that were past their prime, but were still good for hauling and fixing. These, plus their two new coils, would give them six hundred feet of reach the first day, and still let them descend to sleep on the ground a final night. Not that they would be covering six hundred feet today. The bottom section was going to be consuming. And the middle section, too. And the headwall. Seven days, easily.

While Lewis carted the rope to where their climb actually began, Hugh started the elaborate process of taping up. You could go through a lot of skin on a big wall. Lewis would be using cowhide work gloves with the fingers cut off. But Hugh, the better free climber of the two of them, and the one who would be handling the bulk of the leading, needed more freedom than gloves would allow.

First he painted a sticky tincture onto the bottom knuckles and the web of his hand. Then he taped each individual knuckle in special configurations to distribute the stress on each joint, and at the same time protect the flesh. Finally he joined the interlaced finger strips under broad bindings of tape across the back of his hands and palms. The finished product looked like a boxer's fist, and, with some extra patching of more tape, would last for days. At the end of the climb, he would need a knife to cut away the shell of tape.

Hugh flexed his fingers. He slugged his fists into his palms, getting the tape job snug and stretched. The eastern sky was losing stars. Soon the black would ease to cobalt and then the pastels would mount. For now they continued using their headlamps.

Hugh pulled on his seat harness, and fanned the rack of gear apart to choose the few pieces he'd need on the first pitch, or rope length. Lewis laid out his stirrups and jumars for ascending the rope, and tied his shoes.

"I'm ready," he announced. His voice was eager and antsy and scared. He wanted to get under way, and his tone pressed at Hugh.

"You can have the first lead then," Hugh said.

Lewis snorted. "What, and steal your precious legacy?" The first pitch was beyond his abilities and they both knew it.

"Don't be shy," Hugh baited him. "Give it a shot. Miracles happen. Did I ever tell you about the time I saw a gorilla get up off his knuckles and walk? It was an amazing sight. Didn't last long, of course. But what a gallant sight."

"Yeah, you," said Lewis, "you and the other stick people."

Even forty years ago, when he wasn't so strapped with gym muscle, Lewis had been too big for what he called the dainty moves. His veins would bulge as he grappled holds that thinner climbers—stick or bone people, or Biafrans, or Twiggies, all in his lexicon—danced up on with ease. He was like a circus strongman among high-wire acrobats. His specialties were brute hand-and-fist cracks, fearless hook moves, and the hauling of massive amounts of baggage from the depths.

"Still touchy, are we?" said Hugh.

"Have you seen them lately? Bulimic little

twists, nothing but toothpicks for legs. Cut me off at the waist, I could climb what they do."

"You're saying I'm half the man you are?"

"Oh, not you, Glass. You've always been a kingly specimen. Except you have no calves. Or thighs."

They bantered some more while they sorted and compacted what they had spread on the ground. There was a method to their collecting, though it required no discussion, not after so many climbs together. Every object had its exact place, small to large, front to back, and each man had it memorized.

Hugh had grown so used to being alone that companionship should not have come so easily. But as he and Lewis handled the ropes and slings and hardware, he realized he was still known by at least one person in the world. It made him glad to have turned away Rachel.

"What do you think, lad?" said Lewis, closing up the haul bags with his sailor's knot. "Will we be better men after the climb?" It was always Lewis who asked, always the same words. Then Hugh was meant to reply aye, and quote Shakespeare's Harry about once more unto the breach.

"We always were," Hugh answered him quietly, "after every climb. You just forget."

A wound opened in the night, a streak of purple low along the east. They both noticed it, and hurried. Hugh took off his approach shoes and trod in his socks up the slope, carrying his climbing slippers to keep dirt off the new sticky-rubber soles.

Lewis produced a scratched orange helmet. It surprised Hugh, because Lewis had managed to keep it hidden until the last minute, and because it was next to worthless on this route. The wall angled out so much that most debris would be falling well away from them, into the trees.

Lewis strapped it on with a sheepish look. "I promised Rachel," he said.

Hugh knew it was Lewis's promise to himself, though, the last of an illusion of love. He remembered whispering to pictures of Annie at night, whispering to the emptiness of his house in Dhahran, until finally, firmly, he had managed to put her away from him. Out with the pictures, out with her lemon marmalade and Nutella, out with her Joan Armatrading and Mozart tapes. He'd even bought new sheets for the bed. A clean sweep. A new beginning.

Again Hugh was glad to have chosen against Rachel last night. She was right in what she'd finally said. Through Hugh's loss, maybe Lewis could learn how to live without her. Just now, in the darkness before dawn, that seemed worth more to Hugh than any beauty or excitement she could have brought into his life.

The purple sliver ran red. Hugh turned off his headlamp. The trees were gray. The stone was gray. His partner was gray. But over two-thirds of a mile above them, the summit reaches flushed the faintest pink.

Hugh pulled on his shoes and laced them tight. Lewis had already uncoiled one rope into a loose pile, and Hugh tied into one end.

"No headlamp?" Lewis asked. He had backed against a rock and anchored himself there. The rope ran from him to Hugh.

"It wouldn't help. Either I remember or I don't." Memory was everything. Without it there was nothing.

Hugh faced the wall and began tracing his fingertips along the blank surface. This morning, especially, he required the Braille approach. He needed to feel for the secret passageway.

Even in full daylight, the holds defied ordinary sight. That had been part of Anasazi's notoriety. The creation had no rational origin, no crack or dihedral or obvious flakes. It had freaked people out. He'd spent days just sitting and watching the mute stone, even fasting, at one point, to force a vision. The changing shadows had finally revealed a fold at one hour, a seam or a crystal knob at another hour. Like in a fairy tale, once you touched them, they turned real.

He went on touching the rock, hunting for holds, hunting for himself. His body was balking. Both feet felt shackled to the ground, like some instinct warning him away. It would have been unnatural not to be frightened. He told himself that. The naked ape had bred itself out of the trees. Humans didn't belong up there. Ordinary humans. He had this argument with himself often.

But the fear was stronger this morning. He kept his back to Lewis, who waited, rope in hand. His fingers continued searching. *Speak, Glass, or forever hold your peace.*

It wasn't the primal fear that bothered him, though. This was different. A voice—not even that, a sensation—was pulling at him. It came from up there, or from within the stone. He felt sung to. Beguiled. Lulled, even. That troubled him.

A swelling in the stone stopped his uneasiness. After all these years, it was still there at shoulder height, a quiet, subtle bulge among all the thousands of creases and risings that textured the base. It cued him.

He slid his fingertips across the stone and found a hidden wrinkle. His left toe nestled upon a rounded nubbin, exactly where he'd left it. El Cap had kept it all just so for him. High above, dawn touched the wall, spilling light everywhere, soaking the stone with illusions and false offerings and glory.

He pulled. The toe held. He left the ground. Hugh had hold of the ladder now. They were in.

EIGHT

Below him, off to one side where Hugh couldn't fall on him, Lewis started whistling Bach or the Trinity Session or some such. It used to drive other climbers batty, but Hugh had learned to live with it. Lewis had a gap between his front teeth and claimed it gave him the ability to whistle a harmonic fifth. *Listen to this,* he'd say, and would whistle a note.

Hugh would lean close, pretending to really study it. *Nope,* he'd say, *that's just air on teeth.*

Hugh went on leaving the ground.

The first pitch of Anasazi was roughly a hundred and thirty feet from the ground to a small perch that was completely invisible until you reached it. Over the years, the pitch had gained the status of a test piece, and had come to be known as Broken Glass, both in honor of its creator and its victims.

Aside from its difficult, unorthodox moves, Broken Glass only offered what climbers now called psychological protection. There were just three threadlike fissures on the polished slab, opening and closing like little wounds spaced far apart. When Hugh had first climbed this pitch, he'd managed to place a single piece of protection in each fissure, a knife-blade piton, a wired copperhead, and the tip of a baby angle. Not one of the pieces would have held a real fall. A number of aspirants had learned that the hard way, breaking arms, legs, spines, and heads while trying to repeat the cryptic moves of a man named Glass.

Apparently the casualties, year after year, had become too much, though. As Hugh worked higher, he came upon bolts, not just a few, but many. Chicken bolts, they were called, the work of pretenders to the throne.

During the golden age, a period of intense discovery that began with El Cap's first ascent in 1958 and ended in the early seventies, the drilling of even a single bolt had been considered an event very close to statutory rape. Many climbers had backed off from routes rather than despoil them with a bolt, preferring to leave the rock pure for those with more talent, or even to never be climbed. Bolts opened new territory, but they could also be used to dumb down the rock. It had mattered very much back then. They'd been reverent as hobbits.

In his entire climbing career, Hugh had placed

only five bolts, though not one on all of Anasazi. Now as he climbed higher, Hugh found nine, then ten, on this first pitch alone. He would have been disgusted if he hadn't been so relieved to have the bolts to clip into. Each bolt could hold an elephant. It was nice to have death or mutilation removed from the equation.

But each time he clipped his rope to a bolt, Hugh heard Lewis's whistling slide off-key. Lewis had always been more of a purist than even Hugh. To him, bolts weren't just an eyesore, they were evil. They were the Machine, the paving of the American frontier, the cowardice of urban weaklings. And they killed your karma.

At the third bolt and the third sour note, Hugh called down, "Problem?"

Lewis stopped his whistling. "Something wrong, Harp?" he said.

The "Harp" was another dig. Long ago, Hugh had become known as Harp, for Harpoon. Only the insiders got a nickname. Harpoon stood for what the younger generation now called a rope gun. A rope gun was the guy you fired at the Great White Whales. They were the ones with steel nerves and titanium balls.

Lewis started piping away again like one of Snow White's dwarves.

Hugh clipped again at the next bolt. Lewis skidded into a sour note. Hugh ignored him. If Lewis wanted the purity of their original ascent so badly, then he should have taken the sharp end of the rope. In which case, they'd still be puttering around on the ground.

For the next two hours, Hugh worked the rock. Sunlight moved down toward him as he moved up toward it. The slab lost its night chill. His tendons warmed. His hips and shoulders gained more flex. His forearms got hard as gourds from handling thin holds.

He never broke a sweat. That was how slowly he moved, deliberate as a reptile. He took his time, resting on the larger facets, a two-inch cube of white quartz here, a ripple there. His memory returned in inches.

There was a wide stem between two nubbins, as wide as he could stretch his legs, so wide that he'd worried the years might have ossified his abilities. But he managed. Elsewhere he crouched on flakes, like a cat, and pounced for a "sloper," and the rounded bulge held his palm and fingers, if only barely.

His anxieties—not just yesterday's omens of death and madness, but a month of bad dreams— all the warning lights quietly self-corrected. Except for the bolts, every hold was right where it was supposed to be. All felt right and good with the world. He belonged here, he really did. He could do this thing.

The little belay perch appeared. Hugh got one foot on the ledge, and anchored himself, and shouted down. "You are the one," Lewis called up to him.

Lewis bustled about, a miniature man down there. While he waited, out of habit, Hugh tied knots using a bit of slack rope.

The Italian hitch, as it was known, hadn't been invented until 1974, six years *after* Hugh and Lewis had established Anasazi. But Hugh had quickly added it to his repertoire and used it on his trips to the Alps, and his expeditions to the Ahaggar range in southern Algeria and to Makalu in Nepal and Everest in Tibet and Cho Oyu straddling the divide.

Down below, whistling away, Lewis was loading on the rack of extra gear and ropes, getting ready to jumar, or "jug," the line. While he waited, Hugh went through his gamut of various knots.

Most climbers were content just to memorize the basic rope craft. Hugh was a true student, though, forever searching out the history of ropes and knots, talking with sailors, weavers, and fishermen, even using a magnifying glass to examine museum relics. As far back as the Stone Age, mankind had been using knots to hold itself together. Square knots had been found in rawhide cords used by Cro-Magnons.

There were special knots for tying prisoners and hanging them, for passing messages on Incan trails, for binding freight to a yak, for closing wounds. The highwayman's knot was used for hitching horses for a quick getaway, the blood knot for flogging soldiers and sailors and for weighting the belt cords of monks. In medieval times, the figure eight, a climber's standby, signified faithful love because of its symmetrical embrace.

Hugh leaned back against the anchor to soak up the heights. Soon enough they would have the valley spread below them. For now, the better view sprawled overhead in a canvas of bright colors and dark water streaks.

The rope tugged and vibrated along Hugh's thigh. Lewis's jugging had the cadence of a march. He slid the jumars up, one at a time, high-stepping in the stirrups that dangled from each handle. Slide, step, slide, step. The jumaring saved time. More important, it conserved their pool of strength. Lewis would arrive rested, ready to take the next lead. Hugh would belay him, then jug up, and they would switch leads again, leapfrogging.

A crow cawed in the trees. It was a quiet morning. He heard the *hiss-click* of Lewis's jumars sliding up, and the tap of his toes against the stone, and the slight jingle of hardware.

Lewis reached him in a burst of white teeth and orange helmet and wide shoulders, all tiger quickness. He wasn't even breathing hard. He'd told Hugh he woke at four-thirty to hit the gym with the red-eye crowd. Twice a week, rain or shine, he rode his bicycle to Estes Park, thirty-five miles each way.

When they were young, the obsession and mountain mania had seemed almost holy. Lewis liked to damn the herds in the valleys and flatness, stuff cribbed straight out of Nietzsche and Kerouac. *We're their saviors if they'll just open their pig eyes. Fuckin' saints, you and me, Hugh. The last of the holy men. This is important. God's hiding up here. We're the only ones with a prayer in hell of finding Him.* Drunk or stoned, or cold sober, it had been too high and mighty for Hugh's taste. But it used to be fun to wind Lewis up and let him rant like a prophet.

The two men crowded side by side and sorted the gear. They were in no huge hurry. Today was their shakedown cruise. Tomorrow they committed.

They sat back in their seat harnesses and helped each other piece together the heights. Much of El Cap had been virgin when they blazed Anasazi in 1968. Now everywhere they looked, grand paths tracked across the broad, towering expanse.

Off to the right loomed a vast, charcoal-colored stain shaped almost identically like the North American continent. Like Spanish missionaries, the first climbers through that region had climbed the Baja stain and along the California "coast," dubbing ledges Mazatlan and Big Sur, and, near the summit, the Igloo. They'd christened their route the North America—or NA—Wall. Later teams had remained faithful to the theme as they conquered the surrounding territory: Pacific Ocean Wall lay to the left of NA, Atlantic Ocean Wall to the right, with Wyoming Sheep Ranch and New Jersey Turnpike branching up through the dark interior.

Lewis reveled in the poetry of it all. "We're among the people now," he said.

To their left, in the direction of the graceful profile of the so-called Nose, the historic first climb of El Cap in 1958, an assortment of routes threaded up through very steep country. Mescalito had been pieced together during the psychedelic seventies. The Wall of Early Morning Light and New Dawn served as catch basins for the first rays of sunshine each morning. Next to South Seas was Tempest.

Anasazi rose between these beautiful monsters. The one route that Hugh couldn't see was the closest one, the unfinished first ascent that had taken the lives of at least two young women yesterday. He craned out, but couldn't spy the dangling body, nor any landmarks of the women's path, not even the vast roof of Cyclops Eye.

By now, Augustine had probably lowered to his girlfriend's body. As a first responder, the man had surely handled death before. But this one was going to scar him in ways he could not imagine. Hugh knew. Love is never lightly lost.

"So what are my chances?" Lewis suddenly asked Hugh.

Hugh thought he was talking about the coming pitch, or their week ahead. Hugh waved his arm spaciously. "Nothing but blue sky," he said.

There was not a cloud to be seen. The cliff swallows were soaring and dipping, reveling in the sunlight. It was another excellent day in paradise.

Lewis didn't smile. His eyes were shielded behind a pair of thin, very hip sunglasses. Too late, Hugh realized he was asking about his conversation with Rachel last night. Hugh let the moment pass. There would be ample time in the coming days to contemplate their lives. And to bury their women.

"The day's wasting," Lewis said. He rolled his head and shoulders like a boxer about to enter the ring. Hugh checked the belay and tapped his shoulder. Lewis continued up.

As the day went on, they made mistakes, crossed ropes, dropped gear, and mixed commands. The mistakes frustrated Lewis. "We've got to move this dog," he said.

Hugh was more forgiving. He wasn't concerned about their slowness. It was Day One. They were still getting their heads back into the bigness of big-wall life.

The two of them had not climbed together for over three decades. The more circumspect approach would have been to climb day routes for a week or so to fine-tune their teamwork. Instead, as if throwing themselves off a cliff, they were throwing themselves up it.

Around four, they called it quits for the day. They'd gotten a start. Four hundred vertical feet wasn't much to brag about. But they'd penetrated Anasazi's defenses and regained some of their old rhythm. It would have been nice to run a pitch higher before sundown, but that risked a descent in the dark.

While they prepared to rappel off, Hugh looked again for any sign of the rescuers.

"You'd think we would have seen something," he said.

Lewis took a swig of water. "Just as well we didn't."

"They were going to call their route Trojan Women. One of the rangers told me."

Lewis grunted. "Talk about jinxing yourself. Prisoners of war and slaves? What a fucking name."

"Come on, Louie. The Trojan women were the ultimate survivors."

"Survivors?"

"The last of an epic war. You know, like the age of El Cap."

Lewis was having none of it. "They didn't survive, Hugh. They're all dead."

Lewis's scorn baffled Hugh. He thought maybe it had to do with the long day. They were tired. And for all their efforts, the bulk of Anasazi loomed over them.

"Give them some credit," Hugh said. "They were audacious as hell. Warriors. Amazons."

"Jesus," said Lewis.

"You're the bard. Where's your sense of poetry?"

"That's not poetry. It's hubris. Rachel fed the same stuff to our girls. Dream big. Eve was framed. You can be president one day. It's like a yeast infection, this goddess-movement stuff. They think they can dance in the flames and not get burned."

Hugh steadied his feet against the rock. The

bitterness was not like Lewis. "If you're saying they didn't belong here, then maybe we don't either," Hugh said. "You want to talk about hubris."

"I'm saying look where it got them."

"Those women gave it everything they had."

"They screwed up, Hugh. They reached too far."

An image flashed in Hugh's mind, the girl lying in the forest like a human sacrifice. "That's not fair," he said.

"I say it like I see it," Lewis said.

Hugh snorted. "See what? You didn't see anything."

"You gave me the tour this morning, thank you. Blood on the rocks. Blood on the trees. End of story."

Hugh frowned at him. "Either one of us could end up like her."

"Not me."

"Really? Talk about hubris."

Lewis let the big rack of carabiners clap in a thicket against the stone. "What are you doing to us, Hugh?"

What *was* he doing? This was no mere tussling, the sort they used to do over Bob Dylan going electric, or which had more value, René Daumal's imaginary *Mount Analogue* or the real K2. They used to worry such things back and forth until they forgot what they were arguing about. This was different. The dead women were just an excuse.

"I think we better get something sorted out

here," Hugh said, though he couldn't put his finger on what the something was.

"Good idea," Lewis said. "I mean, if you want to bail, just say it up front."

"Bail?"

"That's what I said."

There it was.

Lewis was arguing with himself. He was angry about the deaths. They terrified him. They tempted him. In talking about the women's hubris, he was talking about his own. It wasn't Hugh who wanted to bail, the thought wasn't even in his mind. It was Lewis.

You found things out about yourself and your comrades on a big climb. Hugh had been on expeditions that almost ended in murder or suicide. If Lewis had doubts, if he was already psyched out, then now was the time to admit it. The helmet, thought Hugh. He should have known when the helmet came out.

They didn't need to shout at each other. They were grown men. Things just hadn't worked out. There came a time in every relationship when you had to dissolve the union. They could pull the plug on El Cap and go their separate ways, no hard feelings.

Hugh started to say as much, that there was no sense in trying to whip a dead horse. *Viagra for the soul.* They'd been too old for it after all.

But before he could speak a word, just as he was about to terminate their climb, a shadow flashed past. From out of nowhere, a thin, red streak whipped across the white stone.

Both men grabbed for the anchor slings. They plastered themselves tight against the wall. In the same instant, each had the same thought. Rock. Loose rock. If one fell, more might.

The blood didn't register as blood. The shadow was their evidence, that and the now fading buzz-saw hum. Then Hugh peered over his shoulder, and there were feathers drifting in the air. More remarkable, there was a wing. A bird's wing. Not ten feet out from the wall, a single wing.

"What the hell?" said Lewis.

"It must have hit one of the birds."

As if that were not extraordinary enough, Hugh saw the arc of a falcon disappearing across the valley. "Do you see it?" he said. It had been no rock. "God, incredible."

They had just witnessed a kill.

The disembodied wing fluttered on the air current, like the sound—or sight—of one hand clapping. It was an amazing, majestic, terrifying moment.

It should not have come as such a shock. The peregrine falcons made their aeries on narrow ledges, and portions of El Cap were closed for them during the nesting season. Hugh had heard of their "stoops," high-speed dives that could exceed two hundred miles per hour. And there were swallows and swifts everywhere around the walls. The cycle of predator and prey went on all the time, but almost never in plain view. And never so close.

The falcon kill sobered them. It silenced their arguing.

Hugh looked at Lewis, and his face was speckled with the swallow's blood. He reached over and touched Lewis's cheek with his fingertip. His touch broke their impasse.

Lewis turned his sunglasses to Hugh, and he had twin suns for eyes. Hugh showed the smidgen of swallow blood to him. Lewis did the same thing, touching Hugh's face to show him that he, too, carried the blood. They were both marked.

The freedom of the hills was never free. What they were attempting verged on the transcendent, and it would cost them, it had to. Lewis's words echoed from decades ago, all that jazz about the holy and the seraphim. It was true. They were blessed with awful, wondrous sight up here. Suddenly, deeply, he wanted more of it.

But then Lewis spoke. "We should go down." His tone was final.

Hugh's heart sank. It was over? He let out a sigh.

"What more do you want?" asked Lewis, watching that wing drift and tumble on the breeze.

Hugh didn't try to coax more ascent from him. It was reckless to tie into a man who was only half there. No, it was over. They were bailing. *Walk on.* "Okay," he said.

"We need to rest," Lewis said.

Not, Go home. Not, Strip the wall. Not, Erase our presence. Hugh glanced at him, taking hope. Rest.

Lewis was running his finger along the blood beads on the stone, contemplating. "We've got some distance to go tomorrow. And the day after."

"And the day after that," Hugh added.

Lewis cocked his head back at the summit. "Brother, it's a long way out of here."

NINE

As the alpenglow died and darkness tightened, they settled by their haul bags on the dirt beneath an overhang. They made a cold camp tonight, no fire. They kept their voices low.

It had not always been illegal to camp at the base of El Cap.

It seemed like only yesterday when Hugh and Lewis and others had occupied the base of El Cap like pirates or highwaymen. *Fellaheen,* Lewis had anointed them. It meant "people living on the ruins of civilization." The word came from Spengler's *The Decline of the West,* a favorite of sophomore philosophers, which was what they had been.

Hugh would object. *You call this the ruins of civilization? What civilization? What ruins? This is the Valley, not some city in decay.*

Lewis would roar back, *You call this living?*
Meaning yes, grand and absolute.

By day, they would venture onto the virgin
walls. By night, they rested. Minute by minute, they
had just made it all up in their heads.

Living off army surplus C rations, and salami
and wheels of Wisconsin cheddar, they built small
campfires at night, hung their washed clothes on
tree limbs, strummed pawnshop guitars, and listened to those lucky few with girlfriends rutting
under the moon. It was an academy of sorts, as
close as it got to what John Muir had once termed
"the University of the Wilderness." They had read
and debated everything from Wittgenstein, Delta
blues, and the Bomb, to the *Tibetan Book of the Dead*
and *Playboy* foldouts. When their beer and cheap
wine ran out, they made do with river water hauled
up from the Merced. So long as the climbers stuck
to their caves and burrows up here, the rangers had
largely left them alone.

Now, propped against rocks and with food in
their bellies, Hugh and Lewis agreed that today had
been a very good day. Neither mentioned their
argument at the top of the ropes. Lewis could not
get over the falcon kill. It had rejuvenated him. He
was awestruck. He called it a sacrifice to the gods.

"Now we're gods?" Hugh said.

"You know what I mean, the ancient ones. The
avatars and devis. The *anima mundi.* The cosmic jet
stream. Do I have to give it a name? We were meant
to be there, Hugh. Right then at that very moment.

That was no accident in time. We were supposed to see what we saw. You don't feel it? Right before our eyes, an offering of blood. What else is waiting for us up there? I don't know. We've got to find out. We've got to get up there as high as we can."

Here was the Lewis of old, the mile-a-minute, irrepressible, full-of-bull Lewis, lit with the spirit. He fired words like machine-gun bursts, not to destroy but to pierce, to get inside the moment and root for its meaning before it slipped away.

Hugh remembered their pilgrimages to San Francisco in search of Lewis's Beat heroes, his "subterraneans," the hipsters, not the hippies who were just rip-offs. Lewis refused to accept that he was a decade too late, that the Beats had turned to rockers, or died off. He was sure they must still exist somewhere in the city. But the only thing left of them in the late sixties was City Lights, the bookstore where Ferlinghetti had been arrested for selling *Howl*.

While Annie and Rachel went off to trade Yosemite wildflowers for incense or Moroccan kohl for their eyes, Hugh would follow Lewis among the stacks. It was there that Hugh had purchased the leather-bound book of empty pages that became his Bible. The one book Lewis wanted more than any other, the one he was sure would lead to enlightenment, was a copy of the *Black Mountain Review*, Issue 7, with William Burroughs, Robert Creeley, Jack Kerouac, Gary Snyder, and others. Year after year, he never did find it. His solution, ultimately, was to start his own bookstore. *It will come to me with time.*

On the ride back from Frisco in Hugh's blue VW beetle, worn out and happy, the four of them would share their discoveries and acquisitions, everything from Zig-Zag rolling papers to the latest on Vietnam to ayurvedic medicines. Inevitably someone would have found a Ouija board or books on the I Ching and the Kama Sutra.

Hugh lay his head back against a rock. Annie's face came to him, her young face, the one he'd fallen in love with, not the sandblasted mask with red eyes that stared from his nightmares. What a beauty she'd been. At times, he missed her so badly he ached. Tonight he merely ached, every muscle and joint in him. He put her image away. "Go to sleep, Lewis," he said.

Tomorrow morning, they would leave this world to go into another. For the next week, they would take shelter where they could, on ledges or in hammocks. When they surfaced at the top, they would stagger drunkenly, their balance shot. Well after the wall was finished, they would startle awake in the middle of the night, their bodies still vigilant. But for this final night before embarking, they could walk like Homo sapiens and piss freely and feel the ground against their backs.

But Lewis wasn't ready to sleep. The death of the swallow had him going. He recited the paradox of Kant's dove, a bird that imagines how much easier flight would be without air to resist its wings, and ends up plummeting through empty space. It was an all-purpose parable for Lewis, holding various meanings depending on his need. Tonight the dove simply seemed a means of wrapping up the day. Nature was awesome. The Trojan women had flown too close to the sun. Tomorrow was his and Hugh's turn.

"Amen," murmured Hugh, and drifted off.

He woke from a deep sleep, suddenly, not certain why. He lay still, waiting for something more.

The stars boiled in a narrow chute between the wall and the forest. Lewis wasn't snoring. The forest was quiet. Hugh was about to close his eyes when he saw a shape gliding among the upper branches.

The moon wouldn't get full for another few nights, meaning the moon shadows were faint. But enough light lingered to show the thing as it glided from one tree to another. It came to rest high above him, clinging there, resting perhaps, or getting his scent. Hugh didn't move inside his sleeping bag. He tried to get a sense of its size and whether it had wings.

It seemed to breathe with the breeze. Even as its lungs sucked in and out, he saw another of the things approaching on the moonbeams. It made a quick slip higher, then folded, and grabbed on to a different tree. A minute later, a little flurry of white butterflies quivered past. Hugh was baffled. What kind of night creatures were these?

Then he remembered the women's debris.

Descending their fixed ropes, Hugh and Lewis

had looked out across the acres of treetops at the leftovers from the Trojan Women disaster. It was like coming across the remnants of a shipwreck, with gear and clothing spread in a wide fan among the highest branches. A parka neatly outstretched. A spaghetti mess of ropes and slings tangled in the limbs. Plastic bags had sailed among the redwoods like a flotilla of jellyfish.

Here was the last of them, Hugh realized, looking at the ghostly shapes above him. Plastic bags and the confetti of a shredded paperback. It was trickling down like sediment to the seafloor. The snaky stuff like ropes would probably bind up in the highest reaches and, over the coming seasons, slowly bleach white in the sun. Winter would flush the rest to earth where it would disintegrate or mingle with the garbage tossed off by other climbers.

He tried judging the time from the stars, and gave up. They were living without watches or cell phones now. He glanced at the odds and ends that had emptied out of Cyclops Eye. Living on the ruins of civilization.

He was almost asleep again when he heard the ceramic clatter of rock on rock. It made him sit up. He heard it again, the *click-clack* of talus and a low, guttural huff.

Scavengers, thought Hugh. Though probably not a bear. The bears tended to stay closer to Yosemite Village where the pickings were easy.

Another clap of stone. This time Hugh saw a

curl of fireflies among the trees. In Yosemite? In this cold?

A man—or his phantom upper half—materialized in the phosphorous glow. He was a gaunt thing. A forest dweller. That should have tipped Hugh off. But still the sight didn't register. He was too curious to question it out loud. He waited for the specter to leave the trees and come closer.

They weren't fireflies, but a collar of chemical lights.

Hugh switched on his headlamp.

Joshua howled.

He was a startling sight, his mane and beard caked with mud, and a knife clutched in his teeth. The chemical lights dangled against his body hair. Like some junkyard aborigine, he'd painted stripes and circles on his naked chest with what appeared to be lipstick and axle grease. He'd blacked his face, and tied feathers to his straggly hair.

He loped crookedly across the boulders, going for Hugh. He had the knife in his good hand now. The blade was black, like a sliver of night.

"Joshua." Hugh shouted it, trying to freeze the madman with his own name.

Joshua bounded at Hugh with a scream. Hugh kicked to free his body from the sleeping bag, but it tangled his legs. He shoved to his feet, and hopped to the side.

His light beam sluiced every which way. He lost Joshua. He found him. The knife was in midarc. Stone. A stone knife. It glinted.

The knife strobed down through dark and light. Hugh fell back. Joshua slashed again. Hugh rolled and thrashed. The damn bag.

His only weapon was the headlamp. He thrust the light into Joshua's eyes. With his hand, he physically shoved the light at him, and it worked for a moment. Joshua staggered, blinded. He cut at the darkness, cut at the light. Hugh peeled the sleeping bag from his legs.

Absurd, thought Hugh. This couldn't be happening. There was a manhunt on for this guy. He should have been miles away by now. And Hugh, caught with his pants down, barefoot, in his Fruit Of The Loom underwear, hands taped for the climb.

"Lewis," he yelled. Should he run? Upslope or down?

"She told me what you did to her," Joshua said.

The lunatic had strung together a little necklace. Hugh recognized the jade and turquoise and other beads from the girl's hair. The crazy bastard.

"Stop," said Hugh. "You've got me. We'll leave. It's all yours."

The man was an animal. A monster. He thought he owned it all, the forest, the shadows, the stone, the dead souls. Joshua slashed at him again. Hugh flailed with the light beam, flicking at those eyes, whipping at them. He backed against the wall and felt for holds, but it was slick as ice. There was no way he could climb fast enough anyway. The man would hamstring him before he got three feet. Where was Lewis?

"Take our food," Hugh said. The bastard had eaten his pear. In mortal danger, and that rankled him still. "Whatever you want, take it."

Joshua swelled his chest. He was wheezing. The red lipstick and the grease marked his starved-dog ribs like war paint. "No more running. No more hiding."

Joshua scuttled closer, absent his walking stick. Was that what this was about? He fisted the knife, blade down, and raised his arm. Hugh had the presence of mind to note that the blade was made of black obsidian.

"Bismullah." Hugh barked it at him, more an urge than a thought. In the name of God.

Joshua hesitated. The word—the mystery of it, perhaps, or Hugh's commanding tone—astonished him.

"What?" Joshua lifted his head, listening, casting around for voices. "What?"

Dial him into a different reality, thought Hugh. Add another voice to the mix. Scramble his brains. "She was lying there," Hugh said. The girl. The booty. "I covered her up. We met, you and me. Where'd she go, Joshua?"

"She's"—he waved at the air—"out there. Wherever I go." His haunting bride.

"Remember me, Joshua?"

"I know you."

"We're going to be okay. Keep your knife." Give him assurance. Calm his rage. Then break his legs.

"You don't know," Joshua wailed.

"Everything will turn out for the best," Hugh said.

Joshua rocked in place. "We're in for it now, boy oh boy. She's not fooling around."

"Where did you put her, Joshua?"

A dark shape came hurtling from the trees.

Joshua flew from Hugh's light. It was like the falcon strike that afternoon, an explosion that was all aftermath. Talus clapped, men grunted.

Hugh found them with his beam. Lewis was trying to pin down the lunatic. His huge arms wrapped around the emaciated creature.

"He's got a knife," Hugh shouted. He grabbed a rock.

Lewis let go. He threw the man away from him. Joshua got to his feet. Tracking him with his headlamp, Hugh threw the rock. It landed shy. He threw another. Lewis joined him.

"Lie down, you dirty bastard," Lewis yelled at him.

They kept up a steady volley of stones, mostly missing. Part of Hugh wanted to hold back a little. Gruesome as he was, the man needed help. Medication. A room with rubber walls. But also Hugh wanted to maim him or worse, the jackal.

A rock clipped Joshua's shoulder. It stunned him. He fell. On his hands and knees, he pawed at the ground. Hugh threw another rock. With a howl, Joshua galloped into the forest.

Hugh stabbed around with his headlamp beam, but the trees were ranked like a fortress wall. Joshua had escaped again.

"You're dead," Lewis bellowed at the forest. "You got the curse on you now, Joshua." He gasped for air. "The devil's loose. The birds and the squirrels, and the bugs, they're his eyes. You just stepped in the deepest shit of all time. Hear me? He can see everywhere. He's coming for you."

Bent over, catching his breath, Hugh glanced over. "A curse?" he said.

Lewis leaned his hands on his knees. "Psy-ops, man. Fight him on his own ground. He believes in the devil, give him the devil. See how long he can live with that."

"Is that blood? Did he cut you?"

It was only axle grease. Lewis wiped the smears with handfuls of dirt. "What the hell was he doing?"

"Trying to kill me. I don't know. I doubt he knows. He's got voices in his head. He kept talking about her."

"The girl?"

"Her, yeah, the girl. Who else?"

Hugh picked his way barefoot down the slope, searching among the rocks.

"Here it is," he said. The obsidian blade was eight inches long, its edge meticulously chipped, sharp as a scalpel. It had a handle made of antler. "He must have spent months on it."

"Loot," said Lewis. "You vanquished the bastard. You earned it. Keep it."

They went back to their haul bags.

"Now what?" said Hugh.

"Now what, what?" said Lewis.

"You know. What next?"

You could talk a climb to death. Climbers did it all the time, magnifying the risks, spooking each other until it seemed crazy to leave your own kitchen. But he had to give them both the chance to think it through. Things were moving fast.

Lewis shrugged. "He didn't hurt us. We're still whole."

"We could go down and make a report," said Hugh.

"Except we weren't supposed to be camping here in the first place."

"What can we tell them that they don't already know?" Hugh said. "There's a basket case loose in the woods."

"We disarmed him. We put a few dents in him. All they have to do is pick him up."

"Not our job."

They shined their lights on the food and gear lined up in neat rows.

Finally Lewis said, "I'm good for it."

"You know I am," said Hugh.

"That's that, then."

Sleep was out of the question. Dawn was probably only a few hours off. They decided to put their adrenaline to good use and get another early start.

"It's our own fault," Lewis said. "We never should have come down for the night. Once you go, you got to keep going. We made ourselves vulnerable. It's the nature of gravity. Earth sucks, all that. I can feel it right now, like a wasting disease. Inertia. Quicksand. Before you know it, you're trapped flat on your ass in the La-Z-Boy chair watching shadows on a tube. It's a fight for the real reality, Harp. Every breath, every heartbeat, total combat. We've got to get out of here. Immediately." He went on like that, riffing to beat back the night and get traction.

Hugh pulled on his pants. They stuffed their sleeping bags inside the haul bags. Hugh wrapped the knife, a trophy straight out of the Stone Age, in some socks inside a stuff sack.

It was dark as coal. They humped the two "pigs" full of supplies and gear up to the fixed line. Hugh spotlighted the wall of trees along their right, half-expecting to see Joshua's eyes and face painted with auto grease. But he never appeared.

The bottom of the fixed rope was dangling in midair. It rose out of sight, as if magically attached to the night. They donned their harnesses, and Lewis his helmet, and fled from the forest and its troubles.

TEN

As Hugh climbed the ropes, something like respiration moved the trees. Timber squeaked. He heard the sound of wings, very large wings. A twig broke in the high branches. Hugh imagined an owl gripping its perch.

Spinning in a slow circle, he cast his light at the treetops. On second thought, preposterous as it was, fearing a spear or an arrow or whatever might be left in the caveman's arsenal, Hugh turned off his headlamp.

He continued up the ropes. The moon had sunk, and the sun was still well away. It was like tunneling into the underworld.

In a sense, they were entering the subterranean, or a piece of it. El Cap was a plutonic formation made of superheated rock that had bubbled up from the earth's interior like a massive upside-down water drop. Ice ages had sliced through the valley, sculpting what now stood as the largest homogeneous structure on earth.

Hugh kept his headlamp off as long as he could stand it, chasing the stars until the feeling of free fall became unbearable. Then he flipped the switch on and reentered his tube of stone and rope. His light beam wiped out the stars.

Below him, the blackness gobbled up his light. He felt hunted, though not by Joshua. Joshua was already a fairy tale. They'd made their dash through the ogre's woods, and crossed his border. There was no way he could ever touch them again. By the time they reached the summit, the boogey man would be locked in a cage.

And yet Hugh couldn't shake the sense of pursuit. He was out of Joshua's range, completely alone with the wall. But the darkness wasn't empty.

Hanging in place, he swept the light between his feet. His legs threw shadows on the stone, like twin columns of a gateway. He was passing into himself. There was nothing more to fear but the common fears ahead.

Dawn began breaking while he was midway up the fourth and final rope. The stone took on the colors of slow fire. Instead of hurrying his pace, Hugh slowed it. They were entering wall time now. From here to the top, El Cap would govern their progress.

Lewis was still cooling off when he reached the anchor. The smell of raw sweat was starting to override the last of his deodorant, and his whiskers were coming in black and white. The haul bags were tied off one below the other, like big sausage links.

"Don't you look proud," Hugh said to him.

Lewis grinned and patted one of the bags. In the space of two hours, he'd manhandled a combined weight of two hundred pounds up fifty stories' worth of stone. As the days passed and they ate and drank through the supplies, the bags would lighten. By the top, burdened by mere ounces, they'd be flying.

They entered a collection of dihedrals, where long, vertical blocks were stacked side by side like a cubist jungle. Cracks ran up where the squared angles met at the wall. When one crack pinched shut, Hugh simply moved sideways to the next dihedral.

He felt shielded among the dihedrals. They closed off the sense of exposure. For half the day, he exploited the cracks, zigzagging back and forth, and taking a relatively easy gain of over three hundred feet.

At every stop, they ate Met-Rx Big 100 meal replacement bars, which Lewis swore by. They were lighter and easier to eat than their old mainstay of granola mixed with nuts, raisins, and dried apples, and their Slim Jims, and beef jerky. One thing hadn't changed over all the years, the green or red Jolly Rancher candies they sucked on through the day like recovering alcoholics.

Shortly after noon, the dihedrals ebbed away.

The big open books of stone got smaller and finally flattened back into the wall. Hugh set an anchor and called for Lewis to come on.

While he hauled the bags, Hugh tried to spy the ledges he knew lay several pitches higher. The dihedrals had given him hope that they might actually reach the Archipelago, as the ledges were known, by nightfall. But now, faced with this thread of a crack, he remembered how slow things were meant to be on Anasazi.

The hours passed. Hugh watched the play of shadows across the stone. A few clouds appeared in front of the sun, and suddenly great herds were sliding across their vertical Serengeti. An undertow of wind stirred the forest, and sea serpents swam among the treetops far below.

They came to a small ledge where they'd sat side by side through a sleepless night long ago, with Lewis rapping nonstop about ascent as a moral act versus an aesthetic one, and what is art, and what is moral, and shouldn't love have something to do with it?

They might have used the two-man seat again tonight, but to their disgust, it was so fouled with human sewage they could barely breathe. Lewis cursed the perpetrators and all their generations, and finished by declaring, "We've got to move, Glass. We can't stay here one more minute."

They kept going, slowly, slowly, driven away by the sewage, whipped on by the sun. Lewis panted like a dog, sweating by the pint. The walls could hit

110 degrees or more on a summer day. It wasn't
nearly that hot now. Even before transplanting to
the Arabian deserts, Hugh had always been better
with the heat than Lewis, but found himself wishing for shade, and a cool breeze. And more water.
And for evening.

The wall was starting to ingest them. Hugh
sensed his vision and hearing changing in the vast
suspended fields of stone. Mirages—great, long,
plastic mantles that steamed out from the granite—
bent the distances. Towers and roofs slipped in and
out of focus. Reaching out his hand, a giant, faraway flake became a nubbin six inches high at his
very fingertips. He tried touching an ear of stone,
and it was a behemoth hanging a quarter mile off.
Human scale simply didn't work up here.

As the day went by, Hugh imagined tiny dots
of climbers where there were none. He didn't
worry about his sanity. He and Lewis used to see
the exact same phantoms, sometimes even waving
to them and having them wave back. In the
Himalayas, above the classic eight-thousand-meter
level, he'd shared tea with imaginary climbers, a
phenomenon known as the third man on the
rope. Here, Hugh wrote the illusions off as magical
thinking.

El Cap was a trickster. To Hugh the nonexistent
climbers were just another of the pranks the walls
used to defend against trespassers, like water stains
disguised as cracks, and roofs that circled back upon
themselves. And forest animals masquerading as

humans. The mountains hid inside your expectations.

Lewis had his own take on the phantoms. For him, El Cap had always been one vast alternate reality. The unreal climbers were real, just not real at that very moment. They were vestiges of climbers who had passed earlier, like echoes still lingering. He cited Freud about the unconscious being "freely mobile," alive and autonomous and capable of shaping itself. It wasn't the human unconscious he was talking about, though, but El Cap's. *We're no different from them, Hugh. Imaginary climbers. Think about it, we're just the Captain's dreams. We wouldn't exist without this.* And he would slap the stone as if it was the flank of a sleeping whale.

Hugh wasn't fooled. He'd read a lot of the same stuff Lewis had, from the Taoists to Borges, circles within circles. *So if we're just a dream, maybe they're us. They wave when we wave. They call when we call. What if we're looking at ourselves over there? Or we're over there looking at us over here?*

Lewis would suck his teeth, thinking hard. Then he'd see Hugh was mocking him. *Get a job, Glass. This is serious business.*

Now you're talking to yourself, Louie. Has that occurred to you? I'm just words inside your head. Projections of the unconscious.

You could get us killed with that shit, Harp.

Dreams can't die.

That's what I'm saying, Lewis would say.

That's what I'm saying, Hugh would echo.

Lewis would bite his knuckle or flip him off, and brood. Hours or days might pass before he'd try it out again. That was the old Lewis. So far on this climb—except for the peregrine falcon striking at his contempt for Trojan Women, which was how he had chosen to interpret it, as an omen—his mysticism was parked in some rusting junkyard.

Hugh missed the rapid-fire, nonlinear, deep bullshit. It had meant something to be able to talk such talk on top of climbing through the thresholds. It had made ascent more than a simian urge.

By late afternoon, tired from the climbing and hauling, they gave up on reaching the Archipelago before night. From directly below, it was impossible to see the ledges, but Hugh and Lewis knew from memory that only two pitches separated them from spacious, level quarters. At their rate, though, the two pitches would consume another three to five hours, and it was too soon to be stretching their days into darkness. The weather was excellent. They were well stocked, on schedule, and in command of themselves. It didn't get better than that.

They came to a halt in the middle of nowhere. The thread of a crack they'd been following since noon faded to nothing here. The southeast bowl of El Cap that contained them had gone blue with shadow. The stone was cooling in a hurry, and their climbing had slowed, like a clock winding down. Hugh pulled on a sweater while the warmth was there to take, and they began setting up for night.

It had been a long day. They were now roughly eleven hundred feet up, a little more than a third of the way, not quite the height of the Empire State Building. Minus a ledge, they assembled a portable platform, or portaledge. They fitted together the aluminum tubes of the frame, and stretched the nylon mesh taut for a floor. It was a one-man ledge, barely large enough to hold Lewis, who owned it. Hugh hung a hammock several feet above.

As night fell, they sat on the platform and watched the valley deepen with shadows. Hugh felt his age tonight. Thirty years ago, they would have had tired muscles and thirst that overruled their hunger, but not this deep weariness. Hugh's hands throbbed, as if he'd slammed them in a door. He didn't mind. It felt honest.

Lewis said, "I can't believe they shit all over our ledge."

"I heard it was a problem. All the ledges. Blame it on population explosion. We used to do it, too."

"We didn't know better."

"So our shit didn't stink?"

"You know what I mean. The world was still pure. We were innocent."

Hugh glanced over, and Lewis was slumped against the rock, staring into what was left of the forest. "I do know what you mean," he said.

"I thought we could get it back," said Lewis.

"We can," Hugh declared. "We just need to climb higher."

"Yeah," said Lewis, but without enthusiasm. It

was Rachel again. She was going to eat at him all the way to the top unless Hugh put a stop to it.

"I'm serious," Hugh said. "The trick is to never look back. What's done is done. Screw utopia. Screw the days of wine and roses. Forget the infinite highways, and the infinite stone. And the women." Their glorious hippie goddesses.

"But they were our women."

"Resurrection is the game," Hugh said. "It's a job. We climb. Then we climb more. That's what we do. That's who we are. Summit animals."

"And when your fingers get tired? I mean totally worn out. All crooked and bent and useless."

"No straw death," Hugh said. That had been their battle cry, or one of them. The bluster of youth.

Frogs began their nightly chorus. They sounded huge, but were quite small and lived in the cracks. Every now and then, car lights streamed by on the road far below. Stars winked on, one by one.

Hugh crawled into his sleeping bag in the hammock before it got any darker. They spent another half hour handing water and food up and down in their little settlement, waiting for true night.

Their passing of items had a slow, gluelike exaggeration to it. It was a wall instinct, a bit like a game of tug-of-war, but with a purpose. You held on to the water bottle or the can of mandarin oranges a little tighter, a little longer. Your partner had to pull that much harder before you released it. Nothing got taken for granted.

"You want to sleep?" Lewis said.

"I'm halfway there," said Hugh.

"I mean sleep like a baby." Lewis rattled a plastic bottle and handed it up. "Sleeping pills. One tablet and you're out for the count. No hangover in the morning. That bottle's for you. I brought my own. Get yourself all tucked in before you take it. This stuff works fast."

"No doobies? No Coors? No Gallo?"

"You're the one who said no more days of wine and roses. On to the pharmacy."

Hugh checked his knots one last time. He ran his light over the anchor just to be sure. Then he opened the pill bottle and downed a tablet.

Lewis was right. One minute Hugh was gazing up at the black cutout of the summit. The next he was gone.

Annie was waiting in his dreams. She was clinging to the ropes and slings above his hammock like some desert chameleon, only beautiful and young again. Her hair drifted in the breeze. She was watching him, nothing more. Not watching over him, he didn't get that sense. It was colder than that. She was examining him.

He murmured her name. Abruptly she fled across the rock. He woke.

The hammock was rocking gently. Beneath him, Lewis's portaledge scraped back and forth, an inch, no more. The slings were creaking. The frogs had stopped.

Half drugged, Hugh peered from his nylon

cocoon. The moon was wheeling out from the summit. He sat up to look, and a liquid shadow was coursing across the silver stone. That owl, he decided. The hunter.

Lewis was talking in his sleep. "I'm sorry, Rachel," he whispered. "So sorry."

Their women were infesting them. Their memories. It was temporary, just the lower latitudes still trying to pull them back to earth. Tomorrow, surely, they would break free. Tomorrow they would sink higher into El Cap.

Hugh eased back into the hammock. The Milky Way hung in a spray to the south, and it reminded him of desert nights. He drifted off again.

ELEVEN

The day began without them.

Hugh pried open his eyes inside a brightly lit green pea pod. His throat was swollen. He hadn't hurt like this since . . . he searched back . . . since escaping the desert. He reached up from the confines of the hammock.

Below him, Lewis sprawled on the portaledge, his hair jutting out in clumps. He had a cowboy tan to his helmet line. He'd suffered a bad night, wrestling half out of his sleeping bag. That, Hugh decided, would explain their rocking in the middle of the night.

"Lewis, wake up."

Lewis stirred and resisted, then came awake all at once. "Lord," he croaked, "the sun."

"You and your pills."

Lewis stood and shook his head. The platform

swayed with his weight. "I had a dream last night."

"I heard you."

"Rachel was here, right here, hanging on the slings, crawling around, staring at me. I didn't see her face. But it was Rachel, I'm sure of it."

Hugh was quiet. He didn't say anything about dreaming an identical dream, not of Rachel, but of Annie. He tried to remember if he'd actually seen Annie's face, or simply attached it as an afterthought.

"She had long hair."

"Rachel's got short hair, Lewis."

"This was her younger, like the old days."

Hugh said. "Our muses are beckoning to us."

"Not beckoning," Lewis said. "Warning. She was clear. Go down. Get away."

"Our bodies are talking to us," Hugh said. "We're in culture shock. El Cap's a different planet. They're telling us to be careful. The dreams will taper off once we adjust to the wall." He was winging it.

"You had dreams, too?"

"It's just our brains flushing out the system."

Lewis dogged him. "You said 'they.' You said our muses."

Hugh didn't answer directly. Whoever she was, the dream woman troubled him. She was a symptom of something. He didn't know what. The steeping of memories was one thing. Now they were cross-pollinating each other with dreams. It was a distraction. "We've lost enough time already," he said.

"She was so clear about it," said Lewis.

"Lewis, forget Rachel."

"Good, I like that. I'll remember that while I'm sleeping tonight."

"Seriously. Get focused. You've got to clear your head. Control, Alt, Delete. Reboot. Before she kills you."

"But, Hugh, she's my wife."

Hugh had pushed it as far as Lewis was willing to hear. No doubt they'd revisit the issue. For now, they had a morning to catch up with.

He scouted the wall above. A seemingly empty panel separated them from the tail end of a beautiful hand crack. The emptiness was not entirely empty. As they'd discovered long ago, the panel offered a scattering of flakes. Fritos of Fear, they'd named the section. Most of the flakes were no thicker than the edge of a corn chip, just thick enough for hooks, Lewis's specialty.

Hugh untangled himself from the hammock, and stood on the portaledge in his socks. They wolfed down their breakfast of energy bars, and dismantled most of the camp, stuffing their night things into the haul bags. Lewis pulled on his leather gloves with the fingertips cut off and began cherry-picking the heavy racks for what he would need on the panel of flakes.

Just below their knots, Hugh found that two of the ropes had been chewed to the core. White nylon strands showed through the colorful sheaths. "Our little friends have been visiting."

Like the frogs, mice lived inside the wall, traveling up and down the thoroughfare of cracks. It constantly amazed him how high they would climb for a meal. Hugh didn't mind their hunger so much, their stomachs were small enough. But they'd leave droppings in your raisins, that kind of thing.

"How much of us did they get?" Lewis asked.

"Just the ends of the ropes."

"I should have brought my slingshot."

It was an old joke, the slingshot, because you never saw the enemy. At best, you heard their little claws and teeth. While Vietnam was still on, Lewis dubbed them Charlie because they owned the night.

Hugh moved to the far corner and fumbled through his harness and zipper. His urine, what little there was, passed dark as camel piss. It would stay that way for a day or two even after they summitted, until they had binged on gallons of water. They were like an old-time caravan passing through the desert. Water discipline was a fact of life up here. Some big-wall climbers developed kidney stones from repeated bouts of dehydration.

It was only then, as he shook off the last drops, that he saw the others far below. "Now where did they come from?" he said.

Lewis thought he was talking to his penis. "Don't tell me the crabs have got you." Lice for mice. That was another big-wall affliction, along with bad teeth, dandruff, and world-class constipation.

"You better take a look, Lewis."

"I'll pass, old buddy. Small dicks make me sad."

"I'm not kidding. Down there."

There were two of them, five or six hundred feet below, with a white haul bag. These were not mirage climbers, not the way they intersected the shadow line.

Lewis swore a blue streak. "With all the real estate to choose from, why here? Why us?"

Hugh studied them and their distance. Ordinarily, five hundred feet would guarantee a certain amount of privacy. It would keep at least a day between them. But these guys weren't ordinary.

"They're fast," he said. "There was nobody down there last night. They must have started this morning while we were still sleeping. And look how high they've gotten. They're going to run right over us."

"Not if I can help it," Lewis said.

"Maybe they'll slow down and keep a distance," said Hugh.

"Fat chance. We've got to stay ahead of them."

"They're burning up the cracks. Look at them."

"We'll stop them, then," Lewis growled.

"Come on, we don't own the wall."

"They don't either. You've been out of the scene too long. You don't know. These speed climbers, they're thugs, some of them. It's all about them. They'll do anything to break through your party.

Clip onto your gear, pull on your ropes, just totally
fuck with your *wa*."

"My what?"

"Your *wa*, man. Your yin-yang."

Hugh went on ribbing him. "Not my yin-yang,
they're not."

"Go ahead, clown around. I don't want them
above us. You know what's up there. That band of
diorite is trash rock. It peels off if you look at it
wrong. You want to be dodging their bloopers? I
don't. These young kids, they could care less if you
die in front of their eyes."

"You're getting worked up, Lewis."

"It's not going to happen, they're not going
through."

"I heard you."

Hugh couldn't help sharing some of his resentment. They had been in their glory yesterday,
cranking moves, boisterous and lean. They *had*
owned the Captain. Now these young Turks were
going to expose him and Lewis for what they were,
two weekend warriors ambling through a second
childhood, racing to catch up with their own inven-
tion.

Muttering at the trespassers, Lewis tied in to
their best rope. Suddenly there was no time to waste
on dream women and crack mice. This was war.

In his prime, the Great Ape had also been
known as the Hook. The Hook and the Harp, one
wit had dubbed them. Huey and Louie: the Boulder
Mafia.

Aid climbing was basically hook-and-ladder work, a refinement of besieging medieval castles. You placed a piece in the rock, or on it, and then attached stirrups—the ladder—and ascended on your hardware. In this case, the hook-and-ladder technique was going to involve actual hooks.

Lewis fanned open what could have been a torturer's collection of metal claws, talons, and hooks, one or two of which he'd invented himself. Selecting one, he attached a set of stirrups to it, and set the prongs of the hook on a flake. He glanced down again.

"Forget them," Hugh said.

"They're trouble, Hugh."

"Fritos, Lewis. Fritos."

Lewis fussed the stirrups onto his left foot. Ever so delicately, he eased his 210 pounds onto the rung. The stirrups creaked. Something didn't feel right. He returned his right foot to the platform.

He found another flake and reset the hook. He tried again. More protest from the stirrups. Hugh could hear the hook grating on microcrystals of granite. The flake held. They gained twenty vertical inches. It had taken ten minutes.

"Scrotal fortitude," Lewis told himself.

Hugh relaxed a little. The Hook was back. "Go, fat man," he said.

Standing in his stirrups, Lewis looked as if he was walking on prayers. He chose a different shaped hook for the next flake, and slowly transferred his weight to the upper stirrups. Hugh fed out a few more inches of rope through the belay device, miserly with the slack. They both had to be careful.

The sun slid higher. Lewis sorted his way through the flakes. After an hour or so, he'd gone only twenty feet. Hugh made himself comfortable on the platform, lying with his feet against the wall while he meted out slack in careful hanks.

There was no place for Lewis to set protection as he progressed. Just as worrying, there were only a finite number of good flakes linking the route. Rip a flake, and he could seal shut the Fritos of Fear. Then they'd end up having to chicken-bolt their own unbolted classic, or surrender and leave Anasazi for better climbers.

Lewis started whistling, a good sign. It took little physical effort to aid on hooks, just steel nerves, or extraordinary nonchalance. He'd gone past the nerve stage. "Greensleeves," Hugh realized. Harmonic fifths and all. Thirty feet out.

Lewis fell.

There was no forewarning, no snap of rock or ping of metal, no grunt or whispered curse.

Maybe the extra fifteen pounds of muscle he'd added over the years was too much for Fritos. Or, despite "Greensleeves," Rachel was eating at him. Maybe the approaching strangers spoiled his focus.

Hook or flake, something blew. Lewis plunged.

His hurtling body struck the edge of the platform. He went on going. The rope jerked taut where it passed through the anchor. Hugh pitched upward, face-first into the stone. He saw stars, like in the cartoons.

Then it was over.

For a few moments, the creak of stressed rope and slings filled the silence. The haul bags hung from the anchor like a pair of muggers, pinning Hugh against the wall. Hugh held Lewis on the rope, waiting for him to say something or get his feet under him.

He'd been thirty feet up, now he was thirty feet down. Lewis dangled in his seat harness. He clutched the rope to his chest with his leather gloves. Slowly he looked up at Hugh with wide eyes and a raccoon mask of tan lines. His hip sunglasses were missing in action, jerked from his face in the fall.

They weren't in dire straits. Sixty feet of air gave you bragging rights, though each of them had ridden out much longer whippers in the past. And it was Hugh who had taken the worst of this fall, the belayers often did. Blood leaked from his nose, possibly broken. Red beads trickled across his white-taped hands. He had a nice rope burn across his inner arm. All acceptable in the scheme of things. He'd saved his partner. They were okay.

But as he went on holding Lewis, Hugh saw something he'd never seen in his old friend. Lewis had a dumb, stunned expression. He didn't move. He didn't help. He just sat there.

"Are you hurt?" Hugh said.

Lewis blinked at him.

"Lewis?"

Lewis opened his mouth to speak. It was his style to bounce back from near disaster and play the macho smart-ass, doing his primal *yawp*, hamming it up and rendering quotes. They had a team favorite, delivered with a thick accent. *Don't worry, I'm the kaiser, I just came to wash my hands.* It came from a German lunatic who had gained international notoriety by climbing out of three different asylums back in the 1920s. Entering through the fifth-floor window of a screaming woman, he'd calmly introduced himself, washed his hands, and then eaten the bar of soap. It had become something of a motto for Hugh and Lewis. Dangling on a rope, beat up sometimes, down but never out: *Don't worry, I'm the kaiser.* Having their cake and eating it, too.

But this morning no words came out. Lewis hung there, mute. He swayed liked a man on a noose.

Hugh kept his shoulder into the wall, bearing their weight, patiently bleeding onto his hands. His nose hurt like crazy.

Finally Lewis spoke. "Hold me, Hugh," he pleaded.

"I've got you."

Lewis glanced down, then swiftly up, away from the depths. At last, he grabbed one of the haul lines, taking the weight off Hugh. With a sudden rush, he grappled up the rope and straddled one of the haul bags and clung to the slings. Hugh wanted to look away.

Hugh pinched his nose to stem the blood. It didn't feel crooked. Just a solid punch in the snout.

"I think I twisted my knee," Lewis said.

Something inside Hugh crumpled. This was the Great Ape. He had always been indestructible. He'd never admitted weakness or pain. The knee was an excuse. He was scared. He was done.

Hugh said, "That's no good."

He waited for Lewis to disown the climb. That seemed next. It happened all the time among climbers. It was usually the weather that took the blame, or a bad feeling, or weird vibes, or a bum ankle or knee.

"It's probably nothing," Lewis said.

"Have some water."

"If we can just get to the ledges," Lewis said. His hands were shaking.

Fair enough, thought Hugh. "It's only a couple pitches more to the Archipelago," he said. "Why don't I take the lead?"

"Are you sure? You're the one bleeding."

"Rest the knee," Hugh said. But he was thinking, why go up, why risk one more inch, when they were only going to go down? Because he was quite certain that's the way it was about to play out. If they descended now, they could be back at Yosemite Lodge in time for dinner.

"That's all I need," Lewis said. "I'm still good for it, you know." But his face betrayed him.

Hugh looked around him unhappily. He'd flown ten thousand miles for this, for a swan song that ended in the middle of nowhere? Then he decided that the ledges were at least a landmark on the wall. Up there, they could spend the night, drink a lot of water, eat a lot of food, and in the morning start down. Driving out of the Valley tomorrow, he could look up at the Archipelago and mark his high point and say good-bye to El Cap.

He draped the rack of hooks and gear over his shoulders, and took more time than necessary to arrange the pieces. Fritos was supposed to have been Lewis's hurdle to jump. The prospect of sustained hooking didn't thrill him.

While he was trying to rally himself for the flakes, they heard a tiny voice. That second team of climbers had closed the gap during Lewis's ordeal. Only three hundred feet separated them now. What had taken Hugh and Lewis three days to climb, this pair was going to cover in a single day.

One of the climbers was waving at them. The breeze carried off his words. "What do they want?" said Hugh.

Lewis squinted down. He had the better hearing. "I'll be damned," he said. "A rope. Can you believe that?"

"Why would they want a rope?" said Hugh. It made no sense. How could you claim a speed ascent if you borrowed other people's time?

"So they can pass us, why else? Unbelievable." Lewis flipped them the bird.

Hugh studied the pair. The top climber was in

steady motion, his hands dipping in and out of the rock as he churned higher. It was his belayer who was calling and waving to them. They definitely wanted a jump up.

"Maybe they're in trouble."

"Some trouble," Lewis snorted. "They're moving like a whirlwind. Make them do their own grunt work."

The breeze chased around in the vast bowl, chopping the distant climber's words to gibberish. "Let them yell," Lewis said.

Hugh half-agreed. If this was to be his last night on the wall, he didn't want to be sharing the ledges with two strangers. Let them sweat.

Then a word stopped them. "Glass," the depths uttered.

Lewis frowned. "They know your name?"

It came to Hugh who these men were, or at least the one calling to him. Immediately he started tying two ropes together to lower to the climbers. Lewis didn't protest this time. He understood, too.

For some reason, Augustine was racing to join them.

TWELVE

Augustine came first. He sprinted up the ropes in one swift thrust, no rests, covering the three-hundred-foot gap in less than five minutes. Even before clipping to the anchor, he bellowed down, "Now," as if triggering a race.

His face blazed with exertion and sunburn. He hadn't shaved for days, nor slept probably.

"She's alive," he gasped to them.

They didn't have to ask who. His lover, he meant.

Suddenly Lewis was full of good fellowship. He thumped the younger man on the back. "Ah, that's great, man, great. Here, drink."

Augustine had the lungs of a horse. With each breath, his big rib cage pushed at Hugh on one side and Lewis on the other. The three of them sat on the portaledge, packed together. Far below, Augustine's partner was jugging the long line.

Hugh was confused. "You got her?" he said.

Augustine shook his head no. He swallowed another mouthful of water. "Couldn't get in under the roof. I tried everything. But the wall's overhanging, and then there's the Eye. It's like a crater under a roof. I was hanging forty feet out from her."

"What about a helicopter?"

"Same deal, only the rotors would keep you that much farther out from the wall. A waste of time."

"She couldn't catch your throw line?"

"She's injured." He was terse. Stoic. Dealing with it. He bent forward over the ledge. "You're almost here," he shouted down to his partner.

"How bad is she?" Hugh asked.

"She'll be all right once I get to her." Nothing about broken bones or wounds. Just a statement of faith.

Augustine wouldn't meet his eyes. He kept peering up toward the ledges and across to where, somewhere among the shadows and stains, Trojan Women rose. Cyclops Eye remained invisible.

"And the other woman?" said Lewis.

"Dead."

"That's tough," said Hugh.

"She sure looked dead," Lewis said.

Augustine seized on that. "You mean you've seen her?"

"From the meadow," said Lewis. "The morning we started up, they had a big spotlight. She was hanging at the end of a rope."

Augustine shook his mane of hair. "No, no. You got it backward. Andie's the one on the rope."

Andie, thought Hugh. That was the name of the one who belonged to Augustine. "She's the one we saw?"

"That's what I said."

Hugh and Lewis looked at each other. Judging by the way she was hanging, Andie had seemed as dead as it got. And if she wasn't dead three days ago, she surely was by now. Unless by some miracle . . .

"She looked right at me," Augustine said. "She smiled. I told her the plan. She knows I'm coming for her."

"And what about the other one?"

"Cuba? She's still tied in at their camp, way in the back of the Eye, all tangled in ropes. She must have taken the full shock of the fall. I called to her, but didn't get a word or a motion. Like I said, dead." He didn't seem especially torn up about that.

"Did they ever find that girl's body in the woods?" Hugh asked.

"Cass? Still missing."

Cass, Cuba, and Andie. Hugh liked their names. He was glad they hadn't been Sally, Jane, or Britney, not for a wall called Trojan Women. "And the cave-man?"

"Joshua's gone to ground."

"He attacked us," Lewis said. "We were sleeping at the base. He almost gutted Hugh with a stone shiv. The guy's armed and dangerous. Do you have a radio? You should report that."

"They'll find him," Augustine said. The assault didn't seem to surprise or concern him. They were in a different universe up here, with potential violence all around them.

"He's an evil bastard," said Lewis. "I've never seen pure evil."

"You call that evil?" Hugh scoffed.

"He's a necrophiliac, a homicidal, Satanic son of a bitch. He tried to kill you."

"He's out of his tree, that's all," Hugh said. "I've been thinking about him. You know what's scariest? We could be him."

"You better rehydrate, Hugh. Your brain's shrinking."

"Joshua's what happens when the serpent poisons you."

"The serpent being the devil," said Lewis. "Unless I misread my Genesis."

"The serpent being the serpent. Nature. The wilderness." Hugh slapped the stone. "This."

Augustine spoke. He put a stop to them. "They're bringing in dogs. They'll get him."

After a minute, Hugh said, "I just want them to find the girl."

Augustine looked at him. "Did Joshua do that to your face?"

Hugh dabbed at his nostrils. The blood still hadn't quit. Next would come black eyes. He pointed at Lewis. "He's still learning how to climb."

Lewis raised his chin proudly. "Somebody's got to keep you on your toes. You let your guard down. You deserved it."

The big-wall repartee seemed ready to carry them off again. Augustine leaned forward. "What's taking that kid?"

Hugh glanced down at the approaching figure. "What's your plan?" he asked.

"Going down to her didn't work, so we're going up. I hired a gun." A rope gun, Hugh knew. "He's a wall rat, really young, but really fast."

"Why use Anasazi, though? North America Wall travels right under Cyclops Eye. Or you could have followed them up Trojan Women."

"Except nobody knows where exactly their route goes, only where it ended. And this is our quickest access. Anasazi's a milk run." Augustine paused. "No offense."

Hugh shrugged. Every route had a life cycle. Repeated climbing almost always moderated the dangers. Each time climbers hammered a piton in and out, the crack eroded. The obstacles got rehearsed. Bolts got placed. New hardware, new shoes, new techniques, all these things tamed once fierce challenges. Still, it stung. Anasazi, a milk run?

Augustine went on. "Once we hit the Archipelago, we'll pendulum across to Trojan Women, then climb to Cyclops Eye. With a little gusto, we'll reach Andie by dark. I've got a summit team waiting to lower a litter. All I have to do is radio them. We'll catch the throw line, and they'll haul us up, and that's that."

Hugh looked across the valley at Middle Cathedral Rock. The sun line was moving up the buttress. He couldn't believe how fast the day was going by. Lewis's pills, and then his fall, had eaten it up. There were probably four more hours before sunset, and then another hour of alpenglow after that. It wasn't like on the sea where the light just suddenly switched off.

But even squeezing every minute of light out of the day, even pushing his partner, Augustine was going to be lucky just to tag Trojan Women. First they had to reach the ledges, and the pendulums would take time.

Augustine looked down, and said, "About time."

The kid arrived. "Joe," Augustine introduced him.

Joe was thin, almost anorexic. No more than seventeen, he seemed full of self-certainty. He had a pianist's long, thin fingers. His eyes burned a little too bright. Thirty years ago, Hugh might have been him.

"Have some water," Hugh said.

Joe took only a little.

"The whole thing," Hugh told him.

The boy looked at Augustine, who nodded okay. He drank deeply. Then Augustine said, "Are you ready?"

Joe handed back the water. He spent maybe

three seconds judging the rock, then took off like a shot, hooking the flakes as if they were rungs on a ladder.

For the next few minutes, while Augustine belayed his young partner, Lewis hauled up their bag. It weighed hardly anything. He towed it in, hand over hand. "You guys travel light," he said.

"A little water, some sleeping bags, a med pack," Augustine said. He was paying out rope in big lobs, practically throwing it up the wall. The boy scampered like a spider. He grew smaller on Fritos of Fear.

"We brought extra water," Hugh said. "Take a couple gallons. And food. Whatever you need."

"We're all set," Augustine said to Hugh. "Speed is everything. She's waiting."

"Have you thought about a night on the ledges?" asked Lewis. "Rest up. Get a fresh start. You know, 'Preserve Thyself.' " It was the number one rule in rescue work. He was letting Augustine know that he, too, had served among the saviors. For years, he'd been a member of Rocky Mountain Search and Rescue. He saw it as an obligation. *One day that could be me out there.*

"We're under control," Augustine said.

"That's not what I meant. I'd have the pedal to the metal, too. I'm just saying, you've been hitting it hard. And the ledges are large."

"We've got it covered," Augustine snapped.

Lewis shut up.

Augustine jutted his chin at the heights, sorry for his tone. "We were going to get married," he said. "You know that little stone chapel?"

"I've seen it," said Hugh.

"Yeah," said Augustine. "That was two years ago. We kind of postponed things." He tossed another hank of rope up the wall. The kid was streaking the flakes.

Hugh didn't pry. This was personal. Something had gone wrong. Now Augustine was trying to make it right.

Overhead, Joe reached the crack, jabbed in a piece of protection, a single piece, and stormed higher. The entire crack—a two-hour climb when Hugh had done it years ago—took the kid eight minutes flat.

Augustine got ready to go.

"How can we help?" Hugh asked him.

"You've done plenty. You saved us an hour at least by lowering your rope. You gave us water. How about I trail a rope for you guys?"

Lewis pretended to consider the offer. But Hugh could see his relief. This way they could bypass Fritos in one fell swoop. Within a half hour, they could be on the ledges.

"Sold," said Hugh.

Joe's tiny voice peeped. He'd set an anchor. It was Augustine's turn. Augustine lifted his jumars, one in each hand like cardio-shock paddles, and fastened on to the rope.

"Bring her back," said Lewis, and he meant it.

He clapped Augustine on the back. Hugh looked on. In saving his lost love, Augustine was saving all their lost loves, or so Lewis would have it. But to accept that, you had to accept the converse, that to lose one love was to lose all loves.

Augustine vanished up the rope at a near vertical run.

THIRTEEN

Hugh climbed the rope after Lewis. Until the final few feet, there was no hint of a lost world waiting. Then abruptly he was there.

The Archipelago—or Ark—truly was a chain of islands in the sky. The ledges stair-stepped left and right in bunches, all interconnected, most of them flat or even slightly cupped on the outer rim, like rails along a bunk bed. One was wide enough to hold two people side by side. Hugh had heard that as many as eleven climbers at a time had slept here.

Even more magical was the Ark's sand. The larger ledges held layers of soft, powdery white sand, a vestige of the Ice Ages when the walls were being carved. It seemed impossible the sand could have survived eons of wind and weather, but here it lay.

Lewis was rooting through the pigs for their

night supplies. Clorox jugs stood in a neat row, and the stuff sacks with their sleeping bags were clipped to an anchor.

Augustine and the boy had already departed. Hugh saw them swinging in wild pendulums across the blank stone, arcing down and over to Trojan Women like ape men on vines. They disappeared around an immense column without a look back. Hugh raised one hand in a good-bye.

"Hey, amigo." Lewis gave him a little can of peaches. "Eat up. Be glad we're not them. They've got a night of misery ahead, and nothing but death at the end of it. We're in the lap of God here. Two nights of five-star beachfront. It's all downhill from here." Meaning uphill. Up the wall.

There was no more talk about a bad knee. Lewis was back with the program. Augustine's heroic purpose had gotten his blood moving again. It had been a crappy day. He'd slept late, fallen from his hooks, and lost his nerve. The ledges—and Augustine's example—had given them a second life.

They had covered just two hundred feet today, a scant two pitches that they hadn't even climbed themselves. But they were on schedule. Tomorrow got easier, with abundant cracks and stances at most of the anchors. They could take their time fixing ropes up the next six hundred feet, which would put them almost two-thirds of the way to the summit. And as a bonus they'd get to sleep on the Ark tomorrow night, too.

Hugh took off his shoes and socks and sank his

toes into the sand. It held the day's heat, and he let the softness mend him from the feet up. He padded around in the fading daylight like Robinson Crusoe.

There were all sorts of artifacts from other climbers, mostly ancient, frayed bits of webbing and tape, stuff that would eventually crumble to dust. The sand would outlast it all. He expected the same kind of sewage and garbage they'd found lower. But to his relief, the generations had largely respected the Ark. There was a clean granite smell.

Across the valley, the primal landmarks—Cathedral Spires and Sentinel Rock and unseen giants up valley, around El Cap's eastern buttress—flushed orange and red with the last of the light. There are two stages to alpenglow, a first surge that waxes and wanes, fooling amateur photographers into stowing away their cameras, and then a sudden short-lived second rush of colors.

Hugh went on exploring. The Ark was like a castle with all its levels and hidden niches. Near the end of one shelf, out where it was too narrow to sleep, he shifted some rocks. The sand lay deep here. Careful not to spill any into the abyss, he began scooping a hole.

Lewis came over. "You don't think it's still here, do you?"

"I doubt it. I just thought I'd see."

Hugh sifted deeper. After another few minutes, he gave up. "I guess not," he said.

"Wasn't it a little farther out?"

Hugh edged out. This time his fingers struck a metal cylinder just inches below the surface. He lifted an old thermos from the sand. "Can you believe it?" he said.

The corrugated stainless steel was coppery from weathering, and rust had eaten through the base. Cradling it in one arm, he backed on his knees to the larger ledge, and they sat with it between their crossed legs.

"Did you ever in a million years think we'd be coming back to it?"

"Pretty amazing."

"Are you going to open it or not?"

"Don't get your hopes up," Hugh said. He twisted the plastic cap off. Lewis turned on his headlamp.

"Look at that, would you?"

The inner lining had withstood the elements. Their time capsule was intact. Hugh carefully removed the mementoes and spread them on the sand.

There was his old Hohner's harmonica with the reeds split from dryness, and a Marine Corps belt buckle that had belonged to Lewis's father, and a sheaf of poems, and toys from the two boxes of Cracker Jacks they'd brought along, a plastic magnifying glass, and a dime-sized compass. The real prize came last, snapshots, curled from their decades inside the thermos.

Lewis placed his headlamp on a rock. They were quiet for a few minutes, each examining his own picture. Hugh held the snapshot delicately, with grazed, cuticle-split fingers and his knuckles and hands taped with mummy wraps.

The Kodak colors were as fresh as the day they'd buried the thermos. Annie hadn't aged a day. Strawberry blond curls burst loose from the blue bandanna on her head, cascading down her shoulders. He could almost taste those thick, red lips. He remembered. You didn't just kiss Annie. She had been like a feast.

Lewis cleared his throat. "Wait till she sees this," he said, staring at the other picture.

Hugh didn't tell him that Rachel would not be waiting to see anything. By now, she had surely left the Valley. She was probably boxing up Lewis's things in a house that would not open to his key. Hugh found it hard to believe she hadn't broken the news to him. Then again, Lewis had a tremendous capacity for deafness.

Hugh traded him pictures. Rachel was a Venus rising out of the sea, her blouse plastered tight as skin, her arms high, as if she were coiling up into the world of man. "Where did they go?" Lewis said. His eyes were wet. He returned Annie to Hugh. "This was all for them, remember?" He wanted Hugh to weep, too.

But Hugh was past that. You walked away from the lost ones, or risked joining them. "What about before we met them?" he said. "We were climbers first. We had the mountains in our heads and hearts before they ever came along."

"Yeah, but then they did come along. It didn't

make sense before them. We were up fighting the good fight, and we couldn't figure out the big why. We were wandering, and they saved us."

"Lewis, we buried them in a thermos. Nothing stays the same."

Lewis held his picture by the light. "What did they see in us?" he said.

"What did we see in them?" Desire, it was all about desire. And the end of desire.

Lewis wasn't hearing him. "We gave them everything."

"That's over," Hugh said.

Lewis mistook Hugh's resignation for melancholy. He laid down the Rachel photo and gave Hugh's thigh a bracing squeeze. Poor, good, simple Lewis.

"What do we do with all this stuff?" Lewis asked. He lifted a page of his old poems, and frowned at it as if aliens had been revising it.

"We've unearthed ourselves now," Hugh said.

"I guess we can take whatever we want."

"I think I'll leave my half of it." In truth, most of it didn't matter to him anymore. He tried the harmonica, but it sounded like Lewis's fifths, untrained and just wrong.

He slid the harmonica and toys back into the thermos. Lewis donated his Marine Corps belt buckle, and carefully selected his best poem for the ages. The rest, along with his photo, he kept. Hugh almost kept Annie, then slipped her back into the glass liner, out of sight, out of mind.

They made their camp, going around from ledge to ledge and trying out the best beds of sand. Lewis threw open his sleeping bag in the center of the largest island, well away from the precipices. Hugh chose a ledge with a grand view.

The wall plummeted just inches from where he would lay his head. A lip of stone contained the sand, and someone had thoughtfully drilled a bolt here for night lodgers like himself to clip into.

It was too early to sleep, and the night was warm. Part of it was the sand, still releasing its day heat. They lounged by the haul bags for a while, sipping water and snacking. They turned off their headlamps and let the stars take over.

Hugh looked for Augustine's lights, off to the southeast. "I wonder if they're still climbing," he said.

"He's not stopping for anything," Lewis said.

"Do you think she's still alive?"

"What's it matter? This isn't a rescue. It's penance, man. He'll kill himself before he quits." Lewis's voice was tinged with admiration.

"Penance?"

"For her brother. Not that the man has any real choice. Augustine's got to ride it through. Some things are, like, predestined."

"She had a brother?"

"You've never heard about them? I had it figured out the minute Augustine told us his name." Lewis relished a captive audience. "Down in Patagonia?" he said. "You're sure? Augustine and Tim McPherson and Charlie Regis?"

Hugh waited. Lewis had a sip of water. He took his sweet time.

"They were trying a new route on Cerro Torre. It was a standard Patagonia gig, tons of wind, Shakespearean weather, nothing but base camp day after day. Then they got their clear window and went for it. They managed to push to the shoulder just under the ice cap. Of course the weather turned on them. Of course Augustine's partners got sick. But instead of getting them down right away, Augustine decided to solo the ice cap and snag himself the summit.

"It took him three days, totally out there, you've seen the man. He's got the strength of lions. By the time he returned to their ice cave, McPherson had died. Regis was too weak to move. By now, Augustine was in horrible shape, too. He couldn't evacuate Regis by himself, so he went down for help. The weather got worse. End of story. Three went up, only one came home."

It wasn't completely extraordinary. Hugh could think of a half dozen similar incidents: Messner and his brother on Nanga Parbat, Stammberger on Tirich Mir, and others. And yet he'd never heard about this one. "How could I have missed it? When did it happen?"

Lewis went back in his head. "November or December. The fall of '01."

"That explains it," Hugh said. "Nine-eleven."

After 9/11, notions of risk had been transformed. People quit paying attention to thin air and perfect storms. After that, high adventuring had come to seem desperate at best, or just pathetic. In Saudi Arabia, Hugh had watched the world news shrink to a pinhead. The mood among expats had darkened overnight. His Saudi friends had quit speaking to him. They wouldn't shake his hand. Right there in the ARAMCO offices, posters for Islamic charities had popped up like flowers. Contempt was everywhere, on all sides. A tale of Patagonia would have been swallowed up.

"Which one was her brother?" Hugh asked.

Lewis thought. "I don't know. Regis, I'd say. The one he left alive."

The pieces fell into place, the wedding postponed, this hell-bent rescue, and Augustine's insistence that the woman was still alive. "Survivor guilt," Hugh murmured. There was a deadly brew for the unwary.

"Tell me about it." Lewis said it offhandedly, but Hugh recognized the subtext. Lewis wasn't the first to believe Hugh needed to unburden himself of Annie's death, only the most extreme. Some had offered him coffee or a beer. Lewis had offered him El Cap.

"Somebody needs to forgive the man," Lewis said.

"He needs to forgive himself," Hugh said.

"Penance doesn't work that way, bro."

"Survival is penance," Hugh said.

"Sure," said Lewis. He rattled his pill bottle. "Want some candy?"

"All yours," Hugh said. "That's wicked stuff."
He stood and looked out toward Trojan Women.
Augustine was in motion over there somewhere
tonight, racing after the one soul he could never
hope to save, even if he saved her.

FOURTEEN

Far below, some animal's scream ricocheted across the walls, waking him. At first, Hugh refused to open his eyes. Lying on his back with the safety rope snaking down into the throat of his sleeping bag, he just listened. A mountain lion, he decided. They shrieked like Arab widows.

The sand, so comfortable when he'd first nestled in, had packed hard against his hip and shoulder. His head throbbed. His nostrils and sinuses were clogged with dried blood. He wanted water. He would settle for sleep. He turned on his other side. Maybe he slept.

The moon came lumbering over the summit, a vast, white, pockmarked globe. This time he looked. You could almost lay a ladder against it and climb up among the craters.

The smoke entered him like a dream. He

couldn't properly smell, but it had a taste in the back of his throat. It seemed to come up from his lungs.

Now fully awake, he looked across at the paddy tops of the silver-lit ledges, and Lewis was a motionless lump. He peered over the lip. Thirteen hundred feet below, the forest was catching fire.

Even as Hugh watched, a tiny orange flame danced among the trees like some Promethean spirit. He thought it must be a spark wafting on the breeze, though the air was still at this elevation.

The lion cried again. But its scream changed. It yipped and hooted, a whole menagerie of beasts lamenting the fire, perhaps. Or celebrating the moon.

It etched the floor in a slow, thin, ragged line. There was not one thing he could do to halt it, and so Hugh simply watched. As the spark skipped on and the fire grew longer, he sat up, legs dangling in his sleeping bag, back against the wall.

He sat there for a half hour, sure that firefighters would come streaming in any minute. And yet no one arrived. He began to wonder if they were setting the fire themselves. Maybe this was one of their controlled burns. And him with a ringside seat.

A puff of air ruffled his hair. He paid no attention to it. Breezes hit and ran on a whim. They were usually meaningless vagrants, detached from anything larger than themselves.

But what he felt as a breeze came pouring along the valley floor as a wind. It surged through the stone mouth of Yosemite, invisible but explicit. At ground level, the crooked vein of fire detonated.

The forest screamed again, and this time it seemed to him a human scream. It was promptly drowned in a roar. Trees blossomed with light and exploded. Hugh blinked at the sudden brightness. Flames scattered across the bone-dry fuel of summer. That quickly, the inferno took off.

"Lewis, you've got to see this." Hugh scrambled to his feet and picked his way down to the main ledges. Lewis roused for a minute, long enough to say, "The camera, man, this is headlines." Then he sagged and drifted off to sleep again. They had no camera.

For the next few hours, Hugh had the spectacle to himself. He paced back and forth on the islands as flames broke in waves against the base of El Cap. The fire rose like floodwater, moving from the flat floor and climbing up the talus slopes to the forest tucked behind the Nose. Backlit by flames, the enormous prow looked like a woman on her knees, in grief or submission.

He held out his hand, and the heat amazed him. He tried to recall how hot a forest fire burned, a thousand degrees or more, hot as oil fires he'd seen in the desert. At first, the wind shaped the fire, now the fire shaped the wind. It drew in fresh air and expelled it in thermal riptides. Flames coursed in the direction of Yosemite Village, and Hugh decided any firefighters were now protecting the village.

Here and there, tall trees resisted. Their high limbs stood clean of flame, and Hugh chose them to hold out. But the heat was too much. One after another, the giants burst like firecrackers. Centuries of growth went up with a snap, crackle, pop. The roar grew.

He tried again to wake Lewis, but his friend was deep in dream. He murmured the names of his daughters as if answering them. "Please," he whispered. Hugh gave up on him.

Nothing was immune. The flames raged everywhere. They leaped the road in a rush, and finished off the meadow in a few white-hot seconds. After that, the meadow was just a blackened gash in the beautiful orange and red light. Hugh kept thinking he should be terrified. They were rats trapped on a stone raft. But he could not help falling in love with the fire, it was so beautiful.

Boxed between the valley walls, the heat had nowhere to go but up. Hugh didn't have to hold out his hand to feel it anymore. He took off his parka, then his sweater and shirt. Sweat beaded the hairs on his arms.

The flood became an angry sea. Breakers of fire crashed against El Cap's base, sending great masses of sparks up and curling back into the flames. Each time the sparks flew higher. Embers appeared in the space off the Archipelago, dancing like tiny demons. One landed on Hugh's neck, and gave him a nip. He swept it away.

With a start, he remembered their coils of ropes,

their naked ropes. The embers would melt right through them. He started to hide the ropes inside their haul bags, but the bags were nylon, too. Finally he buried each coil in sand. At the end of fifteen minutes, it looked like a small cemetery of mounds.

After the first two hours or so, the first of the animals began arriving. He mistook the early ones for dark ash. But they were winged bugs, grasshoppers and beetles, boosted toward the stars on hot updrafts.

They landed on the ledges, on Hugh, and on Lewis's sleeping form. They crawled in the sand. They rested on mica crystals glittering in the firelight. The wall pulsed with their motion.

Others were carried higher into the night, and somewhere up there, where the hot air hit the cold night, they died and their bodies rained down like confetti. Hugh swept them from his hair and shoulders. He turned Lewis on his side so they wouldn't fall in his mouth and choke him. Soon he draped shirts over his and Lewis's heads.

A whole food chain unfolded before him. The insects brought predators. Bats swept back and forth, gorging in midair. Agitated by the heat and light, swallows, swifts, jays, and nutcrackers flocked upward. Some flew with wings on fire until they suddenly tumbled back into the awful basement. The lucky ones lit on Hugh's islands, their feathers singed, and found a feast. Their avian brains adjusted immediately, turning hell into heaven, and they began walking around like barnyard chickens gorging on the insects.

The birds had their predators, too. He wished for a camera. Falcons struck. A giant gray owl sank from the night and plucked a raven, still cawing and flapping its wings, from the ledge.

The birds, bugs, and fire degenerated into a vision out of Hieronymous Bosch. The mad mix of birdcalls, buzzing wings, and trees rupturing with light wore Hugh down. The Ten Commandments drama of plague and apocalypse grew tiresome, and finally ugly.

The flames muddied. The crystal light silted up with smoke and ash, which packed higher in layers, filling in the lower forest, then burying the treetops, and piling over that. Strangely, as the smoke crawled higher, Hugh felt as if he was leaving the earth. The valley floor seemed to sink into oblivion. The carpet of fire lit the smoke pink as salmon meat.

The wind died as suddenly as it had begun. In the sudden dead calm, the smoke crept up the wall and enveloped the ledges. Hugh's eyes stung. He wrapped one sleeve of the shirt on his head around his mouth to filter out the stink and taste. Above and behind them, the stone appeared to disintegrate. They were stranded.

Dawn seeped into Hugh's awareness.

The sun came up as little more than a dim gray musket ball. The smoke lost color, relinquishing its lovely nocturnal pink and orange glow to the smog

of sepia tones. What had been so beautiful now reminded him of a dirty stray dog.

At last Lewis's sleeping pill wore off. With a
shout, he sat up and yanked the shirt from his head
and looked around. He shouted again, as if he were
still dreaming, and batted at the insects and birds.
"Hugh?" he said.

Hugh handed him some water. "There's been a
fire. The forest is gone."

Groggy and dubious, Lewis crawled to the edge.
There was not one thing to see for the smoke. He
rubbed at his eyes. "Why didn't you wake me up?"

"I tried. Rome burned, you fiddled," Hugh said.
"Remember all your talk about the *fellaheen?* It
came true. Now we really do get to live among the
ruins."

"Was it lightning?"

"There wasn't a cloud in sight, nothing but
stars."

Lewis held up his arms, covered with stunned
insects. "It's an act of God, Hugh."

"I'm pretty sure it was set on purpose," said
Hugh.

"A managed fire? But the rangers would have
told us."

"I guess not." Hugh shrugged. "They were busy
with other things."

"Maybe they were trying to smoke Joshua out.
Give him a fright, flush him into the open. And
then it got away from them."

"This isn't a western, Lewis." The smoke had

congealed. Hugh couldn't quit coughing. His eyes ached.

"Never mind," Lewis said. "It doesn't matter. Don't you see, we were chosen. First the fallen girl. Then Joshua. Now this. It's some kind of purification."

Hugh was in no mood for his gonzo routine. "Don't start."

"Marooned." A light went on in Lewis's eyes. "Rachel," he said. "The girls."

"Rachel's not watching."

"They'll think we've gone up in flames."

"That makes you happy?"

The insects clung to Lewis. He had grasshoppers on his head. Cinders had lit in his hair and singed patches. He sat there smiling.

Then Hugh understood. Lewis was imagining Rachel imagining him dead, and falling back in love with the idea of him. And then Lewis would materialize from the ashes and smoke, and their fairy tale could resume.

"I guess we stay put for now," said Lewis.

"For now." Descending was out of the question. And climbing on seemed too audacious with a holocaust nipping at their heels.

Live embers sparkled in the air. The gray-brown smoke had poison in it, real poison, the dust of poison ivy and oak. Hugh and Lewis took turns flushing each other's eyes, and finally decided it was wiser to conserve their water.

They settled in, slapping at the embers as if they

were mosquitoes. They taped gauze from the first-aid kit over their mouths and noses to filter the smoke, and draped shirts over their heads as little tents.

It was a miserable day. The brown pall obscured the sun. More animals climbed onto the ledge. The species now included lizards, mice, and a scorched squirrel. They tried to give the squirrel some water, but the thing acted rabid. The fire had driven it insane. When it tried to bite them, Lewis kicked it over the edge, and then anguished about killing a fellow survivor. Birds took refuge on the islands, and tucked their heads down or under their wings.

There was nothing to do. The smoke made reading too painful. The gauze kept them muzzled for the most part. At one point, Lewis did try to start a conversation about what limbo must be like, meaning a day like today. Hugh merely grunted at him.

He looked out at their Ark of dying creatures. "It won't last forever," he said. "The fire will run out of fuel."

"What a sad, ugly way to finish," said Lewis. "It's going to be like walking through the last days of Pompeii on our way out."

Hugh had been waiting for this. "Then why go out through it, Lewis?"

"How else are we going to get down?"

"Why go down, Louie?"

Lewis was appalled. "You mean keep climbing?"

"Leave the ugliness and sadness behind you." Hugh was talking about the fire and destruction. He was talking about Rachel. He was talking about life. "Why walk through ashes when we can go into the light? The forest is green up there. Turn your back on the ruins. There's nothing left for us down there."

Lewis peered at him from under his rag of a head covering. He seemed to be straining, as if Hugh was dissolving in the smoke, that or just now assembling from it. "I don't know if I'm ready for that, Hugh," he said.

Hugh put away his expectation. He quit watching for a flicker of pluck to twinkle in his friend's runny eyes. He could have appealed to Lewis with one of their old battle cries, oh you few, you lucky few, dare we roll our trousers. Or bullied him with disappointment or camaraderie. Possibly he could have forced the climb.

But the Great Ape had lost heart. Even if they made it, even if they struck the summit and all went well, the spirit of the thing had changed. It would be like reaching a place with his own shadow, and Hugh didn't need El Cap for that. He could have stayed home for that. "That's okay," Hugh told him.

FIFTEEN

The fire dragged on. The world tightened around them. Hugh couldn't hear the flames anymore. The gloom thickened and the sun shrank to the size of a piece of buckshot. The insects quit moving, smoked to death. Birds toppled over with their little stick claws balled.

Hugh lay on his side, flipping idly through his book of maps and approach notes. Then he began sculpting the sand into little dunes. With his eyes right next to the ground, the Rub' could take him away from this place.

People thought deserts were all the same, just big wide-open sandboxes. In fact, they came in all shapes and sizes and substances. There were ice deserts in the Antarctic, and relic deserts in Nebraska, where the grass had locked the shifting sands in place. While hunting for hydrocarbon reservoirs near Yemen, Hugh had come across so-called radar rivers, the remnants of river systems that dated back twenty million years before the Nile and other great rivers were born, buried so deep only radar could find them. Deserts beneath deserts.

The Rub' al-Khali—the Empty Quarter—held the greatest sand sea on earth. The only one larger that anyone knew existed was on Mars, near the northern polar cap. Besides their immense size, the two planets' sand seas shared the same kind of dune formation, and even the same shade of red.

"Is she in there?"

Hugh lifted his head. Lewis had crept up on him. He was guessing at Hugh's tracings in the sand. Annie, he meant. Hugh didn't answer. The smoke was making him vaguely sick.

"Come on, man. Talk to me."

Hugh was wary. He didn't like going there with people, not even friends. Friends? He'd become a wanderer. Lewis was his last link.

"Somewhere," Hugh answered.

"Let me in, Hugh. Let somebody in. Rachel said you told her Annie had Alzheimer's. We never knew that."

"What more is there to know?"

"You've got to clear your head, man. Control, Alt, Delete. Reboot. Before she kills you." Tit for tat, Annie for Rachel, Lewis was giving him back his own words.

Hugh lifted his finger from the sand. He didn't like the rebuke. But then he thought that Lewis probably hadn't liked it either. "Fair enough," he said.

There were a thousand and one ways to tell that day. He had become like Scheherazade that way, forever weaving a single incident into complicated escape hatches. His storytelling had begun with the goatherd who found him, and continued with the soldiers, then the police, then the expats in the compound, and always with himself. Stories to survive by. Which would he tell Lewis? He turned onto his side, putting the patch of sand between them.

"There are five types of dunes," he started. "Each depends on the wind for its shape."

Lewis sat opposite, holding his gauze mask in place. With one taped palm, Hugh smoothed the sand, and with his finger he began cutting lines in the sand, building a dome, shaping a starfish, then a parabola, describing each. Finally he scooped an arc.

"This is the crescent dune, the most common kind of dune in the Rub'," he said. "Here are the horns, here is the body. Like an ocean wave, very slow, almost frozen, but alive. Because there is always the wind, and so there is always motion. The grains of sand are driven upslope in little skips and hops. They call it saltating. When one grain lands, it dislodges another, and that skips higher, and so on.

"The crest builds until the mass of grains go tumbling down the lee slope, the slipface. The dune moves. There's a formula for how quickly a dune will creep, sometimes as fast as a hundred yards per year, but usually much slower. The wind determines everything. From year to year, in different places, I could recognize individual dunes almost like they were mountains."

"Did you give them names?" Lewis asked.

"They weren't real mountains."

"It's all relative," said Lewis. "If they can be seas in slow motion, why not mountains in fast motion? I would have named them."

"See? You should have visited," said Hugh. "There's a use for poets, after all."

Lewis grimaced. "Have passport, won't travel."

"We can still change that. Remember all our talk about Nepal or Chamonix? It's not too late."

"Quit changing the subject. We were talking about dunes."

Hugh returned to the desert. "On holidays, especially during Ramadan when everything shuts down, Annie and I and friends would drive south from Dhahran loaded with fuel and water and tents and food. At different points along the way, we'd stop and deflate our tires for traction and angle off into the sands and go for days. At the petrol stations, they'd ask you, twelve or thirteen? Twelve or thirteen pounds of air per inch. Thirteen was for road driving. Twelve for off the track.

"At first, the desert was just a playground. We'd drive up the dunes, then surf our Land Cruisers down the slipfaces, and pitch camp and break out the barbecue grills and home brew. Then we began discovering relic lakes. They're just natural desert pavement now, stripped down to the hardpan. But during the Ice Age, lakes existed all through the region and supported whole tribes. We discovered this by finding their projectile points."

"You went hunting for arrowheads?"

"And spear points, and hand axes. We found knives, flakes, and fossils. The early people made their camps along the lake beds. We started pushing deeper and deeper into the desert. Once we crossed into Yemen without knowing it, and the soldiers fired their rifles to scare us away. Anymore, you'd be crazy to go so deep."

"After what happened to Annie?"

"Because it's a migration route for Al Qaeda and others. They come up from the south. There are crosshairs everywhere out there." Maybe he could get them off on to politics.

Lewis refused to give up, though. "Annie, Hugh. What happened?"

"Have you seen *The English Patient*?"

"And read the book."

"Everyone thinks it must have been like that scene with the sandstorm, that we got buried, or she was injured and I went off for help. But it was nothing like that."

"Then, what happened?"

"Nothing. No drama. No storm. No injuries. The sky was clear. The sun was out. Everything was ordinary."

"She just disappeared?"

"Some friends were going to join us, but at the last minute they canceled. I decided to go out alone with her, a change of scenery. Get her out of the compound. We drove, and I set up an awning. She stayed in the shade while I went looking for flints. I was gone for an hour, less, that's all. When I returned, she was missing."

Lewis got up on one elbow. "Just like that?"

"I had made her an iced tea. It was there beside her chair. Ice cubes were still floating in the glass. My first thought was, she's gone off to pee."

"She must have left footprints."

"Yes, and I followed them through the dunes. I went for miles, calling her name. Night fell. I knew better, but I kept walking, sure she'd be around the next ridge. When the sun came up, I realized my mistake and tried backtracking to find her footprints again. Then I lost my own prints."

"How's that possible?"

Hugh glanced at him. Lewis wasn't challenging him, just openly baffled.

"A breeze came up, not much of one, but enough. The wind was no more than ten miles per hour, I learned later. I didn't recognize any of the dunes. I couldn't find the car. I climbed to the crests and looked out, and there were just soft, rounded waves. You said they're like real mountains, but if they'd been mountains, I could have gotten my bearings. I was lost."

"You? The mapmaker?"

"Yes."

"That just makes it stranger."

Hugh dabbled at the sand. "Why is that?"

"Because you're never lost. Since we were kids, you always knew what you wanted, and where you were going, and how you were going to get there. It was me who wandered and got tardy slips and never got papers in on time."

"This time it was me," said Hugh.

"What did you do?"

"Kept walking. It wasn't a situation where you stayed put and waited for rescue. No one was going to come looking for us. I called for her. I let the breeze push me along. I held up a thread from my shirt and went where it pointed. I thought if only I could find her, at least we could die together."

"But someone found you."

"They say it was another night and a day later. I don't remember much. He was an old man, a goatherder, very poor. Somehow he got me to a petrol station along the highway."

"You must have been a wreck."

"They wanted to take me to a hospital, but I refused. If I was still alive, then Annie might be, too. An army patrol came by. They had a Bedouin tracker. These guys are good. We went back out and found the Land Cruiser, but Annie was gone."

Lewis was quiet.

Hugh smoothed over the sand. "Every now and then, satellites spot ancient caravan sites under the sand, and forgotten cities. She'll show up one day, like that iceman in the Alps. People will wonder about her. Maybe they'll invent a name for her."

Lewis was silent a minute. Then he said, "Rachel told me you had some Arab word for sweetheart."

"*Hayati.*"

Lewis repeated it to himself, and quit talking. He offered no sympathy or condolences, which was fine. People usually tried to put closure to it. Lewis taped the gauze over his mouth again. He retreated to his hood of a shirt.

The afternoon passed.

The smoke grew muddier.

At some point, Hugh heard echoes in the abyss. He lifted the rag from his head. Lewis had heard the voices, too. He went to the rim. "They must be coming for us," he said.

Hugh joined him slowly, padding barefoot across the dried insect husks. Lewis started helloing into the depths. The cottony smoke flattened his voice. He sounded feeble.

Hugh glanced over the edge, and there were no depths to see. Visibility stopped at their feet. Unless you knew the edge was right here, you might keep walking and fall through the smoke without really knowing you were falling. Hugh stepped back.

Lewis went on listening, cocking his head from side to side like a man in total darkness, sifting for noises. He leaned out, one big hand clutching an anchor rope, squinting down.

With no warning, a shape—an apparition—
swept across their heads in a long arc. It almost
struck them.

Hugh ducked. Lewis fell to the sand. Whatever
it was slapped at the rock. Just as quickly, the thing
disappeared back into the smoke from where it had
come, leaving only a drag mark of blood on the
stone.

Lewis scrambled back from the edge. Hugh
peered into the smoke. He looked at the blood streak,
the finger marks. He stood up.

"Stay down," he told Lewis.

"What the hell was it?"

Hugh braced his feet. He got a good wrap of the
anchor sling around one arm, and waited.

A minute later, the figure reappeared. It broke
from the gloom and smoke with crimson eyes, and
this time Hugh was ready for him. With one arm,
he hooked the wingless intruder and brought him
to earth.

It was the boy, Joe. His fingers were scraped raw.
He clutched Hugh's arm. "Keep him away from
me," he said.

Before Hugh could ask what he meant, Augustine sloped in from the smoke. Lewis tackled him
before the arc carried him away, and they landed in
a heap in the sand.

Hugh looked at the two of them, reading their
ordeal in the details. What it came down to was
this, the two searchers had returned to the ledges,

empty-handed. They had strayed into the care of their fellow nomads.

"Water," said Augustine, but not before carefully tying the end of his rope to the anchor. Hugh knew what that meant. He was not finished yet.

SIXTEEN

The smoke had blued their faces almost black. Their eyes were so red they seemed to be bleeding. They drank everything Hugh and Lewis gave them without apology or shame or even thanks.

As night gathered, neither of the younger climbers could speak above a cracked whisper. They had not drunk all day, and the reason for that was simple. Augustine had left, deliberately left, their several gallons of water—plus all their food and the med pack and their climbing gear, everything—hanging from pitons on Trojan Women. In doing so, he had taken a huge gamble, betting that Hugh and Lewis would still be on the Ark with water and food that they would share. It was calculating and presumptuous and totally reckless.

"What if we'd already taken off? What if we'd

started for the top?" Lewis demanded. "We could have decided to climb away from the fire."

"But you didn't," Augustine said.

"We almost did," Lewis lied. He couldn't get over the audacity. "No water. No food. In this heat. Breathing this smoke. Are you going for an epic?"

In the universe of climbers, there was nothing more hallowed—or freighted—than the epic. Whymper's descent from the Matterhorn, Herzog on Annapurna, Doug Scott crawling down the Ogre, Joe Simpson touching the void, Krakauer in thin air, the list ran long. An epic was the closest of close calls, often involving the death of partners, the loss of toes and fingers, madness, terrible privations, the whole nine yards. Summits come, summits go, and those were matters of record. An epic, though, that went into the hall of fame.

The irony was that, for all the shock and awe an epic inspired, no seasoned climber ever wanted to be part of one. *No epics:* that was the wise man's mantra. An epic was a freak of nature, like a two-headed snake. Every epic involved two accidents, the accident itself, and the accident of one's survival. Every survivor was meant to have died, but for some reason had not, and whatever that reason was it was necessarily out of one's control, because if it were in your control it wouldn't have been an epic. God—the mountain—ruled. Only a fool, or Rambo, thought skill or strength or readiness let him off the hook.

And so Lewis was not praising Augustine. His

denunciation was clear. Augustine had invited disaster. He'd cowboyed their descent, and put a kid at risk, and that was not okay. Worse, he was a rescue man. He was supposed to stay in charge.

Augustine did not react. Hugh was struck by that. Sitting among the dead birds and insects on the sand in this psychedelic night with the smoke lit orange and pink now that the sun had fallen, Augustine looked like the lord of his land, calm and in command despite the chaos.

"It was farther than I thought, five pendulums, not three," he said. "That dropped us lower on the wall than I wanted. By the time we connected with their route, it was going dark. But we managed to get a good pitch higher. A few more and we would have reached her. She was there."

"Not anymore, she's not," Joe said.

"We should have kept going."

"The fire started," Joe declared. "I was tired."

Augustine shot a hard glance at him, and opened his mouth, then snapped it shut. Obviously they had argued last night. Obviously Joe had forced their halt, like any sane climber. Obviously Augustine meant to return.

"You said it yourself," Hugh said to Augustine. "It was past dark. You were deep into the night."

"We had lights. That's what lights are for."

"When was the last time you slept?" Hugh asked him.

Augustine rejected the excuse. "Not last night, that's for sure. There were no ledges anywhere. We hung in our slings and harnesses. Not a wink. We could have been climbing the whole time."

"You need rest," Hugh said.

He offered a second gallon of their water, and Augustine took it. Gallon by gallon, Hugh was giving away their climb. But really, he wasn't giving away anything. Lewis had terminated Anasazi. They were going down. Hugh accepted that. Now Augustine could have what was left of them.

Augustine locked eyes with Hugh. "She's alive, goddamnit."

"You saw her?"

"Yeah, we saw her," said Joe. "She's all fucked up. Dead. It's seriously heinous."

Seriously heinous? All fucked up wasn't bad enough? For that matter, wasn't dead? "Then you did see her," Hugh said.

"Before she disappeared."

Hugh glanced at Lewis, who took up the question. "Disappeared," said Lewis. "What's that supposed to mean?"

Augustine shot a look at the kid. "We caught sight of her on the fourth pendulum, just before dark, a good six hundred feet up, hanging on the rope. But when we looked again this morning, she was gone."

"You could see through the smoke?"

"We were higher than you are. The smoke was still rising this morning. Yeah, we could see."

"And the rope was empty?"

"The rope was gone."

Lewis said, "Then it's over, brother."

"Not by a mile," said Augustine.

"The rope broke," Lewis told him.

"You're wrong."

"You did your best," Hugh said.

"She doesn't belong to you, anyway," Joe muttered.

Hugh grew still. Joshua had said something very much like that to him. "Say that again," said Hugh. "She doesn't belong to who?"

Something was out of whack. Hell, everything was out of whack. But there was an undercurrent here, Hugh could sense it. *Keep him away from me.* This was something more than a climbers' quarrel over retreating. It was more than the kid surviving Augustine's single-minded quest. It preceded the climb.

The boy carried horror in him. Freaked by the fire, freaked by Augustine, afraid even to sit next to him. He stayed on the other side of Hugh and Lewis, beyond Augustine's reach.

"Nothing," Joe mumbled.

Augustine spoke. "I'll tell you where the rope went. She took it with her. Once Joshua lit the place up, she climbed back to their camp in the Eye, and pulled the rope up after her. Andie's there. She's waiting for us."

"Joshua?" Lewis said.

Augustine held up his radio as if it were proof of all his truths. "The Neanderthal erased himself. They were closing in on him, and he knew it, so he took the forest and Cass with him. You didn't hear him cooking off down there?"

The screams, Hugh realized.

Lewis looked sheepish. He'd slept through all but the aftermath.

Hugh replayed the animal cries in his mind, stunned to have missed the obvious. Joshua, of course, armed with a torch, racing through the dry woods. And then the wind had come.

"What's the news?" asked Hugh. "How bad is it down there?"

"We got the worst of it right below us," Augustine said. "They caught the burn at Manure Pile Buttress, and killed it down the valley with a fire line. They're still working a few hot spots, but the fire's pretty much run its course. Parts of the road melted. The park's closed. Otherwise, nothing's changed."

"No, everything's changed," Lewis said. Because if nothing was changed, they continued on, climbing.

"Down there, maybe. Not here. Not us," said Augustine.

"We've got a massacre on the wall. A body thief. A forest fire. We're cut off from the world."

Augustine brushed it all aside. The fall, the fire, their isolation . . . a million miles away. "We're still fully operational. The summit crew is in position. The litter's assembled, the anchor's set. All I have to do is give the word and they'll lower the litter to us. By tomorrow morning, we can have her off."

We. Us. Hugh heard him. Lewis hadn't yet. He

didn't get it. It was beyond his comprehension. "Go back up? Tonight?"

"What do you think I'm here for?" Augustine practically whispered it.

Lewis gaped at him, finally realizing that Augustine had not returned from Trojan Women to shepherd a frightened boy to safety. He'd come to trade him for a man. Lewis's chin drew into his bull neck. "No." He shook his head. "There's a limit. Absolutely. Limits."

Augustine released him without a word. He had already released the boy. He turned to Hugh.

"There are ropes running all the way across and up to our high point." No invitation. No pleading. No demands. Just the necessary facts.

Hugh didn't shy away from the blood-red eyes. Augustine was measuring him. In turn, he measured Augustine. He measured himself. "It's night. You're talking about a traverse. The smoke would eat our headlamps. We'd be blind."

"We were blind coming across," Augustine said. "That's why it took us all day to get here. It didn't stop us, though. And now the ropes are in place."

"You don't really think she's alive?" Hugh needed to state his uncertainty outright. If Augustine blew up at the challenge, or fell to pieces, Hugh's choice would be made for him.

"I know what I hope," Augustine said. He didn't begrudge Hugh's bluntness. He didn't fake the cold facts to try and win consent. "Maybe she's not. But there's only one way to find out."

The two men stared at each other.

"Leave him alone," Lewis said to Augustine.

Augustine ignored him. He was fixed on Hugh. They were driving a deal. It had nothing to do with Lewis. "Morning," he bargained. "We rest tonight. Let the smoke thin out. Then jump on it, first light. Get it done."

"Screw this, Hugh. You can't bring Annie back."

"Andie," Augustine corrected him.

"I'm talking to my friend," Lewis snapped, "about his wife."

Augustine's face clouded, then suddenly clarified. "Annie," he said.

"I'm not trying to bring her back," Hugh said to Lewis.

"Then rein it in, partner. This was a mistake. We're off the wall."

Hugh liked that, nearly a half mile off the deck, off the wall. He smiled.

"I'm not fooling. It keeps mutating on us. It started out one thing, then changed to another, and another," Lewis said. "Face it. We were doomed before we left the ground."

Hugh studied Augustine. He'd emerged from the desert with eyes as red as his, and lips as cracked, and a voice like rusted metal. But he wasn't Augustine, and Annie—the idea of her—was not remotely present among these girls killed by El Cap. What Lewis could probably never understand was how unnecessary memory was in the end.

Something tugged at Hugh. Trojan Women

whispered to him. Whatever it was saying, he couldn't quite hear. The more he listened, the less he understood. But he felt drawn to go over. The mystery itself pulled him. It pulled him out of himself, out of his cocoon of solitariness.

He'd grown smaller since Annie's disappearance, and that's not how it was supposed to have gone. Where was the sense of liberation? Where was the fresh love, the unshuttered world, the second life? As it was, he did his job, went home to frozen dinners, watched CNN, and prepared for his next escape into the mountains. The drabness had become a relief of sorts, because it seemed to be the only punishment he would suffer for losing her in the desert. At the same time, it bound him so tightly that at times he could barely think. There had to be more. That's what he wanted to hear in the whispering of Trojan Women.

Something, or nothing, was waiting for him over there. He'd reached enough summits to know the emptiness he would find, but it was better than the emptiness waiting below.

It came down to that. He was not finished with the abyss. Or the abyss was not finished with him. He shrugged. "All right," he said to Augustine.

Augustine gave a single nod. Lewis screwed up his face.

There was nothing more to say. Each of them had made his decision, and all that remained was to wait out the night. Augustine called on his radio, and a ranger reported that the fire beneath El Cap had spent itself and that the floor was cooling. Also, they had located two charred bodies in a cave, presumably Joshua and Cass.

Augustine asked about a third body. Hugh respected him for that because he asked it outright, in front of them all. The third body would have belonged to his missing Andie, which would have eliminated this vertical dash for Cyclops Eye. Negative, said the ranger. But they would send a team to the base to search again in the morning.

Augustine explained the new plan. The radio crackled with static. Roger that, the ranger answered. Lewis and Joe could safely descend and walk out tomorrow. They could catch a ride at the road. There would be crews driving back and forth all day.

The climbers divvied up the gear. There was no haggling. Lewis and the boy needed three ropes, one haul bag, some hardware, and a quart of water for their descent. The fifteen or twenty rappels back to earth would require close attention—too many deaths happened on rappel—and time. But they would be down by midafternoon at the latest.

Hugh packed the remaining four gallons, some food, and bivvy gear for his journey to Trojan Women. Augustine said the extra weight would only slow them. Hugh didn't argue, he just went on packing the haul bag. Augustine said, "We'll do it your way, then."

The climbers settled on different islands to sleep. The heat dissipated slowly. No more fever heat, it felt like a summer night now. There were no stars, of course. No summit. No nothing. Limbo.

Somewhat later, a hulking shape came over to Hugh's ledge. It was Lewis, full of repentance and second thoughts. "Say the word, Hugh," he whispered, "I'll go up with you."

Hugh heard the misery in him. Go back to your used bookstore, your poets and quietude, he did not say. "You're doing the right thing," he told him.

"Then why do I feel like a dog?"

"Don't do this to yourself," Hugh said. "We're good, you and me."

"It's just that the flesh is willing, but the mind is not," Lewis said.

"There's only room for two of us anyway," Hugh told him. "You'd slow us down with your knee." The phantom knee.

"There's more to it," Lewis said. "Something's over there, Hugh."

"Yeah?"

"Nothing good. It's like all the bad shit keeps getting worse. The kid comes flying out of the smoke, and what does he say? 'Keep him away from me.' Augustine. And I've been thinking, maybe that's the heart of it. Maybe Augustine is at the center of it all."

"Augustine didn't cause the fall. He didn't tell Joshua to go berserk. He didn't set the fire."

"One domino falls, the rest fall, too."

"You're getting wild and woolly, Lewis."

"But think about it. Guilt has a life all its own.

It has legs and hands and a face. It runs amok. It screams in the night. What if this shit is following him around?"

"Like psychic manifestations? We're seeing projections of a sinner's soul?"

Lewis made a face. "Something bad keeps dogging him, you got to admit."

"But I don't believe in guilt," said Hugh.

Lewis spread his hands, at a loss. His big muscles papered over a frailty he could not help. He was afraid. Rachel had left him, Hugh was continuing on, and he was in free fall. Full of guilt.

"I don't have the stomach for it, Hugh, the climbing, the weirdness. Whatever you're going to find over there. Those girls were my daughters' ages." Them, too, thought Hugh. His girls were gone. His house was deserted.

"You need to go down," said Hugh. "You've got your head on straight. Think of the girls. Everything will turn out."

"I've never bailed on you. I never thought I would."

"I'm the one bailing on you." Hugh tried to make a joke of it. "Only I'm going in the wrong direction."

"Anymore, I don't know what's up or down."

"Look," said Hugh. "You take care of the kid. I'll take care of Augustine. Let's get them through this."

"I'll wait for you."

"Down in the bar," said Hugh. "Tonic water and free peanuts. We'll torture the bartender."

Lewis heard the farewell. The way Rachel obsessed him now, El Cap would obsess him later. But it was over. He retreated back to his own ledge.

That night Hugh dreamed a woman lay buried in the sand beneath him. He dug down, and it was Annie . . . alive. She was nude and young and ravishing. Her arms opened to embrace him. He called her name. When she answered, sand poured from her mouth. She aged. She withered to bone. Hugh tried to pull away from the creature, but she entangled his hand.

He woke with a start. It was cold. He was sweating.

His hand was sunk into the sand. Something was holding his wrist under there. He pulled frantically, and it was just one of their buried coils of rope.

SEVENTEEN

At dawn, the two teams set off from the Archipelago, one up, one down. Lewis gave Hugh a fierce bear hug. "Preserve thyself," he said.

"I always do," Hugh said.

"I'm serious, watch out. There's something in the air. You can almost hear it, I don't know. Bad jazz."

"Just the wings of angels," said Hugh. Another of their chestnuts.

"Be careful." Lewis paused. "With him."

"Augustine?" said Hugh. "He's obsessed, not crazy."

"Have you seen what he's wearing on his wrist? You haven't. You'll see. Ask him what it is. Because I think I know."

"Yeah?"

"It could be nothing." Lewis frowned at his own

fretting. "You'll probably say to yourself, so what's new? How's Augustine any different from old Lewis, you know, our thing for women we thought belonged to us. You'll probably think that."

"You worry too much," Hugh said. What Lewis did was talk too much. He flashed his mysteries and premonitions like card tricks, rarely the same one twice, and normally Hugh found it entertaining. But now was not the time.

There was a tug on the doubled rappel line from below. Joe was waiting. "Train's leaving," Lewis said.

"Chin up," said Hugh, "knots tight. Into the stone. The breach. All that."

"Vaya con Dios." Lewis gripped Hugh's shoulder. "For real, man."

Lewis backed into the maw. As he melted into the smoke with his head shrouded in strips of cloth, he reminded Hugh of the old goatherder who had plucked him from the desert, a figment of a mirage inside a dream. Or a nightmare.

For one barren instant, Hugh wondered if he was making a mistake, and whether or not he should go after Lewis and get away. So far, events had only gotten stranger by the vertical foot. And Lewis was spot on about sharing with Augustine an obsession with women who left them empty. In that sense, Hugh was simply swapping one man's loss for another's.

It was worse than that. Step by step, by coming to Yosemite and going up El Cap, and now by crossing into the unknown with a stranger, he was climbing back into his own loss. Descend now, and he could wash off the smoke, drive away, and be clean of it all. But again he felt it, even more powerfully this morning. Something was waiting for him over there.

Hugh scanned the Archipelago's ledges a final time. Nothing remained of them except for a few footprints, and their buried thermos of mementoes. Even the dead insects and birds were disappearing into the sand, slowly being consumed by El Cap.

He lifted the slack of Augustine's rope, feeling for its pulse. When the trembling finally stopped, he knew Augustine had reached the far end of the first rope, and it was his turn. He clamped on his jumars, stepped into the stirrups, and began climbing away from the Ark.

Through the first few hours, Hugh was essentially alone on the ropes. Visibility was ten feet at best, and Augustine stayed a full pitch ahead of him. At each anchor, Hugh found the haul bag waiting to be lowered across so Augustine could pull it into the heights. Once the bag was gone, Hugh would continue on.

It was his idea, last night, to leave their ropes in place as an emergency backup. If the rescue litter got lost in the smoke, or the route to Cyclops Eye turned out to have fatal flaws, or the radio batteries went dead, or any number of things went awry, the fixed ropes back to the Archipelago would give them a ready exit.

Augustine had agreed to it immediately. He'd

fought his way through two traverses now, the first time in crossing over to Trojan Women, the second time in returning to Anasazi. A rescue from the summit would be easiest and quickest. But if all else failed, the fixed ropes would allow them to retreat to the ledges and call in a helicopter, or descend to the ground. Augustine's quick consent had dispelled any doubts Hugh had about his common sense. Within those Tarzan muscles and sleepless drive, the man was steady.

Hugh let Augustine gallop ahead on the ropes. Because they were heading diagonally, he had to mind the jumars with special care. The "jaws" had a habit of torqueing right off the rope at certain angles, and so he added a prusik loop to the rope, which further slowed his progress. The smoke was his biggest obstacle.

He felt like a hospital patient, or a hostage, with white gauze taped over his mouth and nose, and a rag tied over that. This was industrial-strength pollution, thick with ash and particulates. The first time he tried to hurry the tempo, it left him hunched in his stirrups, gagging and coughing.

It was eerie snaking through the gloom. If not for the rope, he would have been lost. He could have been ten feet above the ground, or ten thousand. A layer of soot coated the wall. Where their haul bag scraped the rock, it left long, white arcs, like the shadows of atomic particles. Hugh passed handprints where Augustine had pressed against the stone.

The smoke had thinned overnight. As the hours passed, the sun regained some of its size, lighting the world in tobacco hues. Now that the fire was dead, the smoke held no heat. The air and rock and the metal hardware at each anchor were all the same hard cold.

At the end of three full rope lengths, Hugh had no idea where he was going. The topography was wildly beyond his memory of even two days ago. He couldn't gauge the heights or depths except by adding sums in his head, and he was suddenly having trouble remembering distances on Anasazi, which was now invisible to him, and translating those to the equally invisible Trojan Women. He and Lewis used to take turns embellishing an old fiction about a team trapped on an infinite wall. Now Hugh felt like one of those castaways.

It was not that he feared El Cap. To the contrary, he still craved the thing. It still made sense to him even though, the further he committed, the less sense it made. He was crossing lines drawn in his head, leaping old borders. It was like straying into Yemen that time, except now he was consciously trespassing.

The wall changed. He could feel the metamorphosis. It seemed more alive than ever as he angled toward Trojan Women. Brilliant neon green and red lichen patches showed through the film of smoke, some shaped like aboriginal petroglyphs . . . palm prints, animals, and dream lines . . . and some like satellite images of great cities and lakes. Black mica freckled the grime. The granite surged and rippled, painted with layers of soot.

Hugh had never seen El Cap like this, so embellished. It was ugly, and yet exquisite. Patterns and exotic tracings wove across its surface. The wall was a gigantic blank tablet, faintly written upon.

Riding on updrafts, insects had landed and traipsed about, marking the wall with tiny, cryptic messages before they died and fell away. A leaf had left its perfect imprint on the powdery surface. Hugh traveled across oscillating bands of soot, across the very rhythm of the fire.

About then he saw, or imagined, a shape in the smog. It moved with reptile stealth, crossing the stone to his left, headfirst. But the instant Hugh stopped to stare at the thing, it froze and seemed to stare back at him.

He rocked ever so slightly on the rope, and the creature wavered in and out of view. Ten or twenty feet off in the smog, everything about it was indistinct. Was that a hand arrested in midpace, or a bulge of rock? It crouched tightly, like a lizard, but with certain human aspects. Rust streaks, surely, became the possibility of hair, long, wild hanks of it hanging down.

For a bad moment, Hugh thought he'd come upon the body of Augustine's lover dangling on the tip of her rope. What if this was the dead woman? Worse, in a peculiar way, what if she wasn't dead? The idea of her still struggling for survival after so many days appalled him. He'd seen it in Annie, the urge to live no matter how degraded and subhuman you became, an urge that positively had no mind.

He stared and tried to penetrate the smoke, unable to make it out. Had Augustine miscalculated so badly? Had he passed right beneath her without knowing it? If it was her, then they'd reached the fall line of Trojan Women. But that couldn't be. The ropes kept angling off to the right, and Augustine was nowhere near. Cyclops Eye lurked distant and higher, much higher.

It had to be some sort of animal. Those were ribs, pulsing in and out. Or were they? Maybe it was just the drift of smoke. He couldn't feel any breeze, though.

A lizard, he decided, something small and primal. He jugged a few feet higher, pushing closer, mystified. The thing suddenly lurched away. That or the hallucination retreated to stone again.

There were markings over there, more markings. He leaned left, expecting a tiny alphabet of footprints at most, or maybe the sinuous line of a tail.

The footprint was so pale—and human—he disbelieved it. It wasn't the whole sole of a foot, but rather the ball and five toes. It was positioned downward, matching the stance of the creature. Which was completely absurd, of course.

Fighting the rope, he craned sideways and touched the print, barely, just the surface of it, and his fingertips went right through to the white stone beneath. The soot fell away where his fingers had run.

Only a shadow could have left a print so fragile, and there were no shadows in this murky land. He tried to think what could have made the mark. A climber's fist, perhaps, with knuckles for toes? But that made no sense, not in the middle of nowhere, with no surrounding prints . . . and upside down. He tried to re-create the print with his own hand, pressing it this way and that, and nothing matched. His curiosity tugged. A gust of superheated air yesterday? The scuff of a falling rock? That had to be it. He was seeing things. He had rushed to read humankind into the bleakness.

His shoes skidded on the dry soot. He started to push back, then he gave up on the print. El Cap had always reminded him of the bottom of the ocean. From a distance, it looked sterile and lifeless, but when you got up close and it became tangible, the place abounded with energy and life forces, from night mice and swifts to hailstones falling from clear, hot skies. The unnatural was perfectly natural up here.

He slid his jumar up, suddenly eager for company. A whisper halted him.

"Hugh." It seemed to breathe from the abyss. He whipped around in his stirrups, searching behind him and under his feet.

"Hello?" His voice boomed against the stone. The smoke was empty. Enough, he thought. Enough with your mind games. Then his name came again.

"Glass," the air peeped. It came from far away, this time from above. "Glass."

With more relief than seemed proper, he realized it was Augustine calling to him.

American climbers never yodel. But Hugh had gotten the habit from Austrians on a side trip to the sea cliffs in southern Thailand. Done properly, you could signal for miles. He undid the wraps and gauze over his mouth and cast his voice, nothing musical, no real signature to it, just the stock "old lady who."

Then he piled into the ascent. *Get your buns out of here*. The rope quivered under his jumar thrusts.

At last, he found Augustine waiting at the high point. A thin, miserly crack seeped up from the anchor and dissolved in the tea-brown smog. This was as far as Augustine and the boy had managed to get before Joshua went apocalyptic.

"Good, you're here," Augustine said. His face was polished black as a coal miner's. A torn shirt covered his mouth. It sucked in and out like a bellows. He was careful not to show his impatience, but it was there in his readiness, in the rack of gear draped across his chest.

To his annoyance, Hugh couldn't quit coughing. It made him sound unfit. But then Augustine started his own hacking, and that gave Hugh some comfort. They were both afflicted by El Cap, equally vulnerable, equally dependent.

"It took longer than it should have," Hugh said. "The knots were loose. I had to redo some of the anchors. Pieces were hanging from the rope."

It was nothing he'd intended to bring up. But

he felt challenged by Augustine's momentum, or by his own slowness, and it was still early in the game, too soon to show his age or weakness. So he put some grievance in his tone.

To this point, he and Augustine had been on the same page. The two of them might even turn out to be friends. But one thing Hugh had learned from his life among the roughnecks, soldiers, contractors, and Arabs—and especially from other climbers—was to always maintain his autonomy.

He was tied in to a partner he didn't know on a route without a map. If push came to shove somewhere above, and it could with Augustine's sleep deprivation and the death they were about to find and the grinding oppression of this smoke, then Hugh meant to make his own decisions and go his own way. That meant, right from the outset, not giving one inch of himself away.

Augustine didn't bridle at the complaint. "Good," he said, "good. I saw the same things."

"What did you see?" Hugh didn't make it specific. He didn't ask if Augustine had encountered some hominid-shaped creature scuttling around upside down on the walls, an animal with hands and feet. He didn't expose his wild imaginings.

"Chewed ropes," Augustine said. "Bad anchors. Loose knots. It's all in the details. We've got to watch ourselves."

Hugh relaxed a little, even as he tensed. Augustine was conceding the need for caution. But on the other hand, if he'd come across problems, why hadn't he tightened the knots and restored the pieces? Was he so sloppy? Or had he fixed the glitches, only to have them work loose as Hugh was climbing?

Augustine held up a hank of haul line, and it was gnawed to the core. "The crack monsters are getting hungry. Joshua's fire bankrupted the whole ecosystem up here. The place is an open wound."

That pretty much answered the mystery. They were voyaging among starving beasts. Infiltrating a wound. They had to watch themselves.

Hugh looked back along the curved rope leading to the Archipelago, and could almost feel the knots untying themselves and the anchors easing from the stone and the animals tracking them for the slightest morsel. Even as they hung in their stirrups, the bridge back to Anasazi was coming apart, turning to smoke.

"How many more pitches to the Eye?" Hugh asked.

"A few. Not many." Hugh could tell he didn't know, and that it didn't matter to him. Augustine looked up at the crack. "Do you have me?"

Hugh took the rope and ran a swift eye through the belay setup. He planted his feet against the wall. "You're on."

Augustine stretched overhead and probed the crack. It resisted him. The crack was sized for smaller fingers, a woman's fingers. Augustine tried stuffing his fingertips into the fissure, and failing that, unable to free the crack, he turned to aid.

"This is going to slow us down," he groused, slotting in a nut.

That was when Hugh noticed what Augustine was wearing around his outstretched wrist. Now he understood Lewis's warning. In ordinary circumstances, he would have passed off the bracelet as braided threads or twine. Climbers wore all kinds of fetishes brought back from their expeditions. But this was different.

The bracelet was made of human hair, a long lock of it lovingly braided, blond, bleached nearly white by a sun that seemed just a memory now. Instantly Hugh knew whose hair it was. His only question was when Augustine had harvested it from her, awake or asleep, with or without her knowing.

EIGHTEEN

They came to a crazed spray of fractures. Each crack led off into the smoke, and there was no telling which led in the correct direction. More precious hours scaled away.

Hugh had depended on Augustine to be the superior climber, but the younger man's urgency and exhaustion made him clumsy. Holds snapped off in his hands. His feet pawed at the rock. For all his reputation as a rescue climber, he had no gift for route finding, and what few clues the women had left were covered with grime. When one crack proved false, he tried a second, and a third, and each time Augustine went up, he had to come down, laboriously undoing his own protection.

"It's almost like they won't let me inside," he said.

They did seem unwelcome. Augustine had tried

the back door from the summit, and now this massive front door stood locked against them, too. The closer they got to the women, the more complicated their maze became.

"We'll crack it," Hugh told him. He had out his leather notebook, still logging details of the last pitch. "These things take time."

"Andie doesn't have time," Augustine said, and without another moment's rest attacked a different crack.

By the time he lowered off the fourth false crack, they'd wasted five hours, and Augustine was fuming. Above all, he was frustrated by his lover's risk taking. "What was she thinking?" he said. "This was so totally over their heads. They must have known they didn't belong here."

"They'd come so far," said Hugh. "And the summit was right there."

"The summit," spat Augustine.

"We get the sun in our eyes, and sometimes it blinds us," Hugh said, all too aware of their present sunless circumstances. "You know how it goes."

He was baffled by the general resentment, first Lewis's, now Augustine's. The hard men, the bigwall mavericks, begrudged these three women their bodacious nerve. It was a way for the two men to regret their various losses, of course, and no doubt to vent some envy. But also the resentment was visceral, as if the women had trespassed beyond some border.

"She had no business being with them."

"It's a free country," said Hugh.

"There was nothing free about it. They had her brainwashed."

Hugh didn't respond. Augustine was the one who didn't belong, at least not in his depleted condition.

"They were witches," Augustine said. "Cuba and Cassie. Cuba especially."

"Isn't that what climbers do?" Hugh asked. "We're in the magic business. Houdini had nothing on us. Escape artists, that's our part in the greater scheme."

"Real witches," Augustine said. "The kind that brew potions. They were always stirring something in the pot, or fermenting mash, or picking mushrooms. Always hatching conspiracies, always pushing it. Cuba, especially. She told people her mother was a *cuarandera*. And maybe it was true, she wasn't born here. They did the El Norte thing when she was a baby."

At one level, it didn't matter a bit as Hugh perched in stirrups with nothing beneath his feet. And yet this *cuarandera* business seemed oddly crucial, not just to Augustine but to their quest, like a missing handhold, one more link. "A shaman?"

"A granny woman, that's what we called them in Arkansas. The old conjure ladies and midwives. They handled snakes and talked in tongues, some of them."

A Southern boy, thought Hugh, finally getting a handle on Augustine's hatchet-and-honey accent.

He imagined Andy of Mayberry, and sultry summers, and a kid with a slingshot. Maybe none of it was so, but he still couldn't help wondering how Opie had ended up in the Valley of giants.

"This Cuba girl," Hugh said, "it sounds like she talked a lot of tall shit. Climbers do that. They come into the hills and invent themselves fresh."

"She did more than invent. She messed with their heads. She wanted a following."

"Like a cult or something?"

"Not a cult, there were only a couple of them," Augustine said. "But she had something they wanted, some riddle of the Sphinx thing. Like you couldn't get past her without becoming part of her. She got Andie with it, hook, line, and sinker. They drank tea made of poison ivy to immunize themselves. They fasted for their cramps. They did yoga in the dirt, and chanted mantras at dawn. Stuff like that."

"The mystical-mountain thing," Hugh said. At some point, serious climbers all dabbled in it. As a teenager, he'd practiced tying knots with one hand, in pitch blackness, in a cold shower, over and over. That was what the great British and German climbers did, he'd heard. He and Lewis used to walk around carrying snowballs in their bare hands to toughen them for winter ascents, and loaded backpacks with their body weight in bricks for training sessions. They'd talked Zen versus Tantric at the bouldering sites, and made blood oaths, and held séances with Rachel and Annie before their big climbs. And, yeah, bayed at the moon. It was wacky nonsense, but innocent, a phase.

"Cuba got an infected tooth," Augustine went on. "She made Andie pull it with a pair of pliers in the parking lot at Camp Four."

Hugh frowned. "A pair of pliers?"

"Like a rite of passage. A blood rite. Think about it. She got Andie to inflict pain in order to relieve it. She gave her power." Augustine went on. "Cassie got pregnant. Cuba gave her an abortion with herbs and mushrooms. They buried whatever came out on top of a mountain. You mean mystical like that?"

Hugh paused. "They did that?"

"Andie was vulnerable. Fragile. Ready to break. You've heard what happened with her brother and me."

Hugh was careful. "Just about nothing. It's not my business."

"You're tied in to me, aren't you? It's your business."

"I'm tied in to you. That ought to say it all."

But it didn't. Augustine was no longer used to trust. The tragedy was eating him up from the inside out. Patagonia was his cancer. His eyes met Hugh's and it was plain that, guilty or not, he was haunted. "After I got back from Cerro Torre, Andie was a wreck," he said. "She didn't know what to think, who to turn to, who to believe. I was in bad shape myself. I didn't know what to say. Sorry? I ditched your big bro in a storm, still alive, bummer? And there were all these other rumors. Have you heard the cannibal one?"

Walking wounded, thought Hugh. He wondered if the Patagonia disaster had marked the beginning of Augustine's rescue work. Penance would explain him. Lewis was right. The rot of guilt. "Screw the rumors. There are always rumors," he said. "That's how people are. They say the worst things when you're down. I know. It's crap."

Augustine darted a look at him, almost hopefully. Then the gleam in his eyes dimmed. He squinted and gestured up into the smoke. "I don't blame her. Andie was hearing all this . . . stuff. She needed help sorting it out, and Cuba came along to heal her. All I could do was watch Andie fall into this, like, weird orbit. I reached out to her, but she just drifted further away. It wasn't out of hate. She never hated me, that was the worst part. She'd just get sad seeing me around. I was this unfinished business, like I'd died along with the others on Cerro Torre, and come back, and she couldn't decide how to get rid of me. Sometimes I wonder."

"What, if you're a ghost?" Hugh snorted. "You look real enough to me."

"Dumb, I know." Augustine dipped his head. "Anyway, this happened."

"Trojan Women?"

"They wanted to be ahead of their time." Augustine jerked a nut from the false crack. "What they really wanted was to show the world how big their balls were. I told her, Andie, the Captain's not a finishing school. It's real life. A new route like this, it takes no prisoners. But Cuba was always right there whispering in her other ear."

Hugh suddenly felt weighed down by the history. It was getting them nowhere. Augustine had issues, who didn't? He was an adult, and, like he said, this was real life. Above all, Hugh was no priest. He had no wisdom to offer, no forgiveness to dispense. "You want me to give it a try?" he quietly asked.

Augustine screwed his face up, as if he'd caught himself begging for pity. He lifted the rack of gear from his shoulders and handed it across. "I'm climbing like puke," he said. "Get us straightened out."

NINETEEN

Hugh took the rack, and turned his thoughts to the rock. For the last five hours, while Augustine had stolen into the smoke and returned empty-handed, Hugh had been trying to sort out the mess of cracks.

The smoke hampered their sight, of course. But he had a feeling that even on a clear day, the route demanded more than mere craft and muscle. The three women had been playing vertical chess up here, inventing gambits, creating moves, foxing their way up the cracks. Never giving in. Bit by bit they'd tiptoed through the labyrinth. *A female labyrinth.* Somehow that was key.

Hugh tried one crack, and quickly decided against it. He couldn't explain why. It felt vacant somehow, discarded and unused. Minus any obvious signs, he was searching for some wordless sense of a woman's exploration. One of them—he didn't know which—had found the way through here. She was the one he needed to dance with in his head.

He tried a few moves up yet another crack, and discarded that, too. The cracks were a false start. Forget normal sight, he told himself. Feel for the way.

On an impulse, he worked left around a bulge, away from anything obvious. And there it lay. On the far side of the swell, tucked from plain view, rose a sequence of knobs, or chickenheads. They were sloped and eroded and minimal, little more than the backs of horseshoe crabs clinging to the stone. But they marched upward. And something about them spoke of a separate awareness. They would require tenacity and counterlogic and grace. It matched his image of a ballerina with steel fingers.

Hugh shaped his fingers over the first chickenhead, and got a toe settled. He reached for the next, and the next, following them into the concealed heights. His focus turned tubular. The sprawling stone with its false offerings and colliding angles folded into blankness. He was left with a single tunnel through the smoke.

The knobs and bumps weren't so hard to climb. They formed a virtual ladder. The problem was protection. He tried cinching a green sling over one knob, but it squirreled loose and fluttered into the void without a sound. After that, he didn't waste any more slings and carabiners on illusions of security. He just climbed.

With each move, he committed that much

more deeply to his choice. If he'd guessed wrong, it was going to be nearly impossible to reverse course and down-climb. He glanced between his feet, and the chickenheads—so obvious at eye level—had vanished from sight. His trail was disappearing behind him.

His knee trembled. "Tetanus" was the technical term. Climbers called it sewing-machine leg. Uncontrolled, you could shake yourself right off your holds. *Get still*, he thought. Not just the knee. The mind. *Smooth it out*. He breathed, in, out. The ripples in his pond grew glassy still. The trembling stopped.

He got on with the waltz, more and more out of options. He had climbed a hundred feet out, and there wasn't a hint of pro between him and Augustine. That meant a two-hundred-foot whipper if he lost a hold, and that would mean a free fall you could measure in tons. There was no way Augustine could catch such a thing. Hugh had entered the suicide zone. He was dancing with a dead woman. He had no choice but to follow where she led.

As a reward for his good faith, almost, a crack appeared in the stone.

Hugh slotted in a nut, clipped to it, and rested his nerves. While he clung there, he stuck another piece into the crack for good measure. Then he continued higher. A little higher, he came upon handprints beneath the tawny soot, and this time they were real, the traces left by gymnastic chalk. His doubts fell away. Here was her path.

The prints were like shadows in a photograph negative, white instead of black. He placed his hand beside her ghost hand, and his long fingers and taped paw dwarfed the pale vestiges of her.

There was no way to repeat her moves exactly. She had a shorter reach, but greater range and more flexibility, which translated into a completely different style using different holds. By this stage of the women's climb, after seven or eight or nine days, however long they'd been at it, she'd probably starved down to half his hundred and seventy pounds. And judging by the girl's body he'd found in the forest, this phantom climber would have been less than half his age . . . Annie's age when he'd first met her.

Hugh resorted to all his best tricks, pushing himself to dance her dance, admiring the hell out of her, whoever she'd been. He had to push to keep up with the nameless woman. It was like a chase. He followed, literally, in her footsteps.

"Twenty feet," Augustine's voice rose up to him. There were just twenty feet of rope left.

Hugh began hunting for her resting place, and it appeared to him in the smoke, a ledge wide enough for the side of one shoe. At his shoulder level, he found slight scratch marks in the crack where she'd placed her anchor. Injecting two cams and a number three hex, he hitched himself in, and called for Augustine to come.

While Augustine climbed the one rope, Hugh hauled their bag on the second rope. It was fifty pounds, likely less. That was the weight of their long-term survival. Four gallons of water, some food, and a little bivvy gear. It was plenty for now, but way short if Murphy's Law decided to kick in.

Augustine's coughing came through the smog. He sounded like a tuberculosis ward approaching. As he materialized on the rope, he stopped to rest and catch his breath and sample some of the rounded chickenheads. He looked up at Hugh and said, "Goddamn."

That made Hugh feel good. It was like the old days again, spearing the great white. "I was starting to think we'd lost them," he said. "But they were just hiding from us." He did not point out that, in praising Hugh, *goddamn,* Augustine was also praising the "witches" who had preceded them.

Augustine scanned the muddy nothingness above. "Still no sign of the Eye. It's got to be close."

"It's getting late," Hugh said.

Augustine reacted. "We're fine. There's still plenty of day left."

Hugh stood his ground. "We spent a lot of time spinning our wheels. Look at the sun."

The metal ball had rolled across the sky and was sinking behind the shrouded prow.

"We're not turning back," Augustine warned him.

Hugh changed the topic. "Let's check on the others."

"Others?"

"Our partners," Hugh said. "I want to know if they touched down."

"Them," said Augustine. "Right." He took out the radio. Preserving the battery had been his excuse for radio silence, but now Hugh wondered if it wasn't simply the silence he was protecting. No communication meant no news, and more important, no countermanding orders. Hugh had this hunch Augustine was fighting the whole world to press on with this deliverance.

Hugh could hear a woman's voice answer the call. Then Augustine pressed the receiver tight against his ear. He asked about Lewis and Joe. "Good," he said. He asked if they'd found any sign of a body at the base of El Cap. The radio crackled. "That nails it," Augustine said. "She's still up here."

The dispatcher said something else.

"I don't need to talk to him," Augustine replied. A different voice came on, and Augustine said, "Chief." He listened with growing impatience. After a minute, he broke in. "Not to worry," he said. "We're closing in on her. We're almost there."

Hugh looked up at the swampy miasma. Closing in on her? They had no idea where on the wall they were.

The chief spoke again. Augustine replied, "That doesn't work for me. And it's my call. I'm the first responder. I'm the one on the scene."

An argument developed. Augustine screwed the receiver against his ear. "Negative," he said. "We're not going down. We're almost there. Tell them, keep the faith. Hold their position up there. Keep

them sharp. When the time comes, we're going to
want them ready."

The chief started to say more, Hugh could hear
his tiny voice. But Augustine turned off the radio.

"What was that all about?" Hugh asked.

"Our guys got down," Augustine reported. "The
rangers found them wandering along the road. Also
they ran a search along the base. No body. It's like I
said. Andie got herself back up the rope during the
fire. She's in the Eye. She's alive."

Maybe, maybe not, thought Hugh. "They want
us to retreat, is that what I heard?"

"A bunch of backseat drivers. They're stressed
out from the fire. And they're rangers."

"Meaning what?"

"Cops. They like to tell you what to do."

Hugh didn't like it. A conservative approach,
right about now, would include some discussion
about alternatives, such as retreat. But there was
nothing conservative about Augustine's repeated
thrusts at the wall. He meant to break through Trojan Women's defenses, and Hugh had known that
when he'd volunteered to cross over from the safe-
ness of Anasazi.

Augustine was watching him. He couldn't do
this alone, and he knew it. Hugh let him wonder
another few moments. He cut his eyes up at the no-
man's-land.

"Your lead," he finally said. They would go on.

"Actually," Augustine said, "you seem to have
a better feel for it."

Hugh kept his expression mild. But it was a pivotal moment. Augustine was subordinating himself. He was admitting that the climbing was beyond him, and that he needed more help than he'd known. Augustine had touched the rounded chickenheads and seen the evidence of Hugh's nerveless run-out on the pitch below. In effect, he was asking Hugh to become his rope gun.

This hadn't been part of the proposition. Hugh had come to lend a hand, not be the Man. He wanted to be a passenger, not a principal. This was Augustine's karma playing out, not his. And yet he found himself sinking deeper into the siren song, pulled along by whispers and dreams.

By this stage, he was beginning to question whether his discovery of the girl's body in the forest was any more an accident than Joshua's fire. He'd been thinking about that a lot. There was too much coincidence in the string of events to call it coincidence anymore. Maybe Lewis was on to something, maybe disaster was following Augustine around. Hugh didn't believe that, necessarily. But there was some larger mystery to this ascent. A welter of trajectories was crossing and connecting the farther he climbed. He couldn't see the pattern to it yet, and had no idea where it was all leading. His one shot at gaining the big picture meant continuing higher.

Hugh took the rack of gear from Augustine. "All right," he said. "For now."

He made himself part of the race, though it was a different race than he'd started. This was no longer Augustine's solo contest with El Cap. That bullshit was over. The Eye and its cold, silent camp—wherever it lay—were just a feature along the way.

From here on, Hugh had a deliverance of his own to see through. He had himself to carry out of the abyss. If he could finish this thing and get to the top, then the smoke would part, and the floor would lie revealed, and he would surely be able to read his own fate.

TWENTY

On the next pitch, a thin flake, the soot was like dry grease. The toes of his shoes simply would not smear upon the outer rock. All his weight went onto his tired arms. Once again, he was forced to run the rope out its full length before finding a place to anchor to the wall.

While Augustine jugged up and retrieved the protection, Hugh hauled the bag. He took out his notepad and added a line to his map. He wrote, "160', 5.10-ish, no bolts, cams only (1–2"), HB." The line of ink hovered on his page, attached below to dots and a cartoon explosion of false cracks and other lines and hieroglyphics. "Many blades and arrows, two rurps, beaks," a note read, and elsewhere, "Rope drag!" and "mantle off beak."

Every detail held meaning to a climber, and Hugh was meticulous with his record. At the same time, he knew the map was gibberish. It had no beginning and would have no end, because they had inserted themselves onto Trojan Women at an indefinite midpoint, and their climbing would halt when they reached the women. Disconnected from the ground and the summit, it was a map of nowhere.

He felt dangerously lost. Navigation came as second nature to him, a habit from his doodle-bugging days in the Louisiana bayou. He always plotted his location, the more remote, the more precisely. Deep in the desert or among nameless mountains, he kept track of his progress as if it were an autobiography. But Trojan Women erased all his reference points. It made a sham of his fragment of a map. His head ached.

Augustine appeared in the smoke.

"One more pitch," Hugh told him. "Then we park for the night."

"It can't be more than one pitch," Augustine assured him.

But at the top of the next pitch, with the tan smog turning coffee, the Eye still eluded them. "One more," said Augustine.

"No. We're tired. This is it for the night."

"But it's right there."

"You're pointing at smoke."

Augustine tapped at Hugh's open notebook. It left a smudge of blood on his map. "Look how far we've come."

"The question is how far we've got to go, and what shape we'll be in when we get there."

"We're on route. They came this way. Those are their chalk marks."

"I'm not climbing in the dark for something I can't see in the day."

"You just said you can't see anything anyway."

Hugh looked at his red eyes. "You're pushing too hard."

Augustine sagged. He whispered. "I'm afraid."

"I know." Hugh placed one hand on Augustine's arm. It was not all that intimate. They were shoulder to shoulder as it was, crowded together by the ropes. When one coughed, it shook the other.

"You think I'm a fool."

"I think you're tired."

"I'm out of bounds."

"That makes two of us, wherever we are."

"I mean out of bounds with you," Augustine said. "I know how this looks to you, like a dumb infatuation. You lost a woman who was your wife. And Andie was just a dream anymore."

Augustine seemed to be preparing himself for the worst. That would mean more for Hugh to haul, more of other men's guilt. "That's what life's all about though, right? The dream."

"There's a difference," Augustine said. "I know it was worse for you."

Hugh looked to see if Augustine was trying to beguile him. But the man seemed earnest, and miserable, with his bracelet made of hair. "Not necessarily," Hugh said. "My wife and I got to live our years. And yours were all ahead of you."

"Maybe once," said Augustine.

They slung the two hammocks, one below the other, and burrowed in. They rigged slings to pass a jug of water up and down. Hugh had to restrain himself from drinking the whole gallon. They weren't out of the woods yet. The darkness gathered.

"Is it true you never found her?" Augustine asked from underneath him.

Hugh grunted. Couldn't they just let the desert lie? His head was pounding. The hammock was squashing him. It was going to be a long night. But Augustine needed to talk.

"Your friend told me," Augustine said. "It was on the ledges last night. He woke me up. He threatened me. He said to take my claws out of you. You're grieving. I'm exploiting you. He said quit for the good of everybody."

"Lewis, my archangel," Hugh said.

"I almost did what he said."

"Quit?"

Augustine's voice grew softer. "What if you're right? What if she's gone?"

They were supposed to be flying on Augustine's hopes. Instead Hugh was carrying them on his wings, leading the way, decoding the wall, keeping them sound.

"The smoke should settle tonight," Hugh told him. "Maybe by morning, we can see what's what. We'll reach the Eye tomorrow. Then we'll deal with it."

"That's what scares me." Augustine was quiet a moment. "How *do* you deal with it?"

Hugh nested his head against the hammock. First Lewis, now this man, each wanted a guide to lead them through their damage. It was as if Augustine needed him, not to rescue a living woman, but to help bury her. Hugh was a rope gun for his mourning.

"You walk on," Hugh said.

"That's it?"

"Leave her behind. The past. Put it away from you." Hugh was firm.

"But you came back."

"Call it a high school reunion."

"This is where you met your wife," Augustine said. "I heard you in the bar."

"And we lived a life," Hugh said, "and then she vanished. You think people didn't talk? I took a woman with no mind into the desert, and came home alone. People talked. No different than when you came back from Patagonia."

"Except you didn't choose to leave her out there."

"Look," said Hugh. "There are no rules in the wilderness. Not in the mountains, not out in the desert." Nor on El Cap, he almost added. Because with Trojan Women, Augustine was carrying double the load of ghosts. He'd failed Andie's brother and now it seemed he'd failed her, too. "There's no good. There's no bad. Forget the chattering class. When we're this far from the world, there are no eyes to see into our hearts. There's no one to judge us."

"That's the worst part," Augustine said, "getting left to judge yourself."

Hugh shoved at the wall with his shoulder. The hammock and the smoke and this burden of desire were smothering him. "That gets you nowhere. Think of it this way. We're left alone by those who couldn't keep up with us. You survive. You shed your skin. You grow a new one. You heal. It just happens."

"Then we might as well give up," Augustine said. He coughed.

Hugh didn't like his tone. Attitude counted. It added up in all the myriad tiny details that stood between them and the summit. As much as Augustine needed him, Hugh needed Augustine. What he needed was for the man to stay glued together until they reached land, whether that was all the way up or all the way down.

"I said to shed your skin, not your spirit. We came to take care of her," Hugh said. "Andie still needs you."

Augustine didn't speak again. Hugh tinkered with a piece of plastic pipe, trying to prop the hammock open, but it wasn't much use. Finally he fell asleep.

He wasn't surprised to be woken late in the night. By this time, he'd resigned himself to a steady diet of nightmares until El Cap was behind him.

He waited in his hammock, mashed against the wall, hurting, and miserable with thirst. He waited for the evening clue. What was it this time? Underneath him, Augustine was murmuring in his sleep and coughing softly.

After another minute, the noise repeated. A chorus of unearthly shrieks and howls rose up from the remains of the forest. It was the coyotes and other predators. They were ripping each other to shreds as they fed on burnt animals in the ashes of the forest.

It shouldn't have bothered him. They were hanging two thousand feet above the savagery. But the blood drummed in his head, and he felt vulnerable and hunted in his little sack of nylon. He wrapped a length of slack rope around his hands and forearms, and held it hard against his pounding heart, and prayed for them to stop, even knowing it was the way of things.

TWENTY-ONE

On one venture deep into the Rub', Hugh and Annie had come upon a perfect reef of coral, preserved in all its details by dunes that had fanned open for a brief span of time. The ancient sea barrier rose like a dolphin's back and dipped back into the sands. It predated their paleo lakes by millions of years. They found delicate fans and sticklike trees of limestone and a wall of mineral polyps like a thousand open mouths shouting at them, the skeletons of silence.

As they continued into the smoke the next morning, he was reminded of that day. The crack had petered away again, and he was climbing on the edges of dirty coins—of nickels and dimes, flakes that thin—when he came upon a vein of olivine. Like his lost reef in the desert, the vein suddenly surfaced from the white-and-tan granite with-

out explanation or fanfare, a relic of deeper move-
ments within El Cap. It curved upward like dark
green vertebrae.

As he picked up speed on the spine of olivine
with its glowing, bony burls, Hugh took heart. Perhaps this morning they might break through to the
blue sky and a bright yellow sun and at least a peek
of the summit.

The smoke was not so thick at this elevation.
Soot still dulled El Cap's colors, but no longer over-
whelmed them. The gray world was giving way to
life. They were escaping the inferno, or its aftermath.

The vein of olivine snaked up and to the right
like the arch of a bridge. As he went, he found
white chalk marks left by whichever woman had
been leading. It was not unlikely that she was his
same dance partner from yesterday. This high on
the wall—this near the summit—the team would
have sorted out its various specialties and assigned
the free climbing to their fastest, most confident
member.

He was growing fond of this woman, or the
combination of women who made her up. Out here
on the sharp edge, the two of them shared the same
exact dangers and suffered the same questions and
renewed their same faith in a pinch of stone. The
only thing separating them was time. With the
blood chemistry highballing his senses, and her
sequence of moves affirming his moves, his contact
with her verged on the sensual. His dancer seemed
to be waiting for him at crucial moments. And the

way he clutched and pulled and grunted and opened himself up on the rock came very close to embracing her.

In a sense, she was seducing him. Part of it lay in their climbing, part in their desire for El Cap, and part in the morbid attraction between the undertaker and his dead. However you put it, she was pursuing him even as he was pursuing her.

Hugh tried to remember the last time he'd felt chased this way, and it was by Annie back in the very beginning, on a rainy afternoon decades ago. He put away her image. This was a different woman. This was now. He gave in to the ferocious, nearly silent game. The only sound was of his breathing and heartbeat and the sigh of rope across stone.

The abyss dragged at his bowels and the saddle of his pelvis and the root of his spine. It pulled at his organs, and hung on his fingers. It filled him with loneliness and mass and fear. But she didn't give up on him. She offered her ghostly prints, and urged his grace. She beckoned.

Every motion was deliberate, right down to his choosing how much to bend his knuckles when he crimped a hold, and where to place which part of his toe and how much to cant it and when to let go. From one instant to the next, he exerted maximum control, and yet he felt completely out of control. It was so easy. He had only to give in to her.

He tried to imagine which of the three women she had been. He'd met one in the forest with silver along her ear, and turquoise in her hair. Was it her, or one of the others? Probably he'd never know. For some reason, in his mind that made her more beautiful.

The rich green stone felt like chunks of treasure in his hands. It didn't belong. Olivine was an orphan rock. It had floated out from some deep, plasmic interior, defying all the chemical and physical processes around it. Yet here it was, a passport through the territory.

After eighty or ninety feet, the olivine receded. The green chunks melted back into the speckled granite. Hugh clung to the last of the holds, a polished jug, searching for her next move.

There were no cracks in sight, no flakes to hook. Her chalk marks vanished. That gave him a start. He'd been so sure this was the way. Had the olivine been a false lead, then? Had she tricked him and backtracked, and now left him stranded? One thing he knew, his strength was running out. He took turns shaking his hands below his waist, pumping fresh blood into each forearm for whatever came next.

His knee wagged. Tetanus. *Lock it off.* He set his foot again, changed hands, craned back his head, scouring the rock for holds. It seemed impossible that she'd brought him so high on such promising holds only to abandon him at the tip of nowhere. He searched for the slightest detail, a fingerprint, anything. What he finally came to see was so immense it eluded him at first.

Ever so faintly, lurking in the smoke, a dark, nebulous crescent loomed above and to his right. It yawned like the mouth of a whale. It was a roof, he comprehended, a gigantic, arcing brow. Without knowing it, he'd reached Cyclops Eye, or nearly reached it. *So close, so faraway.* Clutching at his final hold, he could see no way to enter the monstrous feature.

He leaned out, trying to see around a squared, blind corner to his side. In the distance, there was nothing but smog. The wall had ceased to exist beyond his reach. While he was busy flirting with his dancer, the abyss had closed in all around him, above, below, on every side. For a fleeting moment, dizzied by the smoke, there was no up or down.

He gripped the olivine for dear life, squandering his arm strength. The greatest lesson a climber learns is when enough is enough. On a grand scale, you judge the rock or ice and weigh the outer mountain against your vision of it. You learn when to push and when to back away, and the limits of your body, how far your legs will spread, how much your arms will hold, how hard your heart can pump. You learn not to overdrive the piton with your hammer, nor shove the cam too deep, nor overpower your holds.

Hugh forced himself to slacken his grasp. He prized one hand loose and shook it out. He traded hands. There had to be a next hold. But like the best of magicians, his anonymous sprite had left not a clue to her trick.

Hugh edged to the right. Holding the olivine lump with one hand, he hooked the heel of his opposite foot along the corner, and peered around.

There was another world in there.

Cupped within a great, empty cavity, the brown smoke looked almost blue. It wasn't the blue of sky, but of deeper places. A slight breeze exhaled against his face. It felt even cooler than the stone he clung to. *New territory.* His excitement built.

He returned to the olivine hold and rested, and then tried again. Hooking his heel, he ran his hands up and down the corner, feeling for any folds or flakes. But the stone was blank.

It baffled him. His ape index had to be a full foot wider than hers, giving him far more range, and still he kept coming up empty. What was he missing? How had she done it? He retreated to his olivine jug and rested. His knee trembled. He switched feet. The other knee quivered. He willed it to stop. It trembled again.

He was running out of gas. There was only so long he could swap hands and feet before the law of diminishing returns axed him from the holds. He would have called down to Augustine, but there was nothing to ask for. Augustine couldn't help him. The rope hung from his waist, a lifeless thing, useless for a fall, no comfort at all. He was alone up here.

Hugh stared at the corner. She had mastered it somehow. He looked for pockets of soot that might indicate the tops of flakes, but the rock was smooth.

Again he tried, hooking his heel on the edge and finding nothing. There was nothing there.

His heel hook started to slip, and Hugh grappled his foot higher. Unexpectedly, at shin level, where he would never have thought to look, the butt end of his heel caught on something. He carefully turned his foot, trading his heel for the top of his toe, feeling for the target.

Climbers are used to seeing with their fingers. Shorter, but more agile, his ballerina had gone one better, fishing with her toes. There it lay, hidden away, a slight shelf carved on the far side. Shaking, he retreated to his olivine jug.

The sequence was clear to him now. He knew what had to be done. As a guy, he was naturally inclined to muscling moves. But there was no move to muscle here. Everything depended on finesse. He eyed the edge of the corner, and it was dead vertical. His forearms were practically shot. His nerves were next to fried. She was giving him one last chance. Testing his commitment. Or mocking him.

He went for it, delicately.

He reached across with his right foot. One hand squeezing the olivine, the other gripping the bare right angle of the edge, he spread-eagled flat against the face.

Now. In one fluid motion, he released the olivine, pulled at the corner, and came upright against the edge. His foot rolled flat. The toe seated on the hold.

There he balanced, embracing the intersection

of two planes, taking a sip of air, just enough. Breathe too deeply, and his rib cage would topple him backward. A cough would send him flying. He couldn't even lift the side of his face from the rock to look around the corner.

Perched on one toe, staring back at the chain of olivine holds he could not possibly return to, Hugh stroked the far wall. There had to be something in here. Up, nothing. Down, nothing.

His left hand was slipping. His knee chattered against the rock. Deeper. He reached deeper. He emptied his lungs. The hold was waiting for him.

But gravity, its slender thread, was towing him backward. There was nothing forceful about it. Very simply, he was going to fall.

Two choices flashed through his mind. He could keep hugging this corner until he fell. Or he could fall, but on his terms.

He fell.

He let go with his hands and fingers and the edge of his one shoe on that little shelf . . . all in that order. Toe last. That was crucial. It gave him the suggestion of a trajectory. Eyes wide, he tipped sideways.

The handhold flashed before him, almost an afterthought. Quick as a pickpocket, he snatched at it. His legs swung out. There was a crack farther on. With the last of his strength, he jammed every piece of shoe and tape and human meat into the breach.

Maybe a little part of him died by casting loose.

All the fear he'd kept at bay came rushing at him now. Shouting and cursing, he grubbed deeper at the crack, not gaining an inch. If he could have clawed his way inside the rock, he would have, anything to hide from the monstrous suck against his back.

At last his terror ebbed. He was safe. And now he saw, he had reached their destination. He was inside the fabled Eye.

TWENTY-TWO

From the ground, Cyclops Eye had always looked to him like a cutthroat's den or a cave. It had a dark, overhanging trench marked at its crest by a dagger-like watercourse. But now that he was on the inside of it, Hugh found less a cave than a great, yawning, open socket, thirty feet deep and possibly a hundred feet high. Over the eons, brittle, black diorite had sheeted away from beneath the beetling brow, leaving this giant, raw divot.

The three women—and now Hugh—had entered halfway up a dihedral that formed the left corner of the Eye's lid. The dihedral rose into the swirling smoke, growing darker and thicker as it curved overhead. On another route, in cleaner stone, the roof might have formed a soaring sculpture. Here, rotted and bottomless, the Eye just seemed to brood.

Below, Hugh spied an indistinct ledge in the depths. It was part of an older route, the classic North America Wall. Conceivably the women could have descended to use the ledge as a bivvy site. But it looked too small to hold three people. Besides, they had been embarked on a route all their own, and had proudly refused to borrow from their ancestors. Their camp was tucked somewhere against the arch above, though the smoke obscured it.

Hugh could have set an anchor where he was, and dutifully waited for Augustine to join him and take the lead. He was still shaky from his desperate entrance, and he knew Augustine wanted to be the first to reach the women's final camp. But then again, Augustine had made him the rope gun. He'd earned the right to finish what he'd started.

In effect, the camp was going to be Hugh's summit. From there, he and Augustine would be evacuated to the top along with whomever they found, and El Cap would be over for him. Finishing the Eye was all he had left for a grand finale.

He followed the dihedral up and right, under the roof. The diorite was sharp enough to gut you if you fell, and the holds shifted in their sockets. But the woman's white fingerprints were clearer than ever on the black rock, and Hugh set his mind to the task.

After a few minutes, he caught sight of the remains of their camp. From below and to the side, it looked like a shipwreck in the sky. Hugh edged closer, traversing beneath the roof.

There were no natural shelves under here, nothing like the Archipelago's ledges to sit or stand on. Instead the women had constructed a small, vertical shantytown out of portaledges. There were three platforms hanging one below the other.

The place was in a shambles. Slings hung without motion. One platform was partly upended. The bright red flooring of the lowest had ripped through and hung like a flag of no quarter.

It was no wonder Augustine had been unable to see who was left, much less gain access to the camp. Dangling at the edge of the roof thirty feet out, he would have faced just a huddle of shadows and this mobile of aluminum tubing and bright, cheery nylon.

It looked deserted. If there was a body, it had to be lying on the highest platform. Hugh crept right on holds that grated like loose teeth.

Only now did he notice a long loop of Tibetan prayer flags hanging from the ceiling. Even sun faded and stained by the smoke, their red and blue and yellow and green colors were vivid. There were dozens of them in a bowed laundry line. Hugh knew from his Asia trips that the flags were primitive prayer factories. Each square of cloth was printed with script and the image of a Pegasus creature, a winged horse called a *lung ta,* that carried the prayers to heaven each time it flapped in the breeze.

Hugh tried to imagine their happy little camp with the gay flags. Now the flags hung limp. He eyed the torn floor and tipped platform. Their blessings had stopped. Abruptly.

He traversed underneath their silent ghetto on pockmarks and shallow scoops in the stone. The scoops held bits of rubble and decades of bird droppings and the bones of small animals, slippery as ball bearings. He grew more wary.

Now he angled up, passing by the torn flooring. A body, or possibly one of their haul bags, must have punched right through the platform. The haul bags were missing, he realized, all their life support. In one catastrophic moment, the place had been emptied of life.

A little higher, he leveled the second platform, and started to pull himself onto its flat surface. But his weight set the whole colony of portaledges swaying, each rocking like a cradle. Slings creaked. Aluminum tubing scraped against the rock. Hugh came to a halt.

It was in the nature of knots to loosen when they weren't tended, and this place had been deserted for how long? The wreckage could suddenly unravel and sail off into the depths with him on it. Hugh backed off the platform and onto the stone.

Now he saw that the uppermost platform was not empty. From below, the impression of a body was very plain against the floor. She was lying sprawled on top.

"Andie?" he called. It was a reflex, a courtesy. This was her home. Of course there was no reply. They were too late. Probably they'd been too late even before he found the girl in the forest.

He crouched below and to one side of the top platform, bracing himself for the sight to come. He'd done this before. He'd looked on death, most recently the girl in the forest. But she'd been fresh, and he could not for the life of him remember how many days had passed since then. The forest fire had burned away time. It felt as if weeks had passed.

He slotted a nut into the stone, then more protection, fashioning his own anchor. Something in the women's system had failed, and he dared not attach himself to their wreckage. Best to start from scratch. The carabiner gates clacked like rifle bolts in the close space.

Enough, he decided. He'd brought them to the source. It was not his duty to face the horror alone. Let Augustine have his wish. Let him look first.

Pulling the gauze from his mouth, Hugh yelled, "Off," even though he was as deep inside the beast as you could get and Augustine could never hear him. He gave several long, strong tugs on the rope, a secondary signal. A minute later, the ropes loaded tight. Augustine was on the way.

Hugh pulled in their haul bag and stowed it neatly against the wall, and waited. He looked at the prayer flags. He glanced up at the platform, mere inches overhead. His curiosity mounted. He waited some more. The hell with it. He couldn't resist.

It was going to be ugly, he could smell her now. B movies flickered in his head. What if she was lying by the edge, her head right there? He gave

himself enough slack to stand and peer over the
edge, but only enough. If the shock felled him, he
would be on a short leash.

He stood.

There was not one corpse, but two.

One woman sat against the wall, strapped into a
spiderweb of slings and ropes lashed across her
chest and shoulder. Her eyes were shut, her mouth
hung open. The other woman lay across her lap, a
rope still attached to her harness. She would be
Andie. Hugh recognized her long, white-blond hair
from Augustine's photograph and the braids of his
wrist braid. She had stones woven into her hair, like
the girl he'd found in the forest.

It looked as if someone had arranged them in
this harrowing pietà, one draped across the other's
lap, piled with loose rope. Death had spared their
faces so far, or at least the face of that seated
woman. No rictus, no corruption. He was just as
glad that Andie's face was hidden against her
friend's chest. Something smelled awful.

Hugh's dread eased. Except for the stench, they
could have been a pair of wax figures. He observed
them, trying to read backward from their ending.

He traced their attempted exit from Cyclops Eye.
The roof jutted out from here. The ceiling was hon-
eycombed with pockets and cells, an upside-down
battlefield of finger-and-hand-sized cavities. One of
the women had crept toward the rim. Her chalk
marks disappeared at the edge. Maybe she'd fallen
there. Maybe she'd made it out onto the face above.

The accident had triggered a pandemonium of falling bodies and haul bags. He could translate their last moments from the frayed ends of exploded ropes and scattered gear. And yet there were peculiarities.

To begin with, there was this strange anchor. It defied his mountain logic, his sense of economy. For some reason, they had wildly overprotected the site. A half dozen silvery bolt hangers glittered on the diorite, with twice that many pitons driven into the seams, and that didn't count the nuts and cams wedged behind flakes. Slings and spare rope had been knotted together and woven back and forth like a cargo net.

He ran his eyes over the scene, and found nothing leftover. They'd used every spare piece of gear to sew themselves to the stone. It went beyond caution. "Paranoia" was the word. It was as if they had been forewarned of their destruction.

He turned his attention to the seated woman. Cuba, he remembered. Her face reminded him of smoked meat. It was the color of dark tea. Tangled in slings, she must have strangled.

Oddly, tears tracked down her death mask, cutting through the soot and grime. At least they looked like tears, which was outright impossible. Joshua hadn't started the fire until two days *after* Augustine had spied her in here, lashed in place just as she was now. Maybe the heat of the burning forest had caused juice to leak from her eyes.

But the greatest mystery was Andie. Somehow

she had returned over a hundred and fifty feet from the tip of the rope to this sanctuary. With his own eyes, Hugh had seen her dangling in the spotlight. How had she gotten here?

Could Augustine have been right? Could she really have been alive all those days? Had she hauled herself up the rope when the fire began, fallen across the lap of her dead companion, and then expired? It defied belief, and yet Hugh could think of no other explanation. Just as Augustine had said all along, she had apparently been alive and waiting for someone to come along. If Augustine could have reached her that first day from above, or if the kid, Joe, had kept climbing through the night, they could have saved her.

A thought crept in. What if she was still alive?

"Andie?"

First the fall, then her ascension. Days on end without water or food. She could be in deep sleep, in a coma. A real life Sleeping Beauty, why not?

Hugh pulled closer. He started to reach for her, then held back. Old dreads. "Andie?" She lay still with her long hair like a curtain, and her head pillowed on the other woman's lap.

Hugh stretched to touch her wrist. It was cold. Everything was cold in here. He couldn't feel a pulse. But if she was in a coma, her metabolism would have slowed to a near flat line. He climbed higher, and brushed the hair away from her face.

He jerked his hand back.

Her neck was stretched the length of a sausage.

Those Jim Crow photos of lynched men . . . it was like that. Dark welts on her throat showed where she'd tangled in the rope on her plunge.

Hugh stared at the pair of women. The mystery deepened. Andie couldn't possibly have towed herself up from the depths. And there was no chance in the world that her eyes had opened when Augustine descended and called her name. Beyond a doubt, she had died—instantly—when the line snapped taut. But then how was she here? The strangeness of it almost offended him.

"Do you have her?"

Augustine's voice bounced off the stone ceiling. Hugh glanced between his feet at the climber charging up through the smoke. His face was so open, so full of expectation, that Hugh groaned.

He did not feel sorrow. These were all strangers to him. And death was not always tragic. When Annie had disappeared in the Empty Quarter, it was as if the Holy Spirit had reached down and taken her away, putting an end to her humiliation and confusion and suffering. That's how Hugh had come to view it, as a divine act.

Hugh opened his hand. He started to say, Slow down. Steel yourself. But something stopped him from softening the bad news. Augustine needed to smash against the reality. Hugh's pause was not mean-spirited, or voyeuristic. He didn't crave the grief about to come. At the same time, he didn't intervene. This was a sort of just desserts. Because driven by Augustine's nobility, and his guilt and raw imagination, Hugh had almost destroyed himself reaching this dead end in the sky.

Augustine wouldn't have stopped anyway. The rope jerked and shivered with his jumar thrusts. "Andie?"

Like a sailor reaching up from the depths, he grabbed for the edge of the platform, which set everything wobbling and rocking. A shipwreck, Hugh thought again, surveying the mad rigging of ropes and the bobbing debris.

Hugh looked at the wax statues. Their dream was over. Their quiet would shatter. The litter would descend. These final sisters would be pulled apart once and for all.

Then he saw something. "Wait," he said. Her head was different.

Augustine grappled his way past. "Andie?"

Her head had been bent down. Now it was lifted. That tea-brown face with streaks like tears.

"Andie?" Augustine's voice warped. He saw the awful, elastic neck now.

Her head must have been lifted already, thought Hugh. He'd memorized it wrong, that was all. Or the motion of the platforms had shifted her limbs.

"God, oh God," said Augustine.

The platforms rocked and scraped. Slings creaked. The clues bullied Hugh. He tried to think. Someone had taken the rope from around that boneless throat . . . after her return from the pit. There was only one possible explanation.

In the same instant, the woman's eyes flicked open.

"Jesus," Hugh shouted.

Blood red, the same as theirs.

Augustine was oblivious, fixated on the corpse. "Andie." He leaned to kiss her.

Above him, the woman blinked. Her eyes traveled across Augustine's matted hair to Hugh, and widened in horror. With his black-and-blue eyes and the dried blood in his beard, he must have looked like the living dead himself.

"She's not dead," Hugh whispered.

And still Augustine didn't comprehend. He cast a glance at him, stunned by Hugh's cruelty. Because his lover was very dead.

The woman stared down at Augustine, astonished by her awakening. Or their trespass.

"Let go." Hugh pulled at Augustine. "Leave her alone."

Augustine had an arm under Andie's body. He was trying to pry her loose.

The woman's mouth came unsealed.

Augustine tugged at the corpse.

Her teeth parted. Tea-brown teeth, everything the color of smoke. Except for her red eyes.

Hugh saw the hard, dark tip of her tongue working. He didn't know what to expect, a scream, a curse, or a plea for help. When the air finally came up from her lungs, what escaped was the hoarse cry of a carrion bird.

TWENTY-THREE

At the woman's screech, Augustine straightened in his stirrups and came face-to-face with the survivor. "Not you," he said.

Why not? Hugh wondered. Then he realized this was Cuba, his witch.

Augustine didn't hesitate. He grabbed for the body. Where he meant to take it, Hugh didn't know.

More dead than alive, the woman clutched the body tighter. With what strength? Hugh stared. A shrill keening poured from that dried-up purse of a mouth.

For a minute, Hugh was too shocked to move. She had returned from the dead. They were fighting. A nightmare image surfaced of the wild dogs that spirited through the dunes. And of Annie wandering mindlessly into their midst like some rare gazelle. Of them finding her feast of bones.

She clawed at Augustine. His arm was trapped. "Let loose," he said. He pulled. The body shifted. She clutched at it.

Their tug of war was grotesque, a custody battle for a corpse. Hugh watched, appalled. At the same time, there was a sort of terrible majesty to it. At the edge of the world, on the brink of human existence, they were fighting for a dead soul, a hero's body.

"Please." It was all Hugh could manage, one feeble word.

They began falling to pieces. The upper platform tilted, and almost capsized. The lower platforms bucked wildly, rocking more violently with each swing.

Chunks of diorite scabbed off and dropped into the smoke, rattling on the lower slabs. The raw powder smell of freshly mined rock sparked from the wall. Grabbing at the center of the slings crossing Augustine's wide back, Hugh tried to yank him away from the struggle.

Augustine bellowed. Cuba hissed. Noise everywhere. Lewis had been right in the beginning, the climb was cursed.

The tug-of-war lasted only a few seconds longer. Then the corpse itself intervened. Held by little more than that cylinder of flesh, her head rolled up. Her face appeared.

The birds had taken her eyes while she hung on the rope. Her tongue was fat, extruded meat. Augustine barked his surprise. Her beauty was gone. His love had become hideous.

He reared away from the head, and plowed into Hugh, who lost his grip. A rope slipped, rock popped, something gave way. The two men tumbled from their stirrups and holds.

The middle platform broke their fall, even as they broke the platform. Hugh landed hard on top of Augustine. The floor's taut membrane held, but the poles did not. Like trap jaws closing, the platform buckled, and the sides clapped shut around them. Pinned together, Hugh snarled in Augustine's rope.

The pandemonium went on. The coupled platforms beat at the wall, rocking and jerking back and forth. Metal screamed on stone. Hugh thrashed to get free, sure the whole camp was about to tear loose, and the flimsy rafts would plunge into the gulf. Not like this, he thought, not tangled in junk and madness. This had nothing to do with him. Nothing.

"My shoulder," Augustine yelled. "Jesus, make her stop."

Hugh wrestled partway from the wreckage. Overhead the woman was shrieking like a banshee. He snatched at straps, rope, their haul bag, anything.

The haul bag came loose in his hand. It plunged from sight. No time for that now. Hugh reached for the wall. Holds ripped from his hands. He drove at the stone with his feet.

The bedlam slowed. His broken platform lost momentum. The upper ledge trembled to a halt. The whole contraption of shelves came to rest.

With a yelp, Augustine's shoulder popped back into joint.

In the stillness that followed, the only sound was the woman's birdlike screeches. A side pole unfastened and arrowed down, whistling like a castaway flute. Abruptly she stopped. She had exorcised her devils. Them.

Augustine lay below him in the belly of the ruined platform. They were both panting. Hugh started coughing. "Are you out of your mind?" he said. He was scared and angry. "What were you doing?"

"She's dead," said Augustine.

"One dead, one still alive." Hugh spoke it starkly. He stripped out the emotion, even the names. They needed discipline. Deep in the desert or high above the earth, self-control was your lifeline.

But Augustine had been filled with such hope. His shock was real. "It's all wrong," he said.

"Wrong?"

"She's the one who dragged Andie into this."

And now Cuba was the one who had survived. Hugh understood. "Andie dragged herself into it," Hugh said. "No one forced her. She reached high, and fell. And you almost killed us just now."

Augustine bared his teeth.

Hugh kept his feet planted and the ledges braced. He held them steady. The frenzy receded. "Like wild animals," he said.

The woman, the survivor—the impossible survivor—had the excuse of trauma and solitude. There was no excuse for Augustine. Unless, Hugh conceded, one counted his tireless days-long siege of El Cap, and now his shattered faith and the sight of his lover turned into that horror on the platform above them.

"It's over," said Augustine.

"It's not," said Hugh. "We have a job to do."

Augustine groaned.

"You've done this before," Hugh said. "We'll take care of them both."

"I need the med kit," Augustine said.

Hugh looked down at him. "How bad are you hurt?"

Augustine stayed lying in the pouch of nylon and snapped poles. "There are drugs in the med kit," he said.

That bad, thought Hugh. Now the rescuer needed rescuing. It was all backward and upside down. Hugh had no business here. This wasn't his climb. It wasn't his rescue. Yet here he was at the mercy of foreign violence. From the moment he'd found the girl in the woods, El Cap had been like quicksand, dragging him deeper and darker the higher he went.

"The haul bag fell," he said. "That had all our water and food. And the med kit."

Augustine said, "And the radio."

Hugh got quiet. "No, you were carrying the radio."

"I put it in the bag."

Hugh wrestled up from the wreckage. He stood and held the anchor. His head brushed the upper platform. The floor sagged where Cuba sat with the corpse. Augustine had still not uttered her name.

Hugh took stock. Augustine was injured. A dead woman had come alive. All three of them needed evacuation, and their radio was possibly gone.

Hugh snatched at the haul line. To his relief, it felt tight and heavy. There was still a hope. He started reeling in the rope, hand over hand, smoothly so the bag wouldn't snag on knobs or in some crack.

While he pulled their cargo from the depths, the woman on the shelf above did not move or make a peep, or so Hugh thought. He was too busy with the rope, and figured the hissing sound was the haul bag sliding against the distant stone. Then he detected words, and decided it must be Augustine talking to himself. But when he looked around, Augustine was lying in the wreckage, staring at the red floor stretched above them, listening.

Hugh stopped hauling. Now he heard. It was Cuba whispering through the floor at them.

". . . couldn't stay away," she was saying. "We knew you'd come."

We? She was raving. Roped to phantoms.

Then he saw that Augustine was listening to her. He looked positively tormented. His lips moved in silent response.

"She told me everything," the voice went on. "How you did it. Left behind. Still alive."

Augustine didn't move a muscle. This was between him and his sorceress. Even bound in place with just a scrap of a voice, starved and crazy, she still had a power over him.

How long had these two been brawling over the poor, star-crossed girl? How old was their hate? It felt ancient to Hugh. And useless, now. For all their care and watchfulness, El Cap had lynched their Andie. Neither of them had managed to save her.

"It was an accident," Augustine answered her. "I told you. The wind never stopped. He wouldn't move. I couldn't stay."

Cerro Torre was his Achilles' heel. Obviously Andie's sisters of the forest had been helping her get things straightened out, damning Augustine with every breath. He'd never stood a chance with her.

Cuba went on punishing him. "Augustine," she said, "keep away. Go down. She doesn't want you."

"How would you know?" Augustine said.

"I died," she told him, "I know everything."

Hugh listened to their clash of whispers. Augustine sank deeper into the wreckage. He was freaked, stricken, an untouchable.

Hugh looked back on Augustine's superhuman drive, and remembered Joe's first words when they had retreated to the ledges. *Keep him away from me.*

It was suddenly obvious. Ever since the tragedy in Patagonia, Augustine had been shadowing his ex-lover. He *was* a ghost, at least to her. Trojan Women had been her attempt to break free. But even in death, he haunted her. Now he had her cornered and eyeless. Not quite cornered, thought Hugh. Not with this half-dead banshee to defend her.

"Get away," she repeated. "You're not the one she wants."

"It was him or me. I wished it was me. What more can I say?"

"Leave."

"Enough," Hugh said to him. "Why let her inside your head?"

The whispering quit. Augustine glanced at Hugh. Eyes red. Damned, damned twice now. First the brother, now the lover. A serial killer in his own mind.

Hugh went after the haul line with new urgency. *Get me out of here.* They were hanging by threads, physically, mentally, every which way.

The bag appeared in the murky soup. "We're going to be okay," he announced. He secured the bag and opened it up. The gallon jugs hadn't burst in the fall, a good sign. If your water balloons could take the beating, the rest of your gear was usually okay.

He found the radio nested in a sleeping bag. He examined the outer casing. "It looks okay," he said.

Augustine roused. "Let me see," he said. Hugh handed it to him. He didn't switch it on. "The battery light's green. It will work."

Hugh's spirits lifted. They were back on track. They had provisions. They had communication. The road was clear. "You want me to make the call?"

Augustine laid the radio between his legs. "First things first. You see the med kit?"

Hugh could have insisted. He didn't want to put off the evacuation one minute more. But Augustine was in command of himself again, full of his old purpose. He began dragging himself out of the sagging wreckage. He stood upright in his stirrups.

"Maybe you should stay still," Hugh said.

"We're copasetic. No problem."

Hugh rooted for the med kit. He held it with both hands.

"Open it up," Augustine said. He looked pale and grim in his stirrups. "There should be a bundle of syringes."

"I have them." Several were preloaded with various liquids, ready to use.

"There's one marked Haldol. That's the one I need."

Hugh found the syringe with "Haldol" written on the plastic barrel. "I don't know this one." He wanted Augustine lucid and able to see the evacuation through. But if that wasn't possible, if Hugh needed to take control, he wanted to know before Augustine doped himself. And he wanted that radio.

"I do," Augustine stated.

Hugh had injected an orange for practice once. He'd never done it with a human. "You want me to inject you?"

"I'll take care of it."

Hugh handed him the syringe. Augustine took it in his fist, needle down, thumb on the plunger. He pulled the plastic cap off with his teeth, and spit it out. "Hold me steady."

Hugh held him by his harness. Without hesitation or real aim, Augustine slugged the side of his fist at the nylon bulge overhead.

If Cuba felt the needle, she didn't move or complain.

"What have you done?" Hugh said. "What the hell was that?" Who was this guy?

Augustine opened his fist. The syringe stayed stuck in the ceiling. "A little site management."

Hugh pulled the syringe from her. "What is this stuff?"

"A silver bullet," Augustine said. "Haloperidol, a major tranquilizer. The docs use it for schizophrenics. Out in the field, we use it for a quick knockdown."

Hugh tossed the syringe away. "A tranquilizer, in her condition? She's in shock. She hasn't eaten in a week. You could kill her." Hugh had no idea if that was true, but he couldn't let the stunt just pass.

"We use it all the time. Give them a poke and back off. They get all settled down. She'll be out for four to six hours."

"I thought it was for you."

"Me? I'm driving the bus."

Unbelievable, thought Hugh. And he was tied into this man? *Where have you brought yourself?* He turned away, caging his anger.

The light was dimming rapidly. Despite everything else, that surprised him. It couldn't be dusk already. Where had the time gone? "Dial it in," he told Augustine. "Bring the litter down. Let's get this over with."

Augustine lowered himself back into the wreckage. "Andie first," he said.

"Andie?"

"We have to get her decent. She's not decent." Augustine's paleness made the filth appear to be floating above his skin.

Decent? She was dead. *One crazier than the other,* thought Hugh. *Beam me the hell up.* He wanted off. Down. Away from this aerie with its stink and its strangled dreams. What was it about this place? Maybe Joshua had it right. Maybe the devil did live here.

"We're running out of day," Hugh said. "The light's fading."

Augustine was barely listening. "I'll take her up," he said. "We'll go together, her and me."

He couldn't guide his lover out alive, so he was going to guide her out dead. Cuba had possessed her for a week. Now Augustine would possess her forever.

Hugh considered his options. Reason or fight.

Or go with it. Finish the thing, he told himself. Get shed of this. "I'll do it," he said.

"Do what?"

"What you said, make her decent. I'll go up." He motioned at the bulge above them. "I'll get Andie away from her. You can't, not with your shoulder. I can."

Augustine suspected a trick. "She'll be out cold in twenty minutes. We can wait."

"We don't have twenty minutes," said Hugh. "Look, she doesn't know me. I'm just a face. Not even that, just a dream in the smoke. I'll take care of Andie. You don't want to see her like this. She wouldn't want that."

Augustine considered. "And then?"

"Like you said, take her out of here. You and her."

Augustine looked at him, beseeching. For a moment, his bleak Viking frown loosened, and Hugh saw the boy behind his armor, the innocence before Cerro Torre ate him. He needed Hugh, and not just to beg for the body and to secure them in this wasteland. He wanted everything to be simple, like in the old days. He wanted to let down his defenses and just have his heartbreak.

Hugh relented. *Take some slack, lad. Quit fighting the world.* He swayed gently in his stirrups. He took command, though of what and for how long he could not say.

"Make the call," he said to Augustine. "Bring them down to us. The two of us working together, we'll do what needs to be done."

Augustine nodded.

Hugh gathered a jug of water and a sleeping bag, and started up. "Cuba," he called.

She didn't make a sound.

"Like a baby," said Augustine.

TWENTY-FOUR

Hugh climbed warily, as if entering the den of a sleeping lion. Except, she was awake. The tranquilizer had yet to take effect, that or Augustine had hit the wrong bulge and sedated a corpse. Clutching her swan-necked friend, Cuba watched his approach with fierce red eyes.

"Water?" He showed her the Clorox jug. "You need to drink."

He knew she could speak. *You couldn't stay away.* She merely watched him.

"I'm Hugh."

Nothing.

"Cuba." He spoke her name.

Her face pinched with rage and fear and plain hunger.

He took a step higher. Lashed to the wall, weighed down with the body, sapped by a week of hardship, she was harmless. And yet she scared him. He doubted she still recognized the rag doll in her arms as human anymore, and he was probably just one more hallucination rising to her from the depths. Even out of her mind, though, she was all sinew and willpower.

With fresh eyes, aware this time of her ordeal, Hugh appraised the bizarre anchor. She must have made it after the fall, not before. While she was still sane, Cuba had locked herself into protective custody. Before the shell shock set in, she'd nailed and jammed everything in her possession into the wall to make herself safe from who she was about to become.

It was a miracle that, in her days of delirium, she hadn't chewed through the ropes and dived into the hereafter. But she'd held it together. She wasn't completely gone or she'd be gone.

He started the soothing patter one might offer a stray dog. "You're safe now, Cuba. Everything's pulling together. I'll take care of you." He left Augustine out of the equation. "How about some water?"

It had been summery up here when disaster had struck. He remembered that afternoon. He'd been portering this very jug of water along the forest floor, and it had been chilly in the shadows. But here in the Eye, the sun had been warm. They were dressed for the beach. Andie was wearing a little tie-dyed tank top. Cuba wore nothing more than a sports bra and white tights. A lingerie lace pattern ran along the outside of her thigh. Her bare shoulders and arms and rib cage were laced with old rope burns and yellowing bruises.

Hugh went another rung higher. She didn't reach for the water, and he wouldn't have handed it to her anyway. She wasn't in her right mind and might have pitched it overboard. That aside, she needed taming.

With broad, slow motions so that she could see, he unscrewed the cap. He poured a bit into the taped cup of his palm, just to let her get the scent. Her eyes darted to the water.

He set one knee on the platform.

The water drained through his fingers. She scowled at the waste. Good, he thought. She saw gain. She saw loss. All in his hands.

He got his other knee up. The platform moved.

"I've come a long way to help you," he said. He raised the Clorox jug, and her eyes followed it. She craned her head back.

"Open," he said. He trickled a few teaspoons into her mouth. Her tongue reached for it. She moaned.

He knew from the desert the sweet purity of that first taste. He hadn't suffered nearly as long as Cuba, only a night and two days. But on one level, survival was its own bottom line. You outlived the ones who died, that's all. He gave her a little more.

"Take your time," he said. "I have all you want, Cuba. I'm a friend."

He heard a scratch of radio static through the

floor, Augustine making the call. Cuba appeared oblivious to it.

"Hugh," she whispered.

He rewarded her with an ounce of water across her forehead. "Cuba," he said, as if christening her.

Her eyes rolled back with ecstasy. He remembered the dunes. The white sun had burned him half black. The cool water had steamed on his flesh.

He slid the water out like fingers, and then traded his fingers for the water. He touched her face. She didn't startle or pull away, just the opposite. She pressed her cheek into his hand. "Hugh."

It was cramped kneeling by her, and the death smell was horrendous. But now he had contact. She opened her mouth, and he doled out more sips. All the while, he talked.

They had one thing in common. He spoke to that. "Trojan Women," he said. "You climbed like saints, Cuba. Like the last of the holy men. Women. No fear of God. Do you understand? You've done something for the ages here. I go back a long ways. I was a wall rat before you were even born, and trust me, I've never seen such a thing. You created a masterpiece here. I mean it. The Captain saved the best for last." He went on like that, plundering Lewis and his road rap, laying it on.

"Was that you who led the way into Cyclops Eye?"

She nodded.

"Unbelievable."

She smiled. Pearls of blood beaded up on her

cracked lips. With a lick, it turned to red lipstick. He bathed her eyes with water. He whispered her praises while she drank in invalid doses.

"I followed your chalk marks. It was like having a vision, Cuba. It nearly killed me. I got lost, and my only hope was to think your thoughts. I never could have found the way without you. You led me right to you."

"Yes," she whispered. "I brought you to me."

He washed away her ferocity. "Can you eat? You should eat." He couldn't have stomached a thing with this stench and that terrible, sightless head between them. But she accepted pieces of a chocolate-flavored protein bar, shuddering as the sugar hit.

He wiped the soot from her eyebrows and doe-like forehead and temples. Twenty-something, he decided. After Augustine's witch talk, he'd expected a sun hag, leathery, wrinkled before her time, gaunt from running with the wolves. Basically another Joshua. But she was not berserk or furrowed beneath the grime. As he washed away the bloodshot, her eyes became bright green. Her flesh was ripe.

She followed his face. "Your eyes," she said.

His black-and-blue eyes, and his bloody whiskers, and his smoke-stained flesh. He swiped at his chin, self-conscious. "I'm not always so ugly."

"I'll keep you," she said.

They murmured back and forth. She nestled in his palm. They could have been lovers, exhausted by each other.

He took his time. Her grip on the corpse relaxed. The fire in her eyes faded. The tranquilizer was kicking in.

He laid her head back against the wall. Weary as she was, her eyes stayed locked on his. He stroked her smoky hair.

"Hugh Glass," she said.

He thought back through his words, and not once had he mentioned his last name. "How did you know?"

She smiled. Mona Lisa with rope burns and a shag cut.

Augustine's voice rose through the floor. He was arguing over the radio . . . again. "That doesn't matter," he was saying. "Work it out. Talk to them. Get us now."

Hugh tried to listen, but Cuba craved attention. She drew him to her with a whisper. "Don't leave me alone," she said.

Poor thing. "You're going home," he told her. "People are waiting for you. They have a team up top. The litter will come. It's going to be a cruise from here. Lie back, enjoy the ride. We're almost home."

That light flickered in her eyes again, the tiger tiger burning bright. She shook her head slowly, knowingly. "It's not that easy, Hugh."

He thought she was objecting on principle. Another five hundred feet and she and her sisters would have finished their climb. Now all was for nothing, halted by the fall. Even their grand title, Trojan Women, would get buried and forgotten. Because by tradition, the naming belonged to the party that finally forced the whole passage, and the parties were no doubt assembling already.

By this time, with the forest fire as a sideshow, the route would be legend. News of the accident would have shot through the community. Trojan Women, or whatever it would come to be called, was now a certified people eater, and that made it a serious prize. The fact was that after *Into Thin Air* was published, the price of a guided Everest climb had actually gone up.

"We can't leave just like that," she whispered.

"I'm sorry," he said. "But we can't stay either."

The string of prayer flags stirred. Hugh glanced out from the platform. Little eddies appeared in the smoke. He felt a soft breeze.

"It's not over." She spoke it like an omen.

"It is," he said. "You can always come back. It will still be here next season." What the rangers had told him. But it was a lie, and he knew it.

Hugh could imagine the big-wall bravos—hard men like Augustine, and long ago, himself and Lewis—phoning and emailing each other, laying plans for an immediate assault on this wall even before the dead and wounded were carried off. Ascent was like that, fundamentally Darwinian. That had always appealed to Hugh. The fittest survived. Conquest ruled. It was a meritocracy of flesh and blood in a kingdom of stone. In this case, though, he regretted Cuba's loss. She and her friends had forged the way. They deserved better than to be a footnote in someone else's history of their own climb.

"We called for you," she said. "You came."

Her eyes were getting dopey, but she still wielded that dominion Augustine hated so much. It was ingrained, her magical theater. She had presence and grit. Hugh liked that.

"Here I am." He smiled. Then he recollected a whisper in the trees around the girl's body. And the next morning that song in the stone too soft to really hear, calling him into the heights. And higher upon the wall, more than once, his name surfacing in the middle of the night. It was almost as if someone *had* been calling.

Her eyes sobered. She was fighting the drug. "I didn't bring you here for nothing," she told him.

He stroked her hair. "You said it yourself, Cuba. I couldn't stay away."

She smiled her blood-bead smile and murmured something. He put his ear closer, certain he hadn't heard right. It was an endearment, surely.

"What was that?"

She spoke again, and it was almost loving. "You fucked up, Hugh Glass."

He jerked his head away. They were back to square one, the two of them. Him the master, her the savage femme lodged in her world of ghosts.

"You don't have to fight me, Cuba. You're saved. Believe me."

"She talks to me, you know," she said.

Hugh looked at Cuba's sole possession, her one companion, this lifeless weight. Her embrace with Andie had become a plague. Literally, she was carrying death upon her. This wild child was going to need therapy for years to come. "Don't worry, Cuba. She's going with us, too."

Her face muscled up. The fear made her ugly for a minute. "She doesn't need us for that. She comes and goes as she pleases." Alive, thought Hugh, then dead, her imaginary companion. Dangling on a rope, now sprawled across her lap.

Augustine spoke to his radio. "After? But that could be days. This *is* an emergency. We need it now. Today." There was a pause, and he said, "But there must be someone."

Hugh had a sinking feeling. He started to ask what was happening. But Cuba suddenly grabbed his hand. It surprised him.

She reminded him of Rachel in the bar that night, reading his lifeline. But there was no softness here, no flirtation. The muse's grip was primal. Her hand was battered and calloused and hard as a hoof. With a jolt, he saw that she had epoxy-glued three torn fingernails back into place sometime during her climb. Nothing stopped her. This woman was a force of nature.

Then he saw the fresh cuts in her palm, and it hit him. Here was the answer to their mystery. Here was the explanation for a dead woman's ascent.

Wasted and dying, Cuba had somehow summoned the strength to pull up the rope holding Andie's body. The forest fire must have spurred her to action. She could have left the corpse dangling far below, out of sight, out of mind. Instead, with her bare hands, Cuba had saved her friend from that floor of fire.

"You've done all you could for her, Cuba."

"It's a big sacrifice."

"You've sacrificed enough."

"We're all part of it. The whole thing's arranged. Like a wedding banquet."

"I understand." Whatever she was talking about.

"You don't." Her whisper went on like rust flakes falling. "She kept me alive for a reason."

Yes, thought Hugh, and what a grisly trade-off it was. The corpse had kept her alive; she had kept the corpse alive. They had talked each other through the long nightmare. Now the nightmare was over. "I'll take care of her, Cuba. She just wants to go home."

"Too late for that. Way too late."

"We're almost there. A little more."

"She borrows me," Cuba confided.

That stumped him. "Andie?" he said.

"Her, too. And Cass. We're all just borrowed. We didn't ask to be part of it."

He didn't want to encourage her nonsense, but he had to ask. "Borrowed for what?"

"Her pound of flesh."

Hugh frowned. He heard Augustine fall silent underneath them. She was still locked on Cerro Torre, still battling Augustine for possession of this battered husk of a woman.

"You have to let go of that," he told her. "It's over."

"Tell her yourself."

"I'm telling you, Cuba. You're the one who hears her."

"We didn't ask to be part of this," she said.

"Then let it go."

"You don't believe in sin?"

Augustine muttered something. Hugh felt squeezed between them. He was caught in the middle, but someone had to finish this business or they would fall to pieces.

"I believe in survival." He spoke it loudly for Augustine's benefit, and to halt her rambling. "That's what this is all about. Survival."

She smiled at his ignorance.

"It's time to sleep," he said.

"Come closer, Hugh."

The breeze surfaced again, much stronger this time, a cold breeze. He thought she was running her fingers through his hair, but she wasn't. The cotton flags snapped briskly, scattering prayers.

"Don't leave me." Her eyes were glazing over.

"I'm not going anywhere."

"Promise."

"I do."

"I can't be alone," she whispered.

"I'm right here with you."

"You don't know what it's like."

They were getting nowhere with this. She was nodding off, but not fast enough. And the sweet nothings were a fraud. He wanted forward momentum. Closure. Exit.

"I brought a sleeping bag for her." He unzipped the bag and laid it lengthwise on the platform.

"She doesn't sleep." A murmur.

"She needs to rest, Cuba. Let's do this together. Help me."

She allowed him to roll the body from her lap onto the opened bag. The platform rustled with the shifting weight. Guy lines and aluminum tubes squeaked. The flags beat back and forth. Below, at the tail end of their wreckage, the platform with the ripped floor skittered in the breeze.

In climbing, you live with a constant symphony of groaning pack straps and ropes bullwhipping and slings under stress, small notes to go with the rough and tumble of waterfalls and avalanches and geological violence. But up here, under this bottomless alcove, even the tiny squeaks and squeals sounded like a machine about to fly into pieces.

As Hugh moved the body from Cuba's legs, he was startled to find a bright, wet fan of blood across her lap. His first thought was that the body must have bled onto her. But except for the broken neck, Andie showed no wounds.

Which left Cuba. The blood could only be coming from her. Had she ruptured something, or been gored by the spiky rock? She seemed not to notice the wound, wherever it was, and he didn't point it out. One thing at a time. The platform was too crowded. Separate the dead from the living. Go from there.

Hugh zipped the bag shut. It was his sleeping bag, a Marmot, extra long. He'd bought it new in a Sherpa trek shop in Katmandu, on sight, no haggling. It was big and full, with extra inches to cover his head during cold nights. After this, he'd never use it again. Cuba wanted sacrifice. Here it was, his treasure of warmth.

The sleeping bag swallowed Andie's slight body with room to spare, even with her long, stretched neck. He zipped it shut and crisscrossed a rope under and around the length of the bag, tying off the sorry sight and much of the smell. When he was done, it made a slender package.

"Everything will be better now," he said.

The tranquilizer took over. After a week of demons, Cuba finally got her first real mercy. She slumped in her cobweb of ropes and slings. Her face softened. Behind that harpy mask lay a girl in a dream too big to be true.

TWENTY-FIVE

"It's done," Hugh announced.

"You got her?" Augustine said. His fingers appeared along the border.

It was Hugh's border. That was what the rim of the platform had become for him, a boundary line. He required the separation. A little at a time, like it or not, this was becoming his territory. On this flat rectangle, he was creating an outpost of sanity and order. Beyond its perimeter hung the ruins and chaos and nothingness.

Augustine's eyes surfaced at the far edge. It was safe for him now. The horror was sewn from sight. He rose higher.

"When does the litter arrive?" Hugh asked.

"They're getting back to us on that."

He'd heard Augustine arguing on the radio. It wasn't hard to guess the concern. The sky was in motion.

Gusts of breeze were stirring vortexes in the smoke. As fast as they appeared, the vortexes flattened out from west to east, the direction of the wind, like riptides in the void. High above their sea of smog, clouds were building and blocking the sun. That explained the premature darkness. A storm was coming. What next, thought Hugh, frogs and famine?

"So you have the radio on," Hugh said, knowing otherwise.

"I'm saving the juice."

"How can they get back to us then?"

"We'll get back to them."

"Did you tell them we have a survivor?"

Augustine didn't respond.

Hugh pressed. "They're not coming, is that what I'm hearing?"

Augustine touched the cocoon holding Andie.

Sharply now. "Damn it, stay with me. We have to get out of here."

Augustine jerked. "They said to wait."

"We can't wait. She's bleeding," Hugh said.

Augustine pushed Cuba's legs apart. He smelled. "Menstrual blood. She's having her period." He wiped his fingers on her pants.

Hugh felt foolish. Suddenly, among all the primitive smells—the wood smoke, the body odors, the smell of this granite cathedral—the scent of Cuba's ripeness was potent, practically a lure to him.

"See what I mean about her?" Augustine pointed at the woman's wrists.

Hugh had seen the tattoos, but not asked Cuba about them. They ran down across the back of her hand to the middle finger, like the henna patterns Annie had learned from her Arab dancers.

"Celtic slave bracelets," Augustine said. "Like she was the priestess of the woods."

Augustine's eyes strayed back to Andie. She mesmerized him. Hugh was tempted to dump the body overboard. Clear the man's mind. But then he might dive after the corpse, radio and all.

"The weather's changing," Hugh said. "Something's going on out there."

"It's the front's rolling in," Augustine said. Like it was old news.

"I thought we were working together," Hugh said.

"Absolutely."

"What fucking front, then?"

"You were there. I thought you heard."

During the radio communication yesterday, Augustine had argued with his chief about something. Now Hugh realized they had been warning Augustine to retreat. "What have you gotten us into?" he demanded.

"It's a delay, that's all. And we couldn't ask for a better place. We have a roof over our heads. We'll be out of the rain. Then they'll come for us." His eyes went back to Andie.

Hugh trimmed his emotions. Just the facts. He reasoned it out. The coming storm was big enough to show on their Doppler screen, big enough that

Augustine had known to keep it secret. They should have rapped off, not pressed on. Now the rescue team on the summit was balking. Things were getting epic.

"When are they coming?" Hugh asked.

"Probably not tomorrow."

A big mother, Hugh guessed.

Suddenly he couldn't bear the thought of one more night on El Cap, especially not in this dismal cul-de-sac. There were no reference points in here, no sky, no high noon, no north. And no retreat. Even if their bridge of ropes back to the Ark was still in one piece, they didn't have a prayer of getting down, not with Cuba tranquilized and the body to lower and Augustine half out of it. The Eye was closing in around them.

"Is the team still on top?" asked Hugh.

"They were."

"Give me that radio."

"I told you what they said."

"You told me what you wanted. You put me on the sharp end and kept me climbing, and now there's trouble rolling in." Hugh tilted the cocoon partway off the edge. He let the rope slip an inch.

Augustine croaked his alarm. "Careful."

"The radio," said Hugh. Ransoming a corpse, the dead for the living. He let the rope slip a few inches more. He hated this, the lowness of it, bargaining with one lost soul over another in this open graveyard. But they were at war now, with each other, with time, with the elements.

"All right," Augustine said. "Just . . . easy with her." He ducked from view.

"First item," Hugh instructed him, thinking out loud, "pass up the med kit." The last thing he needed to worry about was Augustine's arsenal of needles pricking through the floor. "And the haul bag, too." Now was the time to raid the larder. Once he surrendered the body, there would be no more bargaining chips.

Without a word, Augustine handed him the med kit, and the haul bag, and the radio. Hugh never even saw his hand. The supplies and gear came to him like salvage bobbing up in a fog.

"Now take her." Hugh lowered the body quickly, eager to keep Augustine down below, at bay. Crowded by the haul bag, pressed against Cuba, he was in no mood for more company.

Andie weighed little more than a child in the Gore-Tex shroud. Hugh paid out rope until the line went slack. Augustine took possession of her.

Hugh switched on the radio. The dispatcher was right there. When he identified himself, she sounded relieved it was him, not Augustine.

"We need an evacuation today," Hugh said.

"I hear you, Hugh." She was calm. She used his name the way he'd used Cuba's, as a sedative. They were afraid he was on the edge of losing it, too.

Fine, he thought, let them be afraid.

"There's a major weather system heading our way," she said. "You need to dig in, Hugh. You can do that, can't you?" As if he were a child.

"You want her to die?" he said.

That changed her tune. As he'd suspected, Augustine had said nothing about Cuba's survival. The dispatcher started over. "Report your situation, please."

"We have one injured survivor," Hugh said. "We have one dead. Plus Augustine." He let that final implication hang in the air.

"Say again, Hugh, you have a survivor?"

"Her name is Cuba," Hugh said. "She's alive, but bleeding and unconscious." He didn't share that the blood was menses nor describe Augustine's sneak attack with the Haldol. Let them think the worst. Whatever it took to get them down here. "She may have other injuries. I haven't assessed her yet. She's still fouled in the ropes. Before they fell, the women made a hanging bivvy, but it's mostly destroyed."

"Hold please. Don't go anywhere, Hugh."

He heard shouting in the background. As he'd hoped, the news was galvanizing a second judgment.

"Where is the blood coming from, Hugh?"

"I can't tell. Her groin area." He added, "Something abdominal." He knew from Lewis that emergency workers' worst dread was the word "abdominal."

"Did Augustine get Cuba's vital signs?"

"No. Negative. He's . . ." Hugh searched for a neutral word, something besides shock or breakdown. Because Augustine was down there, listening.

"Stressed?" the dispatcher suggested.

They knew. They'd been tracking Augustine for days. "Profoundly," Hugh said.

"Loud and clear, Hugh. The summit crew is discussing options. Please hold."

"There's only one option," Hugh said. He put a hint of panic in his voice.

"Understood, Hugh. Can you get a pulse for me?"

"I don't have a watch."

"Do you know how to take a blood pressure reading?"

He did. And the stethoscope and blood pressure cuffs were right there in the med kit. But Hugh didn't make a move for them. All in all, Cuba looked pretty strong, considering her ordeal. And the whole idea was to keep the gun at their head.

"We need a ride out of here," he repeated.

"You're doing fine, Hugh." She was buying time. He was the proverbial passenger in the cockpit. They were trying to figure out how to land him safely. "Is her airway clear?"

"Yes."

"Has the bleeding stopped?"

"I can't tell."

Another voice broke in, deep and male. He introduced himself as the operations chief in charge of staging the actual rescue. Hugh's hopes rose.

"We've been listening in," he said. "Here's the deal. It's going on night. The storm is a concern. Our rescue team has broken down the summit anchor and they're halfway back to the valley floor.

I know you're in trouble. But I want you to take a deep breath. Assess your situation. Can you stabilize the victim? Can you weatherproof your camp? Can you outlast the storm?"

"How long are we talking?"

"I won't shit you. It could be two days before we reach you. It could be three."

"What about a helicopter?" Hugh asked.

"In this soup? We've got zero visibility. The good news is, the storm will clear the smoke. The bad news is, they can't fly in a storm. That makes this a land operation. It puts my people at risk. Do you understand? I need to know, can you wait?"

Hugh understood perfectly well. They wanted him to gut it out. Under different circumstances, he would have bunkered in without a qualm. But in fact he felt real danger here. It was more than all the weirdness hounding the climb. The Eye really did have bad juju. El Cap had them in its iron sights. He'd never sensed it so acutely on any wall or mountain. He was being watched.

"Negative," he said. "We're a sinking ship."

There was silence. Static. He knew they weren't going to John Wayne a rescue. Nobody was going to commit suicide getting here. They had a window, and it wasn't closed yet, or else they wouldn't be on the radio with him asking him if he could or could not hang tough.

The voice returned. "We've got a volunteer to descend with the litter. The team is on its way back to the summit. This will require some prep time.

Keep your radio on. We will be advising you during the operation." He signed off.

Hugh holstered the radio in a chest harness and clipped it to the wall. "They're coming for us," he said to Augustine. There was no response. All Hugh heard below were broken aluminum tubes piping in the wind.

He glanced over the edge, and it was like peeking over the wall of an asylum. Augustine was weaving a long nest of rope to bind Andie's body to the wall. He looked like a spider clambering back and forth, quietly placing cams and nuts and tying knots everywhere.

A chill shot through Hugh. This was Cuba's same paranoia in action. The man was duplicating her mindless anchor. He was bracing for monsters.

"Did you hear me?" Hugh said to him. "They're coming."

Augustine barely glanced up. "It's getting windy," he said, and went back to work.

TWENTY-SIX

Now that their rescue was under way, Hugh acted as if it wasn't. The litter might arrive in a few hours or another week. Anything could go wrong.

He was cautious to the point of superstition about such things. There was a mountain adage about old climbers, and bold climbers, but no old, bold climbers. No matter where he went in the world, Hugh made it a habit to plot ahead and calculate the risks versus the rewards, and to never rely on others. Know where your water is, that was one of his rules. Expect the worst. That was the morality of survival.

The storm would strike from behind the summit, like the infamous *foehns* that ambush the Eiger *nordwand*. Even if it passed swiftly, the storm could kill them if they weren't prepared. He had much to do, and quickly.

In theory, the camp was a mere transit station, to be jettisoned once the rescuers swooped down. Many climbers would have waited idly, counting down the seconds. Not Hugh. Their house, their fortress—this flimsy craft of tubes and fabric—was not in order. Cuba's platform was tipped down at the far corner. For all the mad zigzag of webbing and ropes, her anchor looked threadbare. Carabiners had jawed open. Protection had wiggled from cracks. Knots practically worked loose before his eyes.

The chaos was both a threat to them and an affront to his pride. The tangled mess would reflect upon him directly. Search-and-rescue types always looked for cause and effect. They homed in on the tiniest details, the untied shoelace, the untucked shirttail, any slight sign of the victim's disintegration . . . and he was not a victim. Let them judge—and they would—Augustine by the wreckage below. At least they would find Hugh's territory trim and well governed.

He let Cuba doze among her lattice of slings. Later he would take her blood pressure and write it in ink on her wrist, above the Celtic slave bracelet tattoo. For now, sitting upright, her breathing was even and she was in little danger of aspirating if she vomited. She could be stored to the side while he secured their haven.

He began with himself, checking his knots, and worked from there. He drove pitons at each corner that touched the wall, and resized the guy lines, leveling the floor. Where the lacing between the fabric and aluminum tubes had frayed, he made swift stitches with pieces of cord. He pulled the remains of the broken platform from below—right past Augustine, who was still hurrying back and forth—and cannibalized its parts. He cut the nylon floor free of the snapped side poles, and draped the membrane over the guy lines to make a three-sided lean-to, with the wall as their fourth side.

As Hugh finished closing himself in with Cuba, the blue light faded. The wind reached under the Eye's deep roof and found their hiding place. The skeleton of the third platform lofted out from the wall like a kite. Up and out it floated on its tether of rope, spinning and trilling through its hollow tubes, before clattering back against the wall. The floor of Hugh's platform bellied up and sucked down.

The temperature was dropping fast. Hugh dug through the haul bag, pulling out everything from sweaters to a pair of clean socks and a plastic poop tube. The pile held Lewis's protein bars, foil packets of Charlie the tuna, and even—wrapped in an Ace bandage—Joshua's flint knife.

He divided the goods. He layered on a turtleneck and sweater and parka, and placed a portion of food, water, and his private possessions in a stuff sack that he attached to the wall. Augustine's sleeping bag he confiscated for Cuba. Whatever was left, he scooped into the empty haul bag. He opened one corner of the makeshift tent.

"Augustine," he yelled. He poked his head outside.

The smoke was gone, completely swept away. The air was cold and fresh and clean. With more light, Hugh could have made out details of the burned forest. Across the valley, dim spires stood like headstones. It was impossible to see the sky for the black roof of the Eye.

Fifteen feet below, Augustine had finally come to rest. He sat among the ropes holding the body. He looked freezing, dressed in nothing but a white T-shirt and canvas shorts. He didn't seem aware of any presence but Andie's.

Hugh dangled the haul bag down to him. "Get warm," he yelled over the wind. "Layer up. Hat. Gloves. Socks over the gloves. Put your legs in the haul bag. Drink. Eat. Have your headlamp ready." It was baby talk, and Augustine was the professional. But he merely looked reminded.

Hugh watched until he took firm possession of the haul bag, then laced the tent shut again, just as glad Augustine was rooted in place where he was. There was no vacancy up here. Snapping on his headlamp, he turned to Cuba.

She was deeply asleep. He tried slipping the ropes and slings up and over her head and limbs, but she had knitted herself tight. He opened his Swiss Army knife and tried to lock-pick her knots. But what had not fallen to pieces was suddenly seized as tight as fossils.

He began cutting through to her with the

rough-and-ready precision of a field surgeon. Mindful that if he sliced the wrong rope, the whole anchor might come unraveled, he felt for tensioned lines and tried to trace pink rope and lime green rope and rope checkered like rattlesnake skin. If there was a logic binding it all together, he couldn't see it.

Starting at her waist, he moved up across her small rib cage. He lifted her bruised arms, and slit the ropes across her shoulders. His hands cast shadows, making it hard to place the blade.

He straddled her, and made more cuts, and suddenly noticed bright drops of blood speckling her arms. It was on the back of his taped hands, too. And her forehead, like beads of sweat. He drew back the knife, certain he'd cut her.

Another drop fell. He dabbed at his nostrils, and the blood was coming from him. He wiped her forehead with his sweater sleeve, and hurried to finish the job.

With a final cut, she slumped onto him, heavier than he'd expected. Her head lolled, and in catching it to his shoulder, he nearly jabbed his eye with the knife. The blade flashed. He dropped the knife. It bounced on the floor and fell through the lacing and was gone. He no longer needed it. But the blunder, however small, reminded him that the void lurked in constant wait.

Awkwardly, half-falling with her in his arms, Hugh laid the young woman on the open sleeping bag. He felt her breasts sliding against his chest, and smelled her animal breath. It unsettled him. In the midst of everything else, it surprised him that he even noticed. The wind was mounting, the temperature dropping. She was just so much baggage to be stowed. And yet she made him pause.

Move by move, he had chased her image up the stone and through the smoke, and finally caught her. For the moment, asleep and in his care, this barbarian princess belonged to him.

He had grown up schooled in Samaritan acts. There had been the Boy Scouts, and church projects, and the widow lady's sidewalk next door to shovel and her lawn to mow. Once a month, Hugh's mother had bundled him off to the soup kitchen on Larimer Street to feed the drunks and whores. He had learned to give to beggars, to pull over for hitchhikers, to stop at accidents.

It had taken him years to purge the impulse. It was Annie's descent into Alzheimer's that had really taught him the limits of giving yourself away. The world was a famished place. Beyond a point, you simply starved yourself for the suffering that never ended. The best you could do was snatch what shelter you found, like this bottomless cave, and then climb on.

His tiredness hit him all at once. He needed warmth and sleep and a respite, just a few moments of peace, from fighting gravity. The wind was driving harder. Night was on. The rescue seemed less likely by the minute. Sliding his legs into the sleeping bag, he folded Cuba against him, and turned off his headlamp.

It was only to keep her warm, he told himself. But it was more than that. The smoke was like musk in her hair, and the even rise of her rib cage against his chest was practically a forbidden fruit. Finally he'd outrun his gauntlet of nightmare women. He could rest. All he wanted was to lie still, and hold her, and ride out the wind. He pulled her tighter.

His eyes closed.

When the radio squawked, he woke confused, in a black cage under assault. He flipped on the light, driving thoughts into place. The platform was shuddering in the wind. The tent walls were sucking in and out like a lung. Cuba lay in his arms.

A second squelch stung him to action. A voice said, "Talk to me."

Hugh wrestled from the sleeping bag and reached for the radio. "I'm here," he said. "We're here. Do you read?"

". . . thought we'd lost you." Hugh could barely hear the voice over the hurricane roar up top. He strained to hear the update. The team had mustered again at the summit rim.

"Say again," he said, "say again."

"We have our mark," the chief yelled. ". . . still assembling the system . . . Cuba's condition?"

"Unchanged," Hugh said. "She's still unconscious."

". . . stabilized. Prepare to . . ." The radio drowned out.

"Say again."

". . . throw line."

They were coming. They needed him to catch their throw line.

"Affirmative," Hugh said. "We're ready. How long before the litter comes?"

The radio went static. Then it came alive again with another voice. "Hang tight, Harp," it boomed. "The cavalry's on the way."

"Lewis?" His voice made no sense. Then Hugh understood, or thought he did. Lewis must have gone to ranger headquarters to catch the latest, and they'd tapped him for communication.

"You picked some fine fucking weather," Lewis said.

"It's almost over," Hugh assured him.

"Not until the fat lady sings it ain't. Listen for me, brother. Be ready . . . buy me a steak."

The reality hit Hugh. "You're the volunteer?"

Wind roar snarled the radio. ". . . you poor, sorry stick people. Somebody's got to."

Hugh couldn't fathom it. "What are you doing, Lewis?"

Lewis must have crouched against the wind. His voice suddenly came through clearly. "Rachel was waiting for me, Hugh. She changed her mind, don't ask me why. Something you did, or something I didn't do, I don't know. We're going to make it work. I get my happy ending."

"Tonight?" Hugh was trying to catch up with it all, the little circles spinning into bigger circles. He'd jilted Rachel, and now she'd taken Lewis back, and here was Lewis preparing to descend.

"We laid pipe for hours," Lewis crowed. "She's back. You saved my life, man."

This changed everything. It was Lewis casting himself into the maw, not some nameless stranger. Hugh scanned around him, suddenly alarmed. Cuba was traumatized, and hungry and dehydrated. But they had water and food for her, and Hugh could nurse her. Dying? Hardly. She was young. Already she looked stronger.

"Don't do this, Lewis." He had lied to get the rescuers off the dime. Now he heard the force of the storm and understood their fear, and it was Lewis at risk.

"I've got no choice, mate. Rachel said it, too. This one's for Annie."

The tent walls snapped in and out, faster. The platform shook. It was getting mean out there.

Hugh hit the transmit trigger. "I was wrong," he said. "She's not injured. She's asleep. We drugged her. Everything's under control. We can make it through. Do not come down at this time. Repeat, do not come. Abort the rescue. Do you read me?"

They did not.

Lewis, being Lewis, had gone right on speaking over him. ". . . so, Hugh, you holy bastard, what do you say, will we be better men after . . ."

"Abort," Hugh repeated.

But at that instant, just as Augustine had feared all along, the battery died. Hugh clapped the trigger and stared at the radio in disbelief. Whatever he had set in motion was coming to be.

TWENTY-SEVEN

Their little raft chopped up and down on the surge of wind. Crouched against the stone, with one arm looped through the anchor ropes, Hugh pried open the radio and tucked the battery against his stomach to warm it. In the Himalayas, they slept with their radios to keep them from freezing. This battery was shot, though.

He shook the radio and banged it on the rock like a monkey. Too late, he thought. Too late. Lewis was sinking through the maelstrom, and there was nothing Hugh could do about it.

He fumbled with the tent lacing and thrust his head out to alert Augustine. The sight below stopped him cold. In the beam of Hugh's headlamp, Augustine seemed to be sailing off into the blackness with his dead lover.

Bundled in a parka and wearing a Peruvian

wool cap, with clean white socks on each hand, he had pulled the empty haul bag over his legs, and woven himself sidelong into the ropes with the body. The hammocks were apparently useless to him. But with the waste-not mentality of a climber, he'd clipped them to his anchor, and now the hammocks bulged and whipped about like spinnakers in a tempest.

Hugh wagged his headlamp from side to side, shouting, but Augustine never noticed. He went on riding his skiff of ropes, running with the storm, going nowhere. Maybe in his mind they were heading for day, or he was simply charting a course through the pitch-black valley.

Hugh pulled his head back inside, exhausted by the madness. He sagged against the rock, with Cuba under his knees, and tried to assess his own welfare. He was sleep deprived and hungry and thirsty. His hands ached, and his throat felt skinned from coughing up the smoke in his lungs. The wind was deafening.

He had climbed high and fought hard, and overcome every trial and tribulation El Cap had thrown at him. He had found reasons for things that defied reason. He had justified the disembodied whispers and midnight banshees and the unraveling knots, and escaped Joshua's murder attempt and outlived the fire. He had placed each odd egg in its own box, and stored it away as accidental or imaginary, and then gone on pretending the walls were just offering their normal fare.

But there was no denying the obvious anymore. At last he had to admit the climb really was cursed. No one had this much bad luck. Something—some outer purpose—was hunting them. Each event, large and small, from the women's disaster to the pitons creeping out of their sockets, from whiffs of breeze to the fire and this storm, all were part of some deep, violent design. He could not fathom why it was happening, unless Lewis was right and it was punishment for the hubris of Trojan Women, or Cuba was right and it was an eye for an eye for whatever Augustine had committed on Cerro Torre.

Even as he thought these things, Hugh worried about his own sanity. A conspiracy of nature? A feral consciousness? It wasn't rational. Suddenly he was thankful Lewis was braving the night. Because Hugh's only hope was to flee before he got swallowed whole.

Abruptly the red tent burst into light.

One minute, Hugh was crouched with his headlamp in the nylon lean-to, dissecting the arabesque of misfortunes. The next he was blinded and groping for slings. His first thought was that something had exploded, or that he'd fallen into a deep sleep and the storm and the night had magically passed.

But this sun was too bright. Lit from below, it was as if he and Cuba were suspended on a membrane of pure color. White beams stabbed through every gap in the platform.

Then a gigantic bird—or an angel, or a devil—cast its shadow on the tent wall. Just as quickly it swept away. It tore off into the maelstrom. Or he'd imagined it, which was entirely possible. He was trying so hard to keep the reins tight on the Captain. But when you mess with gravity, things get loose.

He faced the brilliant red screen, wondering what other phantoms El Cap would throw at him. It was as if the girl's fall had cracked open the earth and unleashed a flood of spirits. One after another, the climbers around him had fallen prey to a quiet mass hysteria. Now was his turn, so it seemed.

The black shadow dived at his wall again. It was huge. And then it was small, and then huge again. It bounded in the wind, reaching for him, then swimming away, a crazy concoction of outstretched wings, dangling legs, and arms with hands and fingers. Its head was a rounded bullet. No little horns, at least, Hugh thought. No spiked tail.

Then he saw the marionette strings from above. It was Lewis out there. They had placed their big SAR spotlight down in the meadow.

Hugh shoved his head through the opening. Instantly the wind and naked light mugged him. He shielded his eyes and peered through his fingers. The scene was unearthly.

What had been a murky crater in the wall was now a scoop of light. The band of diorite stood starkly black against the white granite. Every spur and spike cast a razor shadow. Every freckle of mica sparkled. The prayer flags, lit from behind, flailed in a blur of colors. A good night for wind horses and prayers, Hugh thought.

Thirty feet out, beyond the crest of the over-hanging roof, Lewis and the litter—his metal wings—dangled by threads. He was next to helpless, tethered upright to the edge of a long, narrow craft made of metal ribs and chicken wire. Tossed every which way, he looked battered and disheveled, like a man in need of rescue himself.

Hugh crawled from the tent and wrestled his feet into stirrups that were blowing sideways. He inched his jumars down the rope to where Lewis could better see him, and Hugh could catch the throw line.

Lewis started to wave to Hugh, but the wind twisted him face out to the void, then back to the wall, then off to the east. Looking over one shoulder, then the other, he spun like a moth crazed by the light. At each edge of the spotlight beam, he vanished into blackness. It made Hugh sick just watching.

For all the abuse he was taking, Lewis looked gloriously happy. When he could be seen, he was luminous, like a Greek god or a Hollywood hero. His shoulders were a mile wide. Someone had loaned him a helmet with a bulls-eye painted on top. He was daring the heavens. Here was his arena.

Lewis shouted something to Hugh, but the storm ripped his words away. He lifted his radio and held it to his ear. Hugh signaled back with a slash at his throat. His radio was dead. Lewis understood.

Pumping his legs and shoving at the litter, Lewis struggled to correct for the wind. Finally, realizing there was no controlling the hurly-burly tide, he quit swimming and went with the flow. He got down to business.

The throw line was as simple as it got. A bean-bag weighted one end of a long, thin cord. All you needed was a good arm, and a good catcher.

Lewis's very first cast was nearly perfect. Just as the wind thrust at the Eye, he hurled the beanbag and it struck Hugh square on the foot. Hugh dove head down, but the beanbag was already gone. Off to one side in his cradle of ropes, Augustine did not even reach for it. The throw line arced off into the darkness.

On his next throw, the beanbag snarled in its own rat's nest of cord and fell short. The next ten minutes went to Lewis untangling the mess.

Hugh used the time to descend to a better position. He paused by Augustine. In the hard light, his face looked boiled blue by the smoke and cold and wind.

"Help me," Hugh shouted. "It's almost over. Just this little bit more."

"We made a mistake," Augustine said. The wind was poisoning him. He'd returned to Cerro Torre all over again. He was trapped with the dead and dying.

Hugh tried to rally him. "We're going home. Together. No one gets left behind."

Augustine shook his head no. Hugh had to bend close to hear. "Too late."

Hugh pulled at him. "Get up."

"She sucked us in. It's part of her plan. An eye for an eye." Echoes of Cuba.

Hugh's eyes darted to the roped shroud dangling from the anchor. Augustine wasn't talking about Cuba. Andie was his ghost. For hours, he'd been lying by her body, haunting himself, listening to her voice in the wind. Which made it all the more urgent to escape.

"Clear your head," Hugh shouted. "She's gone."

"She's here. You can't hear her?"

"Listen to me." Hugh held to his rope. "The lost souls are lost. Put her behind you, no looking back."

Augustine kept lying in his spiderweb.

"Look at Lewis out there," Hugh said. "He's fighting for us. Get up. Fight for yourself."

Augustine didn't move. Hugh kneed him in the back. "You keep saving everyone else. Now save yourself."

"It won't work."

"You've killed men before," Hugh said. "Don't you kill us."

Augustine flinched. Hugh had struck the raw nerve.

"Join the living," Hugh said. "We need your help. Help us."

Augustine began struggling with the ropes. Hugh helped free his legs from the haul bag. Augustine planted his rump against the wall and faced out to the wind.

Hugh lowered farther and off to the side. He

bared his hands to catch the throw line. It was better down here. He could look up at the litter instead of down into that spear of light.

Augustine leaned into the wind like an outfielder floating in space. Hugh's fear eased. With two pairs of hands, they would surely snare the throw line. They were practically home. *Don't worry, I'm the kaiser.* He felt almost giddy. The inmates were escaping from the asylum.

Lewis hefted the beanbag and pitched it again. It shot like a rocket . . . into the night. He reeled the line in, threw, and missed. He patiently coiled the cord. He tried again and again.

Hugh felt an insect sting, and another, then more. Silver tinsel suddenly streaked the light. The rain was arriving.

He'd been praying that when the storm finally unleashed, it would cut straight to snow. Snow you could beat from your jacket and legs and brush from your hair. With snow, you could hedge time and stretch the odds. Rain, though. On a night like this, with the cold still mounting, rain killed.

Hugh wiped at his eyes. No more giddy kaiser. The epic was in earnest now.

Lewis threw. He wound it in and threw again. Each miss gobbled up more minutes.

The silver streaks changed direction, like schools of fish, driving down, then sideways, then up. The roof of the Eye provided some slight shelter. But Lewis was naked to the storm. That didn't stop him. He threw again.

Thunder cracked through the valley.

Body and mind, Hugh stopped. The wind had the tang of ozone. It was going to be that kind of storm. They were getting caught among the electric trees and voltage snakes. He searched for lightning, but the SAR light blew his night sky.

Lewis toiled away out there, fearless, willful, defiant. They must have called him, because he put down his beanbag and picked up the radio. He put it to the edge of his helmet and listened, and then tossed it back into the litter. They called him again. He grabbed the radio and put it to his ear. Hugh had no question about what the chief was commanding him to do. *Preserve thyself.* Their summit rig was a lightning rod. They wanted to abort. It was over.

Somehow Lewis bought more time. With a pull, they could have drawn him up, and he would have had no choice. But the litter stayed. Lewis went back to coiling the line.

Hugh tried fashioning a throw line of his own with rope and a weight of carabiners. But pressed against the wall, he had no leeway to make the throw, and the rope was too heavy, and the wind too fierce.

Lewis missed again, missed by a mile. The Great Ape was wearing down. This was crazy. They were creating risks within risks.

Hugh's head was soaked. Water ran down his neck. His fingers were slowing. He'd been fooling himself. Even if they managed to catch the throw line, they were fifty stories shy of the summit in the middle of a tempest. He had to release Lewis, who would otherwise fight until doomsday. Everyone needed to take shelter.

Hugh bellowed monosyllables. "Lou. Quit. Go." The wind invaded his mouth. Howling, not words, came out.

Squall bursts began dimming the spotlight. The bright beam flickered. The Eye jumped time. It was night, it was day, night, day.

Hugh slashed at his throat again. He hand-signed a phone, thumb to his ear. He stabbed upward. *Call up. Ride out.*

Lewis shook his head no. He took aim and missed again.

The ozone smell built. It blossomed all around them, sharp and sweet. Hugh's body tingled. His skin turned electric. There was current in his hair, in his spine. *God.* He started shedding every metal thing on him, extra carabiners, some leftover pennies in his jacket pocket.

He'd met lightning survivors. He'd seen their burn wounds and heard their slurred speech. *Not another Joshua,* he thought. He clenched his teeth.

The lightning struck like velvet. It painted the edge of the roof with blue-green light.

On all his mountains, in all his storms, he'd never seen real St. Elmo's fire. There was that passage in *Moby-Dick*, and woodcuts showing alpinists kneeling before glowing crosses on their summits. Here it was.

The electricity guttered like flames dancing through fumes of rum. Slowly the wide length of it shrank inward and coalesced, and then began to descend along the stone, sliding under the roof. It was a whimsical thing. It meandered among the horns and flakes, taking its time, finding its way.

Hugh coughed rainwater. He closed his mouth. He couldn't take his eyes from it.

Cuba emerged from the tent. The tranquilizer had worn off, or the thunder had awakened her. Her strength was back. She stood on the edge of the platform, unroped. The platform shuddered.

Augustine said something to do with witches.

The ghostly fire sank along the wall. With one touch, her whole anchor of ropes and slings lit cold blue. Like a child, she reached for it.

There was no time to warn her. The spellbinder was spellbound. Rapt. Hugh watched, dreading what came next. She would burst into flame. She would explode or be hurled into the pit.

The cold light climbed her arm, and she held it out like a torch over the abyss, Prometheus in a sports bra.

Maybe it burned. Her mouth opened with a scream. Hugh couldn't hear for the screaming sky. Augustine wasn't lying. The wind was filled with voices. Furies. Dead spirits. She was joining her voice to theirs.

Hugh started up the rope for her. They had come too far to lose her. She was their muse.

The blue fire ebbed. She collapsed against the makeshift tent. In a minute, she would go sliding into the depths.

Hugh threw himself upward, past Augustine standing frozen. Water sprayed from his jumars.

Her arm dangled from one edge. The platform beat up and down, ridding itself of her a few pounds at a time. Her head appeared, hair lashing.

He cast himself across her body. Or was cast. A clap of thunder detonated against his back. His bones seemed to melt. The shock wave doubled him over the platform.

The wind quit. It hadn't quit. He was deaf. Numb. He opened his eyes, remembering, and looked.

Lewis was out there beyond the riot of prayer flags.

The volts were still convulsing him. Head back, teeth bared, he was gripping the metal litter with all his might. His muscles bulged. He made the world seem still for a moment.

Then the night sucked him from view. A minute later, it returned him in a lazy arc.

What had been a man was now a limp puppet. Whoever held his strings above had fled. His limbs flopped. His back arched. A bobble head. As he spun in a circle, the parts of him sprawled stupidly, as if he had never shown grace on the stone or recited poetry or chased the sun.

"Lewis," Hugh pleaded. It wasn't possible. A man was dead. A noble fool. His dearest friend.

Cuba stirred. He lay folded across her. She spoke. He became aware of that. His ears were ringing. "What?" He pried loose of her.

"Don't leave me, Hugh."

"What have we done?" Maybe he shouted at her. He was having trouble thinking.

She opened her arms to him. "Don't cry," she said in his ear. "You're with me now."

TWENTY-EIGHT

After witnessing Lewis's death, the rangers turned off their big spotlight in the meadow. The summit team ran for their lives. Once again, night fell on El Cap.

Light-headed with shock, Hugh followed Cuba into the tent. In her hunger or drugged confusion, she had emptied his stuff sack onto the floor. Chaos, he thought, chaos everywhere.

The edge of his makeshift tent wall snapped like gunshots in the wind. The laces were coming untied on all sides. Their covering was tearing away.

Thunder filled the deep canyon. The stone vibrated with it. Seal out the storm, he thought. Make order from darkness. Begin again. Before drawing the tent shut, he pushed out partway with his headlamp in hand.

"Come up," he shouted to Augustine. The platform was barely large enough for two, but they could make do. "Leave her."

But Augustine had already sewn himself into the ropes beside Andie. With his legs tucked into the haul bag and his hood pulled tight, and those two red hammocks billowing and straining in the wind at his feet, he was once more navigating the underworld.

Hugh gave up on him. Augustine had made his decision. If his lover would not join him, he would join her. By dawn, they would be married.

Hugh searched the night for his old friend. They'd left him hanging with the litter. At the farthest reaches of Hugh's light, armored in his helmet and jacket and plastic white skin, Lewis glittered in the rain.

"Christ," said Hugh, trying to think it through. Rachel had probably been among the rangers manning the spotlight in the meadow, the wife of the daring volunteer. They would have given her binoculars to watch, and maybe a big, yellow SAR jacket for the rain, and a cup of thermos coffee. They would have made her one of them. She would have seen the lightning strike.

Walk on. But she had already walked on once. She had emptied her heart of Lewis and left him on his walls. For whatever reason, maybe drawn by the fire or inspired by steadfast Augustine, she'd circled back and found her husband. And sent him up into the teeth of a storm, in memory of a woman who had lost all memory of herself. Love ruled, that was their notion. Hugh felt sick. After this, guilt would consume her. Her great beauty would wither. Better by far if she had never looked back.

Lewis arced from sight, batted by the wind. Snowflakes appeared in Hugh's light. The last thing he saw outside were the furious prayer flags. Hysteria on a string. He finished stitching shut the tent wall.

Cuba had changed yet again. She sat by the wall, clutching the anchor slings. The priestess, or mad fury, whoever had seized the St. Elmo's fire in her hand, was now in a terror. One moment she was the queen of the dead, the next a frightened survivor.

"I can't do this anymore," she said.

"We're going to beat it," Hugh said.

"She knows we're in here. Listen."

"That's thunder." Every storm feels personal when you get caught out like this. But to Hugh, this one seemed especially point-blank. The wind scoured the Eye so fiercely that he could hear rocks tumbling, like on a river bottom. Loose rope bullwhipped against their tent and the stone. It cracked in the air. The platform's outer edge bucked. If not for the pitons he'd nailed at the corners, they would have been smashed against the roof.

"Don't leave me alone. She's like this animal. Hungry." Andie's ghost again. He didn't know how to fight it.

"You're not alone, Cuba. I'm here. All this will pass."

"Keep her out. Please."

She was on the edge of completely losing it. Haldol, thought Hugh. Or morphine. Whatever it took to put her down. They couldn't take another of her tantrums, their fragile shelter would rip to pieces. But the med kit lay scattered in his lamp beam, and the bundle of syringes was nowhere to be found.

As he pawed through the shadowy mess and tossed things into the stuff sack, Hugh found empty wrappers and jugs. Cuba had been ravenous when she woke up. She was the hungry animal. All that remained of their supplies was a gallon of water and two protein bars. They were meager pickings, but rationed carefully could last them three days, or four.

There were other things missing, too, though in his daze Hugh could not remember what they were. His bible of maps was gone. He searched for it. All those decades, all those journeys, gone. For a moment, its loss went beyond the loss of Lewis, and that was a selfish thing, he knew. But in a real sense, that little journal had been the heart of him.

His T-shirt lay stuffed in the far corner, the last of his dry clothing. Cuba was sopped and shivering. Her skin was all goose bumps. "Put this on." The floor whanged against the stone.

Cuba ignored the offering. She stared at Hugh with frightened eyes.

He laid the sleeping bag open for her. It wasn't quite a straitjacket, but if he could just get her zipped inside, they were half safe. He patted the bag.

"It's snowing, Cuba." Even as he spoke, the storm's pitch changed. Hail rattled on the tent wall like buckshot.

"Lie down. Get warm." He touched her bare shoulder, and despite her trembling, she was hard as a rock. The cords of her forearms stood in ridges. That curious slave tattoo looked like something etched on bone.

"If you leave me, I'll die. She'll kill me like the others," she said. "Don't leave me."

In Saudi Arabia, he and Annie had adopted a jet black Saluki pup they'd found wild in the desert. Back in the compound, five times a day, it wailed when prayers were called from the minarets, which amused all the expats. Diesel, as they named it, had bonded to Annie like glue. Every slight motion she made, that dog was watching. Diesel slept in their room on Annie's side of the bed. Whenever they left the house, the dog had to be chained outside, where it dug deep holes to cower in until their return. Even after Annie quit recognizing him, Diesel stayed by her side. The same day Annie disappeared in the desert, while Hugh was still traipsing through the dunes, Diesel broke his chain and escaped from their neighbors. Hugh never saw him again.

That was what Cuba reminded him of. She needed Hugh in her sight every minute. After this nightmare, her separation anxiety would probably never quit, she would just transfer it to the next person, and the next. And who could blame her, the way the Captain had brutalized her?

"Cuba," he said.

"Promise."

"We'll see this through. We're together to the end, you and me, kid."

"Oh, Hugh." She breathed at him with her witch's voice, husky and low. "I've heard that before."

Her eyes glittered in his headlamp beam. They seemed to ignite, as if pure oxygen had hit a flame. Hugh tipped his headlamp, thinking the battery had surged or the bulb was flaring. She still crouched by the wall. Her iron grip held to the slings. But her vulnerability was gone. It was as if she had changed skins.

"I'm with you, Cuba, right here beside you."

"You say that to all the girls," she said. It jarred him. She was playing? In this storm? After what had just happened?

"Get in the bag," he said.

"I'm cold, Hugh."

"I'll zip you shut. You'll warm up."

"Lie with me." She cut a glance at him.

Why these games? The floor shuddered. Lewis was swinging by a rope out there. Any moment, they might be torn from the wall. "I'm soaked," he said. "You'll be warmer alone."

She let go of the slings.

The tent flashed red. It seared his eyes. Thunder slapped the stone. Night fell again. His ears buzzed.

When he could see again, she was kneeling in his tunnel of light, feral, watchful. Half naked. She had stripped off her sports bra. Ripped on the abyss.

He didn't mean to stare. Where the dark tan line stopped, her breasts were honey gold. They were large for an athlete, with a shadow between. She gave him the spectacle of her nipples and flesh. The wind rocked them. She watched him working to break free of the sight.

She smiled, feeding off the storm. Blood beaded on her lips. She took the shirt from his hands, and balled it to her nose. "Hugh Glass," she said, as if recalling his scent. She pulled it on.

He didn't touch her. But they were inches apart, and he could smell her black hair. The rain had cleaned out the smoke and sweat and death stink. She was fresh and clean, at least for a big wall.

"Lie down," he repeated.

She stretched out on the sleeping bag.

"They'll come for us again," he said. "Everything will be all right."

He started to close the bag over her. She caught at his neck and pulled. She kissed him.

The force of it—the starvation in it—startled him. He tasted the blood on her split lips. He pulled his head away.

"I thought you loved me, Hugh."

He wanted her to be sane. Or wild, but in controlled doses. But there was no way around it. She was crazy.

"Be still."

"Hugh." Like a broken record.

He considered. By embracing her, he would have his greatest safety. He could rest. If she moved, he'd know it. If she struggled, he could hold her still. And they could keep each other warm.

"We need to sleep," he said. He shed the wet parka and shoes. He lay behind her and wrapped the bag over them.

She did not so much nestle as burrow into him, taking his arm for her pillow. He turned off the light. "To save the battery," he said.

"You're not going to leave me, Hugh." A statement of fact.

"Go to sleep," he said.

She fidgeted. Her rump foraged at his loins.

He thought about Lewis rocking in the wind. "Listen to the storm, Cuba." The tent wall hummed with the wind's vibrato.

The ferocity calmed her. She settled in his arms. He started to get warm.

The rattle of hail turned to hissing sleet. Sleet gave way to silence: snow. Those were the sounds Hugh listened for, glimmers of what was going on out there. The wind was full of other sounds, too, but the shrieking and howls were nothing to him, just points of contact between the earth and sky.

Hugh closed Lewis from his mind. The platform bucked less violently. He held on to Cuba, still as a mouse now, and let the delirium take over.

At very high altitude, above eight thousand meters, it could get this way, with the violence and elements, but especially with the loss of jurisdiction. The world turned slippery. From minute to minute, you forgot and remembered and forgot again. Hallucinations took away the pain.

Hugh found himself in the desert, raging at the sun. The dunes had come alive. Great sea waves rose and fell. He saw himself digging in the sand for one of his water bottles. His hand came out with a pear, a shriveled black mummy of a pear.

Annie—mindless Annie—was stalking him through the sand. She'd never done that before. He ran from her. She sprang out and clutched his arm.

"Hugh?" It was Cuba. She was gripping his arm, waking him.

"It was a bad dream. I'm sorry. We're okay."

"I'm cold."

"Stay close."

It went on like that for hours. They shared the storm like fever victims, taking turns singing and groaning and reassuring each other. At one point, Hugh could not be sure she was even alive. He felt for a pulse, but the whole world was pulsing. He listened for her breathing, but the wind was howling. Finally he shook her, and she whimpered. On a night like this, that was all the proof he needed.

TWENTY-NINE

The storm passed. The world lay still. Hugh opened his eyes. Their raft had beached.

All night he had held Cuba. Now she was holding him. Hoar frost—their collective breath—coated the interior.

He tried not to think about Lewis. They needed one of them functional. Unbroken. He was it.

He tried to get free without waking her, but she gave a start. "Wait a little," she murmured. "It's so cold. The sun will come." Sensible enough, if only she possessed her senses. It was him in command now. He had to take the bull by the horns.

"What sun?" he said. Between the fire and the storm, how many days had slipped away in gloom? They had lost their way back to the surface.

She let go of him. No pleading or clutching. No

seduction. She had returned to herself, it seemed, the mortal girl, not the Weird Sister.

He surrendered. It was too soon to be cold, and they had nowhere to go. He felt groggy with her warmth and smell. "A few minutes more," he said. She pressed against his back.

"You must be hungry," he said. His stomach growled. Time to tighten their belts.

"We were going to celebrate with shrimp and Beaujolais," she spoke in his ear.

It was climber chat, freewheeling through the rewards for your self-inflicted punishments. She was mending fast. It gave him hope.

"Lewis and I were going for T-bones and Coronas," Hugh said.

"That was his name?"

His chest tightened. "He was my best friend." The last of them.

She put death away from them. "We were planning expeditions," she said. "Have you ever seen pictures of Nanda Devi?"

"I climbed it once."

"For real?" she said.

"She's a beauty. You should go."

She got quiet. Counting her dead, he figured.

"Where else do you think about?" he asked.

"Places. The planet. Far away. The mountains are just an excuse."

"I've always wanted to go to the headwaters of the Yangtze," Hugh said. More climbers' games, inflicting grand ambitions on one another. "Start in

Shanghai and go by boat, and then by car, and then by foot. You'd end up with yaks."

"Baffin Island," she nominated, "walls twice the size of El Cap."

"The Transantarctic Mountains," he said. "Seashells at nineteen thousand feet. Meteorites from Mars."

They traded dreams. He liked her voice, husky and tinged with her mother's Spanish. Soon enough they returned to where they were.

"It was only another four pitches," she said. "Cass climbed the roof and yelled down to us. She could see the summit. It was ours."

There was much he wanted to ask about the fall, but he didn't go there. They might be stranded here for another day or two, and she was too volatile. And the camp was so fragile.

It had been like this during his final months with the stranger who had once been Annie. Too much stimulation, the wrong music, even a wrong word, and their peace would shatter. He'd lived becalmed until it seemed he'd lose his own mind.

Cuba wanted to talk about her disaster, though. While he lay staring at crystals of white frost on the tent wall, she gave a blow-by-blow account of the fall and her exile among the dead and disembodied.

"At first, I thought it was Cass coming up to me from the woods." Her ghost again, thought Hugh. "I mean, she landed right below us, a half mile down, right?"

"Probably." He didn't tell her that he'd found her.

"It would make sense that she was the one. That she'd want to finish business. Do I sound whacked out or what?"

They were in psychological overload, himself included. Yes. "No."

He let her talk. Except for the events of the fall, there was little chronology to her tale. The forest fire blended into her long isolation and the birds and cloud formations she had found magical. She matter-of-factly told of hauling Andie from the depths.

"You thought she was still alive?"

"God, no. After all those days, I knew."

Then why? "You did the right thing," he told her, even though in Cuba's place he would have left the body hanging as far from view as possible. Indeed, he would have cut the rope to get rid of the reminder.

"It wasn't that," she said. "It wasn't for Andie."

"Were you lonely?" He asked it without accusation, the question of her sanity.

"I wish," she said. "By then I just wanted to be left alone."

"But you brought her up."

"She was afraid you wouldn't come," Cuba said. "So I pulled up what was left. Like bait, you know. She said it would bring you in."

They lay there. Hugh didn't move a muscle, barely breathing. *Bait?*

Her fairy tale about a meandering companion spirit was one thing. This whispering ghoul was something else, like some kind of vertical plague. Cuba was sick with it, her eye for an eye. She was so certain, the way she said it. And the thing was, they'd taken the bait. Augustine had come, with Hugh in tow.

"Why do you hate him so much?" Hugh asked.

"Who?"

"Augustine."

"Hate him?" All innocence.

"Come on."

"There's only so long you can lick your wounds," she said. "And it was probably for the best."

Her wounds, she meant. Hugh frowned. "How do you mean?"

"He's intense. I'm more intense. We were never going to last forever. I couldn't see it at the time. But once he dumped me, things got clear."

Hugh lay there, trying to connect the dots. The stars of frost. "You and Augustine were involved?"

"That sounds so antique."

"You know what I mean."

"We were hot. You wouldn't believe, hot as fire. But then Andie came wandering in, this sweet lost thing, always lost, and that was the end of us."

It made him dizzy. "He left you for her?"

"Don't worry, Hugh. I got over it a long time ago. Because we would have burned each other to a crisp. I finally decided Andie had saved us, him and me both. But then her brother died and she was lost again."

"So you took her in."

"The Valley's small, and mostly guys. Us girls stick together."

Hugh stared straight ahead. He emptied the neat boxes in his mind, each article of this climb, from his discovery of Cass to the slaughter of Lewis. No more boxes. He shoveled the events into a jumble and tried to arrange them in some order. Somewhere lay the thread out of this maze.

Cuba patted his shoulder. She whispered in his ear. "It's almost over."

The sun stayed hidden. The tent wall did not light up. The frost did not scale away. He could have lain there all day, captivated by her warmth and his futile puzzling.

"I should check on things," Hugh finally said. He eased from the sleeping bag and neatly tucked it around her. Her green eyes followed him, like Diesel watching Annie.

"Hugh Glass," she said, as if naming him anew.

The icy parka stood in one corner like a giant insect shell. He beat the verglas from its sides and drew it on, zipping it to the throat and pulling up the hood. He shivered until his body heated the fiberfill and the parka became part of his armor once again.

The laces holding the sidewall had frozen tight. His pocketknife could have picked them apart easily, but he'd dropped it while freeing Cuba last night. His fingernails were ground to the quick. He resorted to gnawing the cord, like an animal. One knot opened, and that was enough to give him a peephole. He peered through.

A crystal world waited outside. The stone, the ropes, their metal protection, everything was glazed with ice. The Eye—probably the entire valley—was socked in by clouds. The misty light was cold and blue. Nothing moved out there. After last night's tempest, the silence made Hugh nervous.

There are moments in the mountains and the desert when things quietly, invisibly reach a state of critical mass. Snow layers a slope just so, waiting for a noise or a footstep to unleash the avalanche. Sand builds at the crest of a dune until that instant it exceeds the angle of repose, and crumples, and the whole dune shifts forward, burying your footsteps and whatever else lies before it. Accidents don't happen, he'd learned. Nature isn't unnatural. Mechanisms get triggered, that's all. Understand the cause and you could master, or at least try to escape, the effects.

Hugh struggled to decipher the stillness. He could feel something primed and waiting out there. But what? They'd traded smoke for mist, fire for ice. The storm had layered their hiding place in glass. The saturated blue light told him that the clouds weren't burning off today. Everything was at peace. But it was the peace of the bell jar, artificial and enclosed. And watched. He could feel it. Something.

"What do you see?" Cuba asked.

"The Ice Age. We're locked down for the day."

"Come back with me."

"Not yet." They were in greater danger than ever. He couldn't put a name to it, whatever inhabited the void.

"Where are you going?"

"Nowhere, Cuba. I'm just looking."

He forced the hole wider and scooted his upper body from the cocoon. Half in, half out, holding on to loose straps, he surveyed their station. The pit plunged into infinite blue.

Remarkably, the storm had not swept Augustine away. He still hung beside Andie, fused in a crystal spiderweb. Her shroud of a sleeping bag had loosened, or Augustine had reached inside. Or the ghost of her had tried to worm loose. Her golden white hair was plastered to the stone in a long glassy stream. The red hammocks hung in tatters.

"Augustine?"

Augustine's eyes opened. He stared up at Hugh from the hollow of his helmet. His face was mottled blue. His hands, clothed in socks, had a death grip on the ropes.

Cuba's voice came from inside the tent. "She let him live?"

Augustine's eyes moved, nothing else. He blinked. For the moment, neither man spoke to the other.

Hugh turned his attention to the mist. Thirty feet out, past the motionless prayer flags, at the brink of the ceiling hung with icicles, Lewis dangled in midair, welded to the litter.

The ropes slowly spun him. Bent backward, he

twisted to face Hugh upside down. His mouth hung open. It was filled with loose snow. Flakes spilled from his lips, his poet lips, and fluttered into the depths.

"Christ, Lewis," Hugh whispered. The great heart, all for one, one for all. For nothing.

The wind had ransacked him. Lewis was naked from the waist up. His flesh was dark red, his veins bright blue. They had left him in place. With his big weight-room muscles, he looked like a side of beef.

Hugh glanced down to where Augustine was turning to stone and ice, dissolving into mist. It was like a myth where humans petrified or turned into trees or animals. El Cap was consuming them.

"We can't stay here," Hugh said.

No one moved or answered. The very air was paralyzed. He felt suffocated.

"They've written us off, postponed us, whatever." He didn't blame them. *Preserve thyself.* "They'll fetch us once it clears. By then, we'll all be dead. That's where this is heading."

Cuba whispered from the sleeping bag. "Make me warm, Hugh. It's too cold to be alone."

"We have to leave," Hugh declared. The mist flattened his words. "Do you hear me?"

After a minute, Augustine stirred. He wrenched his helmet and Tarzan hair from the wall. Ice fractured around his shoulders. His jaw moved. It broke his walrus tusks of snot and rime. A puff of frost came out, but no words. He tried again. "How?"

Hugh didn't know yet. He was trying to strike a

spark among them, little more. No good would come of their waiting and listening to their bones knock and their stomachs growl. But were any of them capable? Were any of them really sane? He was just as crazy as the other two now. But did that matter, so long as they shared the same dementia?

Inside the tent, Cuba had begun droning *om mane padme hum*—the Buddhist chant every mountaineer carries home from the High Himal—over and over. But the prayer flags were frozen. The wind horses stood still. Time had stopped.

Hugh considered lowering off, but that could take days. And Cuba had told him that they'd spied the summit above. They were close.

If only they could lift this lid of stone from their heads. The roof was a dead end. What had protected them last night was killing them now. It blunted their imagination. It killed their hope.

The answer came to Hugh slowly. Their salvation hung in plain sight.

"Lewis," he said.

Augustine's helmet turned to the distant figure. He settled back against the stone. "No use." His teeth chattered. "Too far. All wrong."

Augustine was thinking of a throw line, Hugh knew. And by that measure, he **was** right. Even if they could throw a line and somehow snag the litter or lasso Lewis's body, they would still have to tow it close enough to grab. But the arc would never work. Lewis was parallel to their camp, and the roof was thirty feet deep, meaning never the twain shall meet.

"We don't bring Lewis to us," Hugh said. "We go to Lewis."

"What, we fly?"

"Climb," said Hugh. "If we can reach where his ropes run along the outer wall, then we just climb the ropes."

Augustine traced the idea, his eyes following the roof to its edge. "The ropes are iced. The jumars will clog. It could take hours. It could go into the night."

"Stay here then?"

Augustine muttered.

"We can do this thing," Hugh said. Break the curse. Sneak from the underworld. Reach the sun.

"What about Andie?"

That again. Hugh wanted to argue. They would be leaving Lewis's body behind, why not hers? They could bind the two victims side by side in the litter and leave them for the rescue crew to draw up later. But he knew Augustine would never agree to such a bed, and Hugh needed Augustine's help.

"Andie goes with us," Hugh decided.

Augustine patted her woodenly. "It could work," he said.

It would not be easy, Hugh knew. The ceiling looked deadly with its poxlike holes and black horns and daggers of ice. Even if he managed to exit the roof and gain the headwall and grab one of Lewis's ropes, there was the small matter of five hundred vertical feet separating them from the summit. As Augustine had pointed out, the jumars would clog with ice and that would cost more time. And they were weak. Cuba was chanting. Augustine was haunted. On top of that, they would be burdened the whole way by Andie's corpse.

But it would be worse to stay. Far worse. Cuba was exhibit A, in and out of reality. Too much time among the ruins. Inertia kills.

"We've got to move," Hugh said.

"Move," Augustine repeated. Hugh could see the struggle in his face. The temptation was so strong. Lie back. Wait.

"It's up to us."

"Yes." But the cold hurt. Augustine didn't move.

"We came to save the day, remember?"

Augustine's face grappled with the noble thought.

Abruptly Cuba's drone halted. She was listening, but not to them. To the mountain.

A vast hum descended from the heavens.

Hugh stared into the mist.

All but invisible to them, a huge spectral presence swept by, like a glass ship in deep fog. As it passed, slowly, much too slowly for a falling object, the air pushed at them.

Hugh knew the sound. It was ice from the summit rim, a giant sheet pried loose. It sailed by on translucent wings, probably a half acre wide and several tons heavy.

The monstrous hum grew smaller. It seemed a full minute went by. Then one edge of the ice hull touched the lower wall. A sharp explosion snapped far below.

It was like a prehistoric Fourth of July celebration. Hugh listened to the crackle of shrapnel strafing the stone. It ended with a roaring finale as the main mass of ice struck the ground.

It would go on like this all day, until the summit finished shedding its casing, or night locked the remnants in place. It would mean climbing in fear, through fear, through a fog besieged by giants with wings. But Hugh knew from his desert ordeal that it took a stone heart sometimes. You had to resist temptation and second thoughts and the voices of weakness, even to the point of ruthlessness. You had to slay all doubts. You had to execute the plan.

Augustine was protecting Andie's body from the ice, even though the ice could not reach them in here.

"There's no hiding from it," Hugh said. "The Captain knows we're here."

That did the trick. Augustine nodded his head. Clots of hair jingled against his helmet. Blinking and twitching, he broke apart his sheath of ice.

Hugh glanced inside the tent, and Cuba was watching him. "It's almost over," he said to her.

She didn't answer. She just watched him.

THIRTY

Everything hurt.

Nothing was easy.

First they had to break the ice and reclaim their gear from the stone. It took an hour or more to ransack the anchors, and assemble a proper rack of hardware, and pull free enough rope to climb with.

The cold plagued them. They were clumsy as astronauts. Bundled and gloved, they had to monitor each move. Twice they fumbled handing pieces to one another. A Z-shaped leeper piton went ringing into the mist. A chain of carabiners snaked from their fingers. Luckily—hopefully—they only needed to go a little more than the thirty feet of the roof before reaching Lewis's ropes. From there, the climbing would shift. Beyond the roof, the only tools necessary would be jumars and stirrups and muscle.

Hugh kept wishing his joints would loosen up. His knees creaked. His fingers were half crippled with arthritis. Tendonitis hitched his elbows and shoulders. It was as if he'd aged fifty years in a night.

After his night in the open, Augustine was in even worse shape. He moved like the tin man, rusty, ungainly, and in pieces. He kept kicking the stone, trying to get sensation back in his feet. But he never complained.

"We should take a look at your feet," Hugh said.

"And then what?" said Augustine. Hugh was glad for his stoicism. Now was not the time to be treating cold wounds. If his feet were frostbitten, it would only make matters worse to thaw and refreeze the tissue.

"A few hours more," Hugh promised him.

But even the slightest act required an effort. The carabiners snagged on bulky clothing and nipped at the tips of their gloves. They flexed ice from the sheath, but the rope remained stiff and unwieldy. It was like trying to tie knots with steel cable.

"Are we ready?" Hugh said.

"Wait." Augustine took off his helmet. "Here."

It was an excellent day for helmets, especially on the outside of the Eye. "Keep it," said Hugh. "You'll need it."

Augustine shoved it at Hugh. The giving was important to him, more than a mere shell of protection. It was tribute. He was grateful.

"You'll get this back," said Hugh.

He peeked in the tent and Cuba was sound asleep. Soon enough, she'd need all her strength. For now, at least, she wasn't whispering spells at Augustine. A sense of normalcy returned, as much normalcy as you could ask from a world struck dumb with ice.

Hugh didn't fool around trying to free-climb. Where it wasn't wet or sealed with verglas, the rock was loose and iffy. His climbing slippers would have been useless on the few holds, and baring his fingers would have been suicide. Besides, he wasn't here to dance with Trojan Women. This was a getaway, pure and simple.

He selected a half-inch baby angle from the rack, nosed it against a seam, and hammered it neck deep. Clip in . . . gate down and out . . . step up in the stirrups. His helmet knocked against the ceiling.

He craned back beneath the ceiling, searching for his next placement. There were no tidy cracks to follow, nothing but a wasteland of junk rock to nail and nut and tie onto, one Hail Mary move after another. No running allowed.

Out past the roof, another sheet of ice sang by. The air sucked at the skin of his face. A half mile down, the calved ice roared. Hugh screwed his attention on to the wilderness above.

As he moved across the ceiling, he was essentially walking in the sky, held by nails and small wires and tidbits of airplane metal. It was awkward going. Stretching backward, balancing with one hand or foot against the ceiling, he probed for any flaw to exploit, and sorted through his rack to find the most likely fit. Sometimes he had to try two, three, or four different pieces.

Mistakes were made. He dropped a number two copperhead, then a pink one-inch Camelot. Then a lost arrow bounced loose on his first tap with the hammer. The next one he overdrove, and the flake split away and he lost that piton, too.

More ice fluttered through the blue soup. More explosions. *Fire and ice,* he thought. *You've paid your dues on this one, Glass. Take it home.*

He was acutely aware of time passing, and just as aware that he had slipped into a separate reality. Up here, time got measured in quarter-million-year increments and in miles per hour and vertical feet. In the back of his mind, he tried counting how long it took the ice to strike earth, and it was always different, relative to the aerodynamic shape of El Cap's summit stone, in reverse, the shape of the ice.

It had been like this in the desert as he trekked out from Annie, gauging the sun, consulting his GPS, following his map, step by step calculating his exit from madness. There are degrees of being lost. Understanding that was the key to any labyrinth. Your sense of self was everything.

He looked back at where he'd come from. His rope ran through a crooked row of carabiners dangling from the stone. Like his steady march of footprints out of the dunes. The row grew longer. The edge drew closer.

Hints of an exterior appeared. The subterranean gloom changed. The mist took on a different, lighter blue. Out and above, he knew, the headwall towered. Laid hard against it, braided together and glazed over by the storm, Lewis's ropes were waiting for him.

Stretching with his hammer, he slashed at the icicles fencing the rim. Sticks of chandelier ice tinkled against the metal litter that now hung almost directly below Hugh. He glanced down and saw the row of fine black hairs running from Lewis's stomach up to the plates of his pecs.

He didn't like the wide-eyed surprise on Lewis's face. It made him look foolish. And the snow packing his mouth brought back Hugh's nightmare of Annie with the sand pouring from her throat. He put his back to the abyss. They were gone. He was almost out of here.

His progress slowed. Before freezing, the sleet had run under the roof and filled every cavity along the rim. Hugh had to chisel out the ice with the tip of a piton. Fragments flew in his eyes. His face dripped with melt, which ran down his neck and spine. It took forever to get the next piece in.

Seven more feet, he estimated. Two more moves. Nothing could go wrong from there. The ropes were their freeway to the sun. Never again, Hugh swore. After this, El Cap could sink to the bottom of the ocean. They'd made it.

But then, with what voice he had left, Augustine cried a warning. It was more a bark than a word. Hugh flinched, thinking a rock was falling, or a piece was pulling, or the rope had snarled.

Beaded with sweat and dew and ice melt, he looked back at Augustine. From out here, their little camp with its red tent and the entrails of its wreckage looked far away in the mist, like a dream in decay. Augustine was stabbing at the air, pointing wildly. Hugh wheeled around to see.

Lewis was in motion.

The summit crew had returned. They were drawing the litter and its dead guardian to the top. Smoothly, in utter silence, Lewis glided up from the depths. He was rising into the heavens. His body was going to pass almost within Hugh's reach.

"Wait," Hugh shouted.

Another section of ice fluttered past. The air pressed at Hugh. It carried a scent of trees, live trees, on the summit. They were close.

"Stop," Hugh yelled at them. The roof blocked his voice. The mist muffled it. Occupied with their own commands, and enveloped by glacial clatter, they would never hear him. He could barely hear himself under here.

He shouted in bursts. "Stop. Hello. Help."

Even as the litter slid through the air, a tiny electric voice spoke. "Come in, Litter One. Do you read me, Lewis?" The radio—everything they needed—lay on the bed of the metal basket.

Hugh lunged for it, and went exactly nowhere. "Slack," Hugh yelled down, and Augustine fed him slack, too late. Lewis had already moved higher.

Think. Hugh yanked off his helmet with Augustine's name inked across the back. He took aim and tossed it at the litter with a flick of his wrist. They would figure it out up there, a message in a bottle. They would lower down for the castaways.

But the helmet hit the rim with a hollow clunk, gave a hop, and disappeared into the mist. Hugh started unclipping pitons and nuts, chucking them at the litter, landing some, mostly missing. He quit wasting pieces. The summit team would never read the survivors' presence from a few anonymous odds and ends. Even if they did, the falling ice made conditions far too dangerous. No way would they risk another life today.

Lewis and the litter kept on rising. Desperate, Hugh pitched his hammer at the litter. It had a five-foot keeper sling that connected to his harness. He missed. He tried again. It caught. Handle up, the hammer head snared a corner of the basket.

There was no time for delicacy. The litter was sliding into the heights. Hugh pulled. It would work, or it would fail. The hammer held. Still in motion, the litter sidled toward him.

"Slack," he yelled to Augustine.

One more pull, a few more inches. Time his dive. Grab the radio. Eyes on the prize, Hugh pulled the basket closer.

A breeze kissed him, the backdraft from another wing of ice. More scent of summit pines.

The litter rocked. The breeze banged it hard against the rim of the roof. One of Lewis's arms jerked at the bump. His dead hand flung up and across. As if ridding himself of Hugh, the corpse brushed away the hammer.

Hugh's last link tumbled free.

"Lewis," he whispered.

Lewis's head hinged around. Snow guttered from that crystal mouth. His marble eyes froze Hugh. *Thunderstruck.* Hugh couldn't move. Suddenly it was so hard to breathe.

He could only stare as Lewis rounded the rim, making the journey out. The litter and ropes and body vanished.

Cuba's words returned to him. *I died. I know everything.* Hugh clung to his stirrups and thought, *Everything?* It terrified him.

Then with a gasp, his lungs filled again. He blew out and drew in, starting his clock all over again. The lost souls were lost. He was not. The world was nowhere to be seen in this fog, but he could taste it in the air. It was waiting for him.

Suddenly he knew what to do. With or without his bible of maps, or Lewis's rope, he would find his way out of this purgatory. Pulling up the keeper sling, he took the hammer in his fist. Out there, beyond the shield of this roof, where the ice roamed like dragons, lay his deliverance.

THIRTY-ONE

"I saw it," he lied.

He leaned forward in the tent. He shined his light on their faces. In the fading beam, speckled with mist, Augustine and Cuba looked waxy and yellow and entombed. He was stranded among the damned. Hugh fought his stab of dread. Damned, yes. Stranded, no.

"Tomorrow's the day," he said.

Hugh was exhausted. He should have been hungry and thirsty. But all day he'd been eating icicles and lichen picked from the rock. He had El Cap in his belly and veins and lungs and head.

It was deep night. Sleep was impossible. The three of them sat like peas in a pod, jammed side by side. He had bullied Augustine into the tent. Their backs were against the wall. They shared the one sleeping bag across their legs.

Andie's body hung beneath the platform. She might as well have been lying on their laps. They were possessed by her.

After Lewis and the litter were drawn off, Hugh had kept climbing. He had finished the roof and exited onto the headwall, reaching a crack that ran like a shot up the soaring stone. The blue fog barred any view of the summit, of course. But if Cass had seen it, as Cuba claimed, then it was there.

He had shouted himself hoarse, in vain. By the time he'd worked out from the roof, the summit crew was probably long gone. They had simply been retrieving Lewis and their equipment during what was possibly, Hugh feared, just a break between storms. He was coming to believe Cuba. They were being stalked. The abyss was trying to claim them.

Standing on the outer wall, freed of the Eye for even a few minutes, his sense of hunched slavery had vanished. He'd felt liberated, or nearly so. Now, back among these broken spirits, he realized how lethal this hollow of black stone had become. Tied to the rock, they were getting picked to pieces by their vultures.

"I got a hundred feet up," he related for the tenth time. "The rope is fixed. The crack will go. All the way to the top. It's a good crack. A great crack. Fingers to fists. Cuba, you could do it in your sleep."

"I just don't know," Augustine said yet again. He sat hunched at the far end. Maybe it had been like this in his ice cave on Cerro Torre. All night, he'd been somber and addled. He knew he was going to lose part of both feet. He had diagnosed the extent of the frostbite himself. "They know we're here."

"After the lightning last night," Hugh said, "they probably think we're dead."

"Sooner or later, they've got to come for us."

"That's the crux of it," Hugh said. "Sooner? Or later? You need a hospital. All you have to do is hike the rope tomorrow."

"But we can last."

"Can we? Look at us. We're out of food. Our water's gone." While he was climbing and Augustine was belaying, Cuba had polished off their rations. At this point, she was probably the best rested and strongest of the three of them.

"They'll come," said Augustine.

"What about Andie?"

Augustine's eyes glowed like round yellow moons. "I know what to do with her," he said.

This didn't sound good. "Yeah?"

"I think I should stay."

"And do what?"

"Just stay. With her."

Until death do us part. "Bullshit," Hugh said.

"I'm serious," Augustine said. "Go without me. It's your only way out."

Hugh needed Augustine to mind the rope tomorrow. They had another five hundred feet to climb, and even grief stricken and harrowed by guilt, Augustine was saner than Cuba. "This is Andie's wall," Hugh said to him. "It's not yours to waste."

"She wants me to stay."

"What about resurrection?" Hugh said.

"What?"

"That's what this is all about. You have the power," said Hugh. "Think about it. You can make life out of death. With you for her wings, she can finish the climb. You can make her immortal."

Augustine didn't answer.

Hugh kept the headlamp turned on. They were down to the last battery. It violated his normal moderation, but the darkness was too deep tonight. They were a bubble of light in the void.

Between them, Cuba spoke up. "Don't deceive us, Hugh." Her hair hung in greasy strings. "Don't deceive yourself."

"The summit's there," he repeated to them.

With every heartbeat, a hammer hit his skull. The veins of his neck were so engorged, they stood out on his throat. His cheeks tingled. His tongue felt like a chunk of rubber. He had to work not to slur his words. It was hard to think clearly. He'd experienced these symptoms before, but never below twenty thousand feet.

He felt ready to explode. Every breath was strangled. He had high-altitude sickness, plain and simple. But on El Cap? Maybe there was some freak pressure cell in the storm system. None of the others seemed to be suffering, though. It was just him, the old man.

He wanted to curl into a ball and hold his head. But he had to rally them. He had to occupy them so that the night could not.

"Trojan Women," he said. "It belongs to you, Cuba. All you have to do is cross the finish line."

The notion was outrageous on one level. Augustine's feet were dead white to the arch. Cuba had bound herself among the anchor ropes again. Hugh could barely see through his migraine. They were trapped.

But they could escape. One behind the other, they could cheat the abyss. Augustine could emerge with his lover. Cuba could become a legend. Hugh could return to the desert where he belonged.

"It won't work," she said.

Her omens and fatalism beat at him. He held up one taped fist. "I had my hand in the crack. I could feel the summit in it."

"There's no walking away from this one," she said.

"Terrible things have happened here," Hugh said.

"I'm not talking about here," she said.

Augustine squirmed.

"This isn't a haunted house," Hugh said. "We're going out the door tomorrow morning, and nothing's going to happen to us."

She looked at him as if he were a curious bug. "Then why are you so afraid?"

He was afraid. "I'm not. The dead can't touch us. You have to quit acting like a human sacrifice. We're survivors. We're free from all that."

"Like in the desert?"

He tried to remember telling her about that. His head pounded. Maybe he had. Or Augustine had talked to her. "Yes," said Hugh.

She turned to Augustine. "You're a survivor. Tell us. Is it free?"

Augustine hunched into himself.

"There are consequences," she said. "That's the deal."

Augustine groaned. "I know that," he said.

"You don't just leave the weak."

"I know."

"Let him be," Hugh said. She was ruthless. "Forgive. Forget."

"Apples and oranges," she said.

"What?"

"Forgive. Forget. They're not the same."

"What more do you want from him?" Hugh said. "Bury the past. We're all on the same side now."

"Are we?" she asked.

Augustine may have fallen prey to her, but it wasn't going to work on him. She only knew what you gave away to her.

"The choice is yours," he said. No one could force her to climb, and they didn't have the strength to be pulling two bodies, one living, one dead.

It boiled down to one question. Augustine he could trust, even in his morbid state. Cuba was the wild card. At first light, did he dare share a rope with this woman?

"Are you with us, Cuba?"

"Can I trust you, Hugh?"

He turned the light on his own face so she could see him. "I'm not leaving you," he said. Though he would, and never look back. If she didn't come around, he would have no alternative.

"Promise?" she said.

"Cross my heart."

A soft breeze luffed the tent wall. Hoarfrost sparkled in the light. It was their own breath—their own words—frozen on the nylon and falling back on them. They looked feverish with melt. It ran down his face.

"Your eyes," Augustine said to Hugh. He was frowning, pointing with a sock hand.

"What about them?" Hugh touched the trickle along his nose. He'd thought it was sweat or tears. He looked at his fingertip. He was bleeding from his eyes.

"Can't you feel her out there?" Cuba said.

Augustine lifted his head. "Andie?"

"Andie goes with us," Hugh told him again.

The tent walls pressed in on them. They were diseased with one another. The stillness cloyed. Hugh pulled in a breath. He pushed it out. Under the sleeping bag, Augustine's white feet were dying. The Captain was eating them alive.

"This is what we do." Hugh had gone through it with them. He went through it again. "Augustine goes first on the rope. He trails a separate line to bring up Andie. Cuba goes next. I'll bring up the rear. Then we climb."

He wanted it to sound easy and inevitable. In fact, they would be taking a terrible gamble. The crack could turn mean or seal shut. Even if all went well, their exhaustion and hunger were bound to slow the climbing. If they failed to top out tomorrow, if they got trapped in the open, El Cap would exterminate them.

But they had to try.

"I just don't know," said Augustine.

"It's out of our control," said Cuba. "This is where it comes together."

"Yes, you've said," Hugh said. "Her pound of flesh."

"There's a balance to things," she said.

"We're done giving, Cuba. All of us. We beat her. We made it alive, you'll see."

"There's still tomorrow."

"It's after midnight. This is tomorrow." His stomach cramped. It was the lichen and ice he'd eaten. And the runoff he'd drunk, most likely fouled with climbers' sewage.

"Not yet, Hugh."

"Enough," he said. She was tearing them apart. "No more scapegoats. No more wrath of God. Listen to me. Her ghost doesn't exist."

"I never said ghosts."

"Then what?"

"I don't know."

He put one fingertip in the center of her forehead. "She's up here."

Very gently, she put her fingertip on his forehead. "What about you, Hugh?"

She didn't have a clue, sticking voodoo needles into him, fiddling for a nerve, trying to get inside his head the way she'd done with Augustine. But she was as ignorant of his desert journey as the rest of the world. Not a clue, he told himself.

The breeze went on. The weather was changing yet again, though Hugh couldn't tell if it was for better or for worse. The wind might be returning, and with it a new assault. Or it could be the cusp of a warm front.

The air stunk of the three of them piled against each other. He wanted to open the tent flap at his shoulder for a clean breath. But Cuba had him spooked.

When the headlamp finally died, it was like falling from his body. Their string of voices unraveled. Stray words eroded into grunts and peeps.

And then another sound came to them. A sleeping bag rustled, and it was not this bag across their legs. Something was struggling out there. Beneath them.

They fell silent.

The thrashing quit. Hugh heard the sleeping bag unzipping. Ropes slipped against nylon. Hugh fought the image. *She's escaping.*

Then Cuba reached for his hand with her carpenter's grip, and that scared him more than the sounds. Because she knew.

Slings creaked. It was climbing.

"Not me," Cuba murmured in the darkness. "Not again."

"It's the wind," Hugh whispered.

"What wind?"

"Cuba." *Shut up.*

Rocks shifted in their sockets.

The pressure mounted in Hugh's head. His eyes were leaking. Blood trickled through his whiskers. He felt a hundred years old.

A twig—that dry, that delicate—began to scratch beneath their platform floor. It traced sideways against the nylon, sketching the evidence of them sitting there. Hugh felt it crossing his rump, and grazing the tip of his spine. It poised beneath his anus, and he felt open, gaping open, utterly vulnerable to whatever was down there. He gnawed his lip, tasting the blood in his mustache. *Hold still.* It moved on.

Cuba stiffened beside him.

A minute later, Augustine jerked.

She was making up her mind.

No one moved. Hugh took tiny bird breaths. Not a sound.

Without warning, the platform reared up. Cuba squeezed his hand. Hugh grabbed for the anchor. They crashed down on the guy lines.

The platform bucked. It shook them.

The side tubes buckled. Fabric ripped. Like a wild beast, the abyss fell upon them.

A hole opened. Hugh's legs were sucked right through the floor. He plunged to his waist and would have kept going if not for the rope hitched to his harness. He almost bellowed his fear, but trapped it all inside.

Blind to the others' fate, he felt for slings and pulled. But gravity—or hands, he'd swear—snatched at his ankles. That fast, it had him, like talons closing. The awful weight grappled higher, climbing on him, hauling at his legs. *The lizard king.* This couldn't be real. It crawled to his thighs. It hung from him.

He wanted to yell and kick. To see and at the same time go on not seeing. It was like the moment before you fall. You know it's coming. You hold on. You don't give in.

He groped for higher slings. No one made a sound. For all he knew, they'd dropped through the platform and were being carried off into the night. The slings squeaked. Hugh weighed a ton.

He felt fingers fumbling at his harness. It was untying him from the wall. *What in God's name?*

Augustine saved them. "Andie?" he called.

That suddenly the assault ended. The weight vanished from his legs. Hugh felt himself lifted by his harness, and it was Cuba pulling him back onto the platform. They had been her fingers. Hugh thrust his back against the stone.

"Andie?" Augustine said again.

"Quiet," said Hugh.

"Is she leaving?"

"Let her go."

"Andie?"

The platform quit swaying. No one moved. Without a light, there was no way to judge the damage. Hugh could feel cool air pouring up through the floor. It was torn, the membrane between their slight rectangle of a world and all that yawned below them. He could have felt with his fingers for the destruction. But there was nothing they could do about it in the darkness, and he didn't dare put his hands into the abyss. He didn't want to know what had happened to them, or might yet.

They sat there. Side by side in the pitch-black, they separated into animal solitude. Cuba's shoulder became no different from the rock against his back. The tent walls ceased to exist in his mind. Except for El Cap, there was only the void.

It seemed the night would never end.

THIRTY-TWO

Hugh dreamed about waterfalls, and then he woke and the water was real. He could hear it outside the tent. He opened his eyes, and the tent wall was luminous and red as cherries. He touched it, doubting, but the nylon was warm. The sun had come.

To his right, Cuba and Augustine sat crumpled against their knees and each other, perhaps drawn close by old memories. While the three of them slept, dawn had crept down the wall and under the roof. The spangles of hoarfrost had melted. His headache was gone. It was as if last night had never occurred.

Slowly he discovered the damage. They were crowded together so tightly, he didn't see the bent tubing at first. The tent wall had sagged onto their heads. He pushed aside the sleeping bag and opened his knees, and the floor lay ripped from side to side. A half mile of barrens emptied below.

She was gone. Hugh looked twice. His sleeping bag—her shroud—hung vacant. His neat crisscross of ropes was now just a tangle. Andie had fled.

"Wake up," he said to them.

The water was loud.

Light kept flickering on the tent wall. Colors played on the stone below. With blackened fingernails, Hugh fiddled open the knots. He snatched the tent from his head, and met pure glory. He gasped.

They had been transported to the inside of a rainbow.

Runoff poured from the roof's outer rim, covering the Eye. It sheeted off in a great, long river that reached to the ground. As the currents thinned and thickened, the rainbow rippled.

Hugh finished stripping the makeshift tent from the guy lines, and the membrane floated down, then was snatched away by the waterfall. Augustine held one hand to his eyes. The colors danced on Cuba's cheekbones and black hair.

They stared dumbstruck for a minute. Hints of paradise played through the water, a vision of grand pinnacles and forested gullies and the golden sun. The rainbow was slippery. It swam back and forth, up and down. Spray rustled the prayer flags, colors upon colors. Ice thundered on the valley floor.

In a lifetime of exploring, Hugh had always had to seek out the world's beauty. Never had it come to him like this. He took that back. There had been one other time, a different beauty. Decades ago, one rainy afternoon in Yosemite Lodge, he had looked up from his mapmaking and found Annie standing before him. The rainbow reminded him of that.

"What are we waiting for?" Hugh said.

Beauty did not suffer human contact for very long. No sooner did you embrace it than the illusion withered. One could love too much. He'd learned that. Better by far to walk on.

Augustine peeled away the sleeping bag. Through the gash in the floor, he saw the body missing. "Andie?" he said. He pawed at the chasm.

"She's gone," Hugh said.

"That can't be," said Augustine. "Her knots were tight. I tied them."

"She's gone," Hugh repeated. He had no idea what had happened last night. It was over, that was the important thing.

"I would have taken her up," Augustine protested.

"We'll go faster this way. This is what she wanted."

"They'll come for us now," Augustine said. His feet were dead white. Sacrifices. Pass through the underworld, even stand still among the souls, and you always lost some part of yourself, flesh or spirit. Hugh knew. *Walk on.*

"They won't risk it this morning, not with the ice still coming off," Hugh said. "By the time it stops, we'll be standing on top."

To his relief, Cuba agreed. "It's almost finished." She looked at peace. No more goblins. Her lips had healed, no more beads of blood. The hollows in her cheeks had filled out. Her eyes were bright. They sparkled at him.

In that moment, Hugh almost loved her. The feeling surged through him, crazy emotions, buried emotions. Here, perhaps, was the woman to take Annie's place. He could not wait to cut away his gloves of tape and clean off the blood and smoke and sweat, and to see Cuba bathed and whole.

What would she look like in a dress? Did she wear her hair in braids? How tall was she? He'd never stood beside her. He barely knew her. They'd met in shadow, in ruins, at the ends of the earth. What might they be like out under the sun?

She was convinced she had seduced him into joining her, and that was not a bad beginning. He was twice her age, older even. It didn't have to be forever. Something had started between them up here, a connection. She was wounded. He could heal her.

They could travel to Nanda Devi if she pleased, and to Baffin Island, and the Transantarctic Mountains. Why not? He had the money. He could whisk her away into his world, into the dunes, off to Tibet and Paris and castles along the Croatian coast and Crusader fortresses in Syria, across oceans, under the stars of the Southern Hemisphere. And if it worked. He paused. If it worked, they could make a home somewhere, anywhere.

She might even bear him children who would carry his name.

His heart kept on filling up with her. He couldn't explain it. They'd survived. He'd saved her from death. The sun was out. They belonged together, her hand—with that slave amulet inked from her wrist to her finger—in his hand.

"Can you climb?" he asked her. He didn't wait for an answer. "You have to make the summit first. Not me. Not Augustine. This belongs to you."

She watched him with big, inscrutable eyes. Green as olives, they were solemn eyes, and yet radiant with a dot of sun at the center of each. Did she understand? He was giving her El Cap.

Augustine was straining to get his feet into his shoes. Cuba bent to help him. He sat back, shocked by her compassion or forgiveness or whatever this was.

"Let's not tie the laces too tight," she said. "You're damaged enough, and I'm going to need you up higher."

Augustine looked ready to weep. He looked cleansed. Reborn.

Freedom. Hugh could admit it now. He'd seen the inhuman at work up here. He'd felt the hunger of souls, and heard the voices in the wind. Things he wouldn't have believed in a thousand years had unfolded around him. But whatever had been pursuing them, whatever the haunt, it was over. The curse was broken.

They wrapped a stirrup rung around each of

Augustine's unfeeling feet. Hugh got him fixed to the rope leading out through the waterfall and up around the roof.

Augustine gripped Hugh's shoulder. "You saved our skins."

Time was wasting. "Give a hard tug when you reach the crack," Hugh said. "We'll never be able to hear you through the water."

Augustine scooted to the edge of the platform. He cinched the jumars tight, and stepped off into outer space. Swinging out beneath the immense overhang, he entered the water in an explosion of colors.

The waterfall batted him from the inside to the outside. It was cold. With a roar, he threw back his head, and scarfed a mouthful of runoff. The breakfast of champions.

Just short of reaching the roof, Augustine dipped his head through the water. "It goes," he yelled to them. He was excited. "I can see to the top. The crack goes."

"Go," Hugh shouted to him.

"What?"

Hugh gestured skyward. Augustine vanished above the roof.

"Did you see his face when you helped with his shoes?" Hugh asked Cuba. "He was like a prisoner getting released."

"He *is* released," she said.

Cuba stood above Hugh with her feet spread for balance, taller than he expected. She draped the rack of climbing hardware across her chest, and for the first time looked like a climber, not a casualty. Her recovery was miraculous.

"You look good," he said. Let her take it how she wanted.

The rope tugged from above.

"I'll never forget you," she said.

Hugh's smile faded.

She was saying good-bye. He searched her face, and saw the resolution. She was returning to her world, and it didn't include him. So much for exotic sunsets and far mountains. So much for starting a family to cheer his autumn years. After all his promises not to leave her, she was leaving him. The letdown stung. It embarrassed him. What had he been thinking?

She could have waited for the summit or their return to Camp Four or until he attempted some awkward, candlelit interlude. Instead, alone with him, at the scene of their encounter, before he made more of a fool of himself, she was getting it over with, face-to-face. He respected that.

"Cuba." He paused. *Keep it brief.* What to say? "Once more unto the breach."

She kissed him.

He remembered her other kiss, that grasping, bloody imprint at the height of the storm. This was different, no leathery lips, no desperation. She bent to him. Her scabs had healed. She tasted sweet. It came to him. *Like strawberries.*

She let the kiss linger, and then her hand

released his neck. Straight from the heart, she was letting him go. "I thought you'd never leave me," she said.

He almost protested. Who was doing the leaving here? But he didn't try to change her version. This was hard enough. And really, he decided, it was much cleaner. All for the best. One Annie was enough.

He looked away from her unblinking green eyes. "The prayer flags," he said. "Should we leave them?"

"Take them with you," she said.

A few ounces of cotton prayers for him, a few pounds of climbing gear for her. That said it all. She was retiring him. The deposed queen was taking back her realm. She meant to lead them to the summit of her climb, and that was how it ought to be. She latched her jumars onto the rope.

"Hugh Glass," she said.

"Yes?" A change of heart?

She opened her arms and toppled backward from the platform.

She rode the rope's arc with a secret smile, her eyes still fixed on Hugh. It was a thirty-foot swing, thirty down, thirty out. Back first, she hit the sheet of runoff.

The rainbow burst open. Prism colors sprayed everywhere. A flash of direct sunlight pierced the momentary hole. Then the curtain closed. The rainbow formed again, but now with her blurred silhouette on the far side.

She was like a coiled spring out there, sprinting up the rope. At her pace, they'd make land in a few hours. He couldn't see the rope's outline, only the shadow woman—his dancer—soaring through the air. She merged with the sun. For a moment, Hugh couldn't bear to look at her. Then her shadow darted above the roof.

The rainbow was fading. The day was in motion. Suddenly Hugh felt forsaken in this chamber of stone and water.

The rope tugged. *So soon?* He clipped his jumars onto the rope. Leaning out, he pulled free the string of prayer flags. The storm had whipped them to cotton rags, and the smoke had stained them. But the wind horses raised his spirits. He was galloping off into the heavens. He crisscrossed the flags over his shoulders and chest.

Then he turned to the wall and started destroying the anchor. Bit by bit, he undid their camp, jerking nuts from the stone, unclipping carabiners, loosening knots.

He had promised himself last night. If he could make it through to daylight and be allowed to leave this place, he would erase their presence from the wall. Lewis would have approved. Besides, it was the law. Leave no trace but your shadow.

Webbing and chunks of line and metal fluttered and rang into the depths. The platform, weighted by aluminum and nylon debris underneath, gave a sudden lurch. He hammered free a piton. The platform lurched again.

One last piton to go. The rope was pulling him above. It took all his strength to hang on to the platform sling. He struck at the hardware, sending sparks with his hammer. The piton tick-tocked back and forth. He struck again.

Everything let go at once. The piton sprang from the rock. The sling, weighted by the wreckage of their camp, pulled from his fist. The ruins plunged with a pig squeal, metal on stone, and clattered away into the waterfall. Hugh swung on the rope.

He hit the water face-first. The rainbow smashed open, and on the far side the sky was blue. The sun was yellow.

He came to rest half in and half out of the waterfall. Water poured down his collar and sleeves. It slashed at his eyes. He almost drowned giving a victory shout.

Sputtering and battered, he reached for his jumars. Here was not the place to dally. The water was freezing, and it shoved at him like a mugger. Higher up, on the heated walls, he could dry out. For now, the race was on, the summit or bust. It was all or nothing. One more night on the wall would kill them for sure.

High-stepping with his stirrups, he shoved against the flow. He caught a momentary glimpse of the summit, a neat white line against the dark blue sky. Then the water cut at his eyes again. He hunched his neck and inched higher.

Near the rim of the roof, he jabbed his head

through for a final look at that other world. It was dark inside. The water pounded at his shoulders. The lizard king lurked in there, hungry, always hungry.

Hugh yanked his head back. *Leave it.* He'd escaped again. The water bullied him. He closed his eyes and bullied it back.

The torrent eased against his shoulders. The thundering water softened to a hiss. When he opened his eyes, Cuba was crouching straight above him, at the rim.

With more than half the rope still left to climb, she'd stopped here for some reason. High beyond her shoulder, Augustine stood perched at the crack, looking up. Was she waiting to welcome Hugh? Or simply making sure he wouldn't leave her.

"Here I am," he said.

The water spun him in a circle. He tilted back to smile at her. It was just another few feet before he cleared the overhang and gained solid stone.

The rope kept twisting. Her face revolved. She became the blinding sun, then the water, then a woman again. Her head was cocked. She was studying him almost, making up her mind.

Her hair draped down, and for a moment the black mane lit bright with color, red going on blond. He blinked at the water spray and sunshine. Her hair returned to black, cowling her face from view. He tried to see inside its shadows.

The sun cut at him. The water. Her hair flickered like fire, dark to light. Strawberry blond. *Annie?* He swiped at his face. "Cuba?"

He spun toward the sun, and it blinded him. He craned back to see overhead, and the water whipped his eyes. He twisted in space, fighting the gyre, clamoring to see.

Why didn't she answer? She crouched there, quiet as Annie in the end. Just watching him. Waiting with that infinite, mindless patience. Each time he'd looked back, she was watching him, waiting to be led out from the dunes.

The first night he'd circled back to her. The moon had been full, the air chilly. He lay on top of a dune and looked down at her curled in the sand. He didn't descend. Her hair looked black, her skin silver. She hadn't moved all day. Their footprints tracked in. They led out. But without him, she was lost.

He left her no water. It was a mercy, of sorts. Why drag out her suffering?

She had no idea he fell asleep on the hill above her. When he woke at dawn, she was standing, facing the sun. Again he left her, and went to his cache of water.

The second night he peered over the dune again, and she had crumpled to the sand. At first, he thought it was over, but she began singing. He lay on his back and watched the moon roll by, and listened to her song. It was not a sad song, whatever it was.

On the third morning, she was silent. He kept walking that day, and the next. He knew the direction. Eventually he would cut the highway. A breeze came up. He watched it bury his tracks. He took off his hat and let the sun burn his face and split his lips. At last, it was time to surface from the desert. He approached the goatherder. He had chosen his savior.

Hugh shook his head. He shucked the past. Water flew. "Cuba?"

She reached down a hand. He thought she meant to pull him up. Her fist was wrapped tight, though, and there was something in it.

He screwed his body around, struggling to see.

It was a black thing, glistening, a sliver of night.

That puzzled him. They were paupers up here. Cuba had no possessions. He'd found her nearly naked.

Then he remembered the sack she'd emptied during the storm. His book of maps and the bundle of syringes had been missing. He'd never even thought to look for this unnecessary thing, wrapped in an Ace bandage. It was his souvenir from Joshua.

The obsidian blade jutted from her fist.

"Cuba?" Hugh shoved higher. The water spun him.

She squatted there, facing down, a gargoyle in stirrups. He couldn't see her face. Which mask was she wearing? Which Cuba was this? The sun wheeled. The water hissed.

His jumar butted against the rim. He slapped for a hold, and there was nothing but slick rock and his five-hundred-pound legs and the choking water. He bucked to free the jumar.

She laid the blade against the rope.

He grabbed for the bottom rung of her stirrup, but the water dragged him back. A few inches more, that's all he needed. A few seconds. If he could just breathe.

She whispered. He couldn't hear. The water was sighing.

"What do you want, Cuba?"

She whispered again, ever so patient. She waited for him. He couldn't hear. "What?"

She lowered her head until it was almost between her feet. He stared into her eyes, and still the truth eluded him.

"Cuba?"

Then he saw what she was showing him. Cuba was gone. Borrowed one final time.

Bullshit.

He struck at the water. She didn't back away. He pulled with all his might, squinting through the spray.

They were Cuba's eyes, the same as before, green as olives. And yet there was something in them. Not madness. A glint, not a gleaming.

The water dragged at him. He reached with his neck. He gained an inch. The water parted. He saw what she wanted him to see.

It wasn't her eyes that had changed, but rather their reflections of the sun. They were lit bright, but not with the golden light shining over his shoulders. The spark was white, not gold. He reached with his neck, lifting his head closer, and his mouth fell open.

He recognized that tiny sun on the curve of her green eyes. It was a different sun in a different sky. It didn't belong to this morning. This was the round white star that had burned him on his exit from the dunes.

He searched deeper in Cuba's eyes and they were a lens into her soul. But not Cuba's soul. In that instant, he understood. Here was the last sight of her life, that pitiless desert sun.

"Annie?" he whispered.

"*Hayati,*" she said. The water froze him. *My life.*

Her fist twitched. White fluff burst from the black blade. The rope blew.

The world stood still.

There was no sense of falling. He seemed to be hanging in time and space. All around him drops of water came to a halt in perfect beads. His hands held the stub of rope.

Then he noticed the prayer flags fluttering around his neck.

He was in motion.

As if she'd already forgotten him, as if their paths had never crossed on the high stone, Cuba turned and started climbing. It occurred to Hugh that he would land where the first girl had landed, possibly on the very rock, in the forest now sacked to ash and prowled by muddy beasts.

It amazed him. How could he have been so blind? *An eye for an eye.* From the very start, he'd been warned. *We knew you would come.*

He watched Cuba speed into the heights. Not

once did she look down. She was free at last. He
knew absolutely that she would lead Augustine,
crippled, out of the abyss.

As he fell, Hugh kept his eyes on the dwindling
woman. He preferred to see her soaring toward the
summit, not himself into the darkness. The valley's
shadows rose up.

And still he refused to be damned. The walls
were pure gold up there. He reached past the prayer
flags, up from the darkness, fingers outstretched,
commanding the light to hold him from his fall for
just a moment more.

ACKNOWLEDGMENTS

A book is like an expedition, a confederacy of prior experience, maps, and true believers. In this case, I had the advantage of all three.

I am indebted to Keith Lober—a Colorado boy who went west and became the manager of Yosemite's Search and Rescue unit—for patiently walking me through SAR history, the latest rescue techniques, and the life of a park ranger.

My El Cap partner Cliff Watts once again loaded me up with just the right medical nostrums and fine Georgia humor. Thanks, doc. And long live the Ramones.

I tapped my two brothers—who have lived in Saudi Arabia for a combined thirty years—for details about Arab folklore and Islam, the Empty Quarter, and local customs and language. To Ken, the desert rat, and Steve, the Arabist . . . muchas gracias, bros.

My story's two routes are inventions pieced together from real routes. At all times I kept a copy of Chris McNamara's *Yosemite Big Walls: SuperTopos* by my side, which meant losing more hours than I can count wandering through his masterpiece. For big wall climbers, *SuperTopos* is a must. For non-climbers it is a magic window onto the vertical world, filled with the poetry of El Cap's landmarks, and the wall-rat's love for steep rock. Highly recommended.

My agent, Sloan Harris, is the granite I continue to lean upon. A steadier soul, I have never met.

The pen behind my pen is Emily Bestler, the kind of editor writers dream about, the best I've worked with.

Finally, Barbara and Helena, I am blessed to be tied in with the two of you.

ATRIA BOOKS
PROUDLY PRESENTS

Deeper

JEFF LONG

Coming soon in hardcover from Atria Books

He snapped his fingers. *Let there be light.* And they popped the flares.

The faces of his crew sprang from the darkness, flinching. The flare light hurt their eyes. It painted them green and hungry.

The city of stone materialized around them.

Clemens gave a nod. The clapboard snapped shut like a gunshot. In grease pencil: "HELL, scene 316, take 1. IMAX."

"Dead, all dead," he intoned as the camera panned across the city. It was a bony thing, hard and empty, ancient long before Troy was built, before Egypt was even a word. Walls stood cracked or breached by geological forces. Arches hung like ribs. Windows stared: blind sockets. The camera stopped on him.

Clemens turned his head to the lens. He gave it the tired bags under his eyes, and his shaggy salt-and-pepper beard, and the greasy hair, and the bad stitch job along one cheekbone. No makeup. No concealment. Let the audience see his weariness and the marks of five months spent worming through the bowels of the earth. *I have sweated and bled for you,* he thought. *I have killed for you. And for my cut of the box office.* He put fire in his blue eyes.

"Day one hundred and forty-seven, deep beneath the Mariana Trench," he said. "We have reached their city. Their Athens. Their Alexandria. Their Manhattan. Here lies the center."

He coughed quietly. The whole film crew had it, some low-grade cave virus. Just one more of their shared afflictions: a rash from poison lichens, fouled stomachs from the river water, lingering fevers after an attack by crystal-clear ants, rot in their wounds, and headaches from the pressure. To say nothing of the herpes and gonorrhea raging among his randy bunch of men and women.

Clemens approached a tall, translucent flange of flow-stone. It had seeped from the walls like a slow, plastic, honey-brown avalanche. A carefully placed flare lit the stone from behind. The dark silhouette of a man hung inside like a huge insect caught in amber.

Clemens glanced at the camera—at his future audience—as if to wonder with them. *What new wonders lie here?* He pressed his flashlight against the stone, and peered in. *Through my eyes, behold.*

He moved his light. Inch by inch, the shape revealed its awful clues. This was no man, but some primal throwback. A freak of time. The camera closed in.

Clemens illuminated the pale, hairless legs covered with prehistoric tattoos. His light paused at the groin. The genitals were wrapped in a ball with rawhide strips, a sort of fig leaf for this dreadful Adam. That was the creature's sole clothing, a sack tied with leather cord from front to back across the rump. Leather, in a place devoid of large animals . . . except for man. These hadals had wasted nothing, not even human skin.

"We were their dream," Clemens solemnly intoned to the camera, "they were our nightmare."

He scooted the light beam higher. The beast was by turns delicate, then savage. Winged like a cupid, this one could not have flown. They were more buds than wings really, vestigial, almost comical. But this was no laughing matter. Like a junk-yard mutt, it bore the gash marks and scars of a hunter-warrior.

Moving higher, his headlamp beam lit the awful face. Milky pink eyes—dead eyes—stared back at him. Even though he'd seen the thing while they were setting up the shot, it made Clemens uneasy. Like the crickets, mice, and other creepy crawlers inhabiting these depths, it was an albino. What little facial hair it had was white. The eyelashes and wisps of a mustache looked almost dainty.

The brow beetled out, heavy and ape-like. Classic *Homo erectus*. This one had filed teeth and earlobes fringed with knife cuts. Its crowning glory, the reason why Clemens had picked this one over all the other bodies, was its rack of misshapen horns. Horns upon other horns, a satanic freight.

The horns were calcium growths, described to him as a subterranean cancer. These happened to have sprouted from its forehead, which fit his film's title to a T. Every hell needed a devil.

Never mind that this wasn't the devil Clemens had come looking for. This was not the body of Satan, said to be lying somewhere in the city. Never mind that through the millennia man's demons had been ancestors of sorts, or at least distant blood cousins. Clemens would deal with the family tree later, in the editing room.

"Now they're gone," he spoke to the microphone clipped to his tattered T-shirt. "Gone forever, destroyed by a manmade plague. Some call it genocide, others an act of God. This much is certain. We have been delivered from their reign of terror. Freed from an ancient tyranny. Now the night belongs to us once and for all."

Clemens stood back and gazed upon the horror like Frankenstein contemplating his monster. He held his pose to the count of five. "And, cut," he said.

The cameraman gave a thumbs-up from behind his tripod. The soundman took off her earphones and signaled okay. A clean take.

"Get a few close-ups of our friend here," Clemens said. "Then break down the gear and pack up. We're moving on. Up. There's still hours in the day." A running joke. In a place without sun, what day? "We're heading home."

Home! For once the crew jumped to his command.

The exit tunnel lay somewhere close. It would lead them to the surface in a matter of weeks. For the millionth time, he pulled a sheaf of pages from a waterproof tube and studied its hodgepodge of maps.

The pages came from the daybook kept by a nun, one of only two survivors to emerge from this region ten years ago. It was the ghosts of her doomed expedition that Clemens was chasing on film. Hers had been one of the most audacious journeys in all history, one to rival Marco Polo's or Columbus's, a six-thousand-mile passage through the tunnel system riddling the bedrock beneath the Pacific Ocean. It had been a journey with a punch line, a journey of scientists who bumped smack into an unpleasant article of faith. For here they had found the home of Satan, or the historical Satan, the man—hominid, take your pick—behind the legend. The leader of the pack.

The nun, a fancy scholar named Ali von Schade, had written of meeting him. The city had still been alive back then, the plague not yet released. The last she'd seen of him, he was wearing a warrior's suit of green jade platelets. For three days now, Clemens had been scouring the city for the body or skeleton, looking for his film's money shot, the one that would shock and amaze and bring the story all together in one image. He'd found a suit of jade armor all right, but it was empty, discarded, ownerless, not a bone in it. Despite his disappointment, he kind of liked that. In the end, Satan had been nothing more than an empty suit.

Clemens had made numerous requests to von Schade for an interview, all in vain, always meeting the same polite refusal. *I don't wish to share the details of that disaster.* As if the story belonged to her. As if intellectual property had some sacred protection. Cunt.

He and Quinn, his film partner, had needed her maps and clues to plan this journey. Clemens had tried flowers, dinner invitations, offers of money, even a percentage of the film's net profit—yeah, net not gross, an old Hollywood joke. Nothing worked with her. Zip. Nada. Quinn said leave her alone. Instead Clemens had hired a burglar to steal her journal. If she wouldn't talk, her diary would.

Von Schade's maps were as much memoir as cartography, laced with fanciful tales and ink-and-watercolor sketches of the Helios expedition's progress. Along the way, every time Clemens was sure she must be wrong or had made something up, her maps would prove to be right.

A waterfall thundered in the darkness, hidden in the distance. That was on the map, too. Bound and blindfolded at the time, von Schade had later recorded it in her daybook, an acoustic landmark. Through the waterfall lay their shortcut to the sun.

Long, ghostly strips of clouds drifted overhead. The cavern was so big it generated its own micro-weather. Geologists theorized that millions of years ago great bubbles of sulfuric acid had eaten upwards from the earth's deeper mantle, carving out this labyrinth of cavities and tubes known as the Interior or the Subterrain. The perfect hiding place for a lost race.

Clemens rolled up the pages and switched off his headlamp. They were running low on batteries, and everything else for that matter. But the shoot was largely over. His crew had reached its summit, so to speak, this dead city in the deepest reaches of the sub-Pacific cave system. Now they could ascend, back to the surface, back to the sun. Back to Clemens's faded name and glory.

Most of the kids on this crew hadn't even sprouted pimples when he'd won an Academy Award for his documentary, *War High*, about jackass athletes braving international war zones in their search of the ultra-extreme. After that, he'd coasted on his Oscar laurels, getting work as a second unit director on Hollywood action vehicles.

Then the earth's interior had been "discovered." Overnight, everyone's attention had shifted to this vast, inhabited labyrinth right beneath their feet. The market for movies and books about adrenaline junkies had gone out the window. Clemens learned the hard way that there was no competing with the demons and fiends of religious lore. Within a year, he was bankrupt, divorced, and shooting porn videos for $200 per day.

But then he had met Quinn. Quinn was an old-fashioned explorer who had dipped his toe in the subterranean world and had a film in mind—this film, about an expedition following in the footsteps of an expedition into hell. In a coked-up revelation, it had occurred to Clemens that in order to beat the devil, he needed to be the devil. And so—at fifty-two years old—he'd convinced Quinn to partner with him on the production. Together they had assembled this desperate, calculated slog through the earth's basement. Clemens figured that if *Hell,* splashed upon giant IMAX screens, couldn't revive his career, nothing would. He'd have to go back to work for the skin mafia.

Unfortunately Quinn had proved to be a problem. Quinn the decent. Quinn the grin. Quinn the real McCoy. Quinn the leader. The crew had loved Quinn's easygoing style and his insistence on safety. And his sense of story and scriptwriting that made Clemens look like a dumb-it-down hack. Which Clemens was. But which he didn't need to have the little people snickering about. Thus, Quinn the scream. Quinn the dead.

After his partner's disappearance, Clemens had assumed things would get better. But the crew only grew more disrespectful of him. They suspected him. Idiots. Murder didn't exist in a wilderness with no laws. And besides, no body, no crime. Quinn had chosen a bottomless pit to fall into. It had been easy, the slightest of nudges from behind, barely an ounce of adios, amigo. Clemens had made a few attempts at placating them, even giving them two days to search for their fearless leader. Then it was crack-the-whip time. On with the show.

Joshua. There it was again, that whisper. Clemens whirled around.

He jabbed his light left and right. As always, no one was there. It had been going on ever since they entered the city. The crew was screwing with him, whispering his name with Quinn's voice, winding him up.

"Fuck ya," Clemens said to the darkness.

"Likewise," said a woman's voice. Huxley came striding into his light. "What do you think you're doing?"

"Was that you?" said Clemens.

"Yeah," she said. "It's me. You said we were making camp here."

Huxley was a veterinarian that Quinn had hired to be their medic. It was the pet doctor's unsteady needle that had sewn together Clemens's cheek after a rockfall in the tunnel system. He could guess what she wanted.

"Those wings," she said. She went to the creature suspended in flowstone. "I need to take his measurements and get tissue samples. And I want those wings for my collection. The wings of an angel. A fallen angel. This specimen is unique."

My ongoing rebellion, thought Clemens. The crew was an inch away from outright mutiny. They couldn't wait to get out of here. Daylight was waiting up top. They could practically taste it. And Huxley wanted them to stay?

"You've been saying that about every bone and body we've stumbled across," Clemens said. "We're done here. Onwards. Upwards. Miles to go before we sleep, all that."

"You don't understand," Huxley said. "Wings on men? And we saw that one yesterday with amphibian gills. And the reptile lady."

"What do you want me to say? They're hadals. A dime a dozen down here. A dime a thousand."

"This is going to rock the scientific community," she said. "This is huge. So huge."

"You've got your degree, doc," Clemens said. "What more do you want, the Nobel?"

"Why not?" She was serious.

"Because," he said.

"What more do you want," she asked. "Another Oscar?"

It wasn't Huxley's ambition that Clemens resented. Once this was over, each one of them meant to squeeze the lemon for all it was worth. He'd been hearing their big plans for months. The kayakers were going to buy ad space in *Outside* and *Men's Journal* to lure adventure travelers. There were dark, Class IV tube rapids down here, and river beaches made of polished white marble. The cinematographer wanted to open an art gallery and publish a coffee table book with her still shots of the Interior. Three of the climber types meant to incorporate, raise venture capital, and return to prospect the outrageous veins of gold they'd all touched, but left behind.

In short, there was money and reputation to be grabbed down here. Huxley was no different from the rest of them. Having suffered the darkness, she wanted her piece of the pie. But the thing about Huxley was that she didn't have manners. Just because she'd been Quinn's girlfriend didn't exempt her from the rules. This was Clemens's show now. Everyone else, even the hotshot climbers, had asked his permission to capitalize on the expedition. Not Huxley, though. She treated him like he was stealing the descent.

"We had a deal," she said.

"What deal is that?"

"I came along as a scientist."

"You came along as a medic," Clemens said. "That's your job, to tend the sick and wounded."

"You said we were camping here one more night."

Clemens stared a hole through her. "End of discussion," he said. "We're leaving."

"I'm staying."

"By yourself? In this place?" The flares were dying. The shadows loomed.

"You're not a man of science," Huxley said. "You wouldn't understand."

Clemens thought for a minute, not about staying with

her, but about getting shed of her. He wasn't born yesterday. She was going to try to bring charges against him once they got up top. That or bring a lawsuit against him. This was his retirement she was threatening here.

Clemens shrugged. "You got to do what you got to do, doc."

Huxley blinked. She'd been bluffing. Too late now. Clemens grinned at her. "That's right," she said. "I've got to do what I've got to do. With or without you."

"We'll be on the trail leading up," Clemens told her. "You go through a waterfall and there will be a tunnel. Don't forget."

Huxley lifted her chin. "This won't take more than a few hours. I'll be right behind you."

"You'd better be. I'm telling you, man, don't miss the bus. Because nobody's waiting for nobody anymore. It's dog-eat-dog, Huxley. You hear me?"

She stared as if he'd just confessed. "I'll catch you before night."

Night. There it was again, their strange conceit. Even in this lightless place, they clung to convention, calling their wakefulness day, and their sleep night. Never mind that their bodies had forgotten the sun and they dreamed in shades of blackness.

They left Huxley in a tiny puddle of light. *Good night, sweet princess,* thought Clemens. Fantasizing, he began to write the sad loss of Dr. Huxley into his mental screenplay.

For three days they had been meandering through the city, gathering a bounty of images. It was like Pompeii among these ruins, with this difference. Instead of being locked inside volcanic ash, the dead hung in translucent flux. You could see them underfoot, suspended in the flowstone, hundreds—no, thousands—of them. For three nights they had slept atop the last resting place of the ultimate barbarian. Now they were done with it.

A gigantic waterfall seemed to block the end of the cavern. They shot a flare into the heights. As it drifted down, the spray lit with rainbows in the blackness.

"Lord," one of the kayakers said. That said it all.

Just as the nun's daybook promised, a tunnel lay behind the central waterfall: caves within caves within caves. It was like Swiss cheese down here.

Clemens tried to get his crew to set up the camera and get a shot of him entering the falls tunnel. But they pretended not to hear him. He had been waiting for their muttering and scowls to spill over into actual defiance, and now that it had, now that they had broken from his command, he was relieved. Finally he could quit lashing them deeper. He could just float back up to the world.

The path led up and up in giant circles. The stair steps, carved from solid stone by a subterranean civilization that some scholars dated to 25,000 years ago, had been worn to faint corrugations. The stone was slick from the humidity that blew at their backs on a warm, steady draft.

It didn't take long for Huxley to change her mind about staying behind. Clemens was at the back of the line for a reason. Her voice began echoing up to them after the first hour, but Clemens was the only one to hear it. He couldn't make out her words, but her distress was clear. Maybe her batteries had run out. More likely she couldn't find the tunnel entrance. Bummer.

Soon her echoes grew almost faint enough to ignore. Almost. The whisper still reached him. *Joshua.* How did she do that?

The tunnel walls tightened. The current of warm air quit rushing from below. Clemens could sense the space closing around him by the change in his hearing. Things just sounded closer.

Joshua. He ignored her.

As they went on, Clemens kept looking for debris, bones, or signs of the original expedition. Funded by the Helios conglomerate, the party of scientists, soldiers, and porters had numbered over two hundred at their start beneath the Galápagos Islands.

Following their lead, Clemens and the crew of nineteen had hiked, climbed, and rafted some six thousand miles. They had retraced the Helios expedition's route by its remains, finding clues to its long breakdown in their graffiti, trash, dried dung, and, near the end, their bones. Quinn had likened the doomed explorers to Lewis and Clark crossing America, except the sub-Pacific journey was almost three times as long, and they had been slaughtered by the natives, these so-called hadals of this geological Hades. Only von Schade and the expedition's scout had lived to tell the tale, though they had barely told it. The scout had vanished without saying a word about anything. The nun had gone into therapy, and then academic seclusion. Which had left their story ripe for the picking.

Finder's keepers, thought Clemens. It was his now, the scraps of diaries and logbooks, the rags of uniforms, the broken instruments, the forlorn skulls mounted on stalagmites, the hadal bones lying where the plague had felled them . . . all collected and digitized on large format tape.

Climbing higher, they found hadal symbols cut into the walls or floor. One, in particular, suggested they were on track. It was a simple, recurring ✗ shape. For months, they had been seeing different versions of it, like a blaze mark, only more beautiful and ornate. The closer they got to the city, the more elaborate the symbols had become. Here, for instance, the ✗ was woven so deftly into an arabesque engraving that it seemed to be hiding.

Clemens still found it hard to believe the brutish hadals had once conducted an empire that extended throughout this tubular maze. While humankind was still learning to make fire, the hadals had been busy constructing a metropolis far from the sun. Some experts even claimed the hadals had tutored man at the dawn of agriculture and metallurgy.

A lot of people objected to the notion. *Us? Schooled by them?* Now that he'd spent time down here, though, it made terrible sense to Clemens. Why not get your meat to grow its own food, to breed, and to cluster in villages and cities? Fatten them up before bringing them down.

At a fork in the trail, the group halted for the night. Without a word, the men and women shucked their packs and laid out their sleeping pads. The daybook said nothing about a split in the trail. Indeed, it said almost nothing about the ascent from the city. Apparently the nun had been in shock after her captivity and rescue there. That or she had intentionally concealed where the tunnel exited in New Guinea.

Bobbi, another one of the alpha females, took it upon herself to reconnoiter ahead and determine which of the two trails they should follow in the morning. Within minutes her shout for help rang down the tunnel walls. Immediately everyone got to his or her feet. No hesitation. Out came their motley collection of rifles and handguns.

Not once in five months had they needed to fire a single shot. There was nothing left to shoot down here. The darkness had been sterilized. The Interior was scrubbed clean of threats. Exorcised, as some put it. The man-made pandemic had erased the hadals from existence. Haddie was out of business.

They found Bobbi in a broad hollow, speechless, and pale beneath her subterranean pallor. She pointed up the trail. Clemens watched as the women gathered around their sister and the men flocked ahead with their firearms. They rounded the corner.

"God," barked a man.

A long row of human mummies stood tied on either side of the trail. There were thirty of them, still wearing pieces of military webbing, boots, and uniforms . . . with the sun and wings of the Helios corporation logo on their shoulder patches.

"Finally," said Clemens.

They looked at him. "Finally?"

"The lost patrol," he said. "I wondered where they went."

Clemens's crew had been finding what was left of the Helios scientists for the past three hundred miles, but always absent their hired guns. Here at last were the mercenaries, dried and arrayed for public view, complete with arrows and darts and various death wounds. A black obsidian axe blade with a broken haft jutted from a skull.

"What it this? What happened here?"

"Stone age taxidermy," someone said.

"Custer's last stand, dude."

Their soundman murmured, "Like sinners burning in hell."

Bound with ropes, their jaws agape and flesh shrunken to the bone, they did look tortured. A chorus of the damned. No wonder mankind had feared the underworld. The sub-planet really had contained the torments of legend.

The money shot, Clemens was thinking to himself.

They walked up and down the line like visitors in a darkened art museum, shining their lights on different mummies. The soldiers looked alien to Clemens, like barrel-chested insects with bulging eyes.

Then he saw the incisions. Their rib cages seemed so huge because their abdomens were so small. The men had been gutted. Their eyes had been scooped out and replaced with round white stones that stared into eternity. Their shriveled thighs and biceps all bore the same cut marks, some kind of ritual mutilation.

Their assault rifles lay at their feet, stocks splintered, so much kindling wood. Except they were plastic. Broken into pieces. Clemens could almost see the hatred in it. The hadals had despised these men.

"What's this?"

"Christ, it's his heart. They tied his heart into his beard."

Clemens went over. Sure enough, the dried fruit of muscle was a heart knotted into a man's black beard. "But why didn't they eat it?" Clemens asked. "That and the rest of their bodies?"

Bobbi stared at him. "What are you talking about?"

"There must have been two thousand pounds of meat here when they were fresh," Clemens said. "But instead of eating them, they dried and displayed them. I mean, why go to all this trouble preserving them?"

Hunger ruled this world within the world. No protein went wasted. From what they'd seen, the remains of the scientists, and even of the hadals, were always eaten to the bone, and the gnawed bones broken open for the marrow. And yet these bodies were whole, or mostly so.

Clemens's crew was somber. He listened to them trying to make sense of the atrocity.

"It's a warning," a climber said. "Keep out. Beware of dog. Here dragons be."

"The Romans used to do this. Crucify prisoners on the roads leading into the city. Behave, or else."

"No, no. It's like a trophy case. These are their war souvenirs."

"Why did they do that to their eyes?"

"Jeez-is, would you look, they're castrated, too. The bastards cut their nuts off."

That got them, the men especially. "There, but for the grace of God, go I."

"You think any of them are still around?"

"You saw the city. Nothing but bones. They're extinct. Dead and gone."

"But what if some of them survived?"

"Impossible."

"There are always survivors."

"She's right—the place is one giant hiding place."

Their lights spun this way and that, scouring the blackness.

"Impossible."

They were freaking themselves out. "Go get the camera and sound gear," Clemens said. "The least we can do is record them for posterity."

This time no one balked at his command. When they went, it was all together, leaving Clemens alone with the bodies. He began framing camera angles and composing narrative.

Pan left to right. "These few, these lucky few, our sons and brothers."

He edited himself. People didn't go to IMAX to hear Shakespeare. Give the crowd their boom, bang, ka-pow. He started over.

Shock cut to a mummy's face. Pull back to show the dead. I step from their midst.

"Since the beginning, man has been at war with the dark side. . . ."

He walked down the line, shopping for the right face. Their bared teeth gleamed. The stone eyes stared. Blackbeard, he decided. The one with the heart dangling from his chin.

He strode on and picked his mark, and backed between two bodies. The wall was cool. They smelled like a tanner's shop, and a gym, too. Even dead, their different body odors clung to them. Leather and sweat. Dry as corn husks.

Joshua.

The whisper jolted him. How could Huxley's voice reach him here? Or was it another one of them messing with his *yin-yang*?

He shoved from the wall, out from the carcasses. "Who is it?"

He thrust his light beam up and down the tunnel, hunting for the trickster. But he was alone.

Joshua. Again.

He splashed light across the faces, each grinning his death grin. The air, he decided. It moved in these tunnels. It made them whistle and moan sometimes. That was all. The whispers were just air.

In the middle of the night, Clemens woke with a start. He sat up and shook his head, looking around. This evening's choice of chemical night-light was orange. His little tribe slept all around him in a jumbled orange clump, their limbs tangled and heads pillowed on one another, breathing each other's breath. A fortress of snores and twitches. And guns.

The clustering had become a reflex. By day they were a bold bunch, all muscle and trash talk, itching to beat every cliff, river, or squeeze chute that got in their way. But when it came time to sleep, they huddled like children lost in a forest.

Joshua.

It slid in from the outskirts, a kitten of a sound, barely a breath of a word. He scanned the sleeping pack. None of them was the culprit. The whisper had come from beyond their bubble of orange light.

And then again, *Joshua.* So soft it might have been in his head. Was he dreaming? No. He was wide awake now.

"What?" He kept his voice low.

Joshua. It called to him. Someone was out there.

He counted them and, sure enough, came up one short. Then he remembered Huxley. She'd never showed up. In all the excitement about the mummies, they had forgotten all about her.

"Huxley?" he whispered.

One of the women stirred. She lifted her head. "What's wrong?"

"Nothing," he said. "Go back to sleep."

Her eyes closed.

He sat there for another few minutes, listening intently. But the tunnel was silent again. He lay back and tried to sleep. No dice. Voice or not, Huxley was in his head now. She was alone down there, terrified no doubt, probably lost. She'd asked for it, staying back. Accusing him with her glares.

At the end of a sleepless half hour, Clemens sighed and stood up. He didn't believe in conscience. But the voice had him going now. Screw it, he thought. Bring her in. Maybe she'd show a little gratitude.

He stood up and tiptoed from their orange halo. No sense waking anyone. By morning, he'd be back with Huxley in tow. One more rebel to add to his collection.

As he headed down the tunnel, the image came to Clemens of an immense throat about to swallow him, and for a minute he almost returned to get his sawed-off shotgun. But his knees were bad enough without the extra weight. Besides which, for the past six thousand miles they had found nothing alive larger than a lobster. *Satan is dead. Long live . . . whatever.*

Down he sank through the tunnel. The thunder of the waterfall grew louder.

Huxley was waiting just inside the entrance. Her pale face appeared in Clemens's light. The whites of her eyes bulged. She looked indignant.

"I told you not to stay behind," he said to her.

She didn't say anything. Sulking. Probably hungry. It was going to be a chore prodding her up the trail.

Just the same, Clemens was glad he'd come to fetch her. He would work it into his script, the tale of his midnight rescue. Never mind that it had taken him less than an hour to descend. He'd make it three hours. Hours? Days. Milk it for all it was worth. People would hail his compassion. Reviewers would note his guardian care of the crew. Couldn't save everyone, *poor Quinn,* but not for lack of trying. Everything helped during award competitions.

Huxley went on staring at him. She didn't make a move to come up the trail. "So let's go," he said, descending the final stretch.

She glared at him.

"Can't we just get along, Hux?"

Clemens stopped. He saw the blood painting the spike between her legs. Her mouth was sewed shut. She was impaled on a stalagmite. "Jesus, mother," said Clemens. He stepped back from the mess.

Huxley's eyes followed him. *Impossible.* She was still alive. *Joshua.*

Clemens knifed at the shadows with his light. The darkness parted. It sealed shut again. The walls glistened with waterfall sweat. There was a crevice. Something moved in there. He thrust the light at it.

Eyes glittered back at him. A face in there. It spoke his name again. But this time it was out loud. "Joshua."

Clemens jumped. "What?" The thing didn't answer. For a moment, he thought his buddy in the flowstone had come back to life and broken free. But the eyes weren't pink. There was no rack of horns. He had a tattered, greasy cowl of hair and a ragged beard, years long.

The beast eased from its womb of a crevice.

Stone scraped on stone as it emerged. To Clemens's shock, it was wearing the suit of armor made with green jade that Clemens had found on the ground. The green platelets tinkled like chandelier glass.

The stone tube began crying from above. It was his crew. They sounded like puppies. The men's screams were even shriller than the women's.

Reject. Refuse. Make it go away. Clemens tried to pace his breathing. This couldn't be happening. The city was dead. Killed. Just bones.

Clemens remembered his camera. Even as he backed away, he could not help thinking what a great shot this would have made. In the belly of the abyss, in a city of lost souls, out of sweating stone . . . Satan was resurrecting himself.

Thrillers that leave you on the edge of your seat from Pocket Books

Fury
Robert K. Tanenbaum
Butch Karp tackles his most personal case yet—one in which his family may be only the first victims of a ruthless terrorist cell.

Kindred Spirit
John Passarella
For twins separated at birth, life can be twice as terrifying…

Finding Satan
Andrew Neiderman
A man of science and logic will come to believe—in the power of ultimate evil.

Cobraville
Carson Stroud
A covert CIA mission to infiltrate a terrorist stronghold in the Philippines goes horribly wrong—and now one man must pay the price.

Available wherever books are sold or at www.simonsays.com.

15065